ANGUS DONALD

Blood's Campaign

ZAFFRE

First published in Great Britain in 2019
This edition published in 2020 by
ZAFFRE
80–81 Wimpole St, London W1G 9RE
Owned by Bonnier Books
Sveavägen 56, Stockholm, Sweden

A CIP catalogue record for this book is
available from the British Library.

Paperback ISBN: 978-1-78576-746-3
Hardback ISBN: 978-1-78576-745-6

Also available as an ebook

1 3 5 7 9 10 8 6 4 2

Typeset by IDSUK (Data Connection) Ltd
Printed and bound in Great Britain by Clays Ltd, Elcograf S.p.A.

Zaffre is an imprint of Bonnier Books UK
www.bonnierbooks.co.uk

Holcroft Blood's Ireland

Londonderry

Carrickfergus

Belfast

Belfast Lough

Ballyshannon

River Erne *Lower Lough Erne*

Inniskilling

Newtownbutler

Newry

Dundalk

Upper Lough Erne

Cavan

Longford

Drogheda

River Boyne

River Nanny

Athlone

Galway

Dublin

River Liffey

Limerick

Ballyneety

Waterford

River Blackwater

Killarney

Cork

Lough Leane

Kinsale

The Boyne Battlefield
July 1, 1690

Mellifont Abbey

Tullyallen

Drogheda

Slane

Oldbridge

Rosnaree

Donore

Platin Hall

Roughgrange

Duleek

1 mile

Part One

Chapter One

Sunday, August 25, 1689: 11 a.m.

Captain Holcroft Blood dipped his quill in the ink pot. He gently shook off a drop of excess ink and, with his left hand, he straightened the large sheet of paper in front of him so that its bottom edge was exactly in line with the metal rim of the small folding camp table at which he sat. He composed his thoughts as best as he could in his present disordered state of mind. Then wrote:

Carrickfergus encampment
Sunday, 25th August, 1689

Madam,
*   I have received the favour of your letter of the 17th Inst. in which you informed me of the situation regarding the sad state of the spoons in Mincing Lane . . .*

He recharged his quill and continued.

I am most sensible of the importance of keeping all the silverware in good order for the honour of the household and I regret deeply that your distinguished guest Jongheer Markus van Dijk was unkind enough to take notice of its poor quality when he dined with you and Lady Churchill earlier this month. I am therefore perfectly content that you should purchase an entirely new canteen of silver, should you believe the decrepitude of our existing set truly demands it.

Holcroft wet the nib again, mentally girded up his loins, and scratched out:

As I believe I have informed you on several occasions, you have full permission, as my wife, to draw the appropriate sum from the goldsmith Richard Hoare at the sign of the Golden Bottle in Cheapside. However, as I am engaged in the business of the Ordnance in Ireland at present, indeed as I am in the midst of a siege of the town of Carrickfergus, a dozen miles north-east of Belfast, I do not believe that I should be required to sanction every minor household expense . . .

Holcroft paused, and stabbed the nib into the ink pot again. He knew he had struck the wrong note – he sounded petulant – but such was the peculiar nature of his mind that he could not bring himself to tear up the sheet and start again. He was sitting in the spacious command tent of the English Army in Ireland and, for once, he was quite alone with his thoughts and his letter to his wife. Yet that unusual and most welcome solitary state had not improved his temper.

He was, in truth, furious. But not with Elizabeth. His anger was directed at his commanding officer, General Frederich-Hermann von Schönberg, Master-General of the Ordnance, head of the English Army in Ireland and owner of this cool and comfortable canvas palace. The newly created Duke of Schomberg – the English could never pronounce his family name – was about to let a notorious French spy evade justice. Indeed, Schomberg was now parlaying with representatives of the town's Irish governor, Charles MacCarthy, a parlay that was – to Holcroft's fury – almost certain to lead to the spy's escape.

The Irish governor and his men were supporters of James Stuart, the recently deposed Catholic monarch of the Three Kingdoms of England, Scotland and Ireland, and these men, known as Jacobites, maintained by force of arms that William of Orange, the Protestant prince who presently occupied the thrones jointly with his wife Mary, was a damned usurper. However, to Holcroft's mind, these supporters of King James were little better than criminals. James had abdicated the thrones when he departed from England for France the year before – after a most inglorious coup known paradoxically as the Glorious Revolution. Holcroft had decided, as had millions of his fellow countrymen, that King William and Queen Mary were *de facto* – and also *de jure* – rulers of the Three Kingdoms. These Irishmen were therefore rebels.

This peace conference with them today in Carrickfergus would likely lead to a surrender of the town and the evacuation of all defenders. The rebels would be allowed to march out of Carrickfergus with arms and honour intact. And the French spy, a man known by the codename Narrey, would march out with them.

General Schomberg had initially demanded unconditional surrender from the defenders, an offer which had been considered for the longest time before being politely refused. Holcroft knew, as well as the duke did, that these Irishmen – more than five hundred militiamen – had been ordered to delay the English Army for as long as they could. He also knew that if they chose to be stubborn, the defenders could draw this siege out for weeks, or even months.

After initial success for James's forces in the north, the Jacobites had been driven south when overwhelming numbers of King William's troops – English, Welsh and Scots, as well as Dutchmen, Germans, Danes and soldiers from other northern European lands – had been gathered in England and dispatched across the Irish sea. The old town of Londonderry, or just plain Derry as some local people called it, which had been besieged for three months by the Jacobites had been recently relieved by Colonel Percy Kirke and his brutally efficient infantrymen – nicknamed ironically Kirke's Lambs. The demoralised forces of James, many of whom were poorly trained conscripts, were retreating south.

All that prevented Schomberg from following on their heels to crush the rebellion once and for all was the defiance of this isolated Irish garrison. That was why the half-German general would most likely agree to almost anything the defenders of Carrickfergus asked. And both sides knew it. Schomberg dared not advance south to confront the main part of the Jacobite army if it meant leaving an enemy force behind him that could threaten his communication lines.

It was now late August, and autumn and winter were at hand. The fighting would grind to a halt in October or early November when the weather turned bad. The armies would go into their winter quarters to ride out the cold and rain in as much comfort as they could manage. If the Duke of Schomberg could not vanquish James before the Irish winter stalled the war, he might never beat him. The Stuart King was recruiting fresh men from all across Ireland to his banner. And Louis XIV of France, the most powerful monarch in Europe, who had already committed six thousand troops to the Jacobite cause, might raise another army and send them across the sea to bring aid to his fellow Catholics.

Schomberg had to winkle the rebels out of Carrickfergus fast. If that meant allowing all defenders – including Narrey – to march away unharmed, so be it.

Holcroft understood all this – yet he was still furious with his commander. He had come to Ireland with the express intention of finding Narrey and bringing him to justice – or, if that could not be arranged, then dispatching him speedily to Hell. He had petitioned the duke, begged him, in truth, to be allowed to accompany the Royal Train of Artillery as Second Engineer. And Schomberg had at last agreed to the appointment. But now, just when Holcroft had his enemy trapped and at his mercy, the general was about to let him go scot free.

Holcroft let out a long, heavy breath. He tried to concentrate.

I am very pleased to hear the buddleias are blooming and you may certainly invite a dozen of your friends around for a tea-drinking party in the garden, should you so wish to honour them. Unfortunately, I am unable to tell you very much about the flowers here in this northern part of Ireland, since much of the lands about these parts have been devastated by war. Indeed, the Jacobites have burnt all the surroundings of Carrickfergus almost to the ground to deny us cover, and so the landscape in this region is now very ashy and bleak . . .

The white canvas flap of the tent opened and a lean and dirty officer walked in.

'Blood,' he said, by way of greeting.

Holcroft's response was equally laconic. 'Richards,' he replied.

Jacob Richards was dressed in the same blue Ordnance coat that Holcroft wore, with the distinctive yellow turned-back sleeves. But his coat, his once-white breeches and black leather boots were all slathered with sticky grey mud. He had a scarlet sash around his waist, as Holcroft did, but he was, in fact, his superior officer – a major and the First Engineer of the Royal Train of Artillery.

Richards went over to the oak sideboard at the rear of the tent and poured himself a glass of wine from the crystal decanter. General Schomberg, affectionately nicknamed Uncle Frederick, liked to campaign with all the comforts, as befitted a man past the age of seventy, and the officers of his inner circle were permitted to make free of these home comforts too, within reason.

Richards took a sip of his wine. He watched Holcroft's broad back as he scratched away at his letter for a few moments. 'Parlay's concluded,' he said.

Holcroft put the quill in its stand and turned to look at the First Engineer.

'They surrendered?'

'No, MacCarthy's man defied us. He said: "I don't think we're done with you gentlemen yet!" That's what he said. They're laughing at us. Wasting time.'

A slow grin began to spread over Holcroft's large, sun-browned face.

'So you still have a chance of a crack at your Frog spy.' Richards gave Holcroft the tiniest of smiles. 'Schomberg's incandescent. He wants the assault renewed immediately. Full barrage on the town walls and on the castle itself. But I'm done in, Blood. I've been supervising the gun placements and the digging of the assault trenches all night. The No. 1 Battery is in good order, ready to reduce the castle. No. 2 is bedded in and primed to start on the town gate. So – off you go. Take command. Make Uncle Frederick happy by knocking some bloody great holes in their walls. When I've drunk up this glass, I'm heading for my bed.'

Holcroft stood up and opened his mouth to express his joy . . .

And the world exploded into chaos.

A twenty-four-pound iron ball – blasted from a 'Spanish' cannon with a twelve-foot barrel by fifteen pounds of black powder – makes a formidable missile. The cannon ball ripped through half a dozen guy ropes, punched through the side of the heavy canvas command tent, clipped the edge of Holcroft's writing table, smashing it to matchwood, bounced once then, without slowing, chopped through the central tent pole, a mast-like column of pine, and crashed into the centre of the solid oak sideboard, where Richards was standing at his muddy ease with his well-earned glass of claret. The ball disintegrated the ancient piece of furniture into a storm of kindling and shards of sharp flying oak and then tore a ragged hole in the rear wall of the tent and disappeared.

The powerful wind-wash of the ball's passage knocked Holcroft to the ground and, dizzy and disorientated, he struggled out of the wreckage of the writing table to regain his feet in the gently collapsing tent. Even slightly deafened, and suddenly swaddled in dream-like white canvas, he could hear the sound of Richards' agonised screams. But he could see nothing. Holcroft fought his way free of the sheets of cloth, dragging a clasp knife from his coat pocket, opening it and cutting through the tough material, tearing long holes in the cloth to allow him to see what had happened to his friend. And when he had finally slashed and ripped his way to the First Engineer on the far side of the ruined tent, and had cleared the heavy sheets of canvas, guy ropes, leather straps, and oak splinters away from Richards' prone body, it was clear that the officer was grievously wounded. His coat had been blown away from his right shoulder, leaving a raw seeping wound at the top of his white arm. His lean unshaven face was also slathered in blood. The bottom lobe of his left ear had been neatly chopped off by a spinning sliver of wood. Worst of all, a three-foot-long, needle-pointed spike of oak had transfixed his lower left thigh, just above the knee, pinning him to the floor.

Holcroft hesitated only for a moment as he looked down at Jacob Richards and the monstrous shard of oak sticking up from his leg. Then he grasped the end of the shard in one large hand and with a jerk withdrew it from the wound.

Richards was moaning and muttering something over and over in his pain. Holcroft heard the words: 'Ave Maria, gratia plena, Dominus tecum . . .' and realised the man was praying. He had not known that Richards was a Catholic.

At that moment another ball screamed past, twenty yards to Holcroft's left. The first shot had not been random, then. The enemy was targeting this command tent. They were targeting Schomberg himself. Holcroft had no time to think about that now. He bent down and gathered the muttering officer in his arms. He looked about to get his bearings in the suddenly bright sunlight, seeing the endless rows of other grubby tents, the campfires, the long lines of deep trench-works that surrounded Carrickfergus, and the red-coated soldiery staring out at him from these muddy ditches, their heads at boot height, their mouths agape. As he stood in the puddled remains of the command tent, a big man with a limp, bloody form in his arms, he spotted the regimental flag of a famous guards unit, which gave him his orientation. Then, cradling Richards to his chest, he began to run.

Two hours later, his arms and chest still stained with Richards' blood and mud, Holcroft stepped down on to the No. 2 Battery gun platform. He had left Richards at the mercy of the brandy-soaked barber-surgeon in the hospital tent – a man who refused to guarantee the wounded officer's survival but who had promised to transport him to Belfast Castle as soon as possible where he could be cared for in comfort. Now Holcroft was even more angry than before.

He looked down at the town of Carrickfergus a little over a mile away: it was a roughly hexagonal shape pressed against the shoreline with a flattened front in the north making a seventh side, where the main gate stood. This portal was protected by a fortified gatehouse with twin square stone towers. An eighteen-foot wall, manned here and there by tiny figures in red coats and black hats, ran around the outside punctuated by six bastions, right-angled outcroppings of the wall that would give the defenders the opportunity to fire upon any infantry assaulting the length of wall between one bastion and the next. On the southern side of the town, the Norman castle – a high square donjon, two round towers at the gate and a twenty-foot-high curtain wall – stood on a small peninsula which jutted into Belfast Lough. A quay reached out from the rear of the castle into the sea like a stone arm and curled around to the west, designed to shelter shipping from the weather.

The wide main street of the town ran from the North Gate three hundred yards southwards towards the castle gate towers, with prosperous-looking houses on either side of the wide street.

Holcroft could see a lone old man and a heavily laden donkey making their slow way down the thoroughfare. And now a galloping green-coated fellow on a black horse coming up from the castle and heading for the North Gate, a messenger, no doubt. There was little else stirring on this bright Sunday morning. To the right of the main road was the familiar cross shape of a church – St Nicholas's, he had been told in the intelligence briefings, which he had been asked, if possible, not to damage with his cannon fire. On the left side of the road was a tall, opulent building, a minor palace even, which he had heard was called Joymount House, the residence of the local Protestant magnate Lord Donegall, abandoned at the approach of war.

Joymount House was a squared off U-shape, with the two arms pointing north towards the English encampment. At three storeys high, it was the tallest structure in Carrickfergus, with the exception of the church spire, and the enemy had taken full advantage of its elevation. Holcroft saw a flash of sunlight on brass and a puff of grey smoke on the right-hand roof, and a moment later he heard the boom of a heavy cannon – a twenty-four-pounder to his educated ear. He thought he could make out the line of flight, away to his right, the ball landing near a knot of gentlemen by the deflated command tent, kicking up a spray of dirt, and bounding away between two lesser tents.

He could see that there was a corresponding cannon-shape on the left-hand roof of Joymount House and a group of men tending to it. So ... the enemy had managed to place an attacking battery up there. This was the unit that had been responsible for wounding poor Richards. And it had been no accident of war. It had been a deliberate targeting of General Schomberg's tent and of his staff. *But how did they know which tent to aim at?* Holcroft asked himself.

The answer was plain. Schomberg's intelligencers had their spies in Carrickfergus – and the enemy must have theirs in the English camp, too. Holcroft tucked that piece of information away to be chewed over later. There were more immediate challenges at hand. He hauled out a small, polished brass field glass from one of his deep Ordnance coat pockets, to get a better view of the enemy position and, as he did so, he could hear the ritual chant of the nearest English gun of his own No. 2 Battery crew a few yards to his left.

'. . . Prime the piece . . . Tend the match . . . Have a care . . . Give fire!'

Holcroft loved the ritual words. Exactly the same every time a piece was fired. He found great comfort in their structure and familiarity.

The English gun – one of four of the Train's big cannon that made up the No. 2 Battery – thundered, spewing out flame and smoke and a twenty-four-pound ball, and the heavy carriage rumbled back a yard on its massive iron-bound wheels. The half-dozen Ordnance men serving that particular piece, gunners, engineers and matrosses – the lowliest of gun folk, only semi-trained, who did the heavy lifting of balls and powder – had stood well clear at the shouted command, 'Have a care!' from the gun captain and they now swarmed forward again to begin the complicated reloading process.

The English ball struck the town's north wall a mile away, about ten yards to the left of the gatehouse, the crack it made audible, and a gout of dust flew up and a shower of masonry tumbled down from the strike point. It was not the first time it had been hit. Holcroft had the field glass to his eye. It was a fine shot. In a day, perhaps in two days, a breach would be punched through at that spot, if the gunners did their duty, slowly, methodically, and didn't overheat their barrels.

A second English cannon, a twelve-pounder, one of the two smaller pieces of the No. 2 Battery, rang out, the ball crashing into the wall four paces along and slightly lower than the first hit. They were trying to make an inverted T-shaped pattern of strikes on one section of the defences to the east of the gate – the most efficient way to bring down the wall. Holcroft saw that the damage done by the last strike, by the twelve-pound ball, was understandably less than the bigger gun, but it was not insignificant. At that range, the No. 2 Battery's accuracy of fire was not bad, in fact, not bad at all.

'Smart work, Claudius!' he called out. A roly-poly, red-faced Ordnance officer, who was standing between the two nearest cannon, turned and gave him a grin and a wave of his chubby hand. 'All part of the No. 2 Battery service, Captain,' he called. 'We aim to please!' Then guffawed at his own feeble joke.

Holcroft frowned for a moment, then gave a rather false-sounding chuckle. Lieutenant Claudius Barden, the Third Engineer of the Train, who had command of the No. 2 Battery today, was famous throughout the Ordnance for his poverty, his laziness, his good humour and unquenchable wit. Holcroft had been made aware by several friends of the famous Barden wit: he knew that half the Third Engineer's utterances were designed to amuse – Holcroft's problem was he could not tell which half. To avoid causing offence, or seeming to be what some people referred to bafflingly as a 'cold fish', he tended to smile or laugh in a restrained way at almost anything Barden said.

Turning away from the junior officer, Holcroft swept the glass over to Joymount House, and watched the doll-like figures of the enemy on the twin roofs serving their guns. Two twenty-four-pounders, he noted. *Demi-canon d'Espagne*, the French called them. They were well defended from counter-battery fire by a wall of gabions, huge earth-filled wicker baskets that would soak up any incoming shots, four of which had been placed in two pairs in front of each cannon. *The guns must have been the very devil to get up on that high roof,* he thought. *They must have been at it all night, and working even as they parlayed with us this morning.* He felt a glow of rage at their perfidy.

The two big guns, one on each roof, were a dozen yards apart and between them was a dark gap that fell away to the ground floor.

On each roof, the Irish soldiers were swarming over the guns in a strange undisciplined manner, wielding rammers and sponges, some men approaching with the heavy balls carried on hurdles, others, standing idly by with bags of powder in their arms. He saw one eager man accidentally barge into another leaving them both sprawling on the lead-covered surface of the roof. He could tell that these men were unfamiliar with their big guns – perhaps they were more comfortable with Sakers, Falcons or other smaller fry. Perhaps they were raw conscripts who had never seen a cannon before in their lives. No, that could not be the case. They had hit the command tent with their first shot, and come very close with their second. There was at least one expert gunner at work – even if the bulk of the men were no better than bone-headed farmers. Holcroft swept his glass slowly across both of the roofs. There were two figures on the right-hand roof, two men in dark clothing, side by side, holding themselves aloof from the jostle of red-coated folk around the pieces.

When Holcroft focused the glass on them, he hissed under his breath.

One was tall, broad and bulky, strong-looking and dark. The other was small, slender, almost girlish. Although he had a dark, heavy cloak around his shoulders – on this warm August day! – and a wide-brimmed hat pulled down low over his eyes, Holcroft was able to detect a stray lock of red hair at the curve of his neck. The cloaked man was standing at an easel, a large canvas clamped in place with a paintbrush and palette in his hands – for all the world as if he were on some sightseeing tour of the countryside. Holcroft knew both of the men. The dark muscular one was Major Guillaume du Clos, a French artilleryman who had been trained to the highest levels in gunnery in Louis XIV's elite *Corps Royal d'Artillerie*. He must be responsible for the accurate strike on the command tent. Yet Guillaume du Clos was more than a gunner, he was also the lieutenant, bodyguard and factotum of the second man, the painter, the spymaster known as Narrey – whom Holcroft had identified the year before, at no small cost in blood, as being Henri, Comte d'Erloncourt.

He regarded the two Frenchmen standing together on the roof of Joymount House with a full measure of loathing – but no great surprise. He had long known that this murderous pair were in Ireland, that they had sailed over with James from France in March of this year, landing at the southern Irish port of Kinsale. And Schomberg's own intelligencers had kindly provided him with a description of the only two French officers presently in Carrickfergus.

Don't move. Stay put. Please God, let the two of them remain on the roof.

Aloud, Holcroft said, 'Claudius, would you be so kind as to oblige me . . .'

He stopped and turned, hearing a clatter of many hooves behind him.

A spritely old gentleman in a blue velvet coat with gold trimmings rode up on a huge black horse. He was sporting an enormous grey hat with an orange plume and surrounded by a dozen similarly gorgeous younger officers. It was General Schomberg and these aristocratic cavaliers were his aides-de-camp.

'Captain Blood, sir, have you heard this latest outrage? They're shooting at me now! At me, personally! Their cannon flattened my tent. The effrontery . . .'

Holcroft made a bow to the commander-in-chief. 'I'm aware, Your Grace.'

The Duke of Schomberg looked the Ordnance officer up and down, noting his filthy exterior. 'Are you wounded, sir? You appear to be covered in gore.'

'Not mine, sir. I regret to tell you that Major Richards was wounded when they fired upon your tent after the parlay. He is in the hospital at present.'

'Was he? Is he? The poor chap. I suppose I'd better go and pay him a visit. So the Train is without its First Engineer. Well, you'd better take over his duties, Blood. You'll have to step into his shoes, I'm afraid. Poor old Richards! I suppose I'd best get along and see how he's doing. You'll take over, yes?'

'Yes, sir,' said Holcroft. He looked up at the general's wrinkled face. He seemed particularly old today. Repeating himself in a bumbling manner.

'I told Richards, so now I'd better tell you, Captain Blood. You are to concentrate all your fire, and a brisk warm fire, you understand me, on the North Gate – make me a breach, Captain Blood. One I could march a full company of grenadiers through without touching the sides. Hear me? You have sufficient guns here, I think. Those Catholic dogs had the temerity to waste my time this morning with a parlay – I suppose you heard about that. Well, we will see what they have to say when their walls are tumbling around their ears. I want No. 1 Battery over there to concentrate on the castle defences. Knock their venerable walls to rubble. And your No. 2 fellows here can make a breach for me in the town walls. Yes?'

'Might I have permission, sir, to take a few pot shots at Joymount House? They have a pair of twenty-fours up there; those are the guns that bombarded your tent. I'd like to pay them out for that, and for Richards, sir, if I may.'

'Joymount House, ah, Joymount ...' Schomberg squinted uncertainly at the enemy-held town. 'That's the tall building, is it? On the left, am I correct?'

'Yes, sir, see the bronze gleam; they've two big guns up there on the roof.'

The general was silent for a moment, squinting at the enemy-held town.

'No, Mister Blood, you may not. Time is of the essence. Don't waste it on revenge. Leave them be up there. I want all your battery fire concentrated on the wall by the North Gate. Make me a breach – and I want it by tonight, if possible. Tomorrow morning at the latest. With a hole in their walls, and one or two in the castle, too, we'll have 'em out o' there in no time. Good day, sir.'

As General Schomberg and his gaudy entourage cantered away, Holcroft pondered his predicament. He did not dare disobey a direct order from his commander, particularly as Claudius Barden had heard it as well – he must in good conscience concentrate all fire from the No. 2 Battery on the town walls and make a practicable breach as soon as possible. On the other hand, he did not want this opportunity – one perhaps that was never to be repeated – to go to waste. *Please God, let the two of them remain on the roof!*

What to do? Making a breach was the correct approach, of course, tactically and strategically. With a hole in their walls and a couple of English regiments ready to pour through, the rebels would surely surrender – or, according to the rules of war, they'd face the slaughter of the whole garrison.

Holcroft believed in following orders, indeed, he believed in order in general. Chaos was his enemy. But there was another part of his character that sometimes overrode that impulse: when an idea lodged in his head, he could be mulishly single-minded, even obsessive. He'd come here to bring Narrey to justice, or kill him. Now he had the chance to do just that.

'You heard Uncle Frederick, Claudius. Wants a breach, soon as possible.'

'Yes, sir! Once more unto the breach, eh, sir! Once more.'

Holcroft ignored the lieutenant's silly comment. 'I'd like to borrow one of your master gunners for a few hours, if I may. And five strong matrosses too.'

'Sir? Are you not staying with us, sir?'

'No, Claudius, I am not. With Major Richards out of action I have to be here, there and everywhere. I must check on No. 1 Battery – make sure Lieutenant Field understands his duty, and there are other urgent matters, official, um, business . . .' Holcroft found himself blushing at his blatant lies.

He turned away from the lieutenant in shame and walked to the third gun along the line of the battery, a relatively light and elderly six-pounder piece called a Saker. In fact, it had a more particular name: she was known as Roaring Meg by those who served and loved her. He watched the master gunner, the gun's captain, an old man, bald as one of his round shot, fire off the ancient cannon, covering his ears protectively, and admiring the fall of shot as the ball smashed into the wall halfway up, in the dead centre of the invisible T-target.

He tapped the old man on the shoulder. 'Enoch Jackson,' he said. 'Tell me: have any of the eight-inch Humpties been brought off the transports yet?'

'They have, sir. There should be at least three of them unloaded by now in the artillery park; I saw a gun carriage, an' a wagon-load of hollow-shot, too.'

'Then give old Meg over to your deputy, Enoch, and you come with me.'

Chapter Two

The same day: 4 p.m.

The Irish are no soldiers, Henri d'Erloncourt thought to himself, as he watched a man carrying a bag of black powder trip over a wooden bucket and knock into another fellow bearing a sponge on a long stick, leaving them sprawling on the warm lead roof of Joymount House. *They're bold enough when fired by their foul home-made spirits, but they've little discipline and less sense.*

Major Guillaume du Clos, commander of the rooftop battery, was berating the two tumbled men, bawling and hauling them back to their feet. On the far roof, the eastward one, the big *Demi-canon* roared out again, and Henri, flinching at the sound, watched the line of the shot as it arced through the blue sky and pounded into the English encampment on the hillside.

It gave him great satisfaction to watch the twenty-four-pound ball soar over the nearest lines of trenches, land with a spray of dirt and pebbles and skip through a gap between the lines of grubby white tents and out of sight: he imagined it squelching into a knot of unwary marching Englishmen, ploughing bloodily into a squadron of their cavalry, or smashing a loaded artillery munitions wagon into a shower of broken kindling and spilled black powder. He knew that, in truth, they were not doing much more than disturbing the camp. But there was a moral satisfaction to the cannon assault that went far beyond its limited effectiveness. These two cannon, which had been firing at a relaxed rate of perhaps three or four times an hour, were the only ones in Carrickfergus that had the reach to hit the enemy. And over the course of the day Henri was sure that their impact would have been felt beyond the walls.

Major du Clos had made a genuine attempt to strike at General Frederick von Schomberg personally that morning, to kill him and some of his senior officers, if at all possible – that would have tossed a massive paving stone in the pond! – and the intelligence he had received from the secret agent known as Agricola about the location of Schomberg's command tent had been specific.

But General Schomberg was not dead – *tant pis*; Henri had seen him riding across the skyline in the centre of a pack of bright-garbed aides-de-camp not an hour ago. Nevertheless, it was worthwhile, he thought, to keep up the pressure on the English – to kill or maim as many as they could, to demoralise them – even though the outcome of this contest was in no doubt. Carrickfergus must fall eventually – and King James knew this as well as Henri d'Erloncourt.

The God-ordained ruler of England, Scotland and Ireland would not be bringing his small army of wild, half-trained Irish militiamen and raffish mounted Catholic gentry north to lift the siege here because it would mean facing the might of the disciplined professional English soldiers in open battle. That would be madness. That was exactly what General Schomberg most desired and what Henri feared most. If the Jacobite forces fought a pitched battle, they would most likely be beaten, and the campaign could be over in a single afternoon. No, Henri had decided, they must emulate that great Roman general Quintus Fabius Maximus of the Punic Wars. They must avoid battle at all costs, attack the supply lines, hit the enemy and run. By this clever strategy Fabius had even beaten the great Hannibal himself – and saved Rome.

Not that Henri sought a great victory for King James – indeed he did *not* seek one, at least not immediately. The Comte d'Erloncourt served King Louis XIV, first and foremost, and thereafter his loyalties lay with the Holy Roman Catholic Church. He was here in Ireland to further France's interests, for no other reason, and it was in France's interest that this war be prolonged as much as possible.

An intact and potentially dangerous Jacobite army in Ireland, one that continued to refuse battle, Fabian style, meant that Dutch William was forced to expend his resources here on this damp Celtic island rather than in the Low Countries, where Louis XIV had more important designs. A nice, long drawn-out war was what Henri desired. That was the goal he was striving towards.

And he had identified just the men to help him achieve his ends. They were known as raparees, after the half-pikes, the heavy spears or, in Irish, *ropairí*, that many of them carried. Some were no better than bandits, attacking Protestant and Catholic alike without discrimination. Killing and stealing at will. Others were more disciplined and operated like first-class light cavalry, as scouts and raiders, gathering forage and garnering intelligence for the main army. These were the men who would bleed the Williamite forces to death. These were the men who could keep the war here bubbling away for years.

Henri became aware that Major du Clos was at his side.

'The English are starting to make a breach, monsieur le comte,' he said. 'Look yonder, to the east of the gate.'

Henri pulled a long telescope from his pocket, opened it and rested it on the horizontal top clamp of the easel in front of him. He trained the glass on the town wall and followed the top line until he came to a crumbled dip slightly to the right of the gatehouse and a cloud of dust above it. As he watched, a ball cracked into the far side and the curtain of thick, mortared stone gave a shudder.

'How long, would you say, before the breach is practicable, Guillaume?'

'Not today,' du Clos replied. 'They will cease at nightfall and bring up more powder and ball during the night, and then continue bombardment at dawn. I'd say by noon tomorrow it will be wide enough to permit an assault.'

'Noon, then. Yet maybe there is a way we can slow them down.'

'You desire me to fire at the enemy battery, monsieur?'

Henri thought about his lieutenant's suggestion for a few moments. There were several factors to consider. 'You believe you could destroy it from here?'

'With this rabble of peasants? Unlikely – unless we were very, very lucky.'

Du Clos might have added that the clever Gentlemen of the English Ordnance had created an excellent fortified gun platform for their No. 2 Battery, defended by banks of earth on either side, guarded by half a dozen gabions in front as well as a rock-hard packed-earth slope called a glacis designed to bounce balls harmlessly over the heads of the crews. But he held his tongue.

'No, then. We will continue as before harassing the encampment till dusk. Every Englishman we kill will improve our negotiating position at the end.'

'Yes, indeed!' Major du Clos turned away, and made to leave.

'One more thing, Guillaume,' said Henri. 'A technical question. Could these two noisy cannon be brought to bear on walls or a town gate, if necessary? Could they be depressed sufficiently to hit them with case shot, for example?'

'They could, monsieur. It might take a little time to reposition them, but certainly the guns could be fired on the gates. Do you wish me to redeploy?'

'Not just yet, Guillaume, not yet. But I do desire you to send a man to the castle and summon Colonel MacCarthy up here to me, if you please.'

'Very good, monsieur!' Major du Clos saluted and conferred briefly with a red-coated Irish soldier, who nodded and made off towards the tunnel that connected the twin roofs and also contained the stairwell that led to the ground floor. Du Clos followed the messenger out of sight into the tunnel but a moment later he appeared on the other roof, where he took charge of the cannon there, berating the gun captain in strongly accented English for his Irish idiocy.

Henri put the telescope to his eye, scanning the upper northern hillside where the English and a few battalions of William's Dutchmen, too, were spread out in a smear of tents, horse lines, baggage carts, files of redcoats on the march, piles of equipment and the campfires of several thousand men.

Closer to the town, two lines of deep trenches had been cut parallel with the walls but a few hundred yards distant, and dozens of teams of mud-caked sappers were already pushing ahead, digging more trenches forward towards Carrickfergus, which would ultimately branch out sideways to make the third parallel line of trench works to surround the city. On the eve on an assault, these trenches would be filled with thousands of redcoats – mostly armed with muskets, although a few still carried sixteen-foot pikes – who, driven by the beat of a drum, would surge out and storm the town walls.

Henri swept the glass to his extreme left, over to the sea and focused on the six sleek warships of the Royal Navy, which he could just make out riding at anchor in Belfast Lough. He moved the glass inland to the old square Norman castle and beyond the western walls of Carrickfergus he could see another God-damned battery of English guns pecking away at the castle's ancient walls.

Scanning into the town of Carrick itself, he noted the church spire of St Nicholas – that heretical Protestant approximation of a House of God – and a large stock pen on the far side of the main street. Taking his eye from the telescope, and rubbing it gently, Henri looked naked-eyed on the square open stockade and the hundred or so reddish-brown cattle that were enclosed. The beasts seemed agitated by the gunfire, moving constantly and occasionally crashing into each other and against the stout wooden bars of their pen. Henri could hear their distressed lowing clearly.

He lifted his eyes to the damaged part of the walls and saw with mild alarm that the breach had grown larger in the few minutes since he had last observed it. It might be wide enough to storm

before noon tomorrow at this rate. He imagined a horde of Englishmen bursting through the wall, scrambling over the rubble, firing
as they came. A wave of bloodthirsty enemies flooding the town
bent on revenge.

I should not be here, Henri told himself. *I'm not a man made for
the blood and filth of a battlefield. At heart, I am an artist, a seeker
after beauty.*

He examined his work on the easel with a critical eye: a sweeping
landscape of the town walls and the English positions, in browns
and reds. He had captured the scene exactly. The painting was perfect, perhaps, the most brilliant of all his creations – and was there
anybody in this miserable town who was capable of painting a piece
of art that was its equal? No, what an absurd notion. Was there anyone in this arse-crack of a *ville* even capable of half appreciating his
work? No! Well, perhaps du Clos. *Once Carrickfergus has fallen,*
he thought to himself, *with God's grace, I shall return to my little
office in Cork and henceforth run all my operations from that most
civilised of towns.*

Henri had taken the controversial step of setting up the headquarters of his secret department in a medieval tower in Cork – instead
of Dublin or Waterford or even Belfast – when he had arrived in
nearby Kinsale in March. He liked the town of Cork, it was small
enough so that any curious strangers stood out immediately, which
gave him a sense of security, and the local seafood was delicious, he
found, excellent, even, for this culinary-impoverished island – but
it was the port of Cork, with its regular, unimpeded flow of French
shipping that made the southern town most attractive.

In Cork, he received regular supplies of fine wines and fresh
clothes from home. He received weapons and money as well. And
his junior colleagues in the secret department known as the *cabinet
noir* in Versailles provided him with reports, too, on what was
occurring politically in his homeland – who was rising, who was
in disgrace. There was also the knowledge that, with the regular

flow of traffic back to France, if he had to make a swift departure, there would always be a ship handy to bear him away. Up here, at the far end of the country, besieged by enemies, facing capture and imprisonment, he missed sitting at his beautiful escritoire in the little office in the Old Tower in Cork.

What sins have I committed that I should be stranded up here in this drab, uncomfortable and joyless place? Not a one. I have merely done my duty.

Henri d'Erloncourt had a right to be aggrieved – he should have quit the town of Carrickfergus more than a week ago. It was bad luck that kept him here. He had agreed to the meeting with his agent Agricola, in a rare moment of weakness. He had believed the spy's claim that it was urgent and they had met in a deserted barn about halfway between Belfast and Carrick. Henri had come without his usual cavalry escort, at Agricola's insistence, and only protected by Major du Clos. Yet the intelligence that Agricola provided was out of date – Henri already had the full order of battle of the forces that Schomberg had disembarked, thanks to French agents in the English city of Chester. Agricola had then demanded a large sum in gold for any future service, which Henri had provided in little chinking sacks from his saddlebags. Even if Agricola had not proved useful in this instance, this agent had regular access to high-quality intelligence – and that was more valuable than a few *louis d'or*.

After the meeting, on the way south to Newry to rejoin the regular Irish forces holding that town, the French pair had been spotted by an English cavalry patrol, one of several dozen that Schomberg sent out from Belfast to halt the predations of the local raparees. On catching sight of Henri and Guillaume, the English horsemen, hallooing as if they were on a Leicestershire fox hunt, had chased the two Frenchmen and their exhausted mounts into the only safe haven they could find: the rebel-held town of Carrickfergus.

Schomberg had moved the next day, bringing up twelve battalions of infantry and cavalry, and surrounding the walled town. His warships took up stations in Belfast Lough, to prevent any seaborne relief. And a few days later the big guns of the Artillery Train were unloaded from the transports and hauled into their positions. Henri and Guillaume had been in Carrickfergus ever since.

'You summoned me.'

Henri turned and found himself looking up at a burly, angry-looking ginger man of middle years in a yellow velvet coat with a gold-handled sword at his side. 'Colonel MacCarthy,' he said. 'Thank you for coming.'

The big man's hand was on the hilt of his sword, his face was the colour of a ripe plum. The afternoon sun gave the fellow a monstrously long shadow on the lead roof. '*You* . . . had the temerity . . . to summon *me*. I, governor of this town, was ordered like a servant to come to this battery, with all speed, to speak to you – a mere adviser, a bloody foreigner, to boot. You *summoned* me.'

'I did – and here you are. Once again, sir, you have my profound thanks.'

Henri locked eyes with the furious Irishman. He did not flinch from his anger. He knew that Guillaume would be close by, and doubtless had a hand on the long pistol in his belt. Not that violence would be necessary: Henri *was* a foreigner, he was a proud son of France and the servant of Louis le Grand, the greatest monarch in all the world. And this furious ogre was no more than the jumped-up captain of an insignificant outpost, a caretaker of a flyspeck fortress.

Henri d'Erloncourt had the authority to send the French battalions home – the only reliable regular infantry that King James possessed – ending this war with the stroke of his pen. Or, if he felt the need, he could summon more troops from France to support James's efforts. He could even, with the funds and financial instruments at his disposal, pay the entire Irish Army for a year – or let them starve to death, just as he chose. The two men glaring at each other might both enjoy the rank of full Colonel – but there was no comparison in the extent of their true power.

Charles MacCarthy also knew this. 'So, what do you want?' he said.

'I thought you, as a gentleman of refinement, might enjoy admiring this rather good painting I have made. I am calling it *The Siege of Carrickfergus*.'

Colonel MacCarthy glared at the indistinct smudges of reddish brown on the big canvas. It might have been painted with excrement for all he cared.

'Just tell me what you want,' he growled.

'I want what you want, sir. I want to delay the fall of Carrickfergus for as long as possible. That is our duty, I hope you will agree.'

'We shall have to surrender tomorrow, monsieur. You'll have noticed their breach from your fine vantage point. It grows wider by the hour.' He made an angry gesture with one huge hand towards the town walls. 'We shall be forced to hang out the white flag before noon. By dusk, God willing, we'll be gone.'

'I think not.'

'*You* think not?'

'This, my dear Colonel, is what I propose that we do.'

Chapter Three

Monday, August 26, 1689: Dawn

Holcroft Blood peered around the edge of the wall of the burnt-out farmhouse. In the first grey streaks of dawn, he could make out the silhouette of a sentry on the town ramparts a hundred yards away. Keeping his body mostly hidden behind the broken brickwork, he trained his brass telescope sharply upwards at the roof of Joymount House but could see no movement – just the bulky shapes of the gabions and the faint gleam of the barrel of the right-hand cannon.

The guns were silent. Perhaps the crews were still asleep. Perhaps the two Frenchmen had quit their observation post for good and were now snug in their beds inside the castle. Holcroft did not wish to entertain that thought.

It had taken him till the hour before dawn to get himself and his men into position. It could have been much quicker but he had felt duty bound the afternoon before to visit the No. 1 Battery on the western edge of the siege lines to make sure that its commander, Lieutenant Obadiah Field, understood his orders and was battering the castle with sufficient enthusiasm. Then Holcroft had revisited the No. 2 Battery to check that all was proceeding well with the making of the breach under Lieutenant Barden's command, before riding up the hill to the artillery park to supervise the loading of the parts of an eight-inch mortar, its wooden platform, several boxes of hollow shells and barrels of powder on to two ox-wagons and begin the slow process of bringing them down as discreetly as possible to the remains of a burnt out farmhouse by the Antrim Road outside the town walls and a hundred yards east of the Carrickfergus town gate.

They had arrived long after midnight, undetected by the enemy, or so he believed, and in darkness and as near to silence as they could manage, they had unloaded the freight from the heavy wagons and set up the mortar on its square bed. In Ordnance slang, a mortar was known as a Humpty Dumpty, after a famous siege gun used by Royalist forces at Gloucester in the late civil wars, which had been placed on a high, flat wall and which, because it was overloaded with powder or just badly cast, had shattered upon its first firing.

Now, behind Holcroft's craning body, out of sight from the walls, two of his matrosses were using ladles to fill the hollow spherical bombs with loose black powder straight from the open barrel, while the other three were sleeping, curled up in the corners of the roofless farmhouse and its ruined outbuildings. Enoch Jackson sitting beneath a smashed window inside the house was carefully cutting fuses to the appropriate lengths. It was a difficult task requiring great skill and years of practice – but crucially important if his plan were to succeed.

Even if the French do not return to the roof of Joymount House, Holcroft told himself, *it would still be worth silencing the twenty-four-pounders up there.*

He did not truly believe his own words. General Schomberg had ordered him directly to make a breach, and *not* to bombard Joymount, and he had flat out disobeyed him. If he merely killed the handful of Irish militia who worked those guns with his hidden mortar, it would not affect the outcome of the siege. Even if he killed the two Frenchmen, it would be unlikely to change the course of the engagement. He must admit the truth: he was deliberately refusing orders and putting his men in harm's way, to gain a personal revenge.

He looked again at the roof with his glass but his enemies were still nowhere to be seen. *Could they really have abandoned the position?* No – impossible. He would not believe it. It was the perfect spot from which to observe the battle. None of the English artillery batteries had molested them up there – and they were too distant, two hundred yards *behind* the town walls, for any enemy musketeer in the siege trenches to trouble them.

Holcroft decided that he would do nothing until he could confirm that the Frenchmen were on the roof. Once the mortar opened fire, their position would be revealed – to the enemy and also to General Schomberg – and the clock would begin ticking on the time they had to destroy the Joymount battery.

Fifteen or perhaps twenty minutes was all they could reasonably expect. A sortie by the Irish from the town walls – even only a few dozen infantrymen, or a squad of cavalry – and his men would be slaughtered, unless they fled, which would mean leaving the mortar for the enemy to capture as a prize of war.

'Get a tarpaulin over our Humpty, Enoch. It's full daylight. Cover the whole works from any Irish eyes on the wall. And get all the men inside the ruins to rest. I'm going back to the No. 2 Battery to check on Lieutenant Barden.'

If Jackson was unhappy at being abandoned by his officer a bowshot from the enemy walls, he did not show it. All he said was: 'Will you be long, sir?'

'An hour or two, three at most. If I'm not back by noon, that means something has gone wrong and you should all withdraw discreetly, leaving the mortar here. If anyone asks where you've been, tell them you have been acting under my instructions. You cannot be punished if it's your captain's orders.'

'Right you are, sir. You remember your Proverbs, of course: chapter twenty-nine, verse two?'

'Yes, indeed,' said Holcroft. 'See you in an hour or so.'

Holcroft sprinted across a patch of open farmyard and mounted his horse, which was tied up in a half-demolished stable at the rear of their position. As he spurred up the hill back to the English trench lines, keeping the farm between him and the walls for as long as possible, he pondered what Enoch had just said to him. Proverbs 29:2 – 'When the righteous are in authority, the people rejoice: but when the wicked beareth rule, the people mourn.'

This was an old game of theirs, to quote Bible verses to each other as a way of private communication. Holcroft had memorised almost all of the Good Book in idle hours during his youth, and Jackson had been a celebrated lay preacher forty-odd years ago. But as he rode up the hill he wondered – was he actually a righteous man? Or did disobeying General Schomberg's orders make him one of the wicked?

Fifteen minutes later he dismounted at the No. 2 Battery, and was dismayed to see almost no activity. Claudius Barden was seated at a large, empty, upturned powder barrel sipping a mug of ale and reading a small leather-bound book with a fine gilt-decorated spine. The other thirty-odd gunners and matrosses of the No. 2 Battery were scattered around, some sleeping, or cooking breakfast, some chattering with friends, playing dice or mending clothes.

The sun was a finger above the horizon yet the guns were silent.

'What is going on, Claudius? Why are you not firing on the walls?'

'Oh, there you are, sir,' said Barden. 'Morning. Wondered where you'd got to.' He stood up and put the book down on the barrel. Holcroft could clearly read the title that was printed on the spine: *The Pilgrim's Progress*.

'I have been . . . occupied . . . on private business . . . elsewhere.'

'Is that so, Mister Blood? Private business, eh! Don't tell me you've found a nice Irish lass! You are a sly boots, sir. But fair play to you, sir, fair play!'

There was a clatter of hooves that prevented Holcroft from denying this absurd notion. He turned and saw, with a pang of guilt, General Schomberg, with two aides-de-camp, towering over him from the back of his huge black stallion.

'What is the meaning of this? I gave you clear instructions, Captain Blood, to make me a breach as fast as possible. And now I see you, idle as a fire-side hound, amusing yourself with books. Why are you not working your battery?'

Holcroft swallowed. He had no idea why the great guns were cold and unworked. He opened his mouth to try to give some kind of answer . . .

'If you'll forgive me, Your Grace,' said Claudius Barden, 'we've no more ammunition. We used the last ball and last scraping of the powder barrel at dusk yesterday. We've nothing to charge the pieces with, begging your pardon, sir.'

'Nothing to charge them with? There is a park full of Ordnance not a mile up the hill: four thousand barrels of powder, eight thousand or so balls, I have been told, wadding, linstocks, match . . . it's a damned cornucopia of *materiel*.'

'I sent a master gunner up to fetch supplies last night but Captain Vallance, the Quartermaster, was already fast asleep in his tent, and his deputy said he dared not release anything to us without Vallance's say-so until this morning.'

'Incompetence. Sheer bloody incompetence. How am I supposed to prosecute this war if my officers lack even the merest hint of professionalism. You should have woken that lazy dog Edmund Vallance, demanded the powder and ball. Threatened to report him if he refused. Dear God, I despair. And you, Captain Blood, where were you when this absurdity was taking place? Eh, eh? I placed you in charge of the Train after Major Richards was wounded and, frankly, sir, I expected more. Why didn't you do anything?'

One of the brilliantly dressed aides snickered.

Holcroft found he was unable to answer. For an awful moment, he contemplated telling Schomberg the truth. The truth was always the best course.

He said: 'Well, sir, you see, I was . . .'

Barden interrupted him: 'Captain Blood was suddenly taken ill, Your Grace. A stomach gripe. He left me in charge. The fault is all mine, sir. We sent a galloper to the park at first light, so the Ordnance should be arriving within the hour. We'll have the guns going – ha-ha! – great guns in a very short while, sir.'

Holcroft looked at Barden – if the Ordnance was on its way that was something at least. He saw the lieutenant wink at him. *By God, the man truly thinks I've been debauching myself with some Irish trull.* But Holcroft also felt a sense of gratitude. Barden's lies had saved him from disgrace.

'Indeed, sir? Taken ill, eh? You don't look well, Blood, I must say. You look exhausted. And you do not appear to have changed your clothes from yesterday. So, are you recovered, Captain? Able to do your duty like a soldier?'

'I am perfectly well, thank you, Your Grace.'

'Very well. But I want this battery in action as soon as possible. And if Vallance gives you any more trouble, tell him I shall have him shot for treason. Make that breach practicable today, Blood. Today – you understand?'

The General and his aides galloped away. And fifteen minutes later three lumbering wagons could be seen approaching down the muddy track that led to the artillery park. Holcroft left the unloading to his lieutenant, his gunners and matrosses and took out his shiny brass telescope. The breach was, in fact, nearly practicable already. A crumbling hole a dozen yards wide had been smashed in the town walls a little to the east of the town gate and while the enemy had made some efforts during the night to fill the gap with empty barrels, loose masonry and timber planks, Holcroft reckoned that another hour or two's bombardment would give the General the avenue of attack he desired.

He trained the glass on the roof of Joymount House and saw it was an ants' nest of activity. Men with ropes and hand spikes were clustered round both guns and as he watched it became clear they were shifting their position. Slanting both the barrels of the cannon several degrees to the west, lowering the extreme elevation to their maximum depression.

Why? Holcroft asked himself. *Why move them? What is the new target?*

He trained the telescope along the line of the barrel of the right-hand gun and followed an imaginary flight of a cannon ball. *That cannot be right.*

He checked again, performing the same exercise with the second twenty-four-pounder. There could be no mistaking it. The guns were being aimed at the town wall. More precisely, at the half-breach in the town wall that his No. 2 Battery had made the day before. For an insane moment, he wondered if the enemy battery was going to assist in the widening of the breach. That was absurd. Why would the enemy help the attackers? He noticed there were fresh soldiers on the walls, hundreds of Irish musket men on either side of the breach, keeping low beneath the parapet for the most part but their dark, broad-brimmed hats plainly visible from this high vantage point.

Then he had it. They were preparing to resist the English assault on the breach. Repointing the guns so that their lethal fire would crash down from Joymount House and sweep through the breach; and the musket men on either side would add their weight of lead to the onslaught. He felt suddenly cold and sick. When Schomberg had his breach, and judged it practicable, he would send in his regiments and they would charge through the gap in the town walls and be met with the lacerating fire of the two twenty-four-pounders firing at point blank range. It would be carnage. Hundreds would be cut to pieces in the breach, or if the fire was well directed, blown out of it on to the bloody turf outside. It was not quite a trap – Schomberg would expect to bear heavy casualties in storming the breach. But it would be as horrific as a London shambles on a busy market day in the narrow gap in the walls through which the English and Dutch soldiers must attempt to pass.

Holcroft lifted his telescope to the roof of the tall building. And a sly smile spread over his face. The two Frenchmen were back, with another two Irish officers, it seemed. The cloaked slender one – Narrey – was pointing out something to the Irishmen below them in the town. But Holcroft did not care what. He now had a legitimate reason to attack them with his mortar. As well as destroying his two enemies – how good those words sounded to his private ear – he would end the menace of the battery and save hundreds of his countrymen's lives when the massed assault went in.

'Claudius, if I could have a word . . .'

The lieutenant came strolling over; he had a smudge of dirt on his cheek and a wide sunny grin.

'I am afraid that I shall have to leave you once more. I have to go and . . .'

'Why, sir, you *are* a lusty fellow! I never knew you had it in you. At it like a rabbit all last night, and back again for second helpings this morning.'

'No, no, you misunderstand . . .' Holcroft tried to think how he could explain that he had spent the night setting up the hidden eight-inch Humpty just outside the walls. He was too tired to think straight – and Barden would no doubt make some silly joke out of whatever he said anyway.

'Nevertheless, I must leave you again. Only for an hour or two. You *will* get the battery firing on the breach, won't you? Uncle Frederick will have me shot if there is another delay. I *can* trust you to do that, Claudius, can't I?'

'Absolutely, sir. Happy to oblige you: what's sauce for the goose, eh?'

Holcroft had no idea what Barden meant by this last comment; he assumed some sort of jest, so he smiled warily, nodded and went off to find his horse.

*

'It needs another ounce of powder, sir, or you will not make that distance,' Enoch Jackson said. 'I reckon it's at least three hundred and twenty yards.'

'It's no more than three hundred and ten, man, I measured it carefully by eye from the No. 2 Battery. Another ounce and we'll sail over the top.'

Enoch and Holcroft were crouched over the squat, round barrel of the mortar, like witches around a cauldron. Jackson was holding a small wooden ladle filled with black gunpowder, and it was clear to Holcroft that he was itching to add it to the half pound of explosive already packed inside.

From behind them came the reassuring sounds of the No. 2 Battery firing, the crash of the four big cannon, one booming out every few minutes, followed by the thump and rumble of falling masonry as it hit the walls. The breach was nearly wide enough for it to be deemed suitable to attack – and Schomberg now could not complain about the No. 2 Battery's efficiency. Claudius Barden was doing his duty.

'Oh very well, said Holcroft grumpily, 'you may have your last ounce, Enoch.' This particular Humpty was fixed at an angle of forty-five degrees and fired a hollow iron spherical shell filled with black powder. Before the gun was discharged, the fuse in the shell must also be ignited, just moments before the main charge in the barrel was set off. The amount of powder in the propellant charge dictated how far and how high the shell would travel, the fuse in the bomb must be cut to the correct length so that it would explode the shell, scattering its lethal fragments of red-hot iron, just above the target. He and Jackson had already had an amicable disagreement about the length of fuse required to hit such a high target. If the missile landed without exploding, it could be easily rolled off the roof of Joymount House by a kick from a bold soldier, whereupon it would explode relatively harmlessly in the streets below. Holcroft had won that argument, so he was partially reconciled to submitting to Jackson's expertise on the quantity of powder in the main charge.

In truth, it was hardly an exact science, and a good deal more complicated than firing a cannon such as the ones they aimed to destroy. And in the back of Holcroft's mind was the fate of the original Humpty Dumpty. A brilliant French architect called François Blondel had published an elaborate table that gave exact weights of powder for a specific weight of mortar missile over a variety of distances, and Holcroft had studied the man's works while in service in Louis XIV's *Corps Royal d'Artillerie*; he had even memorised much of it. But he knew the quality of the black powder used could make an enormous difference, as could its composition of charcoal, saltpetre and sulphur. Then there was the wind and weather on the day of firing. So a mortar bombardment had always been, and would always be, in Holcroft's view, a game of trial and much error.

Holcroft calculated that they would have twenty minutes, perhaps half an hour at a push, to get it right. Once the position of the mortar was revealed it was only a matter of time before the enemy responded. Holcroft wished he had a company of Royal Fusiliers to protect the mortar, but the infantry arm of the Ordnance had been dispatched to Flanders. Anyway wishing was useless.

The last ounce added, Holcroft beckoned forward two matrosses, who were carrying the shell suspended on two sturdy iron chains hanging from a long iron bar. Behind him Jackson was tending the linstock, a pole with a burning piece of match-cord at the end, which would be used to light the fuse of the iron missile and then fire the touch-hole on the mortar.

'Everyone ready?' said Holcroft. The men nodded; Jackson gave a grunt.

Holcroft flicked open his old brass pocket watch. It was half past eleven. He would give himself till noon, he thought. Then they must retire swiftly up the hill whether the attack had been successful or not.

'In that case, tend the match, have a care . . .' Jackson was already leaning forward with the linstock, ready to light the fuse.

'Halt,' said Holcroft. 'Stand by, everyone. What is that noise?'

Jackson took a step back. The two matrosses stood there gawping into the black mouth of the mortar, holding the iron bar that carried the bomb, ready to lower it into the barrel after the fuse had been lit.

It was a low groaning noise, very loud, like a giant in terrible pain, but many voices, and there was a drumming noise accompanying it. It sounded, to Holcroft, very much like a regiment of cavalry at the charge.

He stepped to the edge of the farmhouse wall, scrambled up a mound of rubble and looked at the town. A vast cloud of dust was rising beyond the breach. To his astonishment he saw a huge bullock, long horned, tawny brown with a white forehead, stumbling up the broken rocky slope of the inside of the breach. It was followed by a dozen other beasts, lowing in terror and surging forward as if making a desperate attempt to escape the town. In an instant, the whole breach was filled from side to side with jostling, bawling animals.

Then the guns on the roof of Joymount House spoke.

The first cannon blast crashed into the herd of cattle in the breach. *Partridge,* was Holcroft's immediate thought. They had loaded the cannon with the kind of shell known as 'partridge', after the ammunition used to hunt wild birds. A score of bullocks were struck down by the hundreds of flying missiles sprayed out by the Joymount gun, which was firing thin metal canisters packed with musket balls point blank into the herd. From either side of the breach on the town walls, the Irish musketeers stood up and poured their fire into the stricken and terrified beasts, felling them by the score. The second gun on the roof roared, flaying the mound of dead and dying beasts that were filling the gap in the town's defences with their dripping carcasses. And yet still more cattle were coming up behind.

Holcroft was struck by the appalling genius of the enemy plan. He recalled Claudius Barden's quip from the day before – 'Once more unto the breach!' – and remembered the rest of the line from *Henry V*: 'Once more unto the breach, dear friends, once more; or close up the wall with our English dead . . .'

They were closing up the wall, and no error. Not, thank God, with English dead but with the slaughtered bodies of more than a hundred prime beef cattle.

The guns bellowed again from the roof, spraying the dead and dying cattle jammed in the breach, lashing them with flying lead. They were mere dumb animals, but it pained Holcroft to see such horrible carnage. And his heart gave a little jump as he saw that the lead bullock – the one with the white forehead that had been first through the breach – had escaped the murderous fire and was galloping across the open ground towards the English trenches.

The big guns fired twice more. The Irish soldiery on either side joyfully peppered the stricken beasts squashed into the narrow gap. Then all fell quiet. The breach in the wall was filled almost to the top with the twitching carcasses of the dying animals; a waterfall of blood flowing down the outer surface.

Schomberg will not be pleased, Holcroft thought as he scrambled down the rubble to rejoin his comrades by the mortar.

He will not be pleased at all.

Chapter Four

The same day: Noon

From the roof of Joymount House, Henri watched the cattle being driven up to the breach and their massacre by the guns beside him with a dispassionate eye. His plan had worked surprisingly well. 'I believe that will give us another day,' he said, turning to Colonel MacCarthy, who was looming beside him.

'Aye, maybe so. That mountain of dead flesh will take some shifting. It was monstrous cruel but – I have to hand it to you, monsieur – a fine *ruse*.'

'Might I suggest, Colonel, that you reinforce the animal remains with barrels of rock or earth, or gabions if you prefer and a few baulks of timber to shore it up. Your men may now, I believe, work in complete safety behind their fleshly barricade. Also, if I may venture to say so, this might be a time to request another parlay. If they agree, perhaps we can even spin a second day out of this reversal of fortune for them.'

'Yes, perhaps. I'll go and see to it,' said MacCarthy, and he turned away and summoning his lieutenant, he went into the tunnel that led to the ground.

'Monsieur, do you desire me to reposition the guns?' said Major du Clos, at his elbow. 'We could continue our bombardment of the English lines.'

'Yes, Guillaume, give the orders. That big Irish bombardier, McCulloch, he can take charge. But you and I have earned ourselves a fine dinner after our exertions this morning. You will join me, will you not, my dear friend: I have a pair of roast capons and a fine vintage from a little village in Burgundy that I would like you to give me your opinion on.'

They moved towards the tunnel.

At that moment, out of the corner of his eye, Henri d'Erloncourt thought he saw a black object flying in the sky over his head. It disappeared into the streets beyond Joymount House and there was a muffled explosion from below.

'It would seem that they are now bombarding the town itself,' remarked Major du Clos. 'Perhaps as revenge for our blocking of their breach with fresh beef.'

'Such pettiness,' sniffed Henri. 'We shall take great care to avoid falling bombs as we make our way to the castle. I shall wait here, Major, while you brief McCulloch about the guns. Then we'll repair to my quarters for dinner.'

'I told you it was too much powder, far too much,' said Holcroft crossly to his master gunner. Enoch Jackson had the grace to look shamefaced. 'Maybe the Devil or some black demon is watching over them – that Narrey bastard is uncanny lucky. Perhaps we might try a prayer before the next shot, sir. "But thanks be to God, which giveth us the victory through our Lord Jesus Christ."'

'One Corinthians 15:57,' muttered Holcroft. 'We haven't got time for a bloody prayer meeting, Enoch. Nor for your silly quotations. Pass me that ladle, I'll measure out the next myself. Get the men to bring up another filled bomb.'

The next one fell short, exploding between the town walls and the bulk of Joymount House. Holcroft cursed. Enoch was wise enough to hold his tongue.

As his master gunner began the slow process of reloading the mortar, Holcroft flicked open his watch. It was five minutes before noon, they had been firing for ten minutes. He had, he reckoned, two or three more shots before he would bring the wrath of the enemy down on his head. There was the filled breach to be considered too. Schomberg would surely visit the No. 2 Battery to encourage them in their efforts to blast through the wall of dead cattle, and if he found once again that Holcroft was not there . . .

He clambered up the pile of rubble by the corner of the farm-house and pulled out his telescope. 'You take over, Enoch,' he said over his shoulder. 'Nothing fancy, go for the highest rate of fire. I'll spot for you from up here.'

He trained the telescope on the roof of Joymount House. The twenty-four-pounders were being moved again. No need to aim at the breach any more. Then to his joy he caught a glimpse of Narrey standing alone by the easel, tapping his chin with the wooden end of the paintbrush, on the right-hand roof before he moved out of sight towards the rear.

Please, God, let him stay where he is, please, God, let him remain up there.

He looked behind him to see what stage the reloading process had reached. Nearly there. 'Tend the match,' Jackson was saying to the matrosse now holding the linstock. 'Have a care. Give fire! May the Lord guide our efforts.'

It was a beautiful shot. The mortar coughed, spitting the missile in a high, elegant arc, a parabola, far over the burnt-out farmhouse, soaring over the town walls and dropping down, down until the hollow iron sphere exploded with a colossal bang exactly over the centre of the battery atop Joymount House.

'Dead on, Enoch,' shouted Holcroft. 'Full on target. More of that, please.'

At that moment, a musket cracked and a ball pinged from a piece of broken rubble beside his cheek, spattering him painfully with grains of brick dust. The Irish musketeers on the walls had, at last, taken notice of the mortar's position.

There was a crack like the breaking of the world, a flash of white light and a red-hot fragment of the mortar shell slashed through the flesh of Henri's upper arm and knocked him into the tunnel that connected the twin roofs. Dazed, but as yet feeling no pain, the Frenchman struggled to his feet clutching his blood-soaked

left arm. He stared in amazement at the destruction that one falling missile had done to the roof and to the Irish soldiers manning
the two twenty-four-pounders. At least a half dozen men had been
killed or wounded, the lead roof was dappled with splashes and
streaks of blood and a shell splinter had smashed the wheel of the
nearest gun, which now leant drunkenly to one side. The screaming
began almost immediately.

Henri started out at it uncomprehendingly. His first thought
was that one of the open barrels of gunpowder had exploded, perhaps by a carelessly dropped glowing match. But his eye alighted
on a curl of orange iron hissing in a pool of gore and one terrible
word slowly dawned on him: *mortar*. He felt a surge of rage – how
dare they! How dare they attack him personally. He was no soldier.
He was not supposed to be a target for the God-damned English
artillery. It was a crime of war! Then the pain in his arm hit him
like a surge of wildfire and he began to mew like an animal through
his teeth.

'Monsieur, you are hurt!' Guillaume was at his side in the gloom
of the tunnel. 'We must get you away from this place immediately,
monsieur le comte. We must leave now. They have our range. They
have it to the yard.'

Major du Clos tried to drag his master away from the entrance
to the western roof. But Henri refused to be moved. He glared
furiously at the scene of carnage outside: some of the unhurt Irish
gunners were wandering around as if stupefied, calling out to each
other piteously and asking for orders. A few others were crouched
beneath the long barrels of the guns. Some cowered at the foot of
the gabions. One or two bold souls had gathered up muskets and
were firing them pointlessly in the direction of the enemy trenches.

'Monsieur. It is no longer safe . . .'

A second mortar bomb exploded with equally shocking force a
few yards to the right of the first one, directly over the eastern roof.
One man was cut completely in half by a spinning sliver of shell

casing, his two parts flopping down some feet from each other. Another half dozen men were maimed, one losing his leg at the knee, four more were killed outright. Soldiers were vomiting, soiling their breeches with fear. One Irishman with half his face ripped away and hanging by a flap ran screaming over the side of the roof, falling three storeys to his certain death. The lead of the roof was slick with blood. The howling of wounded men cut into his head like a knife.

'Now, monsieur, right now!' Major du Clos seized d'Erloncourt by the shoulders, then began wrestling him towards the stairs that led to the ground.

'No, Guillaume. Unhand me. I must save the painting. It is my best . . .'

'One more, Enoch, just one more shot and then we must depart!' Holcroft could hardly hide his elation. Two direct hits on Joymount House and he had seen Narrey up there not ten minutes ago with his own eyes. Unless God was making a cruel jest, he must now be dead or at least badly wounded. He tamped down the wadding over the propellent charge. 'Advance the bomb,' he said loudly and two matrosses came forward with the iron pole and its burden.

Musket balls were cracking into the brick works all around them but, in his savage joy, Holcroft was oblivious to them. One of the matrosses, a Welshman named Evans, had been struck by a ball in the eye as he had incautiously peered out from cover to look at the enemy firing from the walls a hundred yards away. It had been a preposterously lucky shot – or indeed, a preposterously unlucky one for poor Evans, who fell dead immediately with the back of his head a soggy mash of gore and brains.

'Ready, Enoch,' said Holcroft. 'Advance the match. Fire the fuse . . . Quickly now, quick as lightning. Advance the match. Have a care. Give fire!'

The mortar exploded and the bomb flew high into the air, rose, fell and detonated once more over the stricken, blood-washed roof. A few moments later there was a gargantuan crash and a ball of red flame twenty feet high. It was followed by another smaller explosion and the roof was engulfed in smoke.

'That'll be a powder keg, or maybe two of 'em,' said Enoch, clapping Holcroft on the shoulder. 'Job done, sir. A fine job of work done today.'

Indeed the roof was now burning like an enormous torch. As Holcroft watched, a section of the brick work on the corner of the building peeled away and fell with a crash to the street below. Another smaller barrel of powder detonated shooting a plume of black smoke speckled with orange sparks, sixty feet into the sky. Nothing mortal on the roof could possibly live through that inferno.

'Good enough!' said Holcroft. 'Leave the mortar, powder and shells. Get poor Evans into a wagon quick as you can and let us depart before the Irish come out for revenge. As you say, Enoch: good job. We did fine work this day.'

On the journey back to their lines, Holcroft walked his horse alongside the men in the wagons and searched his conscience. Once they were out of range of the crackling of the muskets from the walls, and his battle ardour had cooled sufficiently, he was engulfed by a great black wave of shame.

There had been some twenty Irishmen on that roof who had, perhaps unwillingly, been forced to serve the two guns and who were now, presumably, twisted and charred beyond all recognition – and that image washed any taste of glorious victory from his mouth and left instead a bitter residue.

His friend Jack Churchill, now risen to dizzying heights in the English Army as a Major-General and created the Earl of Marlborough, no less, before being dispatched to the Low Countries, would have been pragmatic: 'This is war,' he'd have said, 'those incinerated Irishmen were our enemies. God willed they should die. You have absolutely no need to reproach yourself.'

Holcroft could hear his friend saying it. Yet, while he was no battle novice, casualties always offended his sensibilities, and needless deaths made him particularly uncomfortable. The only comfort he *could* find was in the fact that at least the two Frenchmen – who to his certain knowledge had murdered, or been responsible for the deaths of several people Holcroft knew – were dead. A kind of justice had been served to them. May God have mercy on their souls.

When the wagons were on the rumbling approach towards the No. 2 Battery, Holcroft lifted his head and felt a distinct chill in his belly at what he saw. General Schomberg was on the gun platform. And, worse, the old half-German warhorse had removed his fine blue velvet coat, which a nearby aide was now clutching, and seemed to be personally directing Lieutenant Barden and the team of gunners and matrosses.

The encounter was not going to go well. But Holcroft resolved, this time, to tell the truth to his commanding officer. He could at least boast that he had destroyed a powerful battery that was menacing the English assault on the breach. He would also claim the scalps of two enemies of King William, two dangerous French spies. It had been, he would vehemently insist, a victory.

He slid off his horse when Enoch drew the wagons to a halt, and strode over to No. 2 Battery gun platform. As he approached, he caught Barden's eye, and the lieutenant, who had his back to the General, made the comical face of a man experiencing appalling terror. Then he grinned at Holcroft and winked.

'Your Grace,' began Holcroft, 'you honour us with your . . .'

His words were drowned out by the roar of the twelve-pounder and he fell silent and watched the ball fly across the sky and land with a meaty slap, a gout of blood and fleshly matter – but little

noticeable effect – on the fifteen-foot-high barricade of beef carcasses where the hard-won breach had been.

'Carry on, Lieutenant,' said General Schomberg. He turned his
head and looked coldly at Holcroft. 'I hold you personally responsible for that godless monstrosity,' he said, jerking his head towards
the reeking wall of cattle flesh.

'Your Grace, if you will allow me to explain—'

'Taken ill again, were you?'

'No, sir, I came to the conclusion that it was crucial to our—'

'I know what you've been up to,' the General interrupted,
'I might be a little long in the tooth but I'm not yet blind. I saw your
little display with the Humpty yonder. I suppose you think I should
be impressed with your skill.'

'No, sir, not at all; but I deemed it absolutely necessary—'

Schomberg rolled straight over Holcroft's words. 'You asked me
yesterday to give you permission to attack the gun battery on top
of that tall house there, the one that is now burning so merrily.
I believe I gave you a perfectly clear answer. I said no. I instructed
you to concentrate your energies on the breach, did I not? Yet you
took it upon yourself to disregard my command and gallivant
around the field with a mortar picking targets more agreeable to
your tastes.'

'Sir, the guns atop Joymount House—'

'Be quiet, sir. Hold your damned tongue. I gave you an order;
you ignored it. As a result the breach was *not* made significantly
wider, your battery ran out of munitions and you were unable to
make it practicable – as I had asked you to. Because of your failings,
the enemy were able to block the breach in that barbaric manner
and we are set back, perhaps several days, in our designs.'

'Sir, I will have that breach cleared in a matter of a few hours.'

'No, sir, you will not. I am removing you from your command.
You henceforth have no authority over even the smallest piece
of my artillery. Frankly, I would not now trust you to command

a blunderbuss. I was warned about you, sir, when I was forming the Train in the Tower; I was told that you were dangerously
independent minded; that you felt yourself above the normal
strictures of military duty. A loose cannon – that was one of the
more jocular expressions used. But I ignored those warnings, sir;
I decided that you could be trusted to do your duty, that you were
a professional artilleryman. I cannot tell you how bitterly I now
regret that decision.'

'Your Grace, if you'll allow me to redeem myself, I'll have the
breach—'

'No, sir! You may not redeem yourself. You will take yourself off
to your quarters and remain there until I decide what is to be done
with you. You may consider yourself under arrest until further
notice. Now – get out of my sight.'

Feeling like a whipped schoolboy, a red-faced Holcroft made
his bow and retreated to his horse. He could feel the gaze of every
man in the battery boring into his back. As he walked his horse
up the hill, back to his tent in the artillery park, far behind the
fighting trenches, he looked over his actions of the past twenty-
four hours. He had disobeyed orders, he had deserted his post,
he had been responsible for the death of Evans . . . but on the
other hand he had destroyed an enemy battery that was threatening the breach. And he had almost certainly killed Narrey and
du Clos.

If he had the opportunity over again, he decided, he'd have acted
in exactly the same way. Schomberg was a fool if he did not recognise his achievements.

In his small A-shaped tent in the centre of the artillery park, he
drank down a glass of brandy, took off his filthy coat and stink-
ing shirt, washed briefly and collecting his spare writing materials
and sitting on a canvas stool at an empty, upturned box of ships'
biscuits began to recreate the letter he had been writing to his wife
Elizabeth before Richards was wounded.

In the relative cool of his tent, he could hear the guns of the No. 2 Battery distantly pounding away at the breach, and at the further reaches of his hearing the guns of the Royal Navy were assisting the No. 1 Battery by pounding the castle from the black waters of the Lough. Nearer by, Quartermaster Vallance was wheedling with a Danish officer, angling to get a fat bribe. He wanted ten shillings in exchange for six barrels of salted beef that had been allocated to the Dane's heavy cavalrymen.

Holcroft blocked all these distracting sounds out of his head and wrote:

My dear Elizabeth,

I received with joy your letter of the 17th Inst. And I wish you to know that you are in my heart every single day that I am away from you. I am very sorry to hear that your distinguished Dutch gentleman friend disparaged our cutlery during his visit to Mincing Lane and I beg you to feel free to buy as many spoons, knives, forks and so on as you deem necessary. I shall write to my bankers, Hoare's in Cheapside, and tell them to expect you to call upon them.

I believe I may tell you that the siege of Carrickfergus will shortly be concluded satisfactorily and I believe I may also inform you that the Frenchman Henri d'Erloncourt who, as you know, was responsible for the murderous attack on our house last summer, has been killed in the fighting . . .

Chapter Five

Tuesday, August 27, 1689

Holcroft slept deeply for an age, awoke refreshed at a little before eleven, ate a large breakfast of fried bacon, eggs and toasted barley bread in the artillery officers' mess and wondered what to do with himself that day. He oiled his brass telescope. He carefully washed the mud and blood from his coat – tending the garment lovingly. He polished the brass buttons until they shone like gold. Then he brushed every inch of the blue wool with long, caressing strokes until it appeared almost pristine. The Ordnance coat, for Holcroft, was much more than a common or garden item of clothing. It was a symbol of his status, his identity, his achievements in life. He wore it every day, at work in the trenches or on the gun platforms, in the proving halls in the Tower of London, at parties and to dinner at friends' houses. He would have slept in that coat had he been allowed to by his wife Elizabeth, and when he was away from her, he was often tempted to curl up in its warm folds at night and remain there.

He felt, almost, as if the coat was his soul. As if the coat was, in fact, *him*.

When there was no more he could do to prettify his Ordnance coat, he put it on, did up the buttons, sat down and wrote to his bankers. He wrote to his friend Jack. He played a game of Solitaire with a greasy old pack of cards. He leafed through a book of John Dryden's poetry that his wife had given him – and found it incomprehensible. After a certain amount of internal debate, he decided that he should not take Schomberg's order – to remain in his tent – completely literally. So, in the late afternoon, he put on his hat, slung his sword, and wandered downhill towards the No. 2 Battery to see what had been happening while he had been at his leisure.

Lieutenant Barden had been diligent. As Holcroft approached the No. 2 Battery he could see with the naked eye that the breach had been cleared of almost all the dead cattle and widened considerably. The guns were still firing but at a slower, more relaxed rate, and it seemed their task was to prevent the Irish defenders from blocking the long hole in the walls.

Barden was busy with the western-most of the twenty-four-pounders on the extreme right of the battery and so, feeling nervous that he might be contravening some rule, Holcroft wandered over to the six-pound Saker called Roaring Meg, which was once more tended by his friend Enoch Jackson.

Jackson was busy with a large bucket of water and a long-handled sponge, his bald brown head shiny with sweat. He was cleaning out Roaring Meg's powder residue-clogged barrel. He dipped the heavy sponge in the water and forced it into the cannon's mouth, ramming it as deep as he could, and out came a constant trickle of thick liquid as black, viscous and evil-smelling as coal tar.

'Breach is made,' said Enoch, nodding towards the town. 'Young Barden has done a fine job, under the General's direction. We are just keeping it open.'

'Is Uncle Frederick about today?'

'Not seen him since early this morning. He's busy getting the troops into the attack trenches.'

It was true. Holcroft could see files of redcoats, muskets at port, advancing through the system of ditches and earthworks to the trenches nearest the walls.

'That's Sir Henry Wharton's regiment in front. They're the Forlorn Hope.'

Holcroft shivered – the Forlorn Hope always bore the heaviest casualties. They were the men who were first into the breach and who would face the full fury of the defenders' musketry. Few would survive – but those who did were guaranteed promotion. There was never a shortage of officers who volunteered for this duty, knowing they'd be dead, wounded or heroes by sunset.

'When is the assault to go in?'

Jackson shrugged. 'Soon as the men are in place, I expect. You know the general is in a hurry. They sent out another petition for a parlay this morning – now that the breach is practicable. Schomberg sent the envoy away with a flea in his ear, that's what Lieutenant Barden said anyway. "Surrender right now," the general told him, "and you can march out unmolested, your arms and honour intact. Or I'll massacre the whole bloody lot of you, man, woman and child." He's a spirited old devil, isn't he?'

'Did you catch any grief for our business yesterday with the Humpty?'

'Oh, no, sir, I was simply following orders.' Enoch made his face appear slack and yokel-stupid. 'My captain told me to do it, sir. I dursn't disobey.'

Holcroft smiled at him. 'Good man! And the others are all right too?'

'All save poor Evans.'

Holcroft's smile disappeared.

He stood next to Enoch in a slightly awkward silence, as the master gunner began once again to clean out the barrel of the ancient Saker. The sun was low in the sky off to Holcroft's right, the light transforming the waters of the Lough beyond the castle into a sea of shimmering gold. The Navy ships were still firing, bombarding the castle, sometimes overshooting to send their missiles skipping through the town. Even their fire seemed less urgent.

'I should go and pay a visit to Major Richards in Belfast Castle,' Holcroft said. 'Just to see they're caring for him properly.' He had no desire to witness the assault on the walls of Carrickfergus. He knew what would happen, and what the result would be. The town would fall but first there would be a terrible slaughter in the breach, many hundreds, perhaps thousands of English troops would die. Then there'd be the sack of the town and massacre of its inhabitants.

'Good idea, sir. You'll give him my regards, sir, and from all of us.'

'I will.'

There was a sound of a far-away trumpet. A strangely joyful sound. 'Look, Enoch, look. At the castle.'

Jackson stopped sponging the cannon's filthy barrel, turned and looked to where Holcroft was pointing. On the square Norman keep in the centre of the castle, the red stag MacCarthy flag was being hauled down. Holcroft and Enoch watched, both holding their breaths. There was a murmur of anticipation, a low hum all across the No. 2 platform. A sense of building tension. Then, a flag began to rise up the tall pole on the castle keep. A white flag, pure as a virgin field of snow. The flag of surrender.

Cheering broke out across the No. 2 Battery, and Holcroft could hear it rolling up in waves from the trenches below as the news of the surrender spread through the assault force. The Forlorn Hope's sacrifice would be unnecessary.

At last, thought Holcroft, *at last they have all come to their senses.*

Jacob Richards looked terrible. He had huge black shadows beneath his eyes and his body was swathed in bandages. His left leg was wrapped in clean linen from hip to calf. His right shoulder was swaddled and his right arm was in a sling. Half of his head was also bandaged where he had lost part of his ear.

He lay in a wooden cot in the great hall of Belfast Castle, another Norman construction, which was the administrative capital of Ulster. The castle had been transformed into a magazine for General Schomberg's munitions, as well as a general military storehouse, and the great hall had been turned into a makeshift officers' hospital. There were half a dozen other patients in the long, oak-beamed room. All of them asleep except one cavalryman who had lost an arm and who was sitting up in bed, drinking wine and singing sadly to himself.

Richards was also fast asleep and snoring softly. Holcroft sat on a stool by his side and watched him. It was past ten o' clock. He wondered idly whether he should have brought his comrade some apples or a bunch of grapes or some other kind of fruit. Something. But it had not occurred to him in time. He also wondered if he should wake the man – he had been sitting there for more than an hour watching him sleep and it seemed to Holcroft a pointless activity. Perhaps he should wake his friend, ask how he was, pass on Jackson's good wishes, ask if he required anything – and then he could ride back to the camp at Carrickfergus and be in his own bed by midnight.

Richards was an efficient man, he would not want Holcroft to waste his time sitting there and watching him sleep. It is what the First Engineer would want – to be woken. Holcroft was almost sure of it. He was just finishing the internal debate when he saw that Jacob's eyes were open and he was staring at him.

'Richards,' said Holcroft.

'Blood,' the injured man replied.

They stared at each other in silence for a few minutes.

'Do you like fruit?' Holcroft said.

'No.'

'That's good. Because I didn't bring any.'

'Well, that is a stroke of luck,' said Richards with the tiniest sliver of a smile. 'What's been happening? Have you made Schomberg his breach?'

'The walls have been breached but, thank God, the town surrendered before the assault began. They'll march out tomorrow. Safe passage to Newry.'

Richards nodded. 'What about your Frenchman – the spy?'

Holcroft grinned. 'Got him. I brought an eight-inch Humpty to a position down under the walls – took me all night – then Enoch and I blew him to Hell.'

'Bravo! That was a rare coup.'

'Uncle Frederick didn't think so. Said I was disobeying orders. That I should have left Narrey alone and worked on the breach. He's suspended me. Said he wouldn't trust me with a blunderbuss. He might well send me home.'

'Nonsense – Schomberg can't afford to lose you. He has few enough trained Ordnance officers already, and with me hurt, out of action . . . and young Barden's an idiot. Field is good but too inexperienced. He needs you. He'll make you sweat for a while, then you'll be back with the guns.'

'I don't know, Richards. He was in a rare bate.'

'He likes you. And he won't choose to be without you. You are now the most senior officer in the Train. Say you're sorry, be contrite, all will be well.'

Holcroft said nothing for a while. Both men stared into space. Richards shifted in his bed and gave a small groan. Holcroft said: 'Are you in pain? Your wounds – do they trouble you? Did they give you something to ease them?'

'It's fine. Leg throbs a bit. That's all. I'll be mended in no time.'

There followed a few more minutes of silence. Holcroft stared at his boots.

'Enoch Jackson sends his compliments, by the way.'

'That's kind of him.'

Holcroft got to his feet. 'So, do you need anything?'

'Not a thing. They are looking after me very well here. And there is one particular person who has been very kind to me . . . Ah, here she is herself . . .'

Holcroft heard steps behind him and turned to see a slim, pale, raven-haired young woman approaching with a lit oil-lamp in one hand and an earthenware mug in the other. The change in Jacob Richards was astounding. Despite his pierced thigh and ripped shoulder he seemed to be trying to sit up in bed, as if to attention. His face became suffused with happiness, so much so that it almost appeared to be glowing.

'Good evening, Major Richards, I've brought you a night-posset. Brandy, honey and some willow bark, with an egg beaten into it to give you strength.'

'Good evening, Caroline. You are most kind. A brandy posset – just the thing. Excellent! Yes, indeed, nothing like a posset to set a chap to rights.'

Holcroft stared at Richards. The normally taciturn soldier was chattering away like a schoolboy. He seemed positively skittish.

'You drink it all up while it's warm, Jacob. It will help you sleep.'

'You really are too kind, too kind. And I am eternally grateful to you, my dear. Such tenderness, it will quite spoil me when I go back to the trenches.'

Holcroft examined the woman. She was pretty, yes, in an elfin sort of way, delicate, high cheekbones, and large tar-black eyes with long lashes. She was slender and held herself well, with her shoulders right back and spine straight. She was, in fact, rather elegant. Holcroft found he could not stop staring at her.

'Who is your friend, Jacob? A fellow Gentleman of the Ordnance, I see.'

'Oh, this is just Blood.' Richards' reticence had returned.

'Are you not going to introduce us properly?' she said.

'Mmpff. Lady Caroline Chichester may I present Captain Holcroft Blood, Second Engineer of the Royal Train of Artillery, Gentleman of the Ordnance.'

Holcroft bowed. The lady curtseyed in response. He found this person, who was clearly an assistant to a Belfast physician or some other sort of medical personage, to be remarkably entrancing. She must have been about five and twenty years old, clear skin, obviously well bred, and well dressed in a plain, well-cut green dress of some silk-like material that exposed her milk-white shoulders. Then she looked into his eyes – and smiled – and it turned his stomach to icy water.

Holcroft frantically searched his mind for something to say. He knew people made witty conversation in situations like this. It was a practice at which he was spectacularly bad. 'Where do you come from, my lady?' he managed.

'Oh, we come from North Devon originally, old English farm-ing stock, but my family have been in Ulster for a few generations now and we have advanced a wee bit. I believe that we must, in all honesty, consider ourselves to be Irish.'

'My father was Irish,' he said. 'Yet I think of myself as an Englishman.'

'Blood was just leaving,' interrupted Richards. 'He needs to get back to Carrick.'

Holcroft frowned at his fellow Ordnance officer, perplexed. He had not said to Richards that he intended to leave. In fact, he did not wish to leave this ward at all. He wanted to spend more time with this interesting Caroline person.

Richards was scowling at him. 'Thank you for visiting, Blood. My compliments to the mess and to General Schomberg. And, ah, so, God speed!'

'You are riding to Carrick tonight, sir?' asked Caroline. 'Might I ask a great boon of you. I know it is a little forward but, might I perhaps come with you? I mean, would you be able to escort me to Carrickfergus? I have a horse and I'm told I'm an accomplished rider. I would not slow you down, I swear it.'

'I am afraid that will not be possible,' said Richards. 'Captain Blood has his military duties to attend to and cannot undertake to escort civilians . . .'

'I don't have any military duties. I've been suspended. I can do as I please. But why do you want to go to Carrickfergus, my lady?'

'My family has property there and I have many friends inside the town. I have visited Carrick a few times since the siege began but, of course, I have not been able to go inside the walls. Now that the rebel garrison has surrendered to General Schomberg I wish to see my friends are well. To help them if I can.'

She is kind as well as attractive, Holcroft thought to himself. *And bold and unconventional, too, to undertake a twelve-mile midnight ride with a stranger.*

'I should be delighted to escort you, Lady Caroline,' he said.

'Please, you must call me plain Caroline. Everybody does so. I shall call you Holcroft. If we are to gallop out together in the dark of night like a pair of wild raparees then I think we should at least treat each other as friends.'

'Very well, then, Caroline,' said Holcroft. He could hear a small gritty, crunching sound – it seemed to be coming from Richards' mouth.

'Are you ready?' said Caroline. 'Shall we leave poor Jacob in peace?'

Caroline put her white hand on Holcroft's arm and turning to Richards she said: 'Make sure you drink up all that posset, Jacob. It will do you the world of good. I shall no doubt see you again in a few days when I return. Sleep well.'

The wounded Ordnance officer smiled at her. A strangely painful grimace.

'Richards,' said Holcroft.

'Blood,' said the other, through his teeth. It sounded much like a curse.

Lady Caroline Chichester was indeed an accomplished rider. And as the August night was warm and the moon nearly full it was a pleasant journey that took no longer than two hours. Caroline pulled on a heavy travelling cloak and helped by a groom in the castle stables, she was soon sitting sidesaddle on the back of a spirited grey mare. Holcroft was on the back of Nut, one of the three chargers he had brought with him from England, which were cared for day to day by the Ordnance stable boys and farriers. Nut was short for The Chestnut, which was the colour of the three-year-old gelding. Holcroft liked the animals, particularly Chestnut, but he was not terribly imaginative when it came to naming them. His other two mounts were called The Grey and The Bay. He also found that it made giving orders to the Ordnance stable boys simpler.

'Make sure The Grey is ready tomorrow morning, John.' And so on.

Holcroft had his small-sword at his side, and he had his Lorenzoni repeating pistol tight against his belly, held by his red officer's sash, and easily accessible to his right hand. The Lorenzoni was a wonderful machine that Holcroft had bought from an impoverished Italian mercenary and which could, if necessary, fire seven shots without needing to be reloaded. He was not expecting trouble – he had seen a few stray riders and a couple of two-wheeled dog carts on the way to Belfast but there were supposed to be Jacobite irregular cavalry, the wild raparees Caroline had mentioned, operating in the area.

As they rode, Caroline told Holcroft a little of the history of the region. She explained that until recently Carrickfergus had been the most important local place, with its sea links to Scotland, England and the Isle of Man, and Belfast had been no more than an insignificant town with only a thousand inhabitants.

Holcroft listened closely. It soon became clear that she came from a powerful aristocratic family – not that Holcroft cared about such matters of class – but what he did enjoy was that she projected no sense of superiority. She was open, friendly and treated him as an equal; she seemed interested in him and managed a feat that few others had: she persuaded him to speak about his relationship with his father, the notorious outlaw Colonel Thomas Blood, and to recount his attempt to steal the Crown Jewels from the Tower of London.

He warmed to her immediately when she said: 'I never trusted Lord Danby – met him as a girl and there was something odd, something off in his manner.'

Holcroft had run up against that unpalatable nobleman when his father had been imprisoned in the Tower after the attempted theft, and Danby had sent an assassin, an old friend of his father's, to murder him in his cell. Holcroft had encountered his lordship again when the man had been plotting to bring William of Orange over to seize the Three Kingdoms. Holcroft had never trusted Lord Danby either.

She also spoke most kindly of his friend Jack Churchill – now Lord Marlborough – whom she had met on a visit to London some years before. 'Such a handsome man,' she said. 'So kind and courteous to me, although I was just a silly provincial girl. He took me to the theatre in Drury Lane, gave me wine and quite turned my head. It was fortunate in that I was well chaperoned that evening or I might have done something foolish.'

Holcroft instinctively disliked the very idea of her doing anything 'foolish' with Jack – but the thought of her doing something foolish with, for example, him, well, that held a definite appeal. He was no satyr, of course. He would not dream of forcing himself on her. And he was a married man . . . But she *was* a most delightful companion. And he'd not seen Elizabeth in months . . .

Caroline broke in on his thoughts. 'May I ask you a delicate question?'

Intrigued, he said that she might. 'Can you tell me what "windage" is? We were discussing his work, and Jacob mentioned it the other day and I did not like to ask what it meant. It sounds like . . . uh . . . an embarrassing intestinal affliction.'

Holcroft was more than happy to explain it to her. Windage, he said, was the gap between a cannon ball and the barrel of the gun. Too much and the ball would rattle around in the barrel as it emerged and would not fly straight.

'But it can also refer to the deflection of the ball in flight,' continued Holcroft, 'caused by, for example, a gust of wind blowing across the direction of its travel, which can make the ball deviate significantly from its true line. It is a fascinating subject. I don't know if you are aware of Blondel's work . . .'

What followed was a detailed and, for Holcroft at least, delightful discourse on the more arcane points of modern gunnery, and Caroline showed herself to be an attentive listener, nodding and agreeing whenever appropriate.

The miles flew by.

Towards the end of the journey – when it was gone midnight – Holcroft said to her: 'Where are you planning to stay in Carrickfergus?

I could give you my tent, if you like, and I would, of course, happily bed down in the horse lines. You would be safe, I assure you. My cot is reasonably warm and comfortable.'

'Oh, thank you, Holcroft but I'm sure that will not be necessary. As I think I mentioned, my family own a property in Carrickfergus. A big house, in fact. I shall stay there – there are bound to be a few of the servants knocking around and I'm sure I shall be quite comfortable. It is only for a day or two, after all.'

Holcroft felt suddenly cold. They were trotting along a wide track with the black waters of Belfast Lough only a few yards to their right and a stiff, salt-tasting breeze gusting in off the cold sea. But it was not the wind that made him shiver. Up ahead to the left he could see the lights of the English Army encampment spread out like a field of glowing embers and the lights of the town and the castle winking away too. The siege over, the men on both sides would be celebrating. He could hear faint snatches of song on the wind. He felt utterly despondent. She was such a fine and beautiful girl. She even seemed to like him, too. And in a moment she would regard him as a monster.

'Is your brother by any chance Lord Donegall?' he said, dreading the reply.

'Why, yes, he is. I thought you knew.'

'And is your property in Carrickfergus called Joymount House?'

'Yes, that's our place.'

'I am sorry, Caroline, but I don't think you'll be sleeping there tonight.'

Chapter Six

Wednesday, August 28, 1689

The Jacobite garrison of Carrickfergus, some three hundred and fifty surviving soldiers together with their women, children and servants, marched out the North Gate of the town they had defended so well, and turned left on to the main road with drums beating, fifes playing and standards flapping.

Holcroft watched them with a jaundiced eye from his position on the edge of the artillery park on the rising ground to the north of the town, lounging on a horse blanket outside his own little campaign tent. He had drunk himself to sleep the night before with a bottle of brandy purchased from Quartermaster Edmund Vallance. The brandy had cost him a gold sovereign – an outrageous amount – but when he had complained, Vallance told him it was after midnight, his stores were shut and he might take a bottle at that price or come back in the morning.

He had felt obliged to confess to Caroline that he had all but destroyed Joymount House with his mortar shelling, and the subsequent fire it had caused, and she had become immediately tight-lipped and silent, eyeing him with what seemed very much like a deep loathing. He regretted his decision to tell her now – but at the time he had felt that honesty was the best policy. If she later found out, she might accuse him of trying to cover up the truth. Of lying to her. And he could not bear for her to think him dishonest. She had grudgingly accepted the offer of his cot and he had gone off and purchased the exorbitant bottle from the quartermaster – that grinning thief – and drunk most of it before falling asleep in a pile of straw in the horse lines. He drank the rest of the brandy in the morning, when he discovered that Caroline had left his tent early, with no kind word, just a cold note saying that she had gone into Carrickfergus looking for friends and relatives who might have survived the barbaric outrages of the siege.

Now, half drunk, half hungover, and feeling mightily ill-used by the Gods of Fate, he lolled outside his tent on a thick, musty-smelling horse blanket and watched Colonel MacCarthy's cheerful Irishmen, their unloaded muskets reversed on their shoulders, as they marched across his view along the old road that led from the flung-wide town gates, along the coast south-west to Belfast.

They were heading, ultimately, for the Jacobite garrison at Newry – one of the last outposts loyal to King James in the north of Ireland. It was a jolly, almost festive column of men, some of the redcoats singing, others calling out old jokes to their mates, others with jaunty wildflowers or sprigs of green leaves tucked into their hatbands, and doing little dance steps of joy. *It is a victory for them.* The realisation came slowly to Holcroft. *Does that mean we lost this battle?*

The column was escorted only by one troop of sullen English cavalry commanded by Sir William Russell. The fifty or so troopers walked their horses in single file along the far side of the column of marching rebels, between the Irishmen and the walls of Carrickfergus. But beyond the horsemen, Holcroft could see that the civilians of Carrick and the surrounding areas, most of them staunch Protestants, were gathering in large numbers to watch their departure.

A hundred yards north of the road, on a patch of muddy turf a little higher up the hill and to Holcroft's left, two regiments of English infantry were formed up in ten companies to witness the march-past. There were civilians gathering on this side of the road, too, knots of tough-looking folk in ones and twos. Some were shouting abuse at the Jacobites – calling them thieves and despoilers. And it was true: the Catholic rebels had burnt all the lands around Carrick before the English landed to deny them cover and forage, and a good deal of plundering had taken place. Somebody threw a clod of earth that smacked into the back of an Irish redcoat.

Holcroft knew he should stir himself and go and retrieve the eight-inch mortar from the ruined farmhouse beneath the town walls before some black thief carried it away and sold it. But he had been infected with a spirit of disobedience and told himself, once again, that he had been relieved of all his military duties by General Schomberg and that collecting the abandoned mortar and its ammunition was, without doubt, a military duty. He knew, of course, that he *would* have to go and get the piece in a while; a spirit of disobedience can only take a man so far. It could not change who he truly was. But in the meantime, for a few minutes on the blanket, he revelled in his private mutiny.

Slowly, Holcroft levered himself to his feet. He put on his beloved Ordnance coat and low-crowned black hat, slung his small-sword at his side and, tying his red sash around his waist, started to walk down the slope towards the road. He would seek out old Enoch Jackson, who was no doubt also watching the march-past and set him to gathering up a few idle men and finding a suitable wagon or two to collect the abandoned Humpty and its munitions.

As he got closer to the road, he saw that the crowds of civilians on both sides had grown more numerous. There were now hundreds of local men, women and children who had turned out to watch the rebels depart. The mood had grown uglier; the chants and taunts against the garrison were constant, people were now throwing rocks and stones. One woman was screaming that she and her daughter had been raped by the Irish soldiery. Holcroft began to feel uneasy. He disliked big crowds at the best of times, and this was beginning to look like an angry mob. He wondered if he ought to try to do something to calm the bellowing civilians lining both sides of the road. The garrison men were hurrying their steps, officers crying, 'Make haste, lads, make more haste!'

Holcroft could see a group of men on horseback approaching from his right – gaudy plumes, bright scarlet coats bedecked with lace and gold. There was General Schomberg himself on his big black stallion. On the far side of the road, Sir William Russell was riding up and down the column with his sword drawn, warning the civilians to stay back from the marching Irishmen. His officers, too, were trying to keep the peace. One man in the crowd, a tenant farmer by his garb, stepped forward and tried to strike a passing Jacobite soldier with his gnarled shillelagh. Sir William slapped the man across the shoulder with the flat of his blade and bellowed at him to stay back or he'd be cut down.

Then Holcroft saw something that knocked all strength from his body.

At first he could not believe his own senses. There, walking nonchalantly in the centre of a group of red- and green-coated Jacobite officers, was the French spy Narrey. Without his customary black cloak and with his left arm bandaged and hidden inside in a grubby white sling, and with his black hat pulled low over his face – nevertheless, it was definitely Henri, Comte d'Erloncourt, alive, if not quite well. And beside him the hulking form of Major du Clos, shepherding his master as the shower of Protestant brickbats rained down upon them.

Holcroft stared at his enemy. He could not quite believe the Frenchman had managed to survive the inferno on the roof of Joymount House. But here he was. Then Narrey caught his eye, stopped and stared for a moment. His gaze locked with Holcroft's. They were separated by a dozen yards and a dozen folk in that mass of soldiery and lines of furious, shouting civilians. Yet for Holcroft – for only a fraction of an instant – it was as if they were the only men on that muddy road.

Narrey smiled coldly. He turned away and continued to walk with the rest of them, allowing himself to be swept past Holcroft on a tide of hurrying redcoats. Du Clos gave Holcroft one brief mad-bull stare and then followed his master, casting the occasional malevolent glance over his shoulder.

Afterwards, Holcroft could never fully explain what happened next. He was still a little drunk, and hungover; he had been ignominiously suspended from Ordnance duty by Schomberg, he'd been coldly rebuffed by Caroline, despite his kindness to her, and he had just received a very unpleasant shock. He was, in that moment, he told himself later, perhaps just a little bit insane.

He whipped his sword from its scabbard and, holding it aloft, he shouted, 'Murdering bastard!' and plunged forward into the stream of marching rebels, blade high, forcing his way through the press, using his considerable bulk, shouting, shoving and shouldering lesser men out of his path.

The crowd of civilians from Carrickfergus and the surrounding lands were an angry, vocal, jostling assemblage, who had so far restricted themselves to shouting insults and hurling the odd stone and stick at the red-coated men who had burnt their farms, stolen their corn, seized their sheep and cattle and raped their daughters. But the big English officer, now charging forward madly yelling with a naked blade in his right hand – it was the glowing slow-match that sparked the touch-hole and ignited the main charge of gunpowder.

The crowd erupted with an animal-like roar, hundreds of folk surging forwards at the same time, each grasping at the nearest rebel, tearing at his clothes, wrenching out his hair in handfuls and raining kicks and punches upon him. The column broke under the onslaught, the garrison men scrambling to get away from the howling civilian mob crying for their blood. Many succumbed and were pummelled and punched, torn and trampled. Some ran to Sir William's cavalry escort on the south side, trying to find cover under the necks of the trooper's horses; others broke away from the scrimmage and pelted north towards the hillside, seeking refuge in the neat companies of disciplined English infantry formed up to witness the capitulation of Carrickfergus.

Holcroft shoved a small running Irishman out of his path; another rose up before him, face to face, bawling at him, musket held across his chest, and Holcroft smashed him down with one savage blow from his forehead. He could see Narrey and du Clos a few yards away – and they could see him coming. Holcroft realised that he was screaming incoherently, he was two long paces from his enemies now, almost within range of his small-sword, and he was already preparing in his mind the thrust that would spit Narrey through and through like a roasted hog, and the slashing withdrawal of the blade that would spill his guts in a steaming heap in the road. He saw Guillaume du Clos turn to face him, square-shouldered, and seize the butt of a pistol that was tucked into his wide leather belt – but Holcroft knew that before the Frenchman could draw the weapon, cock the piece, aim properly and fire, he would be on him.

'Die, die, you bastard!' he was shouting. He pulled back the sword . . .

A huge black horse was suddenly blocking his path. He cursed and slapped at its rump with his free left hand. The horse skittered but stayed in position, the rider controlling it superbly. Holcroft lifted his eyes to the man in the saddle and found himself looking into the pouchy, ageing and extremely angry face of Master-General Fredrich-Hermann von Schönberg, His Grace the Duke of Schomberg. The old man was holding, in a rock-steady liver-spotted hand, a large cocked horse pistol, which was aimed between Holcroft's eyes.

'Control yourself, Captain Blood, or I will shoot you down in a heartbeat. What the Devil, sir – what the Devil do you think you are playing at here?'

Henri found himself being swept into a circle of two score Irish infantry all now with loaded muskets and under good discipline. Guillaume shoved him into the centre of the mass then joined the outward facing ranks, pistol cocked, ready.

'Do not fire unless you have to, lads; do not shoot unless you're forced to!' Henri recognised Colonel MacCarthy's ogre-bellow. 'We've surrendered with all honour and must not break our parole, even if these God-damned Protestant bastards provoke us now beyond all sense and reason.'

There was no sign of the tall Ordnance officer with the sword – Holcroft Blood, it was definitely him, of all people to see here in this damp, godforsaken island. What a surprise! Holcroft Blood, a man who had served with him as a page in the Duke of Buckingham's establishment, a former officer in Louis XIV's elite *Corps Royal d'Artillerie*, who had turned spy and traitor to His Most Christian Majesty, who had fled to England before Henri could lay hands on him in Paris and bring him to his just and severe punishment; the man he had skirmished with in London the year before – *that* Englishman was now here in Carrickfergus and apparently intent on murdering him with his small-sword.

Well, perhaps it was not such a surprise. The English Ordnance was present in full force with the powerful Royal Train of Artillery, and Holcroft Blood, he recalled, was now a celebrated gunner. Yet, it *was* strange nonetheless. He had not thought of the man since he had heard that Blood had beaten a hireling of his, a crude London criminal, to death with his bare hands. Since then Henri had filed this erstwhile adversary away in a compartment of his brain marked 'Unfinished Business', and forgotten about him. Now, here he was, in Ireland, large as life and evidently bent on taking some sort of revenge.

Like a shaft of sunlight breaking through the clouds, Henri recognised that Blood must have been the artillery officer behind the surprise mortar attack on Joymount House. That made sense. It was typical of the Englishman to seek a petty revenge. So he had Blood to thank for his smashed left arm. And if Guillaume had not hustled him into the tunnel in the nick of time and carried him down the stairs and out of the burning building, he would be dead as a stone.

He moved forward, pressing closer to Major du Clos' reassuringly broad back. 'You recognised that English bastard Blood back there in the crush?' he whispered in his bodyguard's ear. 'You saw him come roaring towards us?'

The major nodded. 'I saw him, monsieur. He seems to have gone now.'

Henri stared over du Clos' shoulder. A kind of order had been restored on the road – the angry civilians had been beaten back by the English cavalry using the flats of their blades and the moving bulk of their horses' bodies. The companies of English infantry had fixed their plug-bayonets and been marched forward to make a sort of bladed human corridor on the road inside which the Irish garrison cowered, many of them bruised, muddied and with torn clothing. Scores now without their hats and muskets. Some even lacked their boots.

General Schomberg was prowling along the edge of the road on his big black horse like a highwayman, keeping the warring sides apart with his ferocious scowl and the threat of the pistol in his hand. Henri could see no sign of Blood.

'The march will continue,' Schomberg was shouting, 'the garrison will be allowed to make their way to Belfast, and onwards to Newry, without interference of *any* kind!' He wheeled his mount and glared at a bulldog-ugly Irish peasant woman with murderous dark eyes and a smooth, round river rock in her hand. 'I have given my word of honour that our gallant enemies may depart in peace. And I will shoot dead any man' – on his high black stallion he loomed massively over the old peasant – 'or any woman, for that matter, who causes me to break my sacred vow to these valiant and courageous men.'

The woman dropped her stone, lowered her eyes. Schomberg moved on.

'If you see Blood,' whispered Henri, 'and have a clean shot, put a bullet in his head immediately. Don't hesitate. Shoot him. We'll explain ourselves later.'

'As you command, monsieur le comte. I shall not hesitate.'

'The column will continue the march,' Schomberg bellowed. 'March!'

Henri felt himself and Major du Clos and the whole circle of Colonel MacCarthy's personal guard being moved sideways in a great jostling mass. He lost his footing for a moment as a stone turned under his boot; he staggered and a careless musket butt knocked his wounded arm, sending a bolt of excruciating pain ripping though his body – but du Clos had him upright in an instant, and the two of them joined the flow of men trudging south-west along the road.

'Swear to me, Guillaume,' said Henri, through agony-locked teeth. 'Swear on your soul. When you next see that double-dyed traitor Blood, you will shoot him in the face. Immediately. Damn the consequences. Blow him to Hell.'

'I swear it, monsieur.'

'I like you, Captain Blood, I really do,' said General Schomberg. 'You are a gunner in a thousand, an artist when it comes to the pointing of a cannon, and I have it from all sides that you are normally diligent, obedient, hardworking . . .'

Schomberg had his feet in a basin of steaming hot water mixed with a pungent bouquet of herbs. The resinous, lemony smell was intense inside the newly erected and smaller command tent and it was making Holcroft's eyes water. The general was wearing nothing below the waist but a pair of red silk drawers and seated on a canvas chair his thin, white, veiny legs were sunk deep in a porcelain washing bowl.

'. . . But, quite apart from your disgraceful dereliction of duty at the No. 2 Battery and your blatant disobedience of my orders, I cannot have you attacking prisoners of war after I have given them my solemn word that they may march away with their arms and honour intact. I simply will not allow this sort of wild, unruly behaviour in one of my Ordnance officers.'

It was the evening of the day of the Irish garrison's departure. The English camp was in turmoil with all units packing up and preparing to head south after the retreating Jacobite army. After being arrested in his attack on Narrey by Schomberg himself, Holcroft had been escorted to his tent by a pair of Sir William Russell's troopers and detained there for the rest of the day while the artillery park behind him was turned into an anthill by the orders to march.

'I sent a galloper with a message to First Engineer Richards in the hospital in Belfast, seeking his advice about what I am to do with you,' said the general, frowning at Holcroft through the fragrant mist of his foot-bath, 'and he sent back the most extraordinary message. He tells me that the two French intelligence agents inside the town, in Joymount House, to be precise, were responsible for the murder of a lady friend of yours. Is this true, sir? Major Richards says that you must have been driven temporarily mad by grief for this female person – one Mrs Behn, a notorious playwright and poet, if I have understood correctly – with whom you had an intimate friendship . . .'

Holcroft had been keeping the blade-sharp memory of Aphra's death locked away in his heart for the longest time. But now, as this silly old goat with his lean shanks wreathed in steam, droned on about his misdeeds, he found that he was transported back four months in time to a warm day in London and a visit he had made to a squalid attic room in a house on Drury Lane . . .

He had gone to the decrepit house to visit his old friend Aphra Behn in mid-April. As he mounted the creaky wooden staircase – pausing only once to raise his hat to a half-dressed and very drunk young whore whom he met coming down – he was feeling irritated and out of sorts. Guilty, too. He had been neglecting Aphra, whose health had declined over the course of the winter and who was now complaining of constant pains in her arms and legs. She ascribed this to a condition called sciatica, which made walking and, far worse, writing extremely painful.

He had visited her the week before and brought her a camphor-wood box of crystallised ginger, a treat that he assumed his wife Elizabeth had bought from one of the Cheapside confectioners and forgotten about. He had found the wooden box of sweetmeats in a dining room cupboard and, lacking any other gift to hand for his sickly and impoverished friend, he had taken it and wrapped it in a pretty green silk ribbon. He had not mentioned this appropriation to his wife because Mrs Blood had a deep and frequently expressed dislike of his playwright friend. Elizabeth objected to Aphra on several grounds: she felt that writing witty, salacious plays was not a fit occupation for a lady; and that, as an attractive widow, she spent far too much time drinking wine with married gentlemen – including Elizabeth's own husband. But most of all, she objected to the fact that Aphra lived above a notorious brothel. *On such petty things, a human life does balance*, thought Holcroft.

As it happened, Holcroft and Aphra had quarrelled on the day he had visited and brought her the gift of the crystallised ginger. She was in more pain than usual, and he was distracted with his preparations for the Train's departure for Ireland. The news had recently broken in London that James had landed in Kinsale with his French troops and the mobilisation for war was in full swing.

Aphra had teased Holcroft about his gift: saying she needed cash not sugared fruit to pay a doctor to treat her condition, and no amount of sweet words, sweetmeats, or even sweet kisses would satisfy a London physician. Holcroft, short-tempered, had asked then whether he should take the gift back.

If only she had said yes.

But Aphra had apologised and they had awkwardly patched things up. A week later Holcroft was returning with a heavy purse of silver for her, a much more suitable tribute to a fine woman who had been so kind to him for so many years and who had offered him wise counsel, and a good deal of practical help, too, in the long, lonely years when he had been on secret service in France.

Holcroft knocked at the door, and when there was no answer, presuming his friend to be asleep, turned the knob and poked his head around the jamb.

The smell repulsed him, then drew him inside. A sickly, meaty odour.

It was clear that Aphra had been dead for some days. She was seated on the floor by the bed, legs a-spraddle, head canted back on the mattress. She had vomited blood and some half-chewed yellowish matter and soiled herself thoroughly. She had also thrashed about as she died. Aphra Behn had clearly been poisoned. Holcroft had seen the effects of similar poisonings several times before and knew them all too well. And the cause of her death was lying innocuously on the floor beside her hand, the open camphor-wood box, now half empty of its sweet and deadly contents.

In his grief and anger, Holcroft had quizzed Elizabeth very roughly and the origin of the camphor-wood box had been revealed. It had been given to his wife by Henri d'Erloncourt on the one occasion when they had dined at his apartments in White Hall – before Holcroft had discovered his true identity.

Elizabeth had put the box of sweets away and forgotten it. Until Holcroft had found it, wrapped it in a ribbon, and delivered its deadly contents to Aphra.

If only he had asked Elizabeth about the sweetmeats before taking them. If only Aphra had returned the gift to him, as he had angrily suggested. If only . . .

The guilt he felt at being the agent of his friend's death was like a six-pound ball in his chest. A weight pressing down on his heart. He cursed himself, he cursed God, he cursed Elizabeth, too. She cursed him right back – saying that the death was a result of his consorting with women of her type. *Her type? Her type? There were no women of her magnificent type left in the world! There never would be one like her again!* Holcroft had lost his temper, raged around their house in Mincing Lane, hurling furniture, pictures and crockery at the walls. Trying to smash his grief, to crush his sorrow. When Elizabeth called him a barbarian for his reckless destruction, he came close to striking her; but managed to stay his drawn-back fist in time.

He drank heavily. He neglected his work at the Ordnance. And it was only at a private informal dinner in the Cockpit, in White Hall, with his friend Jack Churchill, before Lord Marlborough's departure for the war in the Low Countries, that he found himself weeping into his brandy glass.

It was Jack who told him that he was not to blame.

'The fault is not yours,' he said. 'The man responsible is Narrey. He poisoned the ginger and sent it out into the world. Narrey hoped the tainted sweetmeat would kill you or Elizabeth. But he did not care who succumbed. It could have been a servant, a tradesman, anybody. The blame lies at his door.'

The next morning, when Holcoft awoke with a throbbing head, he realised that Jack had spoken true. Narrey *was* to blame.

And Holcroft truly began to hate.

'. . . And so, as a result of Major Richards' very generous report, I am minded to be lenient with you, Captain Blood. I should by rights have you stripped of your command and immediately sent back to London in disgrace. But I have decided, instead, to give you a choice. Are you paying attention to me, Blood? Your thoughts seem to be elsewhere. Are you hearing me clearly? I no longer trust you to have command of His Majesty's cannon. You may not remain with the Royal Train of Artillery. So this is the choice I lay before you: you may resign your commission in the Ordnance immediately and return to England as a private gentleman; or you may remain in Ireland and put your talents at the disposal of whomsoever I deem might profit by them.'

Holcroft was silent. He was still musing on his poor, dead friend.

'I am minded to send you to the west, Blood, to offer your services to Colonel Zachariah Tiffin. He has raised an infantry regiment in Inniskilling – one of several fighting units recruited from that big-hearted Protestant town – and he has a great need of experienced officers. Colonel Tiffin is engaged at present with hunting down raparees in the Erne Valley. His men are a wild bunch: brave and eager for the fray but also ill-disciplined, disrespectful of authority and insubordinate – I have no doubt they will match your own character very well.'

Holcroft said nothing. He was now thinking of the last glimpse he had had of Narrey's dirty face before Schomberg's horse had intervened – a frightened face, a face that recognises too late the inevitable approach of Nemesis. He held on to that image in his mind. It comforted him. He smiled coldly to himself.

'Captain Blood, I am speaking to you. You will answer me now. Which do you choose? Will you resign your commission and go home? Or will you go west to serve with Colonel Tiffin's Inniskillingers? I require you to answer me!'

Holcroft looked at the angry old man with his feet in the reeking bath of hot herb water. There was no choice to be made, none at all. While Narrey was at large in Ireland, Holcroft would remain until vengeance had been meted out.

'I *am* Nemesis,' Holcroft said out loud.

'What, sir? What are you babbling? Answer my question this instant.'

'I'll go west, sir, to Inniskilling. I will serve in Colonel Tiffin's Regiment.'

Chapter Seven

Thursday, October 3, 1689

The wagon clattered through the narrow brick tunnel and emerged into the surprisingly large yard that belonged to the Bull, a coaching inn on the main road to Dublin outside the county town of Longford. The Irish driver hauled on the reins and called out soft words of calm in his own language to the team of six snorting, stamping, lather-streaked horses as he turned them in a tight circle and came to a halt by the side of a long low building, pocked with many small, square windows.

A slight man in a heavy black woollen cloak, with a broad-brimmed hat pulled low over his eyes, stepped down stiffly, awkwardly, from his perch on a canvas-covered chest in the bed of the wagon. As his cloak swung open his left arm was revealed to be injured, bandaged in fresh linen and supported by a sling made from sheer black silk. He was followed from the wagon by a larger, more muscular fellow wearing a blue military-style coat, a sword at his side and a tricorn hat on his wigless head, who vaulted down beside him, landing like a dancer, and offered his arm as a support for the other.

The two men – the injured man clutching the robust fellow's arm – made their way into the tap room of the Bull Inn, with the larger fellow calling out a jovial greeting in strongly accented English as they entered and, finding the place deserted, leading his companion to a rickety table by the peat fire and helping him into a chair.

Major du Clos went up to the board and, pulling a pistol from his belt, rapped hard on the counter with the butt and called out: 'God's blessings upon this house! Landlord! Landlord there!'

The innkeeper appeared a few moments later, rubbing a sleep-creased face and staring in stupid surprise at the big man with a pistol in his hands standing at the counter. 'Good day to you, sir,' he said. 'How may I serve you?'

'We shall require your best meal and some wine and a pair of rooms for the night,' said du Clos, producing a gold piece from his waistcoat pocket and placing it on the counter.

The man's eyes fixed on the gold. 'Just as you say, sir: it shall be nothing but the best for two fine gentlemen such as yourselves.'

Du Clos joined Henri d'Erloncourt at the table by the fire. He looked around the long, low, narrow room, noting the thick drifts of greasy sawdust on the floor and the few spindly tables and chairs, many cracked and broken, the damp and peeling plaster revealing ancient faded brickwork, a massive stuffed bull's head mounted on the wall, with a hook protruding from its shiny black nose on which a brass ring was hung, the ring attached to a thin cord reaching to the ceiling. But the most obvious feature of the space was the absence of any other customers.

'Not a soul,' he said to his companion in French. 'Not even a passing beggar or stray dog. What the Devil does the landlord live on, do you suppose?'

Henri looked at him from under his hat brim. 'Oh, John Gaffrey makes a pretty penny in the right season. I suspect our friend ordered him to keep the place empty for our meeting.'

'You told him noon, yes? It must be past that now.'

'He will come, Guillaume; don't be so anxious. He seeks to make an entrance.'

The landlord brought wine to the table and two filthy goblets, along with cheese, butter, oatcakes, a slab of fatty boiled bacon and a bowl of radishes.

Du Clos took a mouthful of the wine and nearly spat it out on the table. He buttered an oatcake, munched it down with a slice of cheese. He took another sip of wine and then got up and began to stab the peat fire with an iron poker, trying to liven the feeble glow without much success. The landlord had disappeared again and the quiet was heavy on the air, smothering, like a thick musty horse blanket. The major began to prowl around the room, peering out of the many square windows at the coach yard outside and the lone wagon – now abandoned by its driver and without the six horses but still with its high load of tarpaulin-shrouded boxes and chests. It was raining again, not heavily but with persistence. The surfaces of the black tarpaulin gleamed silver in the weak light.

'He's not coming today,' he said over his shoulder to Henri. 'He'd be a fool to come out in this. He's at home with a bottle by his own warm hearth.'

'The Irish pay no regard to the weather,' said Henri. 'None at all. And I'm not sure our man has a warm hearth to call his own. He'll come to us, Guillaume. He is only an hour late. That's nothing for a man like him.'

Major du Clos went over to the bull's head. He unhooked the brass ring and taking a couple of steps back he let it swing on its string towards the hook on the animal's snout. The ring missed and swung back towards the Frenchman.

Du Clos frowned. He prided himself on his skill in physical matters. He was an excellent pistol shot and a master of the sword. He could dance well, and wrestle and throw men like a professional, too. He swung the ring again, giving it a sideways push so that the metal hoop moved in a flattened circle up to the hook and then back towards him. Once again, he missed the hook.

'Damn thing,' he muttered. He tried again without success.

He began to take the game seriously now, standing fore-square on and measuring the swing of the ring on its cord carefully with his eye. He released the ring and watched its progress towards the bull's nose. It ran straight as an arrow, chinked off the brass hook and came wobbling back towards him.

He tried again. Another miss.

'Something is wrong with it. Some piece of Irish trickery,' he said aloud. He hurled the brass ring at the bull's head and it bounced off one of the beast's glass eyes with a click. There was the sound of clattering hooves on cobbles, a neighing of many horses and, abandoning his game, Major du Clos turned and strode over to one of the tiny windows.

The courtyard was a mass of horses and movement, there must have been forty men and beasts milling around outside, the riders calling out to each other in high spirits. They were a raggedy bunch, lean, dirty, villainous – but that was to be expected: each dressed in any old style, coats in hues from russet to faded gold, sky blue to mossy green. Hats were broad-brimmed beaver-skin with plumes, or simple plaited straw sunshades, or the huge floppy cloth caps of workmen; some wore old-fashioned Spanish-style Morion helmets, others sported lobster-tail pots; yet others were bareheaded or wore greasy rain-bedraggled periwigs. Each man, du Clos noted, was heavily armed and none of them alike: swords, long knives, short-handled axes were common, and a few bore pikes cut down to the more manageable length of six feet; a fearsome selection of hammers, shillelaghs and nail-spiked clubs dangled from the saddlebows. But few pistols were to be seen and only one man, that he noticed, was carrying a musket – an ancient wheel-lock with its mechanism fouled by rust, dried weeds and mud. It would be more use as a bludgeon than a firearm, du Clos suspected, even if its owner possessed powder and shot, and knew how to load, prime and fire the weapon, which he very much doubted.

Du Clos turned and looked at his master, who had not moved from his place by the fire. 'He's here,' he said, unnecessarily.

Henri d'Erloncourt remained seated but he pulled the black cloak over his injured arm in its sling, and clapped the wide hat back on his red-gold head.

'Bring him to here,' he said, pointing to a spot in front of his table. 'Don't ask him to sit; don't be too friendly; don't offer him anything to eat or drink.'

The chief of the raparees slapped open the inn door and strode into the taproom. He twirled his hand vaguely in greeting at Guillaume du Clos, who was standing by the door, and gesturing in an ushering motion at the more distant figure of Henri d'Erloncourt, seated at the table by the peat fire. The outlaw ignored his sweeping arms and swaggered across the room, jinked behind the counter and poured himself a tankard of reddish-coloured ale from the barrel. There was no sign of the landlord. The man sighed happily, flopped his hat on the counter, a battered tricorn with a long pheasant's feather poked through the hat-band, and drank the tankard to the dregs, before burping loudly, nodding amiably at the two foreigners and immediately pouring himself another drink.

'You'll be the two French gentlemen,' he said. It was a statement not a question. 'Old John Gaffrey gave you something to eat and drink then.'

The raparee nodded to himself, and drank his second pint of ale in three sucking draughts and began to pour himself another potful. He was a sturdy forty-something man of middle height with sun-darkened unshaven cheeks and long, lank greying hair that was swept back from his forehead and fell to his shoulders in a heavy curtain. He wore a coat the colour of a well-grazed field, vivid green in patches and muddy brown elsewhere, with a thick baldrick across his chest from which hung a heavy, curved, brass-hilted cutlass.

'Thirsty,' he said. But once he had filled his pint he set it down on the counter and looked at the men. 'You won't join me in a drop of the good stuff.'

Again du Clos was not sure if this was a question. 'Come and speak with us by the fire, sir,' he said, gesturing towards Henri and his table.

'I'm well enough here,' the man replied, with a smile. 'Close to the tap.'

Major du Clos did not know what to do. He was caught standing in the centre of the room, midway between his master and the man they had come to meet. He briefly considered trying to man-handle the Irishman over to the table by the fire, and abandoned the idea. The man's hard grey eyes were on him, and it was almost as if he could tell what was in the Frenchman's mind.

There was a scrape of a chair on the wooden floor, Henri was getting slowly to his feet. He began to walk – it was more of a pathetic hobble – across the floor towards the counter, his feet dragging through the sawdust a little more than they might do, to du Clos' knowing eye. His hat was pulled low but his cloak had been allowed to fall open and display the bandaged arm.

Ah, yes, thought du Clos, *a change of tactics.*

'You will forgive my sloth,' Henri said, labouring towards the Irishman and the counter, panting slightly as he spoke. 'I was bombarded by the English at Carrickfergus and suffered an inconvenience. I shall be with you momentarily.'

'Jesus, man, my apologies,' said the raparee leaping out from behind the counter. 'That was damn rude of me. Sit down, man. Here, sit yourself . . .'

The Irishman guided Henri back to the fire, into his chair and hauled over one for himself. He went to the counter to collect his pint pot and to du Clos' intense irritation, he paused on the way across the floor to seize the brass ring dangling on its cord and, with a casual flick, send it looping unerringly to tinkle and settle on the hook in the stuffed bull's black nose.

'I am called Narrey,' Henri began. 'Just Narrey, no other name. This is my associate Guillaume. You, I presume, are Captain Michael Daniel Hogan. Correct?'

'I've no commission just at the moment. But I'm a captain of men. And they call me Galloping Hogan. Or plain Mick Hogan. At your service, monsieur.'

'General Sarsfield said you were a good man,' Henri said, smiling warmly at the man in the chair next to him. 'He sends you his dearest love and told me to ask you the name of that charming maid you both met in Borrisokane?'

Hogan laughed. 'Paddy Sarsfield hates my guts. He says I'm an upstart rogue and a God-damned Tipperary thief, and I suspect he'd hang me from the nearest oak if he didn't sorely need me and my men to kill the English for him.'

Henri laughed along with him, a high-pitched sound more like a giggle.

'And the pretty maid?' Henry said, just managing to control his merriment. 'What was her name again? General Sarsfield said you'd surely remember her.'

'He's a sly one, is old Paddy – always with his tricks and signs, his watchwords and tests. But I suppose that's the world we live in. No trust. Too many liars. Too many traitors. You seek to confirm that I'm who I say I am; right, monsieur? You wish to be sure I am truly Michael Daniel Hogan Esquire.'

'That is exactly so, monsieur,' said Henri, suddenly very solemn.

'And what of it, if I'm not Hogan? What then?' He looked over at Major du Clos who was somehow a good deal closer than before, his hand resting on his pistol butt.

'If I'm not himself, if I am some bold impostor pretending to be the great and terrible Galloping Hogan, is the big man there going to shoot me down? With two score of my friends outside this very door? I don't see you as stupid enough to try that. So what will ye do? If I'm not Hogan. I'm just a little curious, you understand? What *can* ye do?'

Guillaume du Clos made a growling noise in the back of his throat.

'And I've another question for the pair of you.' The raparee seemed at ease; he lolled in his chair, the heavy, half-full pewter tankard held low in his right hand like a threat. 'That wagon out there – that would be the load of new muskets that was long promised by Sarsfield, arms for Hogan's men, a mark of gratitude for the Galloper's loyal service to His Majesty King James. Arms for Captain Hogan to continue his glorious struggle against William, the cheese-muncher-in-chief, and all his English lackeys. Would that be about right, monsieur?'

The silence in the room was as heavy as a death sentence.

'You've come all the way out here to make some kind of a deal. That's plain. Why else would you travel nearly eighty miles in the rain on terrible roads to this shit-hole of a town to have a drink with the likes of me? You want something from me. Plainly. You've come to buy something. But I'd like to know what would you do if I were to take the guns away from you and give you nothing in return? To simply lift them. What would you do if I were to tell my men to hitch up that wagon and ride away into the bogs?'

'Perhaps we have made a mistake in coming here,' said Henri. 'I apologise for having wasted your time. We shall now take our leave of you.'

'Answer my question and I will answer yours,' said the raparee.

Henri stood up, pushing back his chair. 'You could steal from us – that is certainly a possibility. But, if we survived the encounter, I should make it my sole business with all the considerable power at my disposal to hunt you down like a rabid dog and have you flayed alive for your impertinence. You could attempt to kill us now; that is also true. But you would surely die in that exchange – Guillaume would make sure of that. And if by some miracle you did not expire, I have colleagues – very dangerous, very dedicated and clever men – who would investigate the matter thoroughly and they would come for you in due course. Then you would pay the full price.'

Henri leaned forward on the table resting the knuckles of his good hand on the boards and pushing his face towards the lounging raparee. 'You should also comprehend, Master Whatever-Your-Name-Is, that I am very well beloved by His Majesty King Louis XIV of France and he would never let my murder go unavenged. The Sun King would have you taken up, even here in the damp depths of your land, and brought before him in Versailles in chains. Then his torturers would begin their long, slow work. Now, sir, I believe we shall take our wagon and depart. I do not think there is anything more of value to be said between us.'

'Esmerelda,' said Hogan. 'Her name was Esmerelda and she was no pretty young maid, she was forty if she was a day and ugly as a bucket of warts. But she was a jolly soul and a game old lass, I'll give her that. She took on young Sarfield after a rollicking supper in the White Horse and wore him down to the nub, then she bedded me too. Game as a champion rooster, that one. We had a magical evening last year in Borrisokane, I can tell you that, monsieur. A grand night. And you can remind Paddy Sarsfield, when you see that fine Irish gentleman, that he still owes me that three shillings and six for the night's reckoning!'

The landlord John Gaffney was roused by one of Hogan's men, a massively bearded, silent fellow named Gallagher, and he brought over brandy and ale to the table – the Frenchmen refusing to drink any more of his wine. Gallagher departed back out to the rain and the three men seated by the fire now displayed all the signs of being perfectly at ease in each other's company, almost like old friends, although Guillaume du Clos had a certain alertness to his powerful frame that even three large cups of brandy could not entirely dissolve.

'There are four dozen new cavalry *fusils*, what you call in English flintlock carbines, packed in pinewood chests out there under the tarpaulin, Mister Hogan,' said Henri. 'As you had correctly guessed. They are a gift from the King of France to you, coming straight from the royal arms manufactory in Saint-Etienne. There are also quantities of powder, shot, ball, flint and wadding and so on, to go with these muskets. There are two dozen pistols – not new, I am afraid, but clean and well cared for, fully serviceable and personally checked over by King James's quartermaster in Dublin. With ball and powder to match. There are also two dozen swords and a bundle of twenty half-pikes.'

'The King of France is most generous,' said Hogan with a mischievous smile, 'and what does he wish in return for his magnificent largesse?'

'He wishes you to prosecute the war against the Dutch usurper with all vigour.'

'With all vigour, eh? Yes, I think I can manage that. I've fought Dutchmen before. In '72 and '73, with your own brave compatriots, as it happens, in the Low Countries. I imagine you would be too young to remember that war.'

'Ah, is that so? I did not realise that you had military experience.'

'Then what is it that you think I have been playing at this past year?'

'I understood, monsieur, that you and your men have been operating mostly in County Tipperary, and in and around the city of Limerick, doing dirty but necessary work, attacking the undefended farms of traitors to King James, burning crops, confiscating goods from travellers, hunting down and hanging our Protestant enemies but . . . it is most excellent news that you have fought with regular troops, in more, shall we say, *conventional* fields of honour.'

There was a long, prickly pause. 'I am an Irish patriot, monsieur. I will fight the enemies of my people in any way that I can. And always with the utmost vigour. So, apart from that, what else does the King of France require?'

'He requires that you consider yourself in my debt for his magnificent generosity. It may be that the time will come when I shall require a service from you. A favour, yes? But apart from that, well . . . no, no, it would not be right for a humble government functionary such as myself to advise such a seasoned campaigner on battlefield strategy, nor on his chosen theatre of operations.'

'But I have a suspicion that you *are* going to advise me, aren't you? Just as you humbly advise the King of France himself in all these warlike matters.' Hogan's smile had disappeared. His posture was distinctly tense.

'I would venture to suggest, that is, His Most Christian Majesty—'

'Jesus, man, speak plainly. Tell me what you want – and don't pretend that the orders are coming from anyone else but yourself. Come on, spit it out!'

Henri stared at him for a couple of slow heartbeats. 'Very well,' he said. 'I wish you – and I have full authority in these matters – to operate on the flanks of the English Army as it pushes south. They're presently encamped at Dundalk – but it would be far easier to show you. Guillaume, where is that map?'

As Major du Clos spread out a tattered canvas map on the table, Henri said: 'I don't suppose, Hogan, you're familiar with Quintus Fabius Maximus.'

'Oh yes, of course,' said the Irishman. 'I know him well.'

'Truly?'

'Aye, isn't he the old, one-armed fella who runs that big ale-house on the Killmallock Road out of Tipperary?'

Henri stared at him. 'No, that's not ... no, he was in fact a Roman general of the third century before the birth of Our Lord Jesus Christ.'

'Ah no, I was after thinking of Quilty MacSeamus.'

'Quintus. Fabius. Maximus. They called him Cunctator.'

'Did they now? Well, that's not a word I like to use in polite company.'

'It means The Delayer.'

'Hmm, but then again old Quilty could talk the hind legs off a donkey. Keep you at the counter for hours. And he was awful slow to draw a pint.'

'Do you mock me, Hogan?'

'Me? No, surely not. Let's have a look at your little map now.'

All three men leant over the table, their heads coming in conspiratorially close together, as Henri traced the route that the bulk of the English Army, their horse, foot and guns, had taken over the past few weeks. Down from Carrickfergus, through Belfast, Dromore and Newry to Dundalk, which was nestled in the top of a wide bay some twenty miles north of Drogheda on the River Boyne, and a full fifty miles north of the Irish capital Dublin.

'They have the sea on their left flank, and that side will be guarded from attack by the ships of the Royal Navy. But their right flank, as you can see, is wide open,' said Henri. 'It is to the west that they will seek forage for their horses, supplies for the men, wood for their campfires and so on. The reports I have received suggest that they are ill-provisioned and that sickness has already broken out in the crowded English encampment at Dundalk, with little provision for those stricken with disease. So they are likely to pause at Dundalk for some weeks and try to gather their strength and restock their supplies. However, the land roundabouts has been ravaged several times over by passing armies and they will find pickings slim. They must bring the bulk of their food and forage, drink and stores, down their supply lines from the north.

'General Sarsfield is in the far west at Sligo and the Duke of Berwick, King James's eldest son, is down at Athlone recruiting a force of infantry from the south. But we – I and the commanding officers of King James's main army, which is at present blocking the route south – should like you and your horsemen to base yourself in this area . . .' Henri stabbed the map with his finger. 'Around Cavan. And we should like you to behave like the Roman General Fabius, the gentleman I mentioned before, to harass the enemy supply lines, cut them if you can, and deny the English food, ammunition and medicines for the sick. We would like you to particularly target forage parties as they come out of the fortified camp at Dundalk. Here—' He pointed again. 'And to hit the messengers and scouts and any stragglers from the marching columns. Along here. Kill them. No prisoners are to be taken. You are to be the invisible menace on their flank, and behind their lines, you are to sow fear and death – but do not try to engage them in a pitched battle. That was Fabius's strategy – to avoid full pitched battles but to bleed the enemy dry with raids and small skirmishes. They will certainly send out cavalry to chase you, and you must run from them. Do not stand and face them. I think you understand this kind of warfare: you strike without warning, come out of nowhere to kill and steal, then disappear back into the countryside. Yes?'

'I'm familiar with this line of work, sure,' said Hogan.

'We would also be most pleased if you chose to raid further up and deeper into Ulster because they will then have to dispatch much-needed troops to defend their supply depots and transport lines from your, um, depredations.'

'I think that could be managed,' said Hogan.

'And we would like you to recruit more men. There is a small iron-bound chest filled with *louis d'or* on the wagon, equivalent to one hundred pounds. You'll use that to pay a bounty to any who join up to serve with your company.'

'I'll use it any way I choose, once you've paid it to me!' Hogan chuckled. 'I could blow the lot on brandy for the boys and shiny baubles for Esmerelda.'

Henri frowned. 'As you wish,' he said and gave a little Gallic shrug. 'But if we – I do beg your pardon – if *I* am fully satisfied with your actions over the next three or four months, there will be another meeting and another wagon loaded with fresh arms and money. On the other hand, if I'm not satisfied . . .'

'Flayed alive, is it?' Hogan chuckled. 'King Louis' lazy torturers?'

'I should like to do business with you, Mister Hogan. I believe we might aid each other. But I require you to take this compact between us seriously.'

'Aye, you're right. Serious, it is. It is a good deal for me and the lads. I accept. Here's my hand on it.' Hogan hawked mightily and spat a huge gobbet into the grubby palm of his right hand and held it out for Henri to shake.

The Frenchman looked at the offered hand as if it were a fresh, steaming turd. 'Your word of honour will be sufficient, I believe,' he said icily.

Hogan shrugged and wiped his hand dry on his breeches. 'We have a deal then, my friend. The boys and I'll be off for County Cavan in the morning.'

'One more thing,' said Henri. 'There is a man, an Ordnance officer who I believe is now quartered among the English troops based at Inniskilling. He is an evil man, a traitor, and very dangerous, too, and I would be willing to pay a bounty for his head of, say, thirty pounds in gold. No, fifty pounds. But you must bring me his head as proof.'

'You'll pay fifty pounds in gold for this officer's nob? You really must hate the bastard. What did he do – steal your favourite horse? Bugger your wife?'

'I do not possess a wife, Mister Hogan.'

'Just my little joke. I can tell you're not the marrying kind. But in all seriousness: what's the name of this poor fella whose head you want so badly?'

'His name is Blood. Captain Holcroft Blood.'

Chapter Eight

Thursday, November 10, 1689

Holcroft Blood watched the men of the fourth company of Tiffin's Regiment of Foot as they approached him across the parade ground. They were marching in unison, each man's step almost a perfect mirror of the next; their new flintlock muskets were shouldered at the same angle, their grey coats, grey breeches and stockings spotless, the metalwork, buttons, buckles and sword hilts polished to a fine gleam; the bright orange turn-backs on their wide sleeves and the orange garters and bows on their black shoes giving them a festive gaiety at odds with their otherwise sombre martial splendour.

Not bad, Holcroft thought, *not bad at all, considering a couple of months ago they were barely trained militia, not much more than an armed rabble.*

Tiffin's Foot had been recruited that summer by Colonel Zachariah Tiffin from the vigorous Protestant young men of Inniskilling, a town perched on an island between two loughs roughly in the middle of the long, curving Erne Valley. The Erne River stretched in a gentle eighty-mile sweep from its rising point a little south of Cavan all the way west and north to the sea in Donegal and formed the approximate frontier between the two warring sides in Ireland in the autumn of 1689. The men of Tiffin's Foot – who were billeted in companies along the river's length – were charged with defending the unmarked frontier and stemming the incursions of raparees who rode up from Leitrim and Cavan to burn crops, murder Protestant civilians and make off with their livestock.

Sergeant Hawkins, a burly, red-faced man, who carried a halberd to denote his rank, bawled: 'Eyes right!' and the sixty-two men of the fourth company snapped their head to the side to stare blankly at Captain Blood as they passed. From the back of his charger Nut, Holcroft examined them minutely. Joe Cully was stepping an instant behind his neighbour, he noticed, but it was still a vast improvement from that bear-like simpleton's first attempts at close order drill.

Jesus, that had been truly shambolic . . .

Holcroft's first few weeks in command of the fourth company of Tiffin's had not been promising. His new colonel was now based in Ballyshannon in Donegal, where the river Erne flowed into the Atlantic. Colonel Zachariah Tiffin had made himself *de facto* governor of that pretty seaside town, far from the main army command structures and, if the rumours were true, he was entirely occupied with enriching himself at the expense of the local Catholic population with no thought for his many and various military responsibilities.

A harassed Lieutenant-Colonel Harry Fenton, Tiffin's second-in-command – the man who actually ran the regiment – had greeted Holcroft at Inniskilling Castle and shown him his quarters and introduced him to the fourth company's other commanders: Lieutenant John Watts, a far-gone roué by the look of his blotched face and bloodshot eyes; Ensign Francis Waters, a weed-thin, nervous youth from a wealthy local family; and Sergeant Jeremiah Hawkins the senior NCO, who was a solid, tough, entirely more impressive character. However, after that brief introduction Holcroft had been left to his own devices. All three of these company men were cool towards the newcomer, polite but unwilling to be friendly, although Holcroft did not register it. They had all heard of his disgrace in Carrickfergus and felt a bad officer was being foisted upon them.

If the officers were merely cool, Holcroft was greeted by outright hostility by most of the private soldiers, the Inniskillinger recruits over whom he had been set in authority, and who felt he was an interloper, a foreigner, and a suspiciously odd one at that.

However, he was blissfully unaware of this general ill feeling, at least for the first couple of weeks after he joined Tiffin's, as he was utterly sunk in on himself, brooding on the death of Aphra, the escape of that bastard Narrey and his own abrupt departure from the Royal Train of Artillery.

The disgrace of having to tell his friends and colleagues in the Ordnance that he had been dismissed from their ranks still burned within him. He felt the shame most keenly when he admitted to them that he was now reduced to serving as a lowly infantry officer in a local militia unit.

He had dropped in on Jacob Richards in the hospital in Belfast Castle on the morning of his exodus, ostensibly to thank his friend for his intercession with General Schomberg, but in his secret heart in the hope that he might encounter Caroline and mend their friendship. He had spent an awkward ten minutes with Richards, during which they discussed little more than the weather – autumn was almost upon them and the almost perpetual rains had begun – then they wished each other well and Holcroft took his leave.

He had glimpsed Caroline once in the back of the ward, and thought that she had seen him too, but she never approached Richards' bed while he was there. When he 'accidentally' took a wrong turn on leaving the castle and found himself in the cavernous kitchen, he thought he caught another sighting of her walking through a doorway into a pantry carrying a wide tray of bread.

He followed her and found her alone in the small room stacking loaves in long dusty shelves, ready for the patients' dinners that afternoon.

'Caroline,' he said. 'I was very much hoping to see you here today.'

'Is that so?' she said, in an unfriendly tone. 'What can I do for you? Are you perhaps here to warn me that you are planning to bombard the castle and reduce it to a smoking ruin?'

'No, not at all, the castle is already in our hands. Why would I do that? I just wanted to say . . .' Holcroft was at a loss for words. He stared at his boots. He looked at the rows of floury loaves for inspiration. Then he said, in a rush: 'I came to say goodbye. I've been kicked out of the Ordnance.'

Caroline said, 'Is that so?' again in a completely indifferent tone and carried on with stacking the loaves on the shelf. Holcroft stared in anguish at the back of her head. Eventually, she turned, saw the dejected look on his face and said: 'I am sorry to hear that, Captain Blood. I know how much you cherished your guns. You must be rather upset. So . . . what will you do now?'

'I've been sent to Inniskilling to join a militia regiment – Tiffin's Foot.'

'Oh, yes, I've heard of it. My brother knows Colonel Tiffin, I believe.'

There was a long awkward silence.

'Well, I should probably be going now,' said Holcroft.

'Yes, I think that's best. It's a long ride to Inniskilling.'

'So, then, uh, goodbye, Caroline.'

'Goodbye.'

Holcroft went to the pantry door, he opened it, and paused in the doorway. He tried to think of something else to say.

'Caroline,' he said. She turned, a loaf in hand, a streak of white flour on her cheekbone that made her dark hair and bright eyes stand out even more.

'What is it, Captain?'

'Would you mind if I wrote to you, from time to time?'

'What would you want to write to me about?'

Holcroft wanted to wipe the flour from her face. And then seize her and kiss her. 'I could tell you about the doings in town of Inniskilling, about Tiffin's Regiment, the officers, the men, our battles . . . It might be diverting for you.'

'Very well, you may write to me, if you wish to. I do not promise to reply.'

'Thank you very much, Caroline.'

'Goodbye . . . Holcroft.'

Holcroft only became fully aware that his company disliked him after three full weeks in his new position. He had vaguely noticed that the men always stopped speaking whenever he was near them and that they were slow to move when he gave them a direct order. If he thought about it, which he rarely did, he put their behaviour down to their lack of military experience or ordinary stupidity and sloth. And when the officers and NCOs demonstrated that they did not wish to engage him in conversation beyond the barest civilities, he was, in fact, rather relieved. In truth, he was acting like an automaton and merely going through the motions of inspecting the company on parade in the courtyard of Inniskilling Castle every morning and dispatching occasional foot patrols in the local area under Sergeant Hawkins or Ensign Waters. But the collective animosity of the fourth company was made plain when a big bald ox called Joe Cully barged into him while he was walking through the north barracks in Inniskilling Castle one evening in mid-September seeking out Hawkins about some minor matter of company administration.

Cully hit him in the upper left chest with his shoulder, a solid strike, as he was walking past, mumbling, 'Beg pardon, sir,' as he moved away.

The heavy blow came as a shock to Holcroft and for a moment he did not comprehend what had occurred. Then he glimpsed Cully's sly, triumphant grin to his mates as he moved away down the barrack room, and saw a dozen men seated on their beds, watching like a theatre audience. He recognised some of them by name – Burns, McNally, Watson – and the realisation of this slight, no doubt boasted about beforehand, shocked Holcroft like a bucket of water dashed into his face.

He reacted instinctively. He took a step after the departing Cully, seized him by the shoulder of his coat with his right hand, turned him and smashed his left fist into the centre of the big man's smirking face.

Cully was hurled backwards, stumbled, tottered . . . but did not fall. He regained his equilibrium, wiped the blood from his suddenly leaking nose and with a bear-like roar he came charging at the officer with his big fists swinging.

Holcroft deflected the first massive right with the outside of his left forearm and, coming inside and under the man's swinging left – letting it hiss past his right ear – he whipped his forehead hard into the enraged man's face, crashing his skull ridge into the soldier's already bloody nose. Cully was knocked back a step, and Holcroft belted him with his right, a great pounding blow that mashed the man's lips against his teeth. Still Cully did not go down. Screaming and spitting blood and phlegm, throwing haymakers left and right, he charged Holcroft again. One blow landed, a hard whack on the muscle of his right shoulder, but Holcroft hunched down low, avoiding the second wild swing, and plunged two hard jabs, left, right into Cully's midriff, knocking him back once more before ending the fight with a colossal left cross, followed by a pistoning right to the point of his chin. Cully flew up and backwards and landed on his back, all the air expelled from his lungs in a loud, 'Huh!'

Holcroft took a step forward and looked down at his enemy. 'Stay down,' he said, aiming a finger at the soldier, 'or I will knock you out of this world.'

He looked around at the Inniskillingers on the bunk beds, all gaping at him. The smell of the barracks hit him then for the first time: old sweat, cheese and gun oil. He felt as if he'd awakened from a deep sleep: a muzziness clearing. His fists throbbed where he had walloped the man on the ground.

Holcroft swung his head left and right; he met every man's eye with his own, a direct personal challenge – and one that was refused every time. Their eyes slid away, or his stare was met with weak, conciliatory smiles. Holcroft steadied his own swift breathing, then he said slowly and clearly, so that every man in the packed barracks room might hear him: 'I believe that Private Cully has had an accident. He seems to have slipped and fallen. He may be hurt. You will see he is treated for his injuries. However, I do not wish to hear any more of this business, ever again. Is that understood?'

One man got up; he was a small, dark, wicked-looking corporal, an Ulsterman who boasted he'd travelled to England and beyond, one of Sergeant Hawkins's cronies. Holcroft recalled his name from a duty list: Horace Turner.

'It's you,' he said, pointing at Holcroft. 'You're the one. Officer of the redcoats, in the Liberty. You're the one who thrashed Paddy Maguire with his fists.'

He turned to his friends and said, 'Told you all about that mill, lads, I told you . . . I saw him with my own two eyes, last autumn in London, in the Liberty of the Savoy, and I swear I'll never see a fight like it again. I saw Captain Blood here knock seven bells out of the hardest man in all London. Mashed him to a pulp. It's him, boys, same fella, and you all just saw him fight Joe Cully.'

He beamed at Holcroft. 'I thought I recognised you, sir. I'd recognise that big right hand of yours anywhere. But you were in command of a half company of fusiliers, searching for French spies, if I recall. How come ye to be here?'

Holcroft vividly recalled the brutal fight against Patrick Maguire in a notorious London slum the year before which had resulted in Maguire's death and his own disgrace and imprisonment in the Tower. There had been a large crowd that night, several hundreds of folk crammed together in the barely lit street, who had witnessed his victory. He did not recognise this small Ulsterman who claimed to have been there too.

'You are quite wrong, Corporal Turner,' he said slowly. 'There has been no fighting here this evening. Cully has merely tripped and injured himself . . .'

Holcroft went over to Cully who was sitting up mopping his bleeding face. 'Is that not correct, Joe? You fell over, did you not?'

The man stared at him as if he were mad. Holcroft let out a long frustrated breath. He'd been rather proud of himself for this piece of quick thinking. Lying went against the grain with him – indeed, he hated all forms of dishonesty. But, despite his natural aversion, he had trained himself over the years to tell untruths when it was absolutely necessary. He was just not very skilled at the art – far from it – but surely even someone as bone-stupid as Cully must see what he had intended with this obvious falsehood.

'Because,' continued Holcroft, speaking as if to an idiot child, 'if there *were* to be a fist-fight between a private soldier and, say, a captain, the private would be charged with striking a superior officer for which the penalty is death.'

Cully was still gawping at him.

'Oh yes, sir, indeed!' said Corporal Turner grinning at him. 'Private Cully fell down and hurt himself. The dozy ox. We all saw it, lads, didn't we?'

There was a slow chorus of approval. Someone said: 'Clumsy bastard.'

Holcroft took a step towards Cully. He leant towards him, extending his right hand. The soldier shrank away as if expecting another blow. Holcroft seized his left forearm and hauled the big oaf to his feet.

'Right,' Holcroft said. He looked at Cully's broken nose, gory mouth and shocked expression. 'No great harm done. I'll bid you gentlemen good night.'

*

The fight in the barracks in September marked a turning point in the relations between Holcroft and the fourth company of Tiffin's Regiment of Foot. The private men began to treat him with a wary respect. Ensign Waters – whose company nickname Holcroft had discovered was Weak-as-Waters – now looked on Holcroft with something approaching hero-worship. Corporal Horace Turner appointed himself Holcroft's personal champion among the rank and file, and prowled around after the captain ensuring that his orders were swiftly obeyed and barking out threats of dire punishment at any hint of insubordination. Sergeant Hawkins, while remaining correct in his manner at all times, condescended to treat the captain as a being of almost equal merit to himself.

Holcroft also changed. He realised that for weeks he had been sorely neglecting the company of men for which he was responsible. He recognised that they were dirty, slovenly and frequently drunk. That their uniforms were uncared for, their weapons were a mismatched combination of different kinds of old-fashioned muskets. They could not march together as a company in step or do even the most basic forms of parade-ground drill. And it was his fault.

So Holcroft put aside his own guilt and misery and went to work.

With the help of Sergeant Hawkins, he began to drill the company twice a day, two hours at dawn and two at dusk. He taught them to march, to turn left and right, to turn about completely, to advance rapidly, halt and fire their pieces. He did not attempt to teach them anything more demanding – the crack Dutch troops of King William, his famous Blue Guards, for example, had devised a system of platoon firing that meant that a regiment could bring an almost continuous rolling fire down on an enemy line. Holcroft deemed that too complicated to begin with. They would start with the basics.

The great virtue of these Ulstermen was their fiery spirit, their wild and reckless courage in battle – which they had amply demonstrated at the Battle of Newtownbutler in July when a force of two thousand irregular Inniskillingers under Brigadier-General William Wolseley had routed a far superior number of Jacobite regulars under Viscount Mountcashel. They were brave men, natural warriors, but they lacked discipline, Holcroft decided. He could remedy that.

So he and Sergeant Hawkins woke them an hour before dawn and they practised infantry drill until breakfast. Breakfast was followed by fitness-building exercises and then cleaning the barracks, and maintenance of their kit, weapons, clothes and themselves. Then lunch. After lunch they practised firing with their weapons and close quarter combat and after that, sometimes, they were allowed an hour's rest before a full dress parade in the castle courtyard in the late afternoon and another two hours drill before dusk. He issued new clothes for those who needed them, and made them wash their coats and uniforms and keep one set clean at all times – Corporal Horace Turner gleefully supervised extra drill after supper for those who came on parade with less than immaculate attire – insufficiently shiny buckles being his particular bête noire.

When Holcroft felt they were beginning to look more like a company in the regular English Army, he rode to Belfast Castle – which was once again the Williamite headquarters, now that the two sides had gone into their winter lodgings – and paid a large bribe in gold to Quartermaster Vallance to ensure that fourth company of Tiffin's were issued with new flintlock muskets to replace the ancient matchlocks and wheel-locks most of them had been using. He used his own personal money for the bribe, since he was a moderately well-off man, and feeling somehow that he owed it to the men he commanded to get them the very best weaponry available. And, despite his deep loathing of army corruption, he knew this was realistically the only way to achieve his aim. Since the regiment possessed no pikemen – a blessing as far as Holcroft was concerned – he further persuaded Quartermaster Vallance to equip his company with sixty-two of the new plug-bayonets, as well.

These instruments were basically knives with a nine-inch double-edged steel blade, a steel crossbar, and narrow tapering hilt that fitted snugly *inside* the barrel of a musket to make the weapon into a makeshift spear or half-pike. The gun could not, of course, be fired when the bayonet was plugged into the barrel but each man was transformed into a pikeman capable of inflicting injuries on enemy infantry and, in tight formation, keeping horsemen at bay.

He began training the men in the firing of their new flint-sparked muskets at the beginning of October. He trained them hard. For weeks that autumn – rain or shine, which meant, mostly, in a continuous soft Irish drizzle – the valleys around Inniskilling echoed with the cries of Sergeant Hawkins and Corporal Turner, and the roar of sixty-odd muskets, which began as ragged popping volleys lasting for a dozen seconds, but which, over days and weeks, became a single exhilarating crash of sound.

Holcroft had the men practise one simple battle manoeuvre again and again, day after day. The company would form two lines – and by now they could do this swiftly and cleanly without the ugly barging and confusion of the first days – and would advance towards a nominal enemy formation, usually a clump of trees or the wall of an abandoned barn. The men of fourth company would go forward in step, with Holcroft or one of the NCOs occasionally darting forward and tapping a soldier on the shoulder to tell him he was dead from enemy fire. Then fifty yards from the barn or copse, they would halt, take the time to dress their ranks, close up the holes made by the 'dead' men, and fire off a volley from the first line, a massive thunderclap, followed by a second volley from the second line – who would fire into the smoke of the first.

Then the order would come – 'Fix bayonets!' – and every man would insert the plug-bayonet into the hot barrel of his flintlock and – 'Charge!' – they would rush forward, the whole company running together, plunging through the smoke towards the outbuilding or small wood screaming their war cries and pretending to slaughter their imaginary Jacobite foes to a man.

The company loved these exercises. The 'dead' cheered on the 'living' to greater glory. The living demonstrated their skill and valour day after day, week after week. And were lavishly praised for it. In November, Brigadier-General William Wolseley, the regional commander, came out to accompany the fourth company on their exercises one blustery afternoon, and having watched them attack and vanquish a small hazel spinney, he took Holcroft's hand and shook it warmly and beamed at the captain's happily exhausted men.

Holcroft paraded the company that evening in newly cleaned uniforms and spotless rig and Brigadier Wolseley and Colonel Harry Fenton inspected them with due gravity and pronounced them heroes fit for the history books. Holcroft – to his astonishment – was awarded a brevet promotion to major and told that he was now the overall commander of the other two companies of Tiffin's Foot, the second and eleventh, which were also barracked at Inniskilling Castle.

Colonel Zachariah Tiffin, however, sent him a disobliging note, ostensibly congratulating him on his promotion but actually reminding Holcroft that a brevet rank carried no extra pay or privileges and that it could be rescinded at any time. The rank had no force inside his regiment and applied only nominally in the wider English Army. He was still a captain in the eyes of his commanding officer, the note said, and *Captain* Blood best not forget it. Holcroft tore up the message. Colonel Tiffin had not stirred from his governorship of Ballyshannon in the three months since Holcroft had joined his regiment. Neither had Holcroft been summoned. Indeed, he'd never even met his commanding officer.

Being busy gave Holcroft a new kind of energy and brightened his mood considerably. He was still angry, deep in his heart, that Narrey had eluded him at Carrickfergus, but he had no time to brood on his failure to kill the Frenchman. He was also absurdly pleased by the recognition that Brigadier Wolseley had given him with his brevet promotion and was determined to do his duty to the regiment as best he could, despite the churlishness of his colonel. He was eager to bring his Inniskillingers into contact with the enemy, for he knew that nothing melds a company into a cohesive whole like the fiery crucible of actual combat.

In mid-November, over a celebratory dinner in the castle with Colonel Fenton, who was visiting from Ballyshannon, and several other officers of Tiffin's, Holcroft found himself seated in the place of honour beside Brigadier Wolseley himself. The great man was solicitous, pouring him wine and asking generally after his family in London – questions which Holcroft did his best to dodge. He had not had time to write to Elizabeth for some weeks and he was feeling guilty about his neglect. Wolseley was an intelligent and sensitive man and soon ended this line of questioning. He asked if there was anything that Holcroft required for the comfort of the men under his command.

'The men are all perfectly comfortable,' Holcroft said, 'as far as I can tell.' He was puzzled by the question. 'Too much comfort is not always good for young soldiers, sir. Makes them soft.'

'There's nothing I can do for you?' said Wolseley. 'Nothing you need?'

At the far end of the table Lieutenant Watts was drunkenly explaining to the Governor of Inniskilling, a Swedish gentleman named Gustavus Hamilton, a dear friend of William of Orange, why Catholics should never, ever be trusted.

'I should like – if you can find the funds for me, sir – to set up a small, local intelligence-gathering unit here in Inniskilling,' said Holcroft.

The Brigadier raised his eyebrows. 'Spies?' he said. 'Is that what you mean, Brevet Major? That doesn't seem . . . well, very gentleman-like. Are you not satisfied with the weekly intelligence reports from headquarters in Belfast?'

'That is the problem, sir, they come from Belfast, which takes a day or two, and they only come every week. They tell us the big picture – that James's main army is standing before Dundalk, blocking General Schomberg's route south; that the Duke of Berwick is at Athlone, recruiting men and holding the line of the Shannon; that the Duke of Tyrconnell is also raising fresh troops down in Munster. It tells us more-than-a-week-old news about the leaders of our enemies. Yet two days ago, for example, in the village of Cooneen, some fifteen miles west of here, a man named Paul Tincey had his farm burnt and two hundred head of prime cattle stolen. His wife was cruelly violated; his eldest son was lynched for bravely resisting the marauders.'

'That must have been most distressing. But the nature of war means—'

Holcroft interrupted his superior. 'Raids like these are happening every week. Rapalees are operating out of Cavan and Belturbet – they ride out freely to burn and loot and kill. They range as far east as the outskirts of the Dundalk encampment itself. Then they disappear into thin air. We only hear about these outrages *after* they have been committed, some days afterwards. And *never* from the weekly Belfast intelligence report.'

'So what are you suggesting, Brevet Major Blood?'

'I am saying, sir, that if we could discover in advance when these raids were taking place, or if we were told about them very soon afterwards, we'd have a chance of hunting down these brigands, or at least of setting traps for them.'

'I see. You would need horsemen, I suppose.'

'That would be helpful in the chase, yes. But most of all we need to have intelligence of their movements. If you agree, sir, I should like to keep the operations purely local, say between here and Monaghan – my Inniskillingers know the lands hereabouts intimately – and to pay out small sums for information from farmers, travellers, tinkers . . . A small fund for this purpose would be necessary. I'd like to recruit a few men inside County Cavan, if I can   disaffected followers of James, or Protestants who've been ill-used by the Jacobite forces. Or just venal men with a love of money . . .'

'I collect that you are familiar with this type of activity,' said Wolseley.

'Yes, sir, but I should also like to send out wide-ranging scouts – if you could spare me a troop or two from Cunningham's Dragoons – we need eyes on every hill, men on the old towers and rooftops keeping watch for activity.'

'It all sounds rather expensive – and requiring a good deal of manpower,' grumbled Wolseley. 'But I'll let you try it. You had better get me some results, Blood, and soon, something I can boast of to Uncle Frederick at the Council.'

'Perhaps it would be best if you did *not* mention my name to General Schomberg, sir. He is not enamoured of me. I suggest that Ensign Waters – promoted to lieutenant – be nominally placed in charge. He can report directly to me.'

Two days later, in his spartan quarters in one of the round castle towers, Holcroft briefed the delighted Lieutenant Waters about his new rank and role.

'You are merely collecting the intelligence, Francis. You are not to move without my permission, do you understand? No matter how promising the material seems, nor how tempting the target, do not order out the troops without my say-so. We are getting some dragoons for our use. Not as many as I'd like but we will make do. But don't let them go chasing after the enemy at the first sniff of a raid. It is easy to be deceived in this game and the consequences of a mistake can be lethal.'

'Yes, sir. Might I make a suggestion, sir? My family has a number of properties, cottages mostly, and smallholdings, scattered around the eastern shores of Upper Lough Erne. It might be an idea for me to go and visit the families who live there – I know many have been robbed – and offer a bounty for reporting any enemy movement. I'm sure they would be eager for a taste of revenge, and a little silver would also not be entirely unwelcome . . .'

Holcroft knew then he had chosen the right man. He decided to trust the young officer with something he had previously thought to keep to himself.

'There is one more thing, Francis. I want you to listen out for one name in particular. Are you paying attention? If you hear anything about this man at all you are to tell me immediately. Even if it is in the middle of the night, come and wake me. If I am away in Belfast or Ballyshannon or wherever I am, send a fast galloper straight away to find me. This is of paramount importance.'

'Indeed? And what is the name, sir?'

'The name is d'Erloncourt. Henri, Comte d'Erloncourt. He is a French officer somewhat loosely attached to James's headquarters in Dublin.'

Chapter Nine

Monday, January 6, 1690

Informers. There could be no other explanation. Bloody-handed, Hell-bound, God-damned informers. There would be a reckoning one day, oh yes. Revenge would be taken in full measure. Michael Hogan was so tired that he could barely sit on his walking horse. His right shoulder was a mass of fiery pain where the pistol ball had creased him, passing – mercifully – clean through the skin and half an inch of meat at the top of his arm, showing lots of gore but with God's grace not too serious. It would heal in a few weeks. In the meantime it was damned painful. He had tucked his thumb into his belt as he rode to take the weight off the wound.

Around him his shattered and dejected men plodded along the road, eyes down, many of them as bloodied as he and roughly bandaged, all of them utterly spent. They were passing through the hamlet of Drumalee Cross, a mile outside Cavan and all the comforts of home, past Jim Mulligan's alehouse, where Hogan had spent many a warm and joyful evening over the past few months. No one in his band raised their eyes to look at the mossy thatch of the inn, no one in the last light of that terrible day suggested stopping for a reviving pint or two. Every man wanted only to return home, to get off his horse, wash and strap up his wounds, eat a little hot soup and sleep for about a week.

The raid had started promisingly. They had made camp last night in a burnt-out barn a few miles east of Newtownbutler, discreet fires had been lit, and a tender young goat roasted, the ale jug had gone round and round, there had even been soft singing before they curled up in ancient straw or drifts of leaves or wrapped their own heavy cloaks and slept the sleep of the just.

In the first light of frosty dawn, they had come down on the farm-house a little outside Magheraveely, sweeping down the hillside, light as a herd of running fallow deer, sixty-two men all a-horse and armed as well as guardsmen, surrounding the big old house and surprising a farmhand at his early morning chores – chopping the day's firewood – and the tenant farmer feeding a bucket of slops to his pigs. Neither man had offered any resistance, although the old 'un had glanced once at the ancient double-barrelled fowling piece that was propped up against the wood pile. Hogan had smiled genially at him over a levelled horse pistol, inviting him to touch the gun if he dared, and the old fella had just shrugged and sat down there and then in the dust in surrender.

They had taken several dozen hams and cheeses, a few sacks of fine-milled flour, a barrel of apples, one of pears; a trio of piglets had their throats slit and were slung leaking in the back of the dog-cart they always brought along for the plunder. Paddy Gallagher, Hogan's troll-bearded lieutenant, had searched the big house thoroughly – making a hellish mess as usual, breaking pots in the kitchen, emptying chests in the bedrooms like a whirlwind – and found himself a small box of copper coins and an old blue enamel brooch with silver chasing. They rounded up fifty sheep and a big truculent ram from the surrounding fields and set them bleating on the road towards home.

Nobody had been killed or hurt, there had been no women folk to tempt the boys into sinful ways, and they had not left the place in roaring flames, as they were sometimes obliged to do. They even left the old fella and his working man a worn-out sow and a half-sack of beans so they wouldn't starve to death.

It had been a grand day's work. Neat, quick, lucrative.

By mid-morning, they were merrily trotting back south towards Cavan, with Hogan already calculating the price the quarter-master's agent, a Dublin man and a notorious cheat, would pay for the herd. The fighting men of King James's army were ever hun-gry, especially now, in the depths of winter, and Hogan meant to drive a hard bargain for the captured sheep. The boys were singing again as they rode along – there would be meat and drink aplenty tonight, and money jingling in their pockets, and the pretty girls of Cavan could no doubt be easily awed horizontal by tales of their derring-do.

They had kept well east of Newtownbutler and were heading south on the main road north of Wattle Bridge, passing through a small patch of woodland, riding easy, keeping the sheep moving along, stopping the animals from straying up the banks and into the thick wood. Hogan was suddenly aware that the trees were full of men, grey-coated men with flashes of orange at their turned-back sleeves and long muskets. Inniskillingers. Hundreds of the bastards. A tall officer with a blue coat and red sash around his waist was standing out in front. His back was turned; he seemed to be ignoring Hogan's band entirely. He simply called out: 'First rank only . . . fire!' and all Hell was unleashed.

Hogan's men were caught by surprise. The initial volley, the thunderous simultaneous crash of nearly a hundred flintlocks, punched out from the tree line, the individual puffs of grey smoke forming a thick fog bank that hid the upper half of the attackers from view. The bullets whistled, hummed and smacked into soft flesh, horse and human. Half a dozen saddles were emptied, men screamed, horses bucked, the sheep fled bawling into the trees on the far side of the road. Chaos.

Hogan had his pistol out and cocked, he aimed into the smoke bank and pulled the trigger, the piece cracked, the passage of the ball twitching the curtain of grey. Hogan shouted, 'Charge, lads, charge! They won't stand!' Dropping his pistol he hauled out his brass-handled cutlass and, struggling to control his panicked mount, he tried to urge the crabbing horse into the trees.

The smoke bank was clearing, and Hogan could see the line of men busy with scouring sticks and white paper cartridges, biting bullets free, pouring the black powder into the barrels, recharging their flintlocks with terrifying speed and efficiency. And behind the reloading infantry, more men in grey – scores of them – coming forward and forming up on the bank of the road in front of the others in a fresh line, a mere dozen yards from him. The tall officer was shouting commands and the new line of men were levelling their unfired muskets. Hogan was aware that his own fellows were milling crazily in the road, some still dazed and bewildered by the first thunderous volley, some fruitlessly trying to round up the last of the sheep, others helping wounded men, staring at their own blood-oozing bodies in amazement; some, however, had swords or their new carbines out and were glaring at the infantry, ready to fight; yet others were galloping away – God-damned cowards.

'Charge them, lads!' shouted Hogan. 'We must get up there at 'em . . .'

A second volley crashed, drowning out Hogan's words. Half-deafened by the noise, Hogan gripped his horse tight between his thighs and forced it to mount the bank on the side of the road, spurring unmercifully, raking the beast's sides bloody, forcing it towards the trees and plunging into the fog of smoke. A twitch of wind revealed the officer in the blue coat, standing at the end of the line of his damned Inniskillingers, shouting at them to reload. He seemed oblivious to the devastation his two volleys had wrought in the road.

Kill the officer and the bastards would be leaderless. Hogan shouted a wild, incoherent challenge. The man heard it and turned fast. He made out the raparee on his horse, two dozen yards away, barrelling straight for him through the smoke, leaning forward along the animal's neck. The officer coolly reached into his red sash and pulled out a long pistol. He cocked it, pointed it at Hogan and fired. The Irishman, hunching instinctively as the gun was aimed at him, felt the bullet rip the pheasant-feather tricorn from his head. He grinned. *Got you, my bonny boy!* He lifted the cutlass, his horse yards from the man.

Hogan expected the officer to run, or duck away – he was on foot, being charged by a snarling enemy on a big horse, an empty pistol in his hand. But the tall officer did not, he looked down at the weapon, seemed to crank a long lever on the side. Then lifted the odd-looking pistol again, aimed, fired – and shot Hogan straight through the right arm, high up by the shoulder.

The raparee captain felt the punch of the bullet but was more surprised than shocked by the unexpected wound. Was it a double-barrelled pistol? It hadn't looked like one. His horse veered away at the smoke and bang of the pistol exploding by its nose, and the beast raced madly past the tall officer, with Hogan unable to lift his sword arm to strike.

He was through the two lines of infantry and in the trees, with nothing before him but a few sergeants, big men with pole-arms staring at him. One red-faced brute slashed at him with his shiny halberd, but the nimble horse avoided the sweep of the axehead with no help from Hogan. He let the beast run on and heard behind him the sound of a third volley crashing out on the helpless riders in the road.

By God, these Inniskillinger bastards are good, he thought. *Three disciplined musket volleys in less than half a minute.*

He wondered how many of his own men had lived through them.

Two miles down the road, by the black waters of a small lough, Hogan gathered the men who had survived the ambush. A bare handful of riders, he counted eighteen men, though he knew there would be more dispersed across the green countryside who would join them if they could as they made their way south. The plunder wagon was gone, the sheep were scattered to Hell and back. Hogan's shoulder was one huge fiery ache. But two of his poor men were dying in the saddle, both shot in the belly, and spilling blood freely, men too stubborn to dismount and expire in greater comfort on the soft green turf.

That was when the Inniskillinger dragoons attacked. Only a single troop of about forty-five men, in grey coats and orange turnbacks just like the bastard infantry but with white cross belts and carbines in holsters at their horses' withers, galloping towards them down a muddy lane by the side of the lough. At their full strength, Hogan's company would have engaged them in a trice – and would have driven them off with ease. Dragoons were not cavalry, indeed they were looked down upon by real horse warriors. They were mounted infantry, paid less than cavalry, less well armed, too; they used their horses merely to move swiftly from one place to another. They dismounted in battle and formed up in lines like the foot-slogging infantry they truly were. In happier circumstances, Hogan's band of sixty seasoned raparees would have torn them to bloody shreds. But today they ran like frightened chickens.

Hogan put back his spurs and the tired horse took off like a rocket down the road. The dragoons were on fresh mounts, and only fifty yards behind them, their excited cries audible over the clattering of their hooves. As he galloped, Hogan craned over his poor throbbing shoulder to watch them gaining yard by yard on his band of panicked men. He realised then that, like the two lines of infantry in the wood, these dragoons had been waiting for him.

The Inniskillinger footmen could not hope to catch his riders, so they had set up a powerful static ambush in the trees – must have been three companies of musket men at least – and once they had mauled his band with their volleys, sending them skedaddling off down the road, the dragoons were waiting by the lough to finish them off. It was as neat a trap as Hogan had seen in a while. Clearly a fine military mind was at work here.

He briefly wondered about the tall officer in the blue coat and red sash, the man who had shot him with the pistol that did not seem to need reloading. Could this be the dangerous man the Frenchman had told him about? Could this be Holcroft Blood himself – fifty pounds of fine French gold on two long legs?

Michael Hogan had no time to ponder the identity of the enemy officer. The dragoons were gaining on them. Only thirty yards behind now. Hogan felt his own horse begin to falter, its dark neck was creamy with sweat. He's been riding all day and the beast was nearly done. He heard a crack behind him and a high cry of pain. Seamus Kielty, the last man in the band, his poor horse already bleeding from a musket ball in its flank taken at the ambush, had been pistolled square in the back by the leading dragoon. As Hogan glanced over his bloody shoulder, the young man arched his back in agony, threw up his hands and slid off his saddle, disappearing under the churning hooves of his gleefully hallooing pursuers. They were approaching another thick wood – part of the lands of Castle Saunderson, which had been burnt to the ground the previous summer. There had been great slaughter of King James's fleeing men here, Hogan recalled, after the disaster of Newtownbutler. They had faced these same God-damned Inniskillingers then, too. But, just maybe, just possibly, the wood might be a refuge. If they could get into it quickly enough. Hogan bawled to his men to leave the road and head right into the shelter of trees, yelling, waving his good arm, pointing urgently, all at a breakneck thundering pace.

They heard him, turned and galloped into the gloom, reckless of the low branches and the closeness of the trees, plunging into sudden darkness, out of sight from the road and their yelling grey-coated pursuers. Out of the corner of his eye, as he dived into the gloom, Hogan saw old Crookback Keegan away to his left smash his knee into a thick bole as his horse charged between two scabrous silver birches. The old man bawled out a filthy curse, his leg smeared and bleeding, jiggling loose and clearly badly broken. But they were deep in the trees and – Thank Mary, Mother of God – the dragoons were reining in, reluctant to charge after them into the tangled depths of the wood with the same reckless abandon as the fleeing raparees.

'On, lads,' Hogan shouted. 'On and on. We must get distance 'tween us and those mad grey bastards.'

The fugitives needed little encouragement. They forged onwards into the stygian woods, at only a slightly lesser pace than before. The dragoons were out of sight by now, hidden by the trees behind, but Hogan had no doubt they would be following. His greatest fear was that they had been herded into this wood by design. Had the tall infantry officer planned all this? Would they emerge from the trees into the sudden roar of enemy musket fire?

'West, boys, we must head west. That way,' Hogan shouted, pointing to a deer track through the thick foliage, and at least some of the men heeded him. They'd go out of their way, sure, but not too far, the Protestants had occupied Belturbet in early December, which was a small town five miles in that direction, and he had no intention of running into one of their patrols in the state his men were in. But they could risk a little westering. Just a little. There were marshes and bogs and pools and ponds that would swallow any horsemen who did not know the country, and the River Finn as well to negotiate. They would head west. There was more danger in doing the obvious thing and heading due south on the main road to Cavan.

Informers. There could be no other explanation. Red handed, God-damned, Hell-bound informers. Somebody was peaching on them to the bloody English. Otherwise how could they know what road they would be on and when? Michael Hogan was determined that he would find out who and give them what they deserved for their treachery. The dusk was falling, and a thin cold rain, and Hogan could see the welcoming lights of Cavan up ahead. They were coming up to a small ridge on the Monaghan Road, and through the drizzle he could see the earthworks and ancient rotten timbers of old Tullymongan Castle up on his left on higher ground overlooking the town. They passed by the guard house, a tiny wooden hut staffed by a sergeant and two private soldiers, with a striped pole across the road. The pole was lifted. Nobody saluted.

Along the street, folk were poking their heads out of their front doors and windows, silently observing the soaking, dejected horsemen, noting their depleted numbers. Hogan did not bother to acknowledge the few souls brave enough to call out and ask for news. A rider in emerald velvet, one of Brigadier Wauchope's officers, came cantering up the main street towards them, splashing through the puddles. He reined in by Hogan, and looked over the thin column of wet, wounded, exhausted men, sneering down his long Leinster nose, or so it seemed to Hogan. There was no love lost in Cavan between the raparees and the regular Jacobite troops commanded by John Wauchope, the town governor, a gruff Scotsman fanatically loyal to King James. Hogan decided that if the long-nosed officer made a single disparaging comment about his poor men he would pull out his boot-knife and stab him straight through the heart – to the Devil with the consequences.

But the man in green merely sniffed and said: 'A visitor to see you, Hogan. A fancy little Frenchman from headquarters. He's waiting in the Town Hall. Says it's urgent. Arrogant sod but there is a smell of money on him, for sure.'

Hogan dismissed the officer with a wave of his hand. He turned his horse in the street and halted the bedraggled column. He waited till all the men were looking at him through the thickening veil of rain and spoke out bold and loud, so that all could hear: 'We had some bad luck, today, boys. Terrible bad luck. We took some cruel knocks. But you've all played your part like men, like true Irishmen. No one could have asked more of you. And I'm proud of you all. Away to your hearths now, get dry and get some rest. Tomorrow is tomorrow and then we'll see what's what. Bless you all, lads, God bless you all.'

'God bless you, Brevet Major Blood, that was fine work. Absolutely first class,' said Brigadier Wolseley, shaking Holcroft briskly by the hand. 'I understand that there were more than sixteen of these bandits killed outright by your men and we have another thirteen fellows in the cells down below, some who were wounded in the ambush and left for dead by their so-called comrades and some who were captured trying to flee cross-country by the dragoons. First-class work, sir. I take my hat off to you.'

Holcroft and Wolseley were in a corner of the great hall of Inniskilling Castle, enjoying a glass of claret before sitting down to supper. Outside the rain was lashing down, fit to frighten Noah himself, as Wolseley had put it.

'Thank you, sir,' said Holcroft. 'You are most generous. If I may ask, what will you do with the prisoners?'

'I shall hang them all in the morning and good riddance to them.'

'Is it absolutely necessary to hang them, sir? They are, after all, enemy combatants, prisoners of war, and by all the usual rules, they should be—'

'It *is* absolutely necessary to hang them, Brevet Major Blood. They are murderers and thieves who make war without uniform and with irregular, and I daresay, highly illegal methods. They rape and kill indiscriminately and are therefore no more than common criminals. Hanging is what they deserve and hanging is what they shall receive. I admire your tender heart, Blood, but I am somewhat surprised at your attitude. You have a reputation as something of a firebrand. I understand you were kicked out . . . that is, you were relieved of your position in the Ordnance, for personally attacking Jacobite prisoners of war after they had been granted parole. Is that not so?'

Holcroft sighed. He'd no wish to revisit what had occurred at Carrick.

'That is so, sir. But with respect to these prisoners, sir, I should like to request a stay of execution. I wish to interrogate them personally over the next few days and weeks to discover what they know about the raparees of Cavan. About their operations, strengths, weaknesses . . .'

Holcroft, in truth, cared little for the fate of the thirteen men who had been captured – they were the enemy and they were, in truth, bandits, just as Wolseley had said – but he hated men to be unnecessarily killed when they were no longer a threat and he did in fact hope to gain intelligence from them.

Brigadier Wolseley grumpily agreed to delay their fates for a week or so until Holcroft had interrogated them all. The Ordnance officer thanked him distractedly – he had something far more important on his mind this evening. Indeed, the news Holcroft had recently received from Lieutenant Francis Waters had filled him with a sense of dizzying excitement.

'Is there any news from Belfast, sir, about the matter I suggested to you?' said Holcroft. *Please let the answer be yes, please God.* He struggled to keep his face calm and relaxed. The answer to *this* request was of vital importance.

Two days ago, Francis Waters had woken him before dawn and told him that their man in County Cavan – an innkeeper called James Mulligan who had a profound love of money and an illogical hatred of his jolly, raucous customers – had some intelligence for them. Jim Mulligan ran a modest establishment outside Cavan, in a one-horse hamlet called Drumalee Cross, and many of his patrons were drawn from the few hundred Jacobite officers and men stationed in and around Cavan. Mulligan supplied ale, wine and brandy, and powerful home-made poteen, too, if required, along with simple meals, bread and cheese, bacon and cabbage, stews, soups and so on. He listened all day to the bored soldiers as they ate and drank, boasted and bickered with each other and passed on what snippets of gossip he had picked up to Lieutenant Waters' man, a Protestant baker from Fairtown who visited Mulligan's every morning to supply him with fresh loaves of bread.

The gossip that morning was this: a very rich, red-haired Frenchman had come to Cavan. He had taken rooms in Brigadier Wauchope's big house next to the Town Hall and looked set to stay put for a while. They said he had brought firearms and money for the godless raparees – although why that rabble should be so honoured was a mystery. An important fellow, this Frenchman, with a fine carriage, which sported the gentleman's coat of arms: a pair of red foxes on a blue background . . .

It was Narrey. Henri d'Erloncourt was in Cavan. No more than thirty miles away. Holcroft was sure of it. And he looked set to remain there.

'So have you, sir, have you had a reply yet from Belfast?' Holcroft could not stop himself repeating the question. 'Have they said we may attack Cavan? It is the surest way to wipe out this scourge once and for all. I'm sure you agree, sir. We must burn the raparees out of their nest as soon as possible.'

'Oh, I quite agree with you, Brevet Major. Take them where they roost, while they sleep. I completely agree. And so, as it happens, does headquarters. General Schomberg has embarrassed himself mightily at Dundalk. He's got nowhere and his poor men have been dying like flies all winter from the bloody flux. He badly needs a victory or King William will surely replace him with someone more competent: so he has, in fact, given his permission for this Cavan attack of yours. But it'd damn well better be a great success or else.'

Holcroft let out a heavy breath. 'Thank you, sir. You've no idea how . . .'

'Wait a moment, Brevet Major Blood. Not so fast. We'll move on Cavan, as General Schomberg desires, the moment the weather begins to improve - but we are not going off half-cock. I want you to plan this properly. We will use Belturbet as our forward base and I want to know everything there is to know about the strength of the enemy before we commit ourselves . . .'

But Holcroft, filled with a glorious, up-bubbling of joy, was no longer listening to his superior. At long last, revenge was almost in his grasp.

Chapter Ten

Tuesday, February 11, 1690

Something was wrong. Badly wrong. Holcroft's intelligence had been clear, and had been confirmed by various sources, including several of the raparees still held in the dungeons of Inniskilling Castle: the Jacobite garrison at Cavan had no more than seven or eight hundred effectives, mostly raw, barely trained, ill-equipped infantry drawn from all over Ireland. But the fat columns of men now pouring out of Cavan – to form up in their companies and regiments north of the town on a slight ridge that crossed the Monaghan Road – contained many more than seven hundred men.

And they kept on coming.

Holcroft watched them with his brass spy-glass take their places on the ridge from three quarters of a mile away, sitting on the back of Nut as his own men of the second, fourth and eleventh companies of Tiffin's Regiment of Foot marched past. Had he been tricked? Had Narrey deceived him again? Had Henri d'Erloncourt somehow persuaded all his informants to give Holcroft the same false information – to lure him and Wolseley to their doom? It was just not possible. Narrey might have got to one agent, perhaps even two. But there was no way he could have unmasked and turned half a dozen of Holcroft's informants without his knowledge. No, this was something else.

The force commanded by Brigadier Wolseley, which had marched out of Belturbet the evening before, had seemed formidable: a thousand infantry drawn from the Inniskillingers and Kirke's Lambs, as well as other English regiments, strengthened by two hundred Dutchmen, a double company of the Blue Guards, King William's elite shock troops. This infantry column had been screened by three hundred cavalry, two troops of Inniskillinger dragoons and three of crack Danish heavy cavalry. Hoping to surprise the garrison at Cavan – which they believed they easily outnumbered – instead of coming directly south-east on the main road, they had taken a long and tiring detour east, crossed the River Annalee at Bellanacargy and come in towards Cavan from the north-east. At a little after dawn, they were marching up the Monaghan Road only a mile or so out from the town and it seemed that their precautions had all been for nothing. The garrison was apparently well aware of their advance and it seemed it had also been forewarned of their attack and massively reinforced.

Brigadier Wolseley came clattering up and reined in beside Holcroft. Without a word, Holcroft handed him his brass telescope and the commander inspected the ridge before them. 'Bit of a cock-up, Blood, wouldn't you say?'

'Yes, sir.' Holcroft was aware of a sinking sensation in his belly. He knew that Wolseley might decide that the odds against them were too great and choose to withdraw without a shot being fired. Indeed, were it not for the fact that he was almost certain of the presence of Narrey in Cavan, Holcroft would have been tempted to do the same.

'Where did they find so many men?' Wolseley asked.

'My guess, sir, would be that the Duke of Berwick marched north and joined them with at least two regiments, maybe three, and a sizeable force of cavalry. There are nearly two thousand men on that ridge. And I think, sir, that you might be able to make out Berwick's standard in the centre.'

'Yes, I see it. Royal arms as befits the bastard son of James, red, blue and gold.' A moment later Wolseley took the glass from his eye and said: 'They are well prepared for us. Were we betrayed, Brevet Major?' He looked at Holcroft.

'I don't believe so, sir. Although we may have been spotted on the march. You can't move a thousand men even on the back roads without making some clamour. I believe the Duke of Berwick's appearance here at this time is just bad luck. Mind you, our attack would have been fairly simple to anticipate.'

What Holcroft refrained from saying was that he should have anticipated the reinforcement by Berwick's men himself. If Narrey had taken up residence at Cavan, it was for a good reason – probably because he was planning larger, more damaging raiding expeditions into the soft underbelly of Ulster. And if that were so, he would probably have demanded additional troops for the task.

'Well, we're here now, Brevet Major. The question is: can we beat them?'

Holcroft took back his glass and looked up at the thick ranks of men on the ridge. Their lines were shaky, their formations blurred, crowd-like. There were dozens of men wandering in between the regiments looking for their place. They possessed no artillery, not one single gun – which was good. But then neither did Wolseley.

'Yes, sir. We can beat them,' Holcroft said, with a confidence he did not feel. He asked himself if he was doing this because Narrey was here. Because if they fought and won, Narrey would be in his sights. No, they *could* win the day.

'Do you truly believe so, Brevet Major Blood? They outnumber us at least two to one and they have the higher ground in their favour.'

'That is so, sir. But if we retreat now, we shall all feel defeated. The men will be ashamed. Morale will plummet and they may never find the courage to fight well again. I say we attack today. And I should like, sir, to lead the infantry assault personally. If I may. If you will permit me that honour, sir.'

Holcroft felt better after making this offer. If he were planning to risk the lives of so many good men because of his selfish desire to get into Cavan town, the least he could do was to risk his own life alongside theirs.

'I believe you're right. We must attack. And I shall take you up on that gallant offer, Brevet Major Blood. You will command the centre: your Inniskillingers and two companies of Kirke's Lambs and I'll give you all the Dutch Blue Guards, too. On my signal, march your men up there on to the ridge and punch a hole through the middle. I shall follow you with the rest of the assault force and we'll sweep 'em all away like cobwebs before a good-wife's broom. You will do that for me, Brevet Major Blood, will you?'

'Yes, sir.'

'Good man. We'll make our dispositions here, all along this hedge line. I believe I'll soften them up with our cavalry. Let the dragoons and the Danish knock some of the impudence out of them first. Right, get it done then, Brevet Major. I shall be observing from that hill. And don't make a mess of this.'

Michael 'Galloping' Hogan looked down at the lines of enemy infantry in the road below the ridge, now making their dispositions along a thick hawthorn hedge that marked the boundary of a muddy cow pasture. A much smaller force, by the looks of it. Any commander in their right mind should beat a hasty retreat when faced with such an imbalance. But these men it seemed were determined to fight. Were they confident in their superiority, man for man? Or were they arrogant idiots, who did not understand that they were overmatched?

Hogan had been ordered this day to take his place on the extreme right of the Jacobite line, in command of the whole cavalry contingent: his own fifty-strong band of mounted raparees, whose numbers had recently been reinforced by a score of new recruits from his old haunts around Tipperary and Limerick, as well as a full regiment of the Duke of Berwick's Horse – a grand title for a ramshackle force of two hundred mounted Catholic gentlemen, proud owners of small parcels of land mostly around Dublin with a sprinkling of well-to-do merchants and lawyers from the capital city itself.

Each gentleman trooper was able to supply his own horse and two remounts, and possessed a servant and at least a sword and a pistol or two with which to defend himself. They came to the battlefield dressed in all their finery, velvet and silk surcoats, topped by long, flowing, leather-and-wool rain-proof cloaks, and broad-brimmed felt hats with extravagant ostrich plumes dyed all the colours of the rainbow. Some wore bits and pieces of mail or plate armour, some ancient, some even medieval – pauldrons, vambraces and the like – as well as more modern steel lobster-pot cavalry helmets, leather gauntlets, long black riding boots. These gently born horsemen were eager for a fight, eager to prove their manhood, and that eagerness allowed them to swallow their resentment at being commanded by such a low-born bumpkin as Mick Hogan.

The low-born bumpkin himself looked to his left along the line of the small ridge. The infantry formations looked decidedly shaky, to Hogan's experienced eye. In the centre, beneath his magnificent standard, the Duke of Berwick sat on a silver-grey horse. A slim, handsome young man in a blinding golden coat and white hat plumed with a gold-dyed ostrich feather, the duke was surrounded by a dozen aides, gallopers and personal guards. And with him was the slippery Frenchman Narrey, also well mounted, and his bruiser Guillaume. *Would the Frenchmen fight,* Hogan wondered, *or were they here to observe?* Berwick and his entourage were stationed a dozen yards behind the duke's three foot regiments, fifteen hundred men, pikemen to the fore, red-coated matchlock men behind, the smoke from their lit matches curling, trickling upwards in the air.

These Jacobite soldiers were recently recruited from Cork and Kerry – some had signed up to serve only a few weeks beforehand – and many did not understand the officers' orders, which were usually given only in English. Their training had been mostly delivered to them on the march from the recruiting depots in the south. As a result, Berwick's regiments were not in perfect linear alignment, some were bulging absurdly in the middle as the men, already fear-ful of the bloody fight to come, crowded together for safety. Groups of sergeants with halberds or poleaxes patrolled the edges of the formations shoving the men this way and that in an attempt to get them back into their correct places. But the result was that bodies of hundreds of men contracted and expanded, shifted and swayed like huge schools of fish below a sea-going boat.

The rain had held off, for once, and it was a bright February morning. A little cold, but dry. That would make the musketry easier, Hogan told himself. Rain often extinguished the burning match cords, unless they were protected, and bad weather rendered a matchlock no more than a heavy lump of wood. Indeed, it treated more modern flintlocks with a similar contempt. Nothing like a good Irish rainstorm to reduce a battle to a muddy, bloody shov-ing match between groups of men wielding only wooden clubs and wicked blades.

On the far side of Berwick's regiments, Brigadier John Wauchope's men were in better order. Their lines were straight, their private men standing almost perfectly still. They had been in Cavan for some months and their Scots commander had made an effort to see they could all at least parade respectably.

They had the numbers, then. But what about the quality of the men? Hogan looked down the slope at the thinner English lines. The Inniskillingers were in the centre, a couple of hundred musket-men in grey, in three small company-strong blocks, and to their left a large single block of men in blue coats with orange facings – Dutchmen, he assumed. King William's vaunted Blue Guards. There were English redcoats to the right of the Inniskillingers, maybe two full companies. Veterans, too, by the look of them. And now the Williamite cavalry was coming forward, grey-clad Inniskillinger dragoons, what looked like two full troops, and some curassiers, three, no four troops of them, steel breast and back plates worn over long yellow coats with red facings, the metal armour blacked to stop it reflecting the sun and giving the cavalry's position away on the march. The curassiers were forming up on the far side of the dragoons, twenty yards in front of the lines of Williamite infantry, dressing their ranks, the trumpeters blowing complicated sequences, a dry riffle of drums now. Hogan thought they might be Danes. He had heard that King William had sent over some first-class Danish mercenaries with General Schomberg's force.

The curassier officer spurred out ahead of the yellow-clad heavy cavalry, and drew his sword. It flashed in the weak sunlight. That was bold – did the curassiers mean to charge? Uphill, against a numerically superior enemy? With no artillery to soften them up? Yes, they did; the dragoons too.

The ranks of the dragoons were moving forward, at walking pace, but it was definitely an advance. An attack. And one in a style he was familiar with from his time as a youngster in the late wars against the Dutch in the Spanish Netherlands. It seemed clear now to Hogan what they planned to do: the dragoons would ride up, dismount at a hundred, or perhaps even seventy yards, if they were brave, from the red Jacobite lines, fire off their carbines, a couple of concentrated volleys perhaps, maybe three, hoping to kill, wound and generally terrorise a large section of the Duke of Berwick's battle line. Then once the dragoons had done their work, the curassiers would charge home into the now disordered ranks, screaming their war cries, firing their horse pistols, swinging their long, straight lethal swords, smashing into the line of weakened men. The Danish curassiers hoped to chop through the enemy lines, right in the centre – and, if they managed that, then the real killing would begin. Broken, fleeing enemy infantry was easy meat for these heavy horsemen to ride down. The English Foot would follow them up the hill, no doubt, and charge into the gap the horsemen had made. And that would be it. The Duke of Berwick's whole army would be done: dead, defeated or driven from the field.

It was a good plan. Berwick's raw infantry *were* shaky. The English could see that. Having a couple of troops of dragoons – a hundred and twenty hard men – riding up and noisily firing off their carbines at your company from close range, seeming to aim at you personally, was terrifying to a novice redcoat. Even if the men held their nerve, they would break and run when the Danes came thundering in, long swords swinging. That would be the end.

Or not. Not if Mick Hogan had anything to do with it.

He turned to his bird's-nest-bearded lieutenant, sitting placidly on a bay beside him: 'Get the boys ready, Paddy. We're going to take a hand in this.'

Hogan turned his mount and trotted over to the captain of Berwick's Horse, a fat, extremely short-sighted fellow named Sir Robert Cleverly, who wore a rich plum-coloured velvet coat and a gleaming lobster-pot helmet from the late civil wars.

'We're going to charge them, Sir Robert. On my command the cavalry will advance and take the enemy in the flank.'

'Excellent news, Hogan. My men will sweep these Protestant rogues from the field. Show them our mettle, eh? So, ah, straight down the hill and at 'em?'

'No, Sir Robert. Absolutely not! Not down the hill. We're not going to charge their formed infantry ranks. We'd achieve nothing except to scatter ourselves across the landscape. We're going to charge their attacking cavalry.'

'Their cavalry, eh? Excellent. And which cavalry would that be?'

Hogan saw the man was peering across the field. Why had this purblind mole been put in command of the Duke's Horse? Hogan knew the answer: Sir Robert was someone's cousin or brother-in-law. Or someone owed him money.

'Their cavalry are advancing – see over there. The dragoons are coming forward. The horsemen in grey?'

'Oh yes, of course. The grey dragoons. I see them clearly now.'

Sir Robert Cleverly was staring at a small copse of silver birches by the side of the main road that cut through the centre of the battlefield.

'I tell you what, Sir Robert. When I give the word you and your merry band of cavaliers follow after me and my men. Stick with us. Is that clear?'

'Quite so, quite so. At the word, we'll come out hot on your heels.'

'Very good.'

The dragoons advanced at the walk. Halfway up the slope they came to the trot. And for the last few dozen yards they were at the canter. Then they stopped abruptly. The Inniskillingers slid from their horses' backs at about eighty yards from their enemy, in front of the centre-right of the line, equidistant between the Duke of Berwick and Galloping Hogan. The Jacobite musket fire began almost immediately, individual pecking shots, barks and flashes, that kicked up mud and earth near the feet of the dragoons or whistled overhead – Hogan could hear the outraged roaring of the sergeants and officers telling their Cork and Kerry men to hold their damned fire.

The dragoons were untouched by the sporadic barrage – muskets, even in the hands of well-schooled men, were notorious for their inaccuracy at anything over fifty yards. One dragoon in ten was designated the horse-holder, and the nine other dragoons calmly passed their reins to him before advancing, walking into the sputtering fire, carbines in hand, to form up at a distance of sixty yards from the Duke of Berwick's men.

The officers around the duke were staring over the infantry's heads at the dismounted enemy horsemen, a hundred yards away, beyond effective range. One aide galloped away along the rear of the line, carrying an order.

The sergeants and officers were shouting again, trying to organise a combined fire, but as many men in the Jacobite ranks were now unloaded, only a weak, raggedy volley sputtered out from their red ranks when the order was finally given. The dragoons ignored the splattering fire as they dressed their line, taking their time to ensure that they were exactly the same distance apart from the man on either side. Only then did they shoulder their carbines.

One dragoon was hit, and fell back like a nine-pin, knocked down by a Jacobite ball, his face a mass of blood, but the rest of the Inniskillingers – a perfectly still grey line of men, muskets levelled – were unscathed.

They fired. A single crashing sound, then smoke plumed from a hundred barrels and a dozen men in the centre of the Duke of Berwick's lines staggered and fell. The dragoons began to reload, calmly, methodically, seemingly without a care in the world, oblivious to the enemy wall of red sixty yards in front of them. And the wall feared them. It was shifting, moving back and forwards. Individuals breaking free and running to the rear. The sergeants were bellowing, 'Close up. Close up. And hold your goddamn fire!' Once in a while a shot would ring out, a lone musket fired off by a fearful man.

The dragoons were reloaded. They shouldered their carbines again, and at a command from their officer of 'Give fire!' discharged them as one in a rippling crash that ripped into the enemy ranks. The wall of redcoats twitched and wavered, another dozen men fell. Some were trying to edge away from the line of fire. Somebody was screaming: a terrifying animal noise.

It was at that moment that Hogan's fifty-odd raparees and the two hundred eager gentlemen of Berwick's Horse cantered on to the field of battle. Their drumming hooves reverberated through the turf. Their war cries could be heard over the crash of the muskets and the screams of the wounded redcoats.

The dragoons, until now so perfect in their discipline, turned their heads at the sound, saw the Jacobite cavalry pounding towards them and . . . panicked. They ran, some hurling their empty carbines away, every man scrambling to get back to their horse-handlers and their mounts twenty yards away, sprinting from the line, desperate to escape before the oncoming catastrophe overtook them.

Hogan's men crashed into them at the full gallop. For the most part the raparees merely rode down the running men, the weight of horse knocking humans to the turf before the churning hooves milled over him. Some runners they slashed at with sabres, other horsemen pulled out their pistols and fired into the backs of their fleeing foes. The red wall of Jacobite recruits was cheering now – revelling in seeing their erstwhile tormentors taking this punishment. Men were trampled, sliced and stabbed by plunging swords, faces back-cut to the bone. About twenty of the Inniskillingers, the fleetest men, had managed to get to their horses, into the saddle and were kicking their frightened beasts down the hillside. A few of the dragoons, bizarrely, ran towards the Jacobite lines, crying out that they surrendered, calling for mercy. The frightened young men from Cork and Kerry waited till they got within twenty yards, then shot them down like dogs.

Hogan's men, with Berwick's Horse mixed in among them, chased the fleeing dragoons off the summit of the hill and north down the grassy slope. The outnumbered dragoons saw the cuirassiers advancing towards them in their neat lines and, recognising their allies, they spurred madly towards their yellow-coated ranks – despite the desperate cries of the Danish officers that the broken dragoons must steer clear to maintain troop cohesion. The grey horsemen, some slashed and bloody, others mad with pain or fear, ignored the Danes' desperate warnings and barged into the ranks of the cuirassiers. They destroyed the neat order of the Danish advance, forcing their bodies into the safe crush of their ranks. In a moment, what had been an orderly attack up the hill which was supposed to crash into the Jacobite lines at the spot that had been weakened by the dragoons' fire, became a rabble, a horde of milling horsemen. With the terror of the sweat-slathered dragoon horses infecting the cuirassiers' fresh mounts, all discipline and order were lost in a few, mad, chaotic moments.

Hogan's horsemen made the most of it.

His men plunged into the Danes' ranks like an axe splitting a rotten bough. The impact of the Jacobite charge destroyed all remaining order in the yellow cavalry and tumbled it down the slope; Hogan's men set about them with sword, pistol and carbine, some raparees wielding half-pikes like lances with a brutal efficiency. Hogan pistolled a curassier in the groin, avoiding his blackened chest armour, as the man rode past. The city gentlemen of Berwick's Horse were yelling, even screaming with excitement, slashing with their fine blades, hacking down Danes and dragoons left and right. Others were battering at their foes with empty pistols and blunted swords. And the mêlée of warring cavalry – Hogan's rough riders, Berwick's ecstatic gentlemen, exhausted dragoons and confused and frightened Danish cuirassiers, all mingled higgledy-piggledy, jumbled in mad confusion, fighting, clawing, killing, dying – slid down the hill faster and faster, inexorably tumbling towards the English infantry lines.

Brevet Major Blood was standing one pace to the right and three paces in front of the fourth company of Tiffin's Regiment of Foot. The company was formed of three ranks of twenty men each, a neat rectangle of grey-coated soldiery. The second company of Tiffin's and the eleventh were on either side of Holcroft's men. Beyond the eleventh, to his right, stood the statue-like ranks of the Dutch Blue Guard. Impressive, clean-shaven, taller-than-usual men with at least seven years' experience of fighting in King William's armies in the Low Countries and elsewhere. They were the Prince of Orange's elite troops, the heart and soul of his armies, perhaps the finest soldiers in all Europe. They were the bravest in battle, the steadiest under fire. The best men. And they damn well knew it.

The Blue Guards were also lined up in three ranks, although the formation was of a double company two-hundred-men strong. Behind them, and behind Holcroft's Inniskillingers, were two companies of Colonel Kirke's Lambs. These redcoats were hardy veterans: forged in battle from the sands of Tangiers, to the slaughter at Sedgemoor, to the siege of Londonderry the year before.

Holcroft watched as the orderly advance by the dragoons and the Danish cavalry was turned into a rolling shambles by the sudden Jacobite flank attack. His heart sank. He had scanned the enemy lines a few minutes before with his glass and was almost certain that he had seen Henri d'Erloncourt in earnest conversation with the Duke of Berwick in the very heart of their formation. He was almost beside himself with impatience to attack. And now it seemed the cavalry had made a God-awful mess of it and been utterly routed. They were now galloping down the hill, enemy next to enemy, no formation at all: curassier and raparee, dragoon and Dublin gentleman, each slashing at the other, their horses biting and kicking, beasts and men barging and banging into each other and all heading towards his company.

Holcroft nodded to Sergeant Hawkins, who bellowed: 'Tiffin's prepare to fix bayonets . . .' and a moment later: 'Fix bayonets!'

A hundred and eighty-six Inniskilling men drew their new plug-bayonets from the stiff leather sheaths at their belts and rammed the handles into the clean muzzles of their flintlock muskets. Holcroft was aware that the sergeants of both the Blue Guard and Kirke's Lambs were barking out similar orders.

'Rear rank only,' shouted Hawkins. 'Just the rear rank, mind . . . that does *not* mean you, McNally, you stand where you are . . . rear rank, about turn!'

The third line of each of the three companies turned around to face backwards. 'Now then, lads.' Hawkins' voice had dropped in tone and volume but it still rang out clearly across the field. 'First rank, kneel! Stand your ground, Tiffin's; grip those muskets tight as your lovers. Prepare to receive cavalry!'

Holcroft edged into the side of the fourth company, pressing close to the end file, and drew his small-sword, adding its shining length to the bristling hedge of plug-bayonets. The front rank was kneeling, musket-butts on the ground, barrel and bayonet pointing upwards at chest height. The second rank, standing, had their bayonetted muskets at port. The rear rank, facing backwards, also presented a line of bayonets. The whole effect was to nearly surround the company with lines of sharp steel blades, a double-sided defensive barrier.

The nearest horseman, a blood-slathered dragoon on a wildly out-of-control horse, was only yards away. The dragoon was screaming, waving the infantry to move out of his path. The kneeling Inniskilling men flinched, ready for the impact of half a ton of horseflesh and the slice of madly kicking iron-shod hooves. They closed their eyes, gripped their muskets and prayed.

The horse saw the hedge of blades and tried to halt its mad momentum, skidding on its back haunches, spraying mud and small stones, neighing madly – at the last moment the frightened beast side-stepped and swept past the company, missing Holcroft's arm by inches, and bearing the astonished blood daubed dragoon past with it.

The horsemen came barrelling in thick and fast: curassiers sawing on their reins, trying to bring their animals under control, raparees whooping and laughing madly, waving their bloodied swords around their heads, whipping up the panic as best they could . . . But no living horse would willingly impale itself on the Inniskilling bayonet hedge and the wide gaps between the three grey companies allowed every one of the galloping horsemen to swerve round the huddled ranks of Ulstermen and horse after horse thundered safely past the clenched infantry and away towards the rear.

When the last of the horses had gone, Holcroft stepped out of the ranks and surveyed the field. Those Jacobite horsemen who had not run madly down the hill and on to the English lines were walking their sweat-stained horses slowly back to their position on the enemies' right flank. They looked utterly spent, exuberant but exhausted. But they had not won much of a victory.

Holcroft's three companies of Inniskillingers seemed unharmed and intact, and the Dutch to his right were also unscathed. Behind him, though, Percy Kirke's veterans had taken a few casualties. A horse – probably shot dead by some marksman in the ranks – had tumbled, dying but with heavy flailing hooves, into the heart of the second company of Kirke's redcoats and there were now two bloodied men lying unconscious on the turf being tended by their mates. And another sitting man seemed to be cradling a broken arm. But it could have been worse – in fact, Holcroft was pleased by the conduct of the men under his command. Now would come the true test of their mettle.

Holcroft looked up and to the right to the summit of a small hill where there was a trio of horsemen sitting placidly and watching events. He lifted his hat from his head and waved it at the figure in a fine gold coat and gorgeous brown periwig, and the Brigadier lifted his own hat in response. Holcroft made a sweeping motion of his hat towards the enemy lines; he made the motion twice. There was a short conference on the hilltop and then Wolseley copied Holcroft's gesture exactly, his hat seeming to wave the troops on into battle.

'Unfix bayonets, Sergeant Hawkins,' said Holcroft, 'and make sure every man is loaded. I'm going to have a word with the Dutch and the Lambs.'

'What's afoot, sir?' said Hawkins.

'We are going up there, Sergeant. All of us. And we're going to push those bastards off that ridge.'

The red line of Jacobites was a hundred and fifty yards away and already the ill-disciplined troops had begun to fire at the advancing enemy. Holcroft's overwhelming emotion – above the common-place terror of death or wounding, above the anxiety that he should fail in this task – was of contempt. These Irishmen might wear red coats and wield sword and matchlock but they were not true soldiers. Their sporadic, individual fire was too early and too disorganised to be effective. Some of the bullets flew wide of the three compact Tiffin's companies as they advanced slowly up the slope, or went high, but most often they fell short, slamming into the turf between the two sides with little kick-spurts of mud. *No discipline. What were their officers thinking?* Not a single Inniskilling man had been hurt so far. *And long may that last.* The wall of redcoats was unnerved by the near-silent advance of the enemy: Holcroft had forbidden any cries until the last moment and the only sound came from the rattle of the drums as the boys beat out the pace, and the snap of the big square standards, held by the ensigns, that flapped in the breeze above their heads.

They were a hundred yards away. To the right of the Inniskillingers, the Dutch guards were advancing slightly slower than Holcroft's men, and consequently they lagged about twenty paces behind. But Holcroft had no worries about these veterans. They would do their duty, and do it well. Fifty yards behind him, two companies of Kirke's Lambs were coming up the slope, with a savage battle-eagerness on their faces, a blood-hunger that was somehow more than a little shocking.

The musket balls were cracking all about them. And one Tiffin's private, John Watson, gave a shout of surprise and, dropping his flintlock, stumbled to the ground clutching at his bloody thigh.

'Close up, there!' Hawkins voice was steady, unsurprised by the tragedy.

The Inniskillingers marched on, close now, seventy yards out. Well within musket range. The rain of shot from the red ranks ahead of them grew heavier. Holcroft felt a ball pass close to his head with a whine like a mosquito. On the far side of the fourth company Corporal Horace Turner was hit. He gave a bubbling cry as half of his evil little face was replaced by a gory mash.

Only fifty yards from the enemy. The private men beside Holcroft, and behind him, were sneaking glances at his back, silently begging him to halt so that they might fire their weapons and end the torment of the advance. Yet Holcroft was unaware of their distress. The crackling of the enemy musketry was nearly continuous now, a ball thumped into the man next to Holcroft. The private dropped to the ground without a sound.

'Sir?' said Hawkins. Forty yards away from the enemy, Holcroft could see the individual features of the redcoats in front of him – this one unshaven, that one with a purple carbuncle on his cheek. His own men were silently willing him to halt. Another type of man would have been able to sense it. Their mute appeal would have been deafening. Holcroft did not. He was oblivious to their unexpressed entreaties.

Thirty yards. They were far inside the usual range for a musket duel.

'Brevet Major Blood?' said Hawkins again. 'Should we not . . .'

Another pace, another yet. Holcroft could see over the heads of the Jacobite line, the mounted forms of the commanders; the gaudy one in gold with all the lace must be the Duke of Berwick, and beside him, staring directly at Holcroft was . . . it was him. Narrey.

The man who had murdered his friend Aphra. The man who had killed dozens of innocent men to Holcroft's certain knowledge. The spy. His true enemy. Narrey was draped in his customary black cloak, with his hat low over his face, but it was definitely him. He looked small, cold and more than a little frightened.

The Inniskillings were twenty-five yards away from the enemy line. It was hailing musket balls. To their right the Dutch had halted, and Holcroft could hear Captain Jan van Zwyk giving the orders for the men to present their pieces. Holcroft fixed his eyes on Narrey. The Frenchman stared back at him. Musket balls dropped two men in the Inniskilling front rank one after the other. A bullet tugged at the sleeve of Holcroft's blue coat.

'Halt!' They were twenty yards away. Holcroft heard the exhalation from two hundred lungs as he gave the order.

'Dress ranks! Close up! Close up!' Hawkins had the men well in hand.

Holcroft ignored the shuffling of the men behind him and the sergeant's cries to level their muskets. His gaze was fixed on Narrey. He pulled the Lorenzoni repeating pistol from the scarlet sash around his waist, half turned to the men. 'I believe I shall take over now, sergeant,' he said quietly.

Then louder: 'Tiffin's Regiment! All companies. First rank only. Give fire!'

Sixty muskets thundered out along the lines and all three Inniskilling companies were shrouded in a thin grey fog.

'First rank, reload. Second rank, two paces forward. Present your pieces. Second rank, fire.'

Another tightly controlled volley lashed out, punching through the fog and smashing into the company of redcoats a stone's throw ahead of them. Holcroft could see dozens of enemy soldiers lying still on the ground; others seated, holding in their fatally punctured bellies, yet more bloodied but standing their ground and firing back like men.

He bawled: 'Second rank, reload!'

A fair proportion of the scarlet enemy line were trying to move back, squirming away from his blocks of firing men, edging into the mass behind them.

On his right, Holcroft could hear the Dutch discharge their pieces, a much greater thunder, even though the Blue Guards were further from the enemy.

'Third rank, forward. Present your pieces. Fire!' Holcroft shouted.

He watched calmly as bullets from his men smashed into the enemy, ripping soft flesh, knocking down men, splashing others with gouts of blood. The press of redcoats was thinner now, directly to his front, weakened by his fire. 'Third rank, reload!'

There were gaps between the red-coated bodies through which he could see the turf and churned earth behind. An Irishman, standing over the body of his dead comrade, hefted his matchlock and fired at Holcroft, aiming for him personally, and he felt the hot wind of the passing ball by his cheek. He filled his lungs with stingingly cold air . . .

'Tiffin's Regiment. First rank, present. Fire!'

'Second rank, present. Fire!'

'Third rank, present. Fire!'

'Inniskillingers,' shouted Holcroft. 'Fix bayonets . . .' A clattering and foul curses as fingers burned on hot barrels. 'Ready, lads? Now . . . charge!'

More than a hundred and fifty men in grey leapt forward, every flintlock tipped with nine inches of sharp steel. They screamed as they ran the twenty yards towards the bullet-battered enemy, releasing all the built-up fear in shrill, high, ululating cries. They smashed into the Irish ranks like a herd of bulls hitting a frail garden fence at full speed, bayonets lancing out to slice faces and spear bellies. Holcroft ran with them, pausing only to shoot a sergeant standing before him with a halberd poised to strike. He reloaded the Lorenzoni with a twist of the lever and shot another man coming at him with a sword.

The Inniskillingers ripped into the disintegrating Jacobite army like a mighty wind, screaming and stabbing, shoving, thrusting, stamping, crushing faces and snapping limbs with the butts of their heavy flintlocks. Others had abandoned their muskets, the bayonets stuck fast into the ribs of their victims and pulling out their swords, they were carving lanes of mayhem through the enemy ranks. Lieutenant Watts, frothing madly at the mouth, was laying about him with his small-sword like a berserker of yore. A green-coated Jacobite officer, with a jet-black plume in his broad hat, pistolled Watts through the body, lifting and hurling the lieutenant back two full paces to land in a heap. Holcroft ran forward, raised the Lorenzoni and shot the officer in the lower jaw, scattering blood and teeth.

He paused for a second, panting, looking over the heads of the few remaining foes before him. The Lambs had come up fast to support the charge, and unfamiliar men were all around him, red coats with green turnbacks, savage blood-spattered faces, hacking with blades, lunging with their bayonets. The Dutch company were assaulting the line, too, forty paces to Holcroft's right, big blue-clad men, barging into the lines of terrified Jacobite recruits . . .

And the enemy dissolved under this combined onslaught. They were running away, fleeing as fast as their terrified legs would carry them. Holcroft suddenly had a vision, a stone's throw in front of him, of the Duke of Berwick on the back of his silver-grey horse, splendid in gold and lace, and beside him Narrey, smaller, and all in night-black, and they were both being led away, other horsemen dragging their bridles, right now breaking into a fast trot.

'Stand and fight me, you bastard!' Holcroft was screaming impotently – on foot and forty yards from his quarry, the distance growing with every moment that passed. He lifted the Lorenzoni and fired, knowing it was too far to be truly accurate. The bullet struck the hind-quarters of Narrey's mount, and the horse reared and bucked, and Holcroft, for one glorious moment, believed that the black-swathed rider would be thrown. He ran forward but Narrey mastered his beast, and spurred away, a tight group of horsemen fleeing from the field of battle. Holcroft called stupidly: 'Stop! Wait! Come back here, you turd.'

And one enemy horseman miraculously answered his call. A bulky man on a bay horse. He reined in, turned his mount and came galloping back to the shattered enemy lines, covering the ground in a dozen heartbeats. Holcroft recognised Guillaume du Clos' big, snarling face. He cranked the lever on the Lorenzoni, but the mechanism stuck, the lever refusing to turn. Holcroft tugged at it, wasting valuable seconds. It was locked tight.

He looked up and Du Clos was almost on him. He dropped the pistol, and reached for his small-sword. He got the blade half out, looked up again and there was Du Clos, looming on the horse, a levelled pistol in his hand, the huge black muzzle pointed directly into his face. The handgun fired; a bloom of orange-red flame and Holcroft only just had time to feel a crushing blow like a mule-kick to his forehead.

Then all was blackness.

Part Two

Chapter Eleven

Monday, May 5, 1690

Henri, Comte d'Erloncourt trotted down the long corridor in the west wing of Dublin Castle, the three-inch heels of his silver-painted leather shoes clicking loudly on the wooden parquet floor. He had for once abandoned his usual night-black attire and, since he was heading for a semi-public meeting, was dressed in the guise of a Colonel of the Régiment Royal-Bombardiers, his official French uniform of silver-white coat, with red waistcoat, breeches and stockings. He felt somewhat exposed in all his military finery but he bore intelligence of the greatest import, which he felt he must convey to King James without delay and there was no time to arrange a discreet private meeting alone with the monarch.

As he clip-clopped along, he glanced down at his left arm in its pristine uniform sleeve. It was finally healed, nine months after it had been mangled at Carrickfergus, and now, strangely, he had almost forgotten the terrible pain. He had not, of course, forgotten the man who had mangled it. He'd congratulated Guillaume immediately for shooting down that brute Blood at Cavan but he had not truly been able to savour the death of his enemy then. The breakthrough by the English on the ridge had led to a humiliating withdrawal at speed for all the Jacobite forces – some might have called it a rout – with the Duke of Berwick leading the retreat, and with Narrey and Major du Clos sticking close to him. Had the English troops not stopped their victorious advance to loot the town of Cavan and drink themselves insensible, it could have been a far more serious disaster. As it was, it had to be chalked up as a failure of Jacobite arms – and a sobering one. Henri was more than ever convinced that a head-to-head clash between the forces of James and General Schomberg would end in disaster.

He was briefly stopped by a pair of raggedy sergeants armed with rusty halberds by the grand wooden doors of the council chamber but, on giving his name and rank, they pushed open the portal and allowed him to enter. The room was long and narrow and brightly lit by three pairs of chandeliers hanging from the gold and sky blue painted ceiling, and half a dozen men, all dressed in equal if not greater splendour to the French Bombardier colonel, were seated at a table covered in a snowy cloth and bearing in a line along the centre a dozen crystal glasses and three decanters of ruby wine. James, at the far end, looked up as he entered but said nothing, turning back attentively to the elderly man in a black wig, who was speaking from his place halfway down the left side.

'. . . I believe it is the course of action with the best chance of success, sire,' said the Duke of Tyrconnell, 'a full-scale invasion of England would not only wrong-foot the usurper, take him entirely by surprise, but also ensure that he cannot cross to Ireland in strength and attack your forces here. The people of England still love you, sire. I have heard from many lips, from many men of the most distinguished lineages, the noblest families, that they would rise in their thousands in support of your righteous cause and flock to your royal banner.'

'Do you truly believe so, sir? I should dearly love to see White Hall again in the springtime. And there are many loyalists in Scotland who would join me, I am sure of it, Viscount Dundee swears it is so, and as their rightful King . . .'

'And how would you get over the water?' A harsh, foreign-accented voice interrupted the King, and there were some audible noises of indrawn breath at the temerity of this man in speaking over royalty. 'How would you transport your army, sire, across the Irish Sea – a sea which the Royal Navy presently controls. Your troop ships would be sunk before they cleared Dublin Bay.'

'I had rather hoped, General Lauzun, that your master, *Le Roi Soleil*, might be persuaded – perhaps even by you, monsieur – to send his fleet to guard us in that dangerous crossing,' said the King. He glared at the squat, muscular, square-headed general, the commander of the French forces in Ireland. 'Or perhaps his enthusiasm for my cause has waned. We await the stores of food and weapons he has promised. And if he truly wishes to see me regain the Three Kingdoms, as he told me to my face little more than a year ago, he must send more men.'

'The food and weapons will come but, alas, not the grand fleet. You know as well as I, sire, that King Louis has more than enough to contend with fighting the Dutch in the North Sea. A fast ship may slip past the Royal Navy's patrols on a dark night, sire, and has indeed done so on many an occasion. But the grand fleet would be obliged to battle the English ship to ship – and how might that end? Besides, sire, my royal master *has* already sent you men. I brought six thousand of the finest French troops with me when I arrived two months ago.'

'And six thousand fine Irishmen were sent to France in exchange,' said a new voice. General Patrick Sarsfield, a handsome energetic officer in a startling grass-green coat, seemed blithely contemptuous of the Frenchman's words.

The Comte d'Erloncourt, his arms folded behind his back, stood by the dark wood panelled wall, ignored by the great men at the table, and watched the verbal jousting in front of him with interest. It was true that Louis had sent James more troops but his powerful War Minister, the Marquis de Louvois – urged to do so in a secret letter from Henri d'Erloncourt – had insisted that to continue their operations in the Low Country against the Dutch and their allies, the shortfall in manpower must be made up by Irishmen.

However, James certainly had the better of the deal. The Irish troops shipped over to France, like almost all of his army, were barely trained, undisciplined, often seriously malnourished and lacked proper arms and equipment. Many in the Irish Army had not been paid for months. For James's coffers were bare – trade had died completely with the departure of the Protestant merchants, and agriculture had almost ceased as the young men who normally worked the land were recruited into the ranks.

A great many of King James's soldiers lived by theft and pillage of their own countrymen. Their officers did not – or could not – restrain them, or control or discipline them, and these gentlemen were faced with a stark choice of either condoning the outrages against their own people or paying their men out of their own pockets.

Many of James's officers, to be fair, were also woefully inexperienced – due to a deliberate policy implemented by the Earl of Tyrconnell, as the duke then was, before the expulsion of James from England in 1688. Established Protestant officers, often men with a great deal of military expertise, had been systematically expelled from the Irish regiments – often with no recompense for the offices they had purchased – by Tyrconnell's government in Dublin. They had been replaced wholesale by Catholic men, almost none of whom had even the smallest amount of training.

Henri caught Lauzun's eye from the far side of the table. The veteran soldier-courtier stared back at him, then raised one eyebrow questioningly.

Henri gave a quick, affirmative duck of his head.

'I believe Colonel d'Erloncourt has something that he wishes to impart to the King,' Lauzun said, and every eye at the table turned to stare at Henri.

D'Erloncourt pushed himself off the wall and straightened his spine.

'As you know, sire, I am fortunate to have a few well-placed friends in the north, even among the ranks of the Dutch usurper's army and, occasionally, I receive confidential information from them concerning affairs in Belfast.'

He paused, and took a breath, looking at James.

'Spies,' said Patrick Sarsfield, 'why not call these people what they are?'

Henri ignored him. 'My friends in the north tell me that William of Orange is coming over the sea to Ulster with an army—'

'We already know that,' interrupted Sarsfield. 'We've known for months that King Billy is on the way, what we don't know is when . . .'

'What you do *not* know, and what my friends have just informed me, swearing on their souls to the accuracy of their reports, is that William will be in Belfast within the month. Early June, mid-June at the latest, and preparations are already in hand for his arrival. He will bring with him an additional fifteen thousand first-class troops, both infantry and cavalry, and a powerful new Train of Artillery. I shall circulate the details of the units to all you gentlemen later.'

'Fifteen thousand men? Here in a month?' James's pale, thin face sagged. 'And the Duke of Schomberg already has, what, about thirty-five thousand?'

'Forty,' said Lauzun. 'And we cannot muster even thirty thousand men to stand against them, even including my French Brigade. Furthermore, we must find sufficient armed men to garrison all the major towns. So I believe, sire, we must swiftly dispense with your ill-judged notion of an invasion of England.'

'We must have more men – King Louis must be persuaded to send more men!' James looked beseechingly at Lauzun. 'And guns. I have almost no artillery, since I was obliged to . . .' He tailed off. James had been forced to melt down most of his cannon to make copper coins to pay his troops but no one was going to say it out loud. Tyrconnell put his old, lined face in his hands.

'I shall certainly pass on your request to His Majesty,' said Lauzun with an icy smile. 'But I doubt very much, sire, that it will be well received.'

'I believe we might be able to recruit more men to your cause, sire,' said Patrick Sarsfield, 'if only you were prepared to limit your ambitions.'

'My *ambitions*?' said the King.

'Sire, if you were to declare that you sought only to rule Ireland. If you were to make a general proclamation renouncing your claim to the thrones of Scotland and England and saying that you simply wished to rule Ireland – a separate, independent Ireland, free from the shackles of England; an Ireland in which all men, of all faiths, could strive together for the common good. The common people would surely fight more willingly for the chance to be free . . .'

'An outrageous suggestion; pure treason, by God!' said the Duke of Berwick, the King's eldest but, unfortunately for him, illegitimate son.

'I am the King of England, Scotland *and* Ireland, Colonel Sarsfield.' James was on his feet, his voice raised almost to a shout. 'I will not dishonour my royal ancestors, nor will I renounce my royal rights, which have been granted to me by Almighty God, in His infinite wisdom. I shall fight for them, I shall fight all of William's legions to the last breath in my body, and any man who does not wish to stand with me may leave my presence this minute.'

Sarsfield flushed red. 'I meant no disrespect, sire,' he said. 'I will fight for you and your cause till my heart fails inside me. But it would make it a great deal easier to raise the passions of the common Irish people for the cause if . . .'

'Enough, General Sarsfield! Either go from my presence or remain silent.' James's usually pale face was glowing with a righteous anger. 'We shall fight them, this is my command. We shall smite the enemy with the help of Almighty God Himself. You will prepare my army, all of you, now, to march. To the North!'

'A word in your ear, Colonel d'Erloncourt, if you please,' said Lauzun, as the council of war broke up, and the great men of James's court began to leave the chamber in their monarch's wake. 'This new intelligence, you stand by it?'

'I do, sir.'

'It comes from your agent, Agricola, is that the correct code name?'

Henri nodded. The last member of the council had left the room and they were now alone.

'What else did this person tell you?'

'That William is said to be in a great hurry. He will drive to capture Dublin immediately, coming south via Newry and the Moyry Pass to retake Dundalk.'

'Indeed. And he will no doubt succeed. And if he then goes on to take the city of Dublin, the war will be as good as lost.'

Lauzun leaned in and spoke in a whisper. 'I must inform you, then, my friend, that Louis le Grand shall not be sending any additional troops to aid King James in his military endeavours. You may take that as Gospel. Furthermore, His Majesty has instructed me that I should not hazard the French Brigade unnecessarily in a pitched battle against the English. Who is that Ancient Roman gentleman you are always speaking of? Fabius, yes? The one who was always running away. We must emulate him. Yes? I wish you to keep General Fabius's strategy in mind over the next few weeks. You are not to risk the lives of Frenchmen in a foolish unwinnable battle. You understand me, d'Erloncourt?'

'Yes, monsieur. Clearly. Should we not then withdraw the whole Brigade, perhaps south to Cork, in preparation for a swift and safe departure?'

'No. Not yet. One day we *will* be forced to withdraw. And we must keep our whole Brigade intact for that day. And if this panicky English mountebank who calls himself King of England, Scotland and Ireland insists on confronting the Prince of Orange's superior forces head on like an angry mule, we must at least be *seen* to support him. His Majesty has always been very clear on that point. But I will *not* have our brave men slaughtered to satisfy James's pride.'

Chapter Twelve

Tuesday, June 17, 1690

Holcroft Blood sat in a wicker chair in a sun-filled corner of the lush grounds of Belfast Castle reading a letter from his old friend Jack Churchill.

The Earl of Marlborough, as Jack was styled, having distinguished himself in the Low Countries, had been made commander of all troops in England and appointed a member of the Council of Nine to advise Queen Mary on military matters while William was on campaign in Ireland.

> I fear, though, that Her Majesty does not trust or esteem me, neither does she seem to care for Sarah overmuch. It seems that she is resolved to exclude me from her private councils when William is abroad, and while I'm determined to win her favour, the lady is so far immune to my blandishments.

Holcroft could well understand why neither William nor Mary should trust Jack – he had, after all, betrayed his former monarch, James, in the cruellest manner when he switched his allegiance overnight to the House of Orange. If he had betrayed one generous master – and James had been very good to him all his life, raising him up from genteel poverty to great estate – why should he prove loyal to another who was, so far, a good deal less open-handed? There was also the matter of Sarah's close relationship with Princess Anne – who, as the younger daughter of James, was next in line to the throne after Queen Mary, and who indeed had a greater claim to the throne than William. Holcroft had heard a rumour at a dinner in Belfast that the joint monarchs greatly feared that Princess Anne might form a powerful rival political faction with the Countess of Marlborough while William was engaged across the seas in the Irish war.

The Prince of Orange – and the rightful King of England, Scotland and Ireland, to Holcroft's mind – had arrived at Carrickfergus three days before and the General Schomberg had met him and escorted him to Sir William Franklin's house, his temporary palace, a few hundred yards from Belfast Castle. Crowds of people gathered to watch his coach arrive but at first they merely gawped silently, never having seen a king before, until the redcoats of the Foot Guard urged them to cheer. That night, huge bonfires were lit all over Belfast, and the King's arrival was celebrated with flowing jugs of ale and nips of strong Dutch gin – fashionable in England and Ireland since the arrival of so many of King William's countrymen and popular because of its high potency and low price.

Holcroft took no part in the revelries. He was still officially on the sick list, with no military duties and neither was he of a gregarious nature. In truth, he hated parties – and particularly parties at which he knew not a soul. While Belfast caroused, Holcroft remained in the castle reading and writing letters.

His eye slid over the passages in Jack's friendly missive about Sarah and the children's wellbeing and about the house they hoped to build when they had the time, but stopped when he came to a passage about his own wife Elizabeth.

Jack wrote:

Sarah has twice encountered your lady wife at social events this spring, once at the Cockpit, when she attended a grand masked ball held by Princess Anne, and once at the races in Newmarket. Both times Elizabeth appeared to be glowing with health and happiness and was escorted by a dashing Dutch officer, Jongheer Markus van Dijk, who has been wounded in the wars and is now recuperating in

England. He seems an honourable gentleman, and very rich, and I never pay much heed to idle gossip, and neither should you. I called on Elizabeth herself at Mincing Lane last month and she sends you her dearest love, and all her hopes and prayers for a swift recovery . . .

Holcroft frowned. He read the passage about Elizabeth's Dutch friend over again: '*He seems an honourable gentleman, and very rich, and I never pay much heed to idle gossip, and neither should you.*'

The sentence made no sense to Holcroft. What should the man's honour and wealth have to do with idle gossip? He thought that Jack must be making some sort of joke or clever witticism and moved on with the rest of the letter, which paradoxically seemed to be filled with nothing *but* gossip of the political kind, who was in favour at court, who was scheming for more power . . .

He was reading Jack's warm sign-off, when a shadow fell over the paper. He looked up and there was Caroline Chichester holding out a broad straw sun hat. 'You must keep the sun from your head, Holcroft. It is warm today, uncommonly so, and your wound might become inflamed by the rays.'

The battle of Cavan had been a victory of sorts, although it had not altered the course of the war to any significant degree, but Holcroft's own personal mission – to kill Narrey and Major du Clos – must be considered an abject failure. Narrey still lived, as far as he knew, and Holcroft had been rendered *hors de combat* for months. Holcroft took the hat offered by Caroline and placed it on his close-cropped head. The bullet from Du Clos' pistol had struck the left side of his forehead and cut a deep groove along the side of his head just above the ear. It had not, by God's mercy, entered the skull. He had been immediately knocked unconscious and had remained so for four days during which time, he learnt afterwards, he had been transported by bullock cart to Belfast Castle and placed in the care of the Army medical staff there. After such a long period of unconsciousness, the doctors feared that he would never awaken, or that his mind might be irreparably damaged in some way. They had shaved his head, cleaned and bandaged the wound and left him to rest in the ward overseen by Caroline Chichester.

It had not been an easy healing process. After an initial period of some weeks when all had looked well, and he had seemed to be on the road to good health, the wound had become infected, angry-red and filled with corruption. This backward step was accompanied by blinding headaches lasting days and of an intensity Holcroft had never experienced before.

The pain in his head had at times become so bad that Holcroft had screamed out loud and the strongest medicines, even a powerful tincture of opium dissolved in brandy, failed to quell the agony. Gradually, over the weeks and months, the wound healed properly and the headaches lessened, became rarer and finally ceased. But Holcroft had continued to shave his head around the long pink scar on his temple and, at Caroline's gentle urging, had gone so far as to buy an expensive real-hair wig from a Belfast perruquier.

His health was now much improved and, but for a shortness of breath due to months of sluggish inactivity, he was almost back to his normal fighting trim.

His relationship with Caroline had also improved significantly since the awkward meeting in the pantry at Belfast Castle. He had written to her several times while he was in Inniskilling and she had even replied a few times, without much warmth but with enough interest in his life and military doings to keep him writing back. When he was first admitted to the ward, still groggy from his long period of unconsciousness, he had been more or less oblivious to her ministrations, but her tender care of him, the way she held his hand, looked into his face and spoke soothingly to him during the worst of the crushing headaches had awakened emotions of deep gratitude, turning slowly to something more profound, which were as powerful and uncontrollable as the pains in his head.

He had not, of course, spoken of his growing feelings to her. Neither was he sure that they were reciprocated. She told him that she had forgiven him for the fiery destruction of Joymount House – war was war, after all, she had said. And she seemed pleased to spend time with him, over and above her duties as his nurse. She brought him small edible treats and drinks, and read to him from the Bible and from improving works of literature – John Bunyan was a favourite author. She also gave a great deal of thought to his physical comfort. Yet she never spoke of love or tenderness or of anything in that vein and she never touched him except in a manner that was brisk and coolly medical.

However, for Holcroft, she was the very centre of his existence: his first thought when he woke in the morning, and his last at night. Caroline pushed other important considerations out of his mind: the Army, his Inniskillinger comrades, several of whom had made the trek to visit him in Belfast – Lieutenant Waters had called on him three times – and the continued existence of Narrey. His violent hatred of the French spy now seemed a pale and distant thing. He remembered the dimensions of his enmity well, like a house he had occupied for a long time, but could not now remember being comfortable in. He had discussed the dimming of his antipathy to Narrey with Caroline, as they discussed many things close to his heart, and she'd joked that the bullet must have knocked the hate clean out of his head. Although it was clearly impossible, absurd even, sometimes Holcroft believed it must be true. They had also spoken at length of his love for the Ordnance, and the hurt he had felt at his dismissal from its ranks by General Schomberg. Although he understood Schomberg's actions, it had felt like a gross betrayal, as if his own family had rejected him.

'Are you feeling strong enough for a visitor today, Holcroft?' said Caroline, leaning in and adjusting the position of the straw hat so that its shade covered his face from the slanting rays of the afternoon sun.

BLOOD'S CAMPAIGN | 153

'Depends who it is,' said Holcroft. He was feeling lazy and sleepy in his comfortable chair and did not relish another visit from Francis Waters who would surely have some intelligence puzzle for him to unravel. Something that would require his brain to work.

'It's a friend of both of ours – it's Jacob Richards.'

It took Holcroft a moment to remember who Richards was. Perhaps Du Clos' bullet had knocked more than just hatred out of his head. Then he had it: Major Jacob Richards, First Engineer of the Royal Train of Artillery. Of course. His friend. How could he have forgotten his friend and his many kindnesses?

'I should be delighted to see Major Richards,' he said.

'I thought we might, all three of us, have a dish of tea together,' said Caroline. 'I believe Jacob has something important he wishes to ask you.'

Richards looked thinner and more exhausted than usual. He seemed worn down by the war and his great burdens of responsibility in the Ordnance.

'Blood,' he said, as he came over and firmly shook Holcroft's hand.

'Richards,' came the ritual reply.

Caroline busied herself with a silver teapot and cups and the men sat in silence for a few minutes both watching a beautiful woman at her business.

Holcroft said; 'So how is the Train, everything running smoothly?'

'Hardly,' said Richards. 'You heard that Obadiah Field died?'

Holcroft had not.

'He took sick in camp at Dundalk, like thousands of our men, and perished soon after. The bloody flux. Bad food. Bad lodgings. Bad logistics.'

'Poor fellow. I am very sorry to hear that. I liked him.'

'I'm the poor fellow – not him. He's with Jesus now. Sergeant Jones died, too. And Lieutenant Hunt went home to England – his father passed away and he inherited the estate. I'm running the Train with half the complement of officers.'

'Sugar?' said Caroline, and Richards declined, accepting a brimming cup.

'Talking of inheritances,' Richards continued, 'Barden has come into some money. A rich uncle died, or something. He's bought himself a fancy sword with an engraved gold handle, and some fine horses too. And all the extra cash in his purse has made him lazier than ever. I have to chase him every day!'

Richards seemed more sorry for himself than Holcroft had ever seen him. He knew his friend was rather poor – but he had never seemed the envious type.

'William must have brought over a few replacement officers for the Train,' said Holcroft after a long pause. 'I heard he had twenty new guns with him. He must have supplied some officers to man them. And the King must know you're short-handed. Schomberg surely told him of the situation.'

'The King brought a few men with him. But none of them are any good. A bunch of spoilt and inexperienced children. Filthy rich, titled yahoos too dim even to find a berth in the Guards. God-damn bastards. Beg pardon, Caroline.'

'Oh, I'm sure God will happily damn all of those bastards for you, Jacob.'

Holcroft picked up his cup of tea and tried a sip of the fragrant brew.

'So you're fit, Blood, are you? Ready to return to duty?'

'Still get the odd headache but I'm basically fine. Looking forward to seeing my Inniskillingers again. Tiffin's boys. No doubt they're missing me.'

'God-damn it, Holcroft. You know why I'm here. Don't make me beg.'

Holcroft looked steadily at Jacob Richards. He did, for once, understand what the senior Ordnance officer was obliquely referring to.

'What about General Schomberg?' he said. 'He's the one who sent me packing. He's the one who kicked me out. What would he say?'

'Uncle Frederick's finished. He's in disgrace. If he were on top of his job the King wouldn't have come all this way to personally over see the campaign. The King is perfectly polite to him, treats him with the respect due to his many years of experience. But William is in command. All the decisions are his.'

'I don't choose where I serve, Jacob. I follow orders, same as everyone.'

'But you *would* come back to the guns, if I could fix it with the King, wouldn't you? You'd have command of the Train, well, under me. You'd be the Second Engineer again. But you wouldn't be able to call yourself a brevet major. I'm only a major, so you'd have to be a captain. But that's the offer.'

Holcroft smiled at his friend.

'If you can arrange it, Jacob, of course I'll gladly come back.'

'And don't expect Uncle Frederick to offer you an apology!'

'I won't expect anything from him at all.'

'More tea, gentlemen?' said Caroline, perhaps a little too smugly.

Chapter Thirteen

Sunday, June 29, 1690

Michael 'Galloping' Hogan stopped his horse on the top of a ridge, near a crossroads to the west of the village of Tullyallen, and looked down at the north bank of the River Boyne about half a mile away. The ribbon of water that he could make out through the trees was a slow-flowing, peaty brown, and he knew that there was a passable ford somewhere down there, where a man on foot could cross without getting either his musket or cartridge pouch wet.

On the south bank of the river was the hamlet of Oldbridge, a scatter of three or four houses, some with walled gardens, with rising cornfields behind and the small hill of Donore, with its church tower visible on the horizon. It was a peaceful spot, idyllic even – meandering river, water meadows and yellow fields of ripening wheat – but it would not remain so for long. Hogan and his horsemen were advance scouts for the whole Jacobite Army – behind his men were some twenty-five thousand troops, horse, guns and foot, moving south on the road to Dublin. And behind *them*, no more than a day's march from the rear guard, came King William's far more numerous force.

Hogan was tired, exhausted, in fact; he and his men had ridden over this same ground not two weeks before – but heading north that time. James and his army had advanced from Dublin in high spirits pushing up to Ardee and on to Dundalk, but the King had hesitated, sending Lord Galmoy ahead to set up a small ambush at the Moyry Pass to surprise the Williamite advance units.

Then, quite suddenly, James had changed his mind about his strategy. The King became terrified by the notion that he could be outflanked by William's cavalry forces coming round through County Cavan, past his left-hand side, to cut off the road to Dublin behind them. If that happened, he would have enemy both north and south of him. Surrounded. So James – panicking shamefully – had ordered a swift retreat down the same route, and back they came, all of them. Foot-sore, food running low, nothing achieved.

The new plan was to defend the main route to Dublin here, at the River Boyne. 'The King sees the Boyne as Dublin's walls,' the Duke of Tyrconnell had told Hogan, when he issued his scouting orders. *God help us if that is true*, Hogan thought. Nevertheless, he had been ordered to make a thorough reconnaissance of the area and find suitable places for the Army dispositions.

But then again ... there were worse battle grounds to fight on, Hogan supposed. The river was a barrier of sorts that could be defended, and the enemy could only cross it here at Oldbridge, or at the well-defended stone bridge downstream by Drogheda Castle, or by a wooden one upstream at the little hamlet of Slane, a few miles to the west. With the right placement of the troops and a little grit and determination, the English could be stopped here and fought to a standstill, if James handled his troops correctly.

However, to Hogan's mind, it was extremely risky to stand and oppose the foe at all. The defeat at Cavan had shown what poor troops the bulk of Irish regiments were, many of the men painfully inexperienced, no more than rustics in red coats – not that Hogan could really criticise them for running. He and his surviving men had run with the rest when the line of the ridge was broken. And he had not stopped galloping for a good ten Irish miles.

More worrying was the great disparity in the size of the two forces. William's army was now estimated to contain more than thirty-six thousand men. All of the swarming bastards well fed, well armed and well disciplined. The Irish Army – admittedly a little better armed since the French had finally delivered a supply of new weapons – was considerably smaller, perhaps only twenty-five thousand men. Strategically, Hogan knew that the Frenchman Narrey was right – raids, hit and run, strike their lines of communication, attack where they least expected it and run for the hills; that was the way to win this war. To drag it out until it became a running sore in William's side. Then maybe the Dutchman would go home and leave Ireland to be run by the Irish.

But what did Hogan know? He was only a lowly cavalry captain, newly commissioned as a troop commander into Tyrconnell's Regiment of Horse. Patrick bloody Sarsfield was behind the new commission, of course. Hogan had had no say in the matter: 'We badly need light horsemen, Mick,' Sarsfield had said to him when he finally returned to Dublin, 'and you and your rogues are some of the best. It won't be for ever. But Ireland needs you. God knows, you've had your fun up in County Cavan. Time to join the colours. Time to come in from the cold. James is calling. You wouldn't want to be letting our rightful King down, would you?'

In among Sarsfield's sweet patriotic words was an unspoken threat. 'Join the regular cavalry, Hogan, or be deemed outlaw, an enemy to all men.'

So here he was on the north bank of the Boyne, looking for camping grounds for the whole bloody Army.

The River Boyne ran across the valley, three miles east to the walled town of Drogheda and the Irish Sea. The river to the east of Oldbridge broadened and deepened and was divided by two small islands – Grove Island and Yellow Island, he remembered them being called last time he had passed by this way. Looking south, to his right-hand side, the Boyne curved round in a bow and then headed off south-west. Ahead of him, across the brown river, the Hill of Donore rose a mile or so away. It would make a fine command post, Hogan thought; the King could sit up there in comfort and splendour and watch his loyal men below doing his dirty bloody work. No, this wasn't the worst spot for a battle, by any means – that is if they were absolutely compelled to fight one.

Hogan spurred his horse and set it scrambling down a steep sunken road that led to the ford. Once in its tunnel-like embrace he could see nothing of the surrounding countryside. And no one would be able to see troops moving on this track, he noted. A quarter of an hour later, at the bottom of the hill, he reined in on the flattish ground beside the reed-covered banks of the river.

He could see the flat stones and shallow patches of the ford, a foot or so deep, near the end of the sunken road, and the track on the other side leading out of the wet towards Oldbridge. Easy crossing. This was the spot to defend.

Hogan heard the neighing of a horse and looked up, expecting to see one of his own men who had followed him down. He saw two men in unfamiliar whitish-grey uniforms. His hand reached to his pistol on the horse's withers – and stopped. To his surprise, he recognised the French shit-weasel Narrey and his gorilla of a bodyguard, walking their horses towards him along the grassy bank. *How the Devil did they get here? I am the tip of the spear.*

'Captain Hogan – well met!' called out Henri. 'Good afternoon, sir!'

'Good afternoon to you, monsieur. It's a grand day for a ride, is it not?'

It was indeed a fine, cloudless day, with a soft breeze that kept the heat at bay. 'So this is where His Majesty wishes to fight, is it?' Henri said casually.

'He means to defend the line of the river – as well you know, monsieur.'

Henri d'Erloncourt smiled warmly at Hogan. His companion Major du Clos stared blankly at the Irishman. Their horses were only yards apart. Hogan could see a vivid splash of fresh blood on the major's grey sleeve. There was more blood spattered on his thigh. 'Are you wounded, monsieur?' Hogan said to the burly artilleryman, indicating the blood with a flick of his index finger. 'Should you like me to summon aid? Perhaps fetch a doctor?'

Major du Clos said nothing. He stared all the harder at Hogan.

'The blood is not his,' said Henri. He gave a careless laugh. 'We have been conducting the interrogations of some deserters in Drogheda Castle.'

Hogan thought about this for a moment. Whatever atrocities the unsavoury pair had been up to, he truly did not wish to know about it.

'And how do you consider our chances of victory, Captain Hogan?'

For one insane moment, Hogan considered pulling his pistol from its holster and shooting down Major du Clos. With him gone, the skinny fop would be easy meat for his sword. There was no one else here. He might be observed by one of his men on the hillside, but none of them would peach. Hogan was not by nature a murderous man. But every instinct was telling him that these men were evil. It wasn't a question of why he should kill them. It was a question of why not. The world would surely be a better place without them.

'I would put our chances at fair,' he said. 'It depends on whether King James holds his nerve on the day. We can stop them if we're well directed.'

Henri nodded slowly as if he were listening to the wisdom of a great sage. 'Tell me, Captain Hogan, do you remember our first meeting at the Bull Inn?'

'Vividly.'

'Do you remember that I gave you weapons and a large sum of money?'

'Jesus, man, it was only nine months ago, of course I remember.'

'And you asked what I – or rather King Louis – wanted in return?'

Hogan said nothing. He was in no mood to play silly games.

'We spoke of you vigorously prosecuting the war against the English – which you have done admirably. I congratulate you, sir, on your labours!'

Hogan remained silent, watching the two Frenchmen. *Now would be the time to do it,* he thought. *Lunge for the pistol and drop the big one. While this arse-worm is enjoying the sound of his own voice so much it's almost onanism.*

'I spoke then of a service that I might ask of you. A favour. Remember?'

It was too late now. The little man had reminded him that Hogan was in the Frenchman's debt. And Hogan always paid his debts, one way or another.

'What is it that you want from me,' he said.

'I am not so optimistic as you, sir, about our chances of victory.'

Hogan shrugged.

'I believe that we shall not be "well directed", as you put it, on the day of battle. Furthermore I predict we shall be soundly beaten by the superior English troops and it shall be as a result of King James's usual folly and incompetence.'

The Frenchman seemed not to care that he was speaking treason.

'The battle will surely be lost, Captain Hogan, and the Irish Army will retreat in disarray – and it is at that moment that I shall require you to fulfil your commitment to me. When the signal is given for a general disengagement and the drums beat for retreat, then shall I require your favour to be repaid.'

'What do you want me to do?'

'When the day is lost, I desire you to seek me out on the battle-field – I shall be with the sole French gun battery, our position should by then be obvious. And you and your men shall escort me and my artillery to safety.'

'I may be dead by then. That is, if we've lost the battle.'

Henri gave a little snigger. 'Oh, I think you are a survivor, Captain Hogan. I'm certain you will live through the day. But in case you do succumb I should like you to instruct your second in command – it's that great bearded lout Gallagher, is it not? – to fulfil your commitment in place of you.'

'And if I refuse to do your bidding – no wait, I remember it now, it is your fearsome French torturers and all that flaying alive business and whatnot, yes?'

Hogan was laughing now, right in the Frenchman's face.

'No, that would not be appropriate – but I shall tell the world that you are a man without honour – a faithless liar, whose sacred word means nothing.'

Hogan stopped laughing. He glared at Henri, the fingers of his right hand flexing open and closed near the butt of his holstered horse pistol.

'You will come and find me on the battlefield, when the drums beat the retreat. You will come then and pay your debt to me in full. Are we agreed?'

Hogan nodded.

'Excellent! Now I have one more thing to tell you. It is a message from the Governor of Drogheda. He says that there is a wooden bridge over the River Boyne about six miles west of here, at the village of Slane. It might be wise to burn it, he says, to deny its use to the enemy. I could not say whether this is the right course or not. I am merely passing on his advice. Good day, Captain!'

Chapter Fourteen

Monday, June 30, 1690

In the ancient great hall of Mellifont Abbey, Holcroft Blood sat on the bench by the wall and observed the milling throng of two score senior officers of William's army. The King himself was seated at the far end of the hall by the fire, a slight figure, in the over-large chair, his face drawn with pain and the pure white bandage on his left shoulder catching the flickering light of the fire.

William had been struck by a cannon ball that morning while reconnoitring the north riverbank of the Boyne with his aides and some of his Blue Guards. Holcroft had been told that the King, in order to show his insouciance and because it had been a warm sunny day, had sat down on the grass by the water's edge for a picnic with his aides. If that was true, it was madness, even though he was out of effective musket range from the enemy. For the Irish, seeing him, had swiftly brought up two cannon – most likely three-pounder Falcons, which being light were the easiest to move in a hurry – and opened fire on William and his party at their al fresco meal. One staff officer and several horses had been killed and a cannon ball had bounced off the ground and grazed the King's shoulder. The doom-laden rumours had spread through the army like lightning: *The King is dead! William is slain by the enemy! All is lost!*

William, after having the painful but, fortunately, non-lethal wound cleaned and dressed by his surgeon – he had lost a good deal of skin and a slice of shoulder flesh but mercifully nothing was broken – was forced to ride through the camp, with the Duke of Schomberg at his side, in great discomfort, but bravely showing his face to the troops to quell the rumours of his demise. Holcroft, who had arrived with the guns from Dundalk after nightfall, had missed the panic – for which he was grateful. But, immediately after he had given his orders to Barden for the dispositions of the cannon on top of the ridge, on the extreme right wing of the army, he had been summoned to this council of war with Richards as the two senior Ordnance officers.

It was clear that William meant to fight the next day. His army was assembled here on the north bank of the Boyne, and James's full force was ensconced on the other side of the river, waiting for them to try to cross. This was the reason William had come to Ireland. A full-pitched battle. A trial of strength between the two sides – and let God Almighty, who made kings and broke them, choose who should triumph on the day of reckoning.

The King stood, shrugging off the helping hand of the Duke of Schomberg, and said, 'Gentlemen! If you please . . .' and the room fell silent.

'Tomorrow is the day, gentlemen, tomorrow we shall face the enemy. And tomorrow we shall be victorious against him.'

There was a general murmur of agreement, a few men even huzzah-ed.

As William cordially invited all his generals to give him their advice on strategy, Holcroft looked around at the faces of those commanders – the Duke of Schomberg, standing beside his royal master; his eldest son Meinhardt, Count Schomberg, who had his own division; there was the Count of Solms, William's most trusted warlord and commander of his elite Blue Guards, and on the far side of the fire the Duke of Württemberg-Neuenstadt, who commanded the left wing – all of them beefy, tough Germanic professional soldiers, but not one true Englishman among them. Not for the first time, Holcroft pondered what had happened to bring his nation to the point where there were more of his countrymen in positions of high command on the far side of the Boyne than gathered in the fire-lit darkness in this crumbling old abbey for a council of war.

Jacob Richards, at least, was an Englishman. Sitting beside him, the lean Ordnance officer seemed eager, coiled, almost straining like a dog at the leash. Holcroft tried to concentrate as the Duke of Schomberg took a step towards the centre of the room and began to outline his strategic vision for the coming fight.

'I am told by my scouts that there is an old bridge at the village of Slane, a few miles to the west, and also a passable ford at a place called Rosnaree, between here and the bridge. Based on that intelligence, I suggest we make a grand flanking march, with say, two thirds of our forces – say, twenty-five thousand men – leaving one third here to hold them, and the bulk of our forces heading west, crossing at Slane or Rosnaree and coming in round behind the enemy. We would have him trapped between two armies. Then we crush him!'

Meinhardt Schomberg loudly agreed with his father.

'My son would be the perfect commander to lead this grand flanking march,' the Duke continued. 'I would do it myself but this crucial and difficult manoeuvre needs a commander of sufficient youth and vigour.'

'Nonsense – divide our forces in the face of the enemy? That would be sheer folly.' Count Solms's words were filled with derision. Holcroft had heard that he and Schomberg were bitter rivals for the King's favour. 'These Irish troops are undisciplined, they are weak, ill-trained. I say we go straight at 'em. Downhill and over the water in one huge determined push. They won't stand.'

'You gravely misjudge our enemies, my dear Count,' said Schomberg. 'They are not the raw, easily frightened troops of last summer. They have had a year to recruit and train their men, to put some fire and steel into them. It would be far better to try a more subtle approach. Meinhardt will lead two-thirds of the army around their left flank, crossing the river at—'

'Poppycock!' said Count Solms, and there was a general intake of breath at his crude language. 'My Blue Guards are the finest troops in Europe. They will slice through these ragtag Irish like a swung sabre through soft cheese.'

'I do not think you quite grasp, sir—'

'What don't I grasp, you old fool? I'll have you know that I—'

'Gentlemen, calm yourselves; gentlemen, if you please ...' William was making placatory gestures with his hands. Holcroft could see that any movement of his wounded left shoulder was causing him a great deal of pain.

'I thank you both for your expert advice but I shall make the final decision. So, yes, flank attack or straight at them? Hmm – yes, this is what we shall do,' said the King. 'We shall indeed send a force, under Count Meinhardt von Schomberg, on a flanking march. That will distract our enemies. But we shall not be dispatching such huge numbers as you suggest, my dear duke, that would be a grave mistake, I feel. So, Meinhardt, dear boy, you may take only the right-wing of our cavalry and Trelawny's Brigade of Foot with you – that will be about, um, seven thousand men, I believe, and you will seek a crossing where ever you can find one in the area of Slane or Rosnaree and once across you will menace the enemy's open left flank. With the Blessing, it should draw off a portion of Jacobite forces from the centre. Is that clear? I shall have your specific orders written out for you later this evening.'

Meinhardt Schomberg nodded obediently.

'However, our main effort must be here, betwixt Oldbridge and Drogheda. The enemy are to our front and we outnumber them. This is where we shall beat them. I feel it in my bones: God will give us victory! General Schomberg, you will command the centre. I shall command the left wing myself. The plan is simple – the Blue Guards will attack the enemy centre and push across the Boyne. Meanwhile, I shall be advancing on our left and will hook round and attack their flank once they are engaged with the Blue Guards at Oldbridge.

'The key to victory, gentlemen, will be timing. I require a full artillery barrage on the positions at Oldbridge to begin at 9 a.m. precisely – do you hear me, Major Richards? Your big guns will open fire at nine, and will continue to bombard the enemy in the centre at Oldbridge for exactly one hour. Destroy their defences, such as they are. At 10 a.m., the artillery bombardment must cease, not another shot, sir, if you please, and the Blue Guards will then make their advance across the Boyne. I do not wish my finest troops to be endangered by wild, ill-aimed cannon fire from our own side.'

Holcroft sat up straight. Did the King truly think the Ordnance were so stupid as to fire on their own attacking men? He felt more than a little insulted.

William was oblivious to his indignation. 'I shall, of course, already be in position by the Yellow Island, ready to cross and flank the Jacobites when they are fully engaged in the centre. Ginkel's cavalry brigade will be on my extreme left, attempting a crossing nearer Drogheda, which will allow them to swing round behind them and cut off their retreat. But all this depends on timing, gentlemen. At about ten of the clock, I am reliably informed, the river will be at its lowest ebb. Easily passable. That is when we attack. God willing, we have a great victory in our grasp – but timings, gentlemen, must be observed.'

Holcroft was still hearing the phrase 'wild, ill-aimed cannon fire' echoing in his mind. He stood up and, raising his hand like a schoolboy, he said: 'Am I right to suppose, sire, that the artillery will fire *only* between nine and ten?'

'Yes, ah, that's correct,' the King peered at him, 'Captain Blood, isn't it?'

'I mean, sire, what should we do after that? Sit on our backsides? Merely observe? Should we not harness up our light pieces and follow the advance?'

'You will do as you are damn well told, Captain Blood.' The Duke of Schomberg clearly had not forgotten Holcroft's misbehaviour at

Carrickfergus. 'The King has given you his orders. You will rain fire on the enemy between the hours of nine and ten; that is all that your King requires of you.'

'With the greatest respect, sire, is that not a waste of our superior artillery power? We have forty guns to their – what is it, five, or maybe six pieces?'

Jacob Richards was tugging urgently at his sleeve, and hissing in his ear for him to be silent and sit down. Holcroft ignored his friend.

'If, after ten o'clock, sire, we were to harness some of our light guns to their horse-teams, the Falcons, perhaps, or maybe a six-pounder Saker, we could follow in behind the advancing troops and give them the support of our guns. We could bombard any defensive positions that the enemy might seek to hold as they retreat, or simply attack their infantry and cavalry rearguard formations. We might be able to make any victory you win, sire, more complete. If you recollect, it was the enemy's ability to move their guns quickly, sire, that gave you such discomfort this morning.'

There was a shocked silence at Holcroft's effrontery. It was tantamount to *lèse majesté*. Was this fellow mocking the King's honourable wound?

Jacobs gave a low groan of despair.

King William looked hard at Holcroft but said nothing. He was thinking.

'Captain Blood, this is no time for you to be advancing your peculiar notions about gunnery,' said the Duke of Schomberg. 'The position of the guns has been set out clearly. The best position. You are not to shift them during the battle. This is not Carrickfergus and the Train is not an eight-inch mortar.'

'No, Your Grace, with the greatest respect, this is *not* Carrickfergus. This is not a siege. This is a battle. Sieges are static – a fortress does not move about during the course of the day; on the battlefield movement is key for the infantry, and the cavalry – so why not for the artillery too?'

'Silence! You will be silent, sir! The King has given his orders. He does not wish for you to quibble and argue, question his royal commands . . .'

'One moment, my dear General Schomberg,' said the King. 'I like the idea of a mobile artillery force. It is novel. Revolutionary, you might even say. It could be useful being able to bring up the guns to where they are needed. But tell me, young man – Captain Blood – if you were to move the light cannon – the Falcons, you called them – if you were to take them down into the thick of battle, what would prevent enemy cavalry from overrunning your guns and capturing them, killing you and your men and bearing the guns away as a battle trophy?'

'Until quite recently, sire, we had a battalion of infantry that was raised specifically to guard the guns. The Royal Fusiliers, sire. That was their task. However, they were sent as line infantry to the Low Countries, to fight under Lord Marlborough's command. The artillery is bereft of them.'

'Do you criticise the King's decisions?' Schomberg had by now worked himself up into a rage, under his huge wig his face was a rich purple colour.

'I merely request that a small force of infantry be assigned to protect the guns. A well-trained company, armed with the latest flintlocks would be best.'

'You have a particular unit in mind, Captain Blood?' said the King.

'As a matter of fact, sire, I do.'

Holcroft's horse Chestnut picked his way through the dark village of Tullyallen, and, as he approached the inn on the left where many of the officers of William's army were quartered, the door swung open and a man, a major, very drunk, stumbled out. He squinted up at Holcroft, a tall shadow on his big horse in the dancing orange light of the inn's wall torch, and said 'No popery?' as if it were an important question requiring a serious answer.

Holcroft touched his hat politely, said 'No, sir. None at all,' then kicked Nut into a gentle trot that bore him away from the drunken fellow. There would be many men this night who would drink their fill before they slept, knowing as they did that tomorrow might be their last on this good green Earth. Holcroft did not despise them for their weakness. He had seen the carnage of battle several times and its horrors never became acceptable to his mind. He had seen brave veterans torn and bloody, screaming for their mothers' succour; and the cavalry horses with their bellies ripped open, still standing, shocked, stunned by the agony, uncomprehending, with their intestines dumped in a steaming pile by their hooves. He'd seen a drummer boy dying slowly, moaning over his folded arms with a musket ball in his groin. Holcroft would have a tot before he slept tonight too. But not yet. He had work to do before he retired to his tent.

To his right, he passed the black bulk of the church on the skyline. Candle light gleamed from the windows and he caught the faint sound of singing. A service in progress. Religion was the other great comfort that many fighting men sought on the edge of the abyss. Others would be rutting with their wives or lovers this night – finding their solace there and obeying the eternal urge to procreate in the face of Death. He wondered what Caroline was doing now.

A few days after the battle and she would have her hands full. The wounded officers of William's army would begin coming up to Belfast within days; by ship, if they were lucky, by road on a rumbling, juddering ox cart, if they were not. His time in her care in the castle now seemed to be a distant dream, the pain and fever forgotten; her presence a light in the darkest night.

He felt a shaft of guilt then. He had thought of Caroline first, not of his wife Elizabeth. Why was that? He had not so much as kissed Caroline, he still had no idea if her feelings for him went beyond friendliness – and he was *married* to Elizabeth, and had lain with her in their conjugal bed on countless times, making love, trying unsuccessfully to make a baby inside her. Why did Elizabeth not spring first to his mind in this time of great peril? He knew the answer, of course, in his secret heart – but he did not want to own it.

He saw the lane ahead, and the gate with a pair of sentries, where he had been told it would be. He reined in Nut and peered through the gloom of night at the two men in grey uniforms with dark turn-backs standing with their muskets across their chests. The man on the right was a huge hulking shape.

'That you, Joe Cully? Standing stag on the eve of battle, when every man in the company is drunk or asleep.' The proximity of Death made Holcroft loquacious. 'Good fellow. Unless it's a punishment. You've annoyed Sergeant Hawkins, haven't you? What d'you do, Joe? Drunk and disorderly. Brawling?'

As he stepped off his horse and handed the reins to a familiar grey-coated Inniskillinger, the sense of homecoming was, for Holcroft, quite overwhelming. Seeing the same old faces for the first time in months: there was Sergeant Hawkins, standing in the fire-glow with a ladle in his hand over a cauldron of gin punch, with Francis Waters, seeming somehow older and longer, lounging on a pile of straw, and the others too, McNally and Burns with sprigs of green tucked in their hatbands. And a few new faces as well. Good men. His men.

He accepted a mug of punch and gave them the news: that the fourth company of Tiffin's Regiment would be detached from the battalion to guard his guns in the coming battle.

'Does that mean, sir, that we won't be fighting tomorrow?' said McNally, a cheerful rogue, red of head but black of heart.

'You won't be part of the main assault. But I do have permission to move the light guns forward, if the frontal attacks are successful and the enemy is pushed back. And if the guns go into the field you lot will be given the task of protecting them – and me and the other gunners.'

'Be a shame to miss *all* the action,' said Sergeant Hawkins, his face red as a cherry from the punch. 'I'll enjoy giving yon Papists a good thumping.'

Despite his words there was relief in his tone. 'You may well get that chance, Sergeant,' said Holcroft. 'We'll be in the thick of it, I'd say.'

'So you are taking over command of the company,' said Lieutenant Waters. Holcroft knew that Francis had been put in temporary charge of the fourth till a new captain was procured from somewhere, but Colonel Tiffin had either forgotten that they lacked a company commander or did not much care.

'You will be in charge, Francis,' he said, 'but you'll report to me. I won't bother you, though. I'll be busy with the guns. The men are still in your hands.'

Holcroft saw the happiness on Francis's smooth face. He knew that for decency's sake the young man could not be raised up to captain so soon after his elevation from ensign, but he also knew that it was unfair to ask a lieutenant to permanently shoulder the company commander's job.

'I've been meaning to give you something, sir,' said Francis. 'Something you lost at Cavan.'

The lieutenant disappeared into the darkness and Sergeant Hawkins began to regale Holcroft with his version of events after he had been laid low on the battlefield at Cavan, some of which he already knew. The Williamite infantry assault had utterly smashed the enemy line on the ridge, with the Duke of Berwich's men fleeing back into the town and some taking cover up into the ancient fort of Tullymongen on the heights. Cavan had then been sacked, with the Inniskilling men running wild, a disgraceful display of indiscipline.

The redcoats and the Inniskillingers – those who had survived the brutal assault – had released their terror in an orgy of wanton destruction. They had looted and raped with abandon, drunk anything and everything they could get their hands on and finally set light to some of the town buildings – and then they had nearly been annihilated when the Irish had summoned their courage and counterattacked in force streaming down the hill from the old fort.

It had been touch and go for a while – but the Inniskillinger companies had somehow re-formed, drunk as they were, and eventually fought off the resurgent enemy with their well-drilled volleys. Fortunately, most of the Jacobite cavalry was already fleeing south to safety, and when Brigadier Wolseley had finally brought up his own horse and re-established control of the town, the battle was over. It had been a victory of a kind that bloody day but, by the time order was established, the town was merrily aflame and Cavan had to be swiftly abandoned, with all the troops pulling back to the safety of Belturbet that night.

'Here you are, sir.' Lieutenant Waters was back in the circle of firelight. Some of the men found this on the ridge after the fight and I kept it for you.'

He handed Holcroft the Lorenzoni repeating pistol, which had been cleaned and polished to a high shine. 'I had a gunsmith look at it in Belfast, sir – he was amazed, sir, quite amazed by the mechanism – but he fixed it up and now it's nearly good as new.'

Holcroft was touched by this kind gesture. He held the unusual pistol in his two hands, his fingers stroking the octagonal barrel, his head bowed over it almost as if at prayer – and felt for the first time in an age the prick of hot tears. He fought them back, blew his nose on a dirty kerchief, and muttered thanks. But that piece of intricate steel and wood in his fingers suddenly brought all the emotions of that terrifying day at Cavan roaring back – the sight of Narrey in his black cloak and hat galloping away as Holcroft stood impotently among the corpses of the enemy line; Major du Clos turning his horse, charging at him. The awful moment when the Lorenzoni had seized, the lever jammed, and he had looked into the orange blossom of flame; into the eyes of Death.

Narrey. The murderer. Holcroft's hatred, long held in abeyance during his recovery in Belfast came creeping over him like the soft hand of a lover, seizing his insides in a cold black loathing. Where was the bloody Frenchman? Was he, even now, down there on the far side of the Boyne with the Irish troops preparing for battle? Would he see him tomorrow? Perhaps within pistol shot? Perhaps, if God was good, there'd be a reckoning between them. Tomorrow.

Chapter Fifteen

Tuesday, July 1, 1690: 8 a.m.

Henri d'Erloncourt, relaxed in the saddle, toyed with one of his leather gloves and watched King James out of the corner of his eye. The monarch was seated at a folding table at his breakfast outside his travelling house, a wooden box on wheels, in which he had passed some of the night in a comfortable bed. Behind the King loomed the old church of Donore on the summit of the hill. It was a quarter past eight of the clock yet already the morning mists were lifting to reveal the promise of a bright, hot and beautiful day.

A horseman came thudding up the steep grassy slope of the hill, a man in a brilliant scarlet coat and broad-brimmed black hat with a scrap of white paper in the hatband, the symbol that all James's troops had been ordered to wear that day to distinguish them from their similarly clad enemies. The man slid off his sweating horse and, first bowing, he approached the breakfast table. The Duke of Tyrconnell intercepted him. After a murmured conversation, the duke went to the King's side. Henri edged his horse a little closer to overhear the news.

'Sire, the enemy is on the move,' said Tyrconnell.

'What, already?' said the King through a mouthful of cold roast chicken. He took a swallow of wine, dabbed his mouth with a lace napkin and stood.

'See there, sire, the dust on the road to the west. Take my glass.'

James put the telescope to his eye. From this high vantage point he could see clearly over the countryside for miles. Even Henri, without the aid of a lens, could see large numbers of troops moving on the far side of the river, thousands of men and horses, in formed columns heading westward.

'By God, there are a lot of them. What does it mean, Tyrconnell, do they mean to flank me?'

'It is difficult to say, Highness. But there are several points at which they might cross the river. The bridge at Slane has been destroyed but the water is shallow there, and the Rosnaree ford is only guarded by a single regiment of dragoons, under Sir Neil O'Neill – not even five hundred men.'

'O'Neill won't hold them. There must be ten or twelve thousand men on the march.'

Henri pulled out his own glass and examined the columns. Not as many as ten thousand, he thought. But it was impossible to say with any real accuracy.

'They must see that we are arrayed strongly in their front at Oldbridge,' said the King. 'They will surely be mauled if they attempt to cross the river there. And my nephew William is a wily bird. He's not one for the straightforward attack. It is quite possible that they are attempting to cross the water in the west and come around behind us. To cut us off from Dublin.'

'It could just be a feint, sire,' said Tyrconnell.

Henri edged closer to the King and gave a discreet cough.

'Yes, Comte d'Erloncourt. You wish to say something?'

Henri bowed to the King. 'Sire, my informants have suggested to me that the Prince of Orange seeks to attack you on more than one front. His most trusted generals have been urging a major flanking movement in council. Even a strategy of encirclement.' Once it was spoken, Henri almost believed his lie.

'Hear that, Tyrconnell? He's trying to flank me. The Comte d'Erloncourt's spies confirm it. William's trying to sneak round and get behind me.'

'I am not so certain, sire,' said the veteran Irish general. Tyrconnell shot Henri a malevolent glance. 'He could be merely trying to draw your men away from the centre at Oldbridge. To weaken us there before he attacks . . .'

'If I might suggest something, sire . . .' Henri shivered. He had always savoured the thrill of his influence. The power of his words to affect events.

'Speak up, d'Erloncourt. Let's hear your counsel.'

'Oh yes,' said Tyrconnell nastily. 'Do offer us more of your *insight*.'

'I think it might be wise to send the French Brigade to the west, sire. If the enemy is trying to flank you, or to come around behind your lines, as he clearly seems to be doing, General Lauzan and his men can stop them. And, if this truly is where the full weight of the enemy punch will land, if necessary, the French Brigade can hold up the enemy there, contain him till you come to our aid.'

'Sire, if we were to strip the meagre defences in front of Oldbridge of the whole French Brigade, I fear we will have great difficulty in repelling . . .'

The King ignored Tyrconnell. He was looking once again at the column marching west. The cloud of dust on the road was huge and unmistakable.

'Monsieur d'Erloncourt, I believe you are right. Where is Lauzan now?'

'General Lauzan is in his tent at the foot of the hill. I believe, sire, he is at his toilet.' Henri felt a glow in his belly. He had served his true master well.

'Then you, monsieur, shall give him my orders. The French Brigade is to deploy to the west, and your guns, too, Comte d'Erloncourt, if you please – we must strengthen our left wing. Tell Lauzun that he is to stop them at the river, if he is able to. If not, he must hold our flank securely until I can come up . . .'

'Sire, I must counsel against this,' said Tyrconnell. 'If the main attack—'

The King overrode him. 'And Lauzan will need horsemen, too. Send Lord Galmoy's men, and General Sarsfield's regiments, Maxwell's dragoons too. Make out the orders, Your Grace, this instant, if you please.'

'Sire, the centre will be dangerously weakened . . .'

'The enemy attack will not fall on the centre, Tyrconnell, it is just about to erupt on our open left flank. Look yonder; are you blind? See the enemy on the road – twelve thousand of them, I am sure of it. I can divine my nephew's mind. Follow my orders, Your Grace, or I will find someone who will.

'Furthermore, I want all tents and baggage packed and ready to go. If we should decide to pull back, it will be in haste. If they succeed in getting round behind us, Tyrconnell, all is lost. If they cut the road to Dublin it would be . . . well, a catastrophe. You must recognise that at least, Your Grace. Now see to it, there's a good fellow. And without any argument, if you would be so kind . . .'

Holcroft Blood looked at his watch; it was ten minutes before nine. From his position on a high bank of earth to the west of the sunken road that led down to the ford at Oldbridge, he could see along the ridge at the gleaming array of artillery. The view of neatly aligned guns to his right gave him a jolt of pleasure.

The Ordnance had been moved into its correct position during the night and the massed guns occupied two hundred yards of high ground on the extreme right of King William's Army. He had three strong batteries on the ridge, each of four big cannon, twelve- or twenty-four-pounders, and at the near end of the line, closest to Holcroft's position, a battery of four stubby eight-inch mortars. Each piece was polished and shined to a sparkle by the guns teams and was perfectly in line with the others in the battery. Half a dozen guns, mostly Sakers and twelve-pounders, had been dispatched with Count Meinhardt von Schomberg and his seven thousand men when they began their westward march after daybreak. And the rest of the Train was snug in the artillery park, a hundred yards behind the ridge, ready to be called forward at need, if some of the guns were hit by enemy fire or were damaged in some way. These reserves included two three-pounder Falcons, which Holcroft had ordered to be hitched to their carriages, with teams of horses and drivers standing by.

The Mortar Battery was captained by Master Gunner Enoch Jackson, who was sitting cross-legged on the earth, his brown bald head bowed low over a box of cut fuses. He appeared either to be examining them closely for defects, or praying to the Almighty that they were cut to the right length to deliver His righteous wrath unto their wicked Jacobite foes.

Beyond Jackson, Lieutenant Claudius Barden, the Third Engineer of the Train, had command of the No. 1 Battery and the thirty gunners and matrosses who manned its two twenty-four-pounders and pair of twelves. That affable young man had been in tearing high spirits all through the night as the big guns were heaved on to the ridge in near-darkness – and the lack of a good night's sleep seemed to have had no dampening effect on his energies.

He saw Holcroft looking over at him and called out: 'Beautiful day for a battle, sir. God is smiling on us from on high. A sign of victory, sir, for sure!'

Holcroft wasn't sure what Barden meant by 'God is smiling on us' – did the Almighty have a mouth? Did God smile? Did he think the sun was God? He assumed it was a joke and gave a weak grin of his own in response.

Holcroft had overall command of these two batteries this day – No. 1 and the Mortar Battery, with Barden and Jackson under him – and Jacob Richards, who he could see was also looking at his pocket watch two hundred yards away at the far end of the line, had charge of the No. 2 and No. 3 Batteries.

Holcroft liked Richards, he really did. But he was aware that the man had developed some sort of absurd boyish infatuation for Caroline. They had had an awkward conversation on the march from Dundalk, walking their horses beside the lumbering Train.

The week before, Caroline Chichester had asked permission of the First Engineer to accompany the Train under his protection, and she and a young maid and an ancient serving man armed with a pair of horse pistols had joined the column at Newry. Holcroft had been too busy to see her but he knew that Richards had dined with her on several occasions in the officers' mess. He had also heard that his senior officer had paid several brief visits to her large and comfortable tent, where he had been entertained by Caroline and her servants. Holcroft had not been entirely paying attention to Richards' words as they approached Tullyallen, but he was suddenly aware that his friend had been talking in vague terms about Caroline and marriage.

'I'm not a rich man, Blood, I believe you know that. But I do have some prospects, my father is not in the best of health and I can expect a pretty decent inheritance when he is called, two or three hundred a year. So I'm not quite penniless. But I loathe the idea that Caroline might think me a scrub – a God-damned fortune hunter. Her family is really very well situated, as you know, Lord Chichester, Earl of Donegall, has estates across Ireland. But I care for her deeply. And my future is reasonably bright, I think, in the Ordnance. I might make full Colonel one day. Do you think she might, well, consider me as . . .'

'Have you spoken to her about marriage?' said Holcroft.

'No, no, good Lord, no. We are on friendly terms, of course and I believe she holds a measure of tenderness for me. But I don't wish to offer myself to her until I'm sure I would not be scorned. I simply could not bear that.'

'I should leave her alone, if I were you. Just forget the whole idea.'

Richards gave him a strangely virulent glare.

'And why would you say that, Blood, I wonder? Why should I just forget about her? To leave the field clear, perhaps . . .'

'I don't think officers who are on active campaign, in the midst of a war, should contemplate marriage, domesticity and so on. For one thing, it may distract you from your duty. For another, you might be killed at any time.'

'Thank you for reminding me of my duty. She won't have *you*, you know. She knows you're married. She would never stoop to concubinage. Never.'

The venom in Richards' words was clearly apparent. Holcroft was not sure how to respond. 'My marriage is not . . .' He was about to say 'entirely happy' and stopped himself. He did not want to think about Elizabeth just then. He said instead, 'the issue here. My wife, whom I married in peacetime, is safe in London.'

'Yes, I know that, all the world knows *that*. And you must also know by now what everyone is saying she gets up to on her own in Town.'

Holcroft stopped his horse. 'What do you mean by that?'

Richards flushed. He reined in. 'I'm sorry. I meant nothing by that remark. It was spoken in anger and I regret it. I apologise, Blood. Forgive me.'

Holcroft knew exactly what Richards was referring to. He felt a glow of anger towards the man. But for the swift apology he might have formally called Richards out and fought him. He took a deep breath, and let it out slowly. He had found a letter, a dirty little note in truth, from an unknown hand, left on his cot in his tent at Dundalk. The letter had, in most unpleasant and graphic terms, informed him that Mistress Elizabeth Blood was the lover of Jongheer Markus van Dijk, a captain of the Dutch Third Regiment of Guards. It was signed 'A well-wisher'. Holcroft had torn the note to shreds and refused to believe it. Just a grubby rumour. Some snivelling worm trying to make trouble. But Richards' mention of the rumour made him feel hot and cold at the same time.

'I'm going to check on the fodder for tonight's camp,' he said to the First Engineer. And he turned his horse and rode off down the column.

It was now almost nine o'clock. On the ridge above the Boyne, Holcroft could hear sounds behind him, many boots scuffing on a stony track. He looked over his shoulder and saw that the sunken road was filling with men in the blue coats and orange turn-backs of the Dutch Guards. Hundreds of soldiers, each with a flintlock musket and a sprig of green tucked into their hatbands. He looked at Richards at the far end of the artillery line and raised his hat. The First Engineer of the Train raised his own hat in return. Neither man smiled.

Holcroft glanced at the village of Oldbridge, half a mile below and slightly to the east of his position on the far side of the Boyne. He could see a large house with a walled garden, and three smaller stone cottages shaded by ash trees. Beyond were golden cornfields, the wheat ripe and ready for the scythe. The enemy were in their positions behind the low walls of the garden – he could just see their heads – and in the hedgerows, some in shallow scrapes in the earth behind barriers of hawthorn and beech. He could see a squadron of cavalry in a motley of uniforms trotting easily across the fields behind the village. Were it not for the soldiers' presence, it would have been a placid scene.

'Very well then, Enoch,' he said to the bald master gunner, who was standing by the nearest mortar and looking expectantly at him. 'Let us begin to reduce—' His words were cut off by the roar of cannon in the No. 3 Battery.

And battle was joined.

Chapter Sixteen

The same day: 10 a.m.

The horse fidgeted beneath Hogan at the sound of the cannon. The old bay mare had been in many a scrap and mêlée but she was not used, on a noisy and frightening battlefield, to the forced immobility demanded by strict regimental discipline. With each thunderous crack and boom of the English guns she gave a little twitch, and occasionally she took a few dancing side-steps. Hogan checked her, soothed her, stroking her withers with his hand and murmuring soft endearments to let her hear his familiar voice in her constantly flicking ears.

Fortunately, the Duke of Tyrconnell's Regiment of Horse, to which Hogan's company was now informally attached, was formed up on the lower slopes of the Hill of Donore a good half a mile behind Oldbridge, where the majority of the enemy Ordnance was falling. For nearly an hour, the tiny hamlet by the river had endured a pounding from the big guns on the ridge above the Boyne and a fog of dust and smoke clouded the air. It was clear to Hogan what the enemy had in mind. They were softening up the defences in Oldbridge – knocking the houses into rubble, destroying the flint walls of the big garden, tearing through the hedges and woodland copses and battering the terrified men who crouched there – in preparation for a massed infantry assault.

What Hogan did not understand, and what nobody could explain to him, was why almost two thirds of the Irish Army had departed earlier that morning and was now marching west. *This is where the attack would fall – here: why were they sending the troops away?* Looking over his left shoulder, he could see the last units of

the French Brigade, a little train of six cannon, accompanied by
thirty mounted artillerymen, marching south-west, along the line
of the river.

Looking to his front, he could count only six battalions of infantry between himself and the Boyne. Perhaps three thousand men.
However, the Irish were much stronger in the mounted arm, which
was a blessing. Apart from Tyrconnell's Regiment lined up beside
his own irregular company there were the horse regiments of
Colonel Sutherland and Colonel Parker, two squadrons of King
James's Life Guards and one troop of horse grenadiers, and behind
him and slightly to his right there were a couple of full-strength
regiments of dragoons.

However, horse alone could not win a full pitched battle and
now that the guns of the French Brigade, commanded by that sly
bastard Henri d'Erloncourt, were gone west, there was no artillery
left to answer the battering being laid down by the English on the
ridge. As he soothed the fidgeting bay, he did the number calculations in his head: he reckoned at best they might have eight or nine
thousand Irishmen between Oldbridge and the Hill of Donore. Far
too few to face the might of William's army. How many did the
Dutchman have: twenty thousand? Thirty? Whatever the exact
number it was still terrible odds.

He thought about what d'Erloncourt had said about his expec-
tation that James would mishandle the battle and feared that it
would come horribly true. He silently vowed to himself that if the
King did order a retreat, 'Galloping' Hogan and his men would
not be slow in obeying. He was no coward, he'd proved that many
a time, but he and his men were raiders not redcoats. They were
light horse whose job was to harry a fleeing foe, scout out ahead,
relay messages. They were not infantry whose role was to stand
and die.

When the trumpet sounded for the retreat – if it did – he and
his fifty men would abandon the Duke of Tyrconnell – to the Devil

with that pompous old arse - and seek out the Frenchman and get him safely away from the battle.

If things completely went to Hell and Damnation, Henri d'Erloncourt could at least get him and his men aboard a boat to France, down south in the ports of Cork or Kinsale. If this war was lost in one mad, reckless, badly managed battle, Hogan did not intend to stick around and answer difficult questions from William's officers about all the farms he had burned in Ulster during the past year. Not that he believed he had anything to reproach himself with – he had never lain with an unwilling woman; he'd never killed a man unless it was necessary. But he was tarred with the raparee brush – and some of his fellow raiders had not been as circumspect as he. He could not afford to fall into English hands. That would be asking for a noose. If it came to it, he and his men would run from the field. Mick Hogan was a patriot – not an idiot.

His mare suddenly lifted its head. Hogan did likewise. The guns had stopped. There was an eerie quiet across the battlefield. Hogan fumbled in his waistcoat and pulled out an ancient watch: it was exactly ten o'clock.

He stood up in his stirrups and, craning his neck, he could make out the ford at Oldbridge, and the gently smoking rubble of a pair of cottages a little way from the river's edge. Why had they stopped? Had they run out of ammunition? No, they couldn't have, after coming all this way. They'd have brought a few extra kegs of powder and cannon balls with them, surely.

He had his answer a moment later. On the far side of the water, from a sunken road that led to the ridge – stepping through a curtain of leafy fronds, the arms of weeping willows – came the forms of men. Marching men with blue coats with bright orange turn-backs and glorious orange stockings, each one gripping a gleaming musket. William's famous Blue Guards. His finest men.

At this distance they looked like children's dolls. Hogan took out his glass and trained it on the far bank of the river. Lined up eight men abreast and countless ranks deep – big men, he could see now, grenadiers, all over six feet tall – the guardsmen came out of the tunnel-like mouth of the road in a slow and steady tramp, like a huge blue caterpillar emerging from a gigantic burrow, and spilling out on to the flat, grassy water meadow before the slow brown river.

There was something stately, even majestic, about the advance of the Blue Guard. They came straight ahead, with a measured tread, paying little attention to the bank of the river, the leading rank jumping straight in and beginning to wade across, water up to their thighs, muskets held shoulder high, the men behind following in their splashes, their legs whipping the water white.

On the south bank, Hogan could see red-coated Irishmen, poking heads up from where they had been taking cover, and their officers were beginning to marshal them. A goodly number had survived the artillery barrage, thank God. Many hundreds. Even thousands. Whole companies, scores of men, erupted from half-crushed buildings, taking their places on their knees by mounds of steaming rubble, levelling their muskets. Other formations, company or even some battalion-sized, were forming up behind the shot-torn hedgerows and crumbled smoking remains of stone walls that had once been little cottages.

Hogan felt a flame of hope burst into life in his heart.

The first Irish volleys crashed out, precise, deadly, and Hogan saw five grenadiers in the front rank of Blue Guards fall, splashing into the brown water. But their places were immediately filled from the wading ranks behind. More volleys. The musket balls whipped into the advancing column, lashing it from the front and both sides now. Lead balls thumping into human meat. Dutchmen fell, again and again, plunging sideways into the water, gouts of red splashing the dark coats of their fellows, the bodies drifting away eastwards with the current. The men of Clanrickarde's Regiment of Foot, the foremost red-coated battalion tasked with guarding the ford, were on their feet near the water's edge, firing as fast as they could, reloading and firing again into the oncoming ranks. Sergeants were screaming, directing the onslaught, and the Irish muskets smashed into the column with fire and lead, and a desperate fear-driven fury.

Still the Dutch came on. Not one man of them had fired a shot.

The water of the Boyne was thick with bodies but the slow blue caterpillar forged onwards, and yet more men were coming out of the sunken road, pushing the column into the withering fire of the enemy. Now, incredibly, tall Dutchmen were stepping out on the dry south bank, diverging left and right, splitting into smaller units, still under a murderous, unrelenting storm of Irish musketry. They were forming ranks by companies, wounded men falling with every beat of Hogan's heart, toppling out of their formation. Others dropping to their knees, sprawling, coughing blood but trying to stand up again and rejoin their comrades. Somehow, in the face of the hurricane of fire, the Dutch ranks were properly formed. Officers and sergeants carefully ordered the lines, with halberd and sword, indifferent to the storm of musket balls that shredded the men all around them. On the right, an elderly officer with a pink sash was shot full in the face. He fell. A sergeant hauled him away and took his place, standing broad shouldered and proud as Lucifer, bawling out his commands.

Hogan was appalled – and awed. These men could not be fully human.

Twenty yards from a hedgerow, which was lined with thirty redcoats, all madly firing and reloading as quick as their fingers could work, the leading Dutch company formed up, calm and cool as if on the wind-swept parade ground outside The Hague. They levelled their pieces, the command came briskly from a sword-wielding gentleman in a silver wig, and the first Dutch volley smashed into the hedge, wiping out all but two of the redcoats pitted against them. The second Dutch rank stepped forward, threading though the first; they straightened the line and a second volley swept away this final pair.

All along the south bank the Dutch were advancing in step, stopping to dress their ranks and firing with a chilling precision. Slaughtering their foes. Some of the blue guardsmen, detached from the main bodies, were throwing grenades, lighting the match fuses on the fist-sized iron balls and bowling them, underarm, towards the enemy-lined hedgerows, where they exploded and did terrible damage, shredding hawthorn and beech to the roots, ripping the flesh off the cowering redcoats behind. The Irish were being pushed back. And yet more of these blue automatons were streaming across the Boyne. There were several hundred Dutchmen now on the south bank in a bridgehead seventy yards wide, thirty deep. The blood-puddled ground, churned to a mire in places, was scattered with dying guardsmen, dropped arms and equipment everywhere.

Clanrickarde's battered men were outnumbered on the south bank and were beginning to make an orderly retreat. This was no rout. No panic. The redcoats would pull back thirty yards, to a fresh hedge or the remains of a wall, reload their muskets, form a ragged line, level their pieces, wait for the command and smash a devastating volley into the advancing Dutch.

Hogan heard the faint rattle of drums and a tinny blast of trumpet over the thump of musket blasts and the screaming of wounded men. He saw that a full battalion of redcoats – six hundred men, King James's own Foot Guards, some of the finest soldiers in the Irish Army – was advancing on this bubbling, smoking cauldron of carnage on the south bank. These big, bold Irishmen, half-pikemen, half-matchlock musketeers would push the Dutch back in the water.

Hogan was sure of it.

And then he scanned the bridgehead with his telescope and suddenly he wasn't so sure. The flow of Dutchmen across the River Boyne had in no way slackened. And many of the blue guardsmen were snug behind the rubble defences that the Irish had recently abandoned. And what was this? Further east from Oldbridge, near the spit of land called Grove Island, Hogan could see more Williamite units advancing to the far side of the river. Musketeers in grey with leather baldricks. Huguenots, he believed, from the split crosses on the flags. Protestant Frenchmen who'd been ejected from France by Louis XIV.

Whose idiot idea was it to send away the bulk of the army?

The Irish Foot Guards were now hand-to-hand with the Dutch Blue Guards in the battered ruins of Oldbridge. The musket smoke, thick as soup, almost obscuring the field, but the regular crash of the volleys and the howls and moans of wounded men were still clearly to be heard. Hogan saw the two companies of Irish pikemen, in a single red block a hundred-men strong, lower their sixteen-foot weapons and begin their advance. Nothing could stand in the way of their phalanx; no body of men could hold without being skewered on the sharp pike points. Then out of the smoke on their left flank, a platoon of twenty Blue Guards appeared as if by magic, straightened their lines and began to maul them with disciplined volley fire as they marched past.

The pikemen could do nothing. Volley after volley crashed into the pacing redcoats. And the Dutchmen to their front – fifty men formed up in the ruins of an orchard – added their fire to the general carnage. Shooting for their lives, rank after blue rank poured their lead missiles into the slowly advancing redcoats. A pair of grenadiers ran forward from the right and tossed smoking spheres into the centre of the pike formation. A boom and spray of lethal red-hot metal shards erupted in the forest of pikes. Ten men fell. Then moments later another bang, another dozen men dead or mortally wounded.

More grenadiers darted forward. More bombs were hurled. More men died. The galling platoon fire ripped again and again into the flanks of the marching pikemen. And savaged from front and flank, and from the heart of the formation, too, the pikemen stumbled and fell, legs lacerated, groins punctured by red-hot iron, tripping on the corpses of their friends in the smoke, blundering out of formation. Blinded by smoke. Battered by musketry from all sides. In a few short moments, the vaunted King's Foot Guards disintegrated into a disorderly terrified mob, the soldiers hurling their unwieldy pikes aside and taking to their heels, haring away south as fast as their pumping legs would carry them.

And further east several hundred grey-clad Huguenots were already halfway across the river, muskets high, wading through the brown water, and there were many more units coming down the hillside behind them – Williamite redcoats this time – streaming down to the river on their left to join the attack.

We cannot hold them, Hogan thought. *This fight is surely lost.*

'Captain Hogan,' shouted a voice to his right, 'Captain Hogan, sir!'

He took the telescope from his eye and turned to see a young pink-faced lieutenant of Tyrconnell's Regiment galloping towards him waving his hat.

'The Duke's compliments, sir, and he desires you to lead your men down to the river to attack those infantry in grey as they come out of the water.'

The pink-faced lad pointed at the mass of Huguenots milling on Grove Island. 'The second, third and fourth squadrons will follow you in support.'

'Very good,' said Hogan. 'And what is the rest of His Grace's Regiment going to do in the meantime. Sit up here with their thumbs up their fat arses?'

The lieutenant's pink face became even pinker.

'I believe . . . that is, I'm not sure, sir . . . but I think . . . His Grace means to charge the enemy at Oldbridge and push the Dutchmen back into the Boyne.'

'Hrmpf,' said Hogan.

'Do you understand your orders, sir?' said the boy.

Hogan ignored him. 'Paddy Gallagher,' he shouted, startling his bay mare into a little jig. 'Get the lads ready, if you please. We're going down in there.'

Hogan's men hit the enemy when they were at their most vulnerable, with only two score musket men from the first Huguenot battalion on the south bank of the Boyne and the rest of the division – the other two battalions – either waist deep in the water or on Grove Island in the middle of the river preparing to cross. The raparees came out of a small patch of woodland at the full gallop, the men shrieking their war cries, whooping and shouting like godless savages, and fell on the disordered Huguenots, shooting off their carbines then mauling the enemy with swinging swords and darting half-pikes.

The horsemen smashed into the grey-clad men from the east, riding them down with the sheer momentum of their horses, or slashing at their faces, necks and scalps as they passed, leaving great flapping, bleeding wounds. Those with spears or cut-down pikes skewered the Frenchmen through the body and left their weapons waggling deep in their Protestant flesh. After the first pass, Hogan rallied his own company, halfway between Grove Island and Oldbridge, and got them back into some semblance of order. The casualties had been mercifully light – two men missing, presumably fallen in the carnage by the riverside, and half a dozen with minor wounds and still in the saddle.

The three squadrons of Tyrconnell's Horse, who had followed the raparees in the charge, were still down at the water's edge, sabring the beaten infantry, hacking and slashing at those desperate men still on their feet.

Yet the Huguenot companies were far from toothless – their advance guard had been more or less annihilated on the bloody, muddy bank but more men were coming across the water, hundreds more. On Grove Island, fifty yards way, there were companies form-ing and beginning their volleys.

The Tyrconnell squadrons were still on the riverbank, the horses milling in circles, the men slashing at the last few cowering victims of the sudden attack. Some men even bloodying their shiny swords on corpses, just for the look of it. But the grey ranks of musket men on the island were keeping up their fire – and steadily taking their toll. As Hogan watched, he saw a dozen grey jets of smoke all in a row erupt from the island and three Irish saddles emptied on the bank. Why were Tyrconnell's men not pulling back? Ah, now he saw it. The senior captain, distinguishable by his scarlet sash, was lying with his legs in the river, hatless, half his head gone. The Tyrconnell squadrons were leaderless.

Hogan had a sudden urge to ride away. They had done their part. Now it was time to find that wee French shite and be gone from this Hell.

He knew he couldn't do it.

'Sound the charge, Paddy,' he said. 'We'll give 'em a little more pepper.'

They went in again, this time more cautiously, carbines empty, but horse pistols out, shooting the men in grey as they came out of the water. Cutting down those who had already made it to the shore when the pistols were spent. Hogan shot a Huguenot in the dead centre of his chest, and pulling out his cutlass, he slashed another fellow across the forehead, the blade chunking into the skull under the hat brim, sticking there a moment till he wrenched it free from the falling body.

Yet the regular banging of the Huguenot muskets on Grove Island was constant and unceasing. The musket balls zipped and whizzed and cracked all around them. And Hogan's men were dying, one by one. There were too many of the enemy, hundreds of faces, still coming on, ever coming on through the brown water under their square orange banners, shouting their barbarous French war cries, some firing off their flintlocks at them when their grey shanks were still in the river. Others, their musket barrels plugged with razor-sharp bayonets, reaching up, snarling, to stab at Hogan's riders as they passed by on the bank.

A flood tide of enemies. Unstoppable.

'Pull back, pull back,' Hogan was shouting at his own poor men and the remaining Tyrconnell squadrons. 'Regroup in the woods.' He saw a big man in water-splashed grey level his musket at him. Fire. And behind he heard a grunt and turning saw that Gallagher had been hit by a ball in the belly. The big man hunched forward over his pommel, swearing, his grubby chemise blooming red.

'Pull back to the tree line,' Hogan was shouting. No one seemed to hear him. He seized Paddy Gallagher's bridle and began to pull the horse after him.

Yet half his own men did heed him, and began to disengage, loosing their last pistol shots over their shoulders and withdrawing to the relative safety of the woods. The rest of them, the regulars of Tyrconnell's Horse, were caught up in the orgy of bloodletting, slashing and screaming, cursing and stabbing their foes on the water's edge when the musket volleys took them. They were overwhelmed, it seemed, in a few moments. The few score men still alive swamped by the grey-clad hordes.

Hogan watched them as he reloaded his long horse pistol at a safe distance of a hundred yards. He looked about him: under the trees were perhaps ninety men, half his original numbers, some of his own, some of Tyrconnell's men, more than he had expected. They were busy binding up their wounds, gulping water or ale from their big round canteens, boasting to their mates of the great deeds they had done that day. They seemed cheerful – even exuberant. Christ! More than half of his men were dead or wounded – it had been a bloody slaughter. That was courage. That was fighting spirit. In that moment he loved them all – every mad-bastard one of them – more than he could ever express.

The battle was not done. A whole enemy battalion, five hundred grey-clad men, was now on the south bank – with another Huguenot battalion halfway across the water coming to join them. Hogan dearly wanted to run. *Had they done enough? Surely they had done enough this day.* Hogan looked at the busy riverbank, where the Huguenots were massing, forming their companies, preparing to advance, the sergeants carrying away the dead – both kinds – and stacking them like cut logs by the water's edge.

Beyond the Huguenots, to the west, the battle still raged around Oldbridge. The redcoats and the blues were engaged in ferocious individual combat in the ruins of the village, soldiers of both sides mingled in the smoke-wreathed mêlée, stabbing with pike and sword and plug-bayonet, pistolling each other at a range of only a few feet, the musket volleys crashing out again and again. He could see the rest of Tyrconnell's cavalry there, swinging their sabres, yelling their hatred, smashing down the Dutchmen. And some men of Colonel Parker's Regiment, too. An orgy of noise and smoke and stench and slaughter. Neighing horses. Gore and filth. The screaming of men unceasing, ringing out like the bells of Hell.

Hogan took a great deep breath. 'One more time, lads,' he said. 'Once more for King James and for our own dear Ireland. Come on, lads, *charge!*'

Hogan's men crashed into a half-formed Huguenot company, tearing it apart, sabring men bloody as they tore through their ragged ranks. And then they hit the formed ranks of a double company as if it was a stone wall; a massed volley smashing into the galloping Irish horsemen like a giant's knock-out punch.

The pistol was blown from Hogan's right hand. His bay mare was bucking like a mad thing, uncontrollable, and with his numb fingers Hogan could barely remain in the saddle, let alone direct his mount. A second volley exploded around him like a lightning storm at sea, noise and fury and streaks of orange light – and he knew then that it was enough. He had had his fill. His men had had their fill. Their courage had reached its end. Those who survived the two volleys were now riding away, galloping back towards the Hill of Donore.

There were few enough alive. A scant two dozen of his comrades and a score of Tyrconnell's riders. *All that blood and death – and for what?* Hogan let the horse carry him from the cheering Huguenots, at a canter, his aching body loose in the saddle, and at three hundred yards he reined in, quieted the old mare and let her graze in a miraculously untouched patch of golden corn.

He turned in the saddle to survey the battlefield.

The once-green turf by the river was littered with the bodies of his own men and dead and wounded horses but the grey ranks were fully formed and were advancing at a slow pace, coming on towards him. He was done, though. His men had done their dying now. Over to the right, by the woods they had briefly sheltered in, yet more of William's men were making the crossing, at least three full battalions. Cavalry too, beyond them. It looked like a general advance. The enemy smelt victory. As well they might. Hogan knew *he* was defeated. He looked left at the smoking, body-strewn rubble of Oldbridge and saw defeat there too. The elite redcoats of the King's Foot Guards had been pushed back. The massed Jacobite cavalry had made their charge and were scattered. The Blue Guards, the few left alive, were in full possession of the field and many more of their comrades were fording the stream. Thousands upon thousands of them, or so it seemed to Hogan. An army of fresh, foreign troops coming to join in the joyous slaughter of his own poor countrymen.

They had tried with all their heart and soul to stop the enemy at the Boyne. They had given their lives for their King, and gallantly spilled their own blood.

And they had failed.

Chapter Seventeen

The same day: 1 p.m.

From the saddle, Henri d'Erloncourt surveyed the English flanking force with his telescope. They were a quarter of a mile distant, on the other side of the small wooded valley. Just seven or eight thousand men – that was his estimate – and they were forming a rough line of battle among the trees. A cavalry regiment, then one of infantry, then another horse battalion, and so on. But there were reinforcements coming up behind them, five battalions of infantry at least. He had seen the blocks of redcoats moving as one man across the green fields south of the Boyne when he had climbed into a tree earlier for a better view. The French Brigade would soon be facing about eleven thousand enemies – a very sizeable flanking force – a small army, in fact. Yet Henri, most unusually, was not the slightest part concerned for his own physical safety.

The enemy had crossed the river Boyne at the Rosnaree ford, some four miles south-west of Oldbridge, and they swung around to head back east along the line of the river, aiming to attack the Jacobite left flank. They were lining up no more than a long musket shot away. He could make out faces of the English scouts on the tree-lined lip of the valley with the aid of his glass.

Henri would have felt less relaxed about the situation but for two things. Firstly, there were thousands of crack troops of the French Brigade around him, moustachio-ed veteran cavalrymen and well-trained line infantry, all good Catholic Frenchmen, even if his six light guns, under the direction of Major du Clos, had been delayed and would not come up in less than two hours. He had also been informed by a passing galloper, that King James would be arriving at this remote place – Roughgrange, it was called – with the bulk of his army, perhaps another ten thousand, within the half hour.

The second reason for his nonchalance was that, although not wide, the valley between the two forces was steep banked and had a muddy stream running at the bottom between two man-deep ditches. The bed of the valley was also treacherously boggy – a place that no attacking force could negotiate with ease or safety. The enemy scouts clambering about on the far slope were discovering this uncomfortable fact for themselves.

Henri had been down there in the mire not a half hour ago – and he knew that the little valley was an impassable obstacle for both of the forces now facing each other: the French Brigade and the English enemy – who, he assumed from the standards, were commanded by General Meinhardt von Schomberg, eldest son of William of Orange's tired and ageing warhorse.

Ridiculous, he thought. *We can see them; they can see us, but there is no way either side can come to blows. Indeed, it is more than a little absurd.*

It was also a triumph of his own secret plans, agreed with General Lauzun, to keep the French Brigade out of harm's way if possible during the main battle.

He was savouring the impasse when he heard the pounding of hooves and, collapsing his glass, he turned to see Patrick Sarsfield cantering up.

The handsome young general, dashing in a bright green coat, to Henri's eye, and with a gorgeous emerald plume in his hat, reined in a few yards away.

'The King has come up, monsieur,' said Sarsfield. 'Half a mile that way, at the old farmhouse.' He jerked his head northwards. 'He's asking after you.'

King James was standing in the over-warm kitchen of the house, leaning with his knuckles on the scrubbed oak table, and staring at a large map. There were men in uniform surrounding him, eating and drinking, chattering with each other, but the King was strangely silent, brooding.

'Sire,' said Henri, 'I understand that you desire my counsel . . .'

'Ah, there you are, d'Erloncourt. You've been up at the valley and seen the situation for yourself?'

'Yes, sire. It is most regrettable. The French Brigade has as yet been unable to attack them and drive them back into the Boyne. Most unfortunate.'

'So General Lauzun has informed me. Although I do not quite see why – with a little honest pluck and fortitude – the valley could not be traversed.'

'The men and horses would be bogged down in the valley for too long, sire,' said Henri. 'Perhaps an hour or two. They would be at the mercy of the English troops above them. They would be needlessly slaughtered.'

'That is what Lauzun said, too.'

A mud-spattered officer approached the table, he offered the King a scrap of paper. James read it and his already ghost-white face seemed to grow almost translucent. He threw the paper angrily aside and once more peered at the map. Tracing the Roughgrange valley with his finger, his hand stopped at a large area of bog, and looped further south.

'Fresh news, sire?' said Henri.

'It appears Colonel Sarsfield is of the same mind as you,' said the King without looking up. 'Apparently even the enemy general agrees. Indeed Sarsfield reports that they are forming up their columns and moving off. Trying to get round, by the road here . . .' He tapped the map a few miles to the south.

Another officer, a colonel but equally besmirched as the first aide, approached the table. He whispered in the King's ear. The King stared at him, aghast. Now there were suddenly many more men in the kitchen. Henri was jostled by a captain with a bloody bandage on his arm. The noise suddenly swelled to a hubbub, a dozen men speaking at once. Some were arguing.

'Silence, I will have silence,' roared James. 'You, sir, over there by the door, I will have your report now, if you please.'

Henri recognised a grey-haired, middle-aged major from the Earl of Antrim's Regiment of Foot. He looked utterly exhausted.

'I bear bad news, sire,' the major said. 'The enemy have crossed the Boyne at Oldbridge and have consolidated their beachhead. The Blue Guards were too strong for us, sire. We were forced to fall back.'

'Tell me you made a counter-attack – surely you came back at them?'

'Yes, sire, we attacked with our foot – all the battalions we had – and the cavalry were magnificent. They made a dozen charges. But we could not hold.'

'I see. And now – tell me, sir. What is the situation now?'

'The enemy have made four separate successful river crossings, sire: the Blue Guard still hold Oldbridge; at Grove Island ten English battalions have crossed over to the south bank; the Danish cavalry came over at Yellow Island in vast numbers . . .' The major swallowed hard.

'Tell me all of it, sir. I will know the worst.'

The man nodded. 'Yes, sire. Indeed. Further to the east, sire, a little over a mile east from Oldbridge, General Ginkel's cavalry – we think at least five or six regiments – have found a passable ford near the town of Drogheda. They came streaming across and easily brushed aside our mounted picquets. They say Dutch William himself has now come over the river with them. We had to pull back, sire, all along the line. There is now fighting on the slopes of the Hill of Donore and in and around the graveyard of the church on the summit. The Earl of Tyrconnell is still up there, sire, and is holding his own with a mixed force of dismounted cavalry and dragoons, or so it was when he sent me here to you.

But the rest of the army is in retreat. Some of the men are running in fear, sire.'

The King said nothing for a moment. He looked at Henri. His eyes were red and moist. The Frenchman was forced to drop his gaze. 'And I am here,' said James, sighing heavily, 'a full four miles south-west from the main attack, with sixteen thousand men who can do nothing but shake their fists impotently at a smaller enemy force on the far side of an impassable valley.'

Bulling his way forward through the crush was General Lauzun, looking red-faced, hot and angry. The noise in the farmhouse kitchen had dropped to a few guilty whispers. Every man was straining to hear the King's next words.

'I came here on your advice, Monsieur d'Erloncourt. You told me that William was planning an assault on my flank. What would you have me do?'

'The Almighty has not favoured us, sire. The day is clearly theirs. And I am heartily sorry if my best counsel has not served you as well as I would have liked.' Henri tried to sound meek. 'Your safety is paramount, sire, and I believe you must withdraw from the field to fight another day. If you remember the successful strategy of the great Roman General Quintus Fabius Maximus . . .'

'You want me to run away?'

'The Comte d'Erloncourt is quite right.' Lauzun had made it to the King's side, puffing slightly. 'Your safety is the most important thing, sire. I have given orders for General Sarsfield's Horse and Colonel Maxwell's dragoons to escort you to Dublin. The rest of the army must concentrate here at Duleek—' Lauzun put his finger on the map at the village he had named five miles due south of Oldbridge, 'we can regroup and fight them off to give Your Majesty time to get away south. Three roads meet at Duleek, including the road to Dublin, and its bridge is the only crossing of the River Nanny for miles. The enemy must come through there and, if we can hold him till nightfall, we stand a chance of withdrawing in an orderly fashion. Much of the army is still intact, sire, and can be preserved to fight again another day.'

'You say that a large part of my army is intact, Monsieur Lauzun, and what you mean by that is that the French Brigade has not yet fought at all.' James was clearly furious with the general. 'Your men have not fired a single shot this ill-starred day. Very well – it is now time for them to show their courage. I wish you, General Lauzun, and you, Colonel d'Erloncourt, to conduct the rear guard. We shall withdraw to fight another day, yes. I shall return to Dublin. But you two gentlemen will hold the enemy here – at this place, Duleek. That is my command, gentlemen. I should like to see if your Brigade can actually fight.'

It had felt horribly wrong to quit the battlefield in the middle of a fight. But Hogan also knew it would have been the very summit of insanity to remain.

The rampant forces of William of Orange were over the river in three or four places and the Irish defences were shattered along the line and those men still unharmed were running for their lives. King James's redcoats had fought like lions, trying to stem the tide of William's legions coming across the shallow water. But it had been an impossible task and they were beaten.

It was not a pretty sight: terrified men were throwing away their pikes and muskets, their packs and ammunition pouches, even their coats and shoes, to allow them to run faster. They streamed through the open cornfields like panicked deer. Some sought false sanctuary in the old church atop the Hill of Donore, regrouping there under the Duke of Tyrconnell's bullet-torn banners, but most were running due south, unimpeded – but hunted by roaming squadrons of Williamite cavalry – until exhaustion or the jubilant enemy horse claimed them.

'Galloping' Hogan and the rag-tag band of horsemen he had gathered on the slopes below Donore – forty-seven men, his own surviving raparees and the remains of the four squadrons of Tyrconnell's Horse, plus a handful of stragglers from Sutherland's and Parker's regiments – had headed west instead.

Above them on the crest of the hill, the fighting was raging in and around the churchyard, among the very gravestones, and Hogan knew it was only a matter of time before Tyrconnell was overrun or forced to retreat further south. It was time, he decided, to seek out the little Frenchman – to keep his sacred word to him – and finally quit this place of death and horror for good.

Yet finding the left wing of the army had not been easy – the men were exhausted and frightened, their animals streaked with white sweat. At one point they narrowly avoided being trapped between a full regiment of yellow-jacketed Danish curassiers and an advancing column of fresh Brandenburger infantry. They had spurred their tired mounts across two trampled cornfields, leaping the hedges and ditches like reckless fox-hunters, with the sound of Danish trumpets right behind them. But on the western side of the hill they found a sunken road that hid even the tallest riders, and allowed them to follow the course of the river down to Roughgrange unseen.

Only in the large courtyard of the farmyard – surrounded by hundreds of his fellow soldiers, a great many of them officers – did Hogan begin to relax. There was discipline here; there were regiments of Frenchmen formed up in grey-white blocks outside the walls of the farm, and cavalry too. Fresh regiments of horse in bold bright colours, untouched as yet by the blood and filth of battle.

Hogan and his men dismounted and began to care for their mounts, keeping together in a corner by the old brewhouse, where there was a series of butts filled with rainwater. Hogan dug out his mare's nosebag and allowed the old girl to eat properly for the first time that day. He found her brush and worked the worst of the mud from her flanks in slow, steady strokes – loosening the girth but leaving the saddle in place. He had told his men that they must be ready to leave at a moment's notice.

A shadow fell across his horse's neck and he looked up to see Patrick Sarsfield, in brilliant green velvet, looking down at him from the back of a magnificent black stallion.

'Still alive then, Hogan?' Sarsfield said, touching his plumed hat in salute.

'No, not at all. 'Tis a terrible shame, Paddy, but my poor torn body lies yonder by the cursed riverbank with all the others. Dead as a stone. What you see before you is a revenant, just a particularly handsome shade, that's all.'

Sarsfield laughed, a loud explosion of mirth, unworthy of the raparee's feeble joke and in truth no more than an involuntary release of his anxiety.

'What news from the field?' he said finally. 'Is Tyrconnell still fighting?'

'The duke was up there on the hill when I made my departure,' said Hogan. 'By the church. But he won't be there now. Dutch Billy's men were swarming up there, thick as the lice on one of your mistresses, Paddy.'

Sarsfield found this less amusing. 'He'll pull back to Duleek,' he said. 'That's where we are all heading now. You too, Mick, if you've any sense.'

'What has the King in mind?' Hogan asked. 'He's here, I take it?'

'He's here. But I've orders to escort him back to Dublin. Maxwell's coming too, to keep the man safe. We're leaving now – any minute, in fact.'

'So it is finished here? Truly – we are properly beaten?'

'The King is quitting the field. Will you ride along with us then, Mick?'

Before Hogan could answer, he heard a querulous voice call out his name.

'There you are, at last. I've been waiting for you! You've delayed me, sir!'

Henri d'Erloncourt stamped across the courtyard, looking furious.

'I believe my instructions were perfectly clear. Well, you're here now. We must make the best of it. We ride in ten minutes, Captain Hogan, ten minutes! You will escort the guns and myself to Duleek. Be sure your men are ready.'

Hogan caught Sarsfield's eye. The Irish general grinned.

'Luck to you, Mick,' Sarsfield said.

'And to you, Paddy,' said Hogan with a heavy sigh. 'And to you.'

Chapter Eighteen

The same day: 4 p.m.

Holcroft Blood put his shoulder to the wheel and heaved. The four-wheeled ammunition wagon was stuck fast, the iron rim of the big spoked wheel caught between vice-like stones in the riverbed. He was no weakling but he couldn't budge it an inch. The cold brown water of the Boyne came up to his thighs, and two paces away he could see the corpse of a Blue Guard, completely submerged, entangled in a tree root and staring blank-eyed up into eternity.

'Get Joe Cully down here, Sergeant, right now – and half a dozen of the men. They can leave their muskets and kit on the riverbank. Lively now!'

The two cannon that Holcroft had brought down from the artillery park behind the crest of the hill – a light three-pounder Falcon and Roaring Meg – and their teams of horses and men were safe and dry on the south bank. But the ammunition wagon, without which the two small cannon were no more than useless metal tubes, was stuck fast. The driver, enthusiastically whipping the six-horse team across the river had, it seemed, driven the wheel into a deep crevice on the stony riverbed.

After hauling fruitlessly for several minutes, with Holcroft and several other private soldiers of the fourth company of Tiffin's Foot giving their aid, Joe Cully had dropped face down in the water and levered a huge boulder out of the riverbed by main strength, freeing the wheel at last. The wagon's horses had responded to the driver's calls immediately and a few moments later the heavy ammunition cart – its vital contents mercifully dry – was creaking and groaning up on to the bank, then trundling south after the two cannon teams.

As Holcroft stepped out on to the muddy turf, and accepted the reins of Nut from Sergeant Hawkins, he saw a red-coated galloper approaching along the riverbank, a captain he recognised from the council at Mellifont Abbey.

'What news of the enemy, sir?' Holcroft called out, as the man spurred his horse into the water. The rider reined in, and glancing round at the wagon and the guns, said: 'The enemy is on the run, sir. He is soundly beaten. But I have grave news, sir, grave news indeed for the Ordnance. General Schomberg is dead. He fell a mile yonder in the mêlée, pistolled by an Irish blackguard.'

The man spurred away across the water and Holcroft digested his news. He felt – nothing. The Duke of Schomberg was dead. The man who had expelled him from the Ordnance was no more. Holcroft had not wished him dead. But neither did he mourn his passing with much grief. *Rest in peace.*

Now that Holcroft was on the battlefield itself, rather than observing it from the heights above, the terrible intimacy of war was apparent. The torn corpses, redcoat and Blue Guard, were curled together in death like lovers, piled in rag-doll heaps. And even though the surviving Dutch troops were briskly clearing away the debris of war, as the small train progressed through the ruined village of Oldbridge, Holcroft and his men were constantly having to shift the bodies of the slain out of the path of their big, slow-churning, iron-shod wheels.

Beyond the immediate battle zone in the village, the trampled cornfield behind was littered not so much with dead men and horses, as with the belongings of those who had fled. The cumbersome matchlock muskets – which the majority of the Irish troops had been issued with – were the first things they had discarded in flight, along with their bandoleers of dangling wooden charge-holders, and their bullet pouches. Not all had made it. As the small gun train rumbled along, heading south along a track around the eastern flanks of the Hill of Donore, they passed the remains of men who had fallen foul of the cavalry, usually marked with hideous wounds to the face and neck, great crimson slashes, some half severing the head from the body. And there were plenty of wounded enemy too. Piteous men crawling and mewling their pain, some lacking limbs, or blind, gore-streaked and desperate.

Holcroft and his men ignored their heart-rending calls for water – or occasionally for the mercy of a bullet – and kept their course. He knew his duty – and it was not to succour the enemy wounded. The battle was not ended.

He had made this point forcefully to Jacob Richards, before receiving his blessing to take the two guns, the ammunition wagon and the whole fourth company out into the field. The foe had been pushed back but Holcroft knew from his maps that they must cross the narrow bridge at Duleek. That is where they would find the enemy – and his duty, he told Richards, was to bring his two cannon into action as swiftly as possible, to aid the other branches of the Army as best they could in crushing the enemy.

There was more to his urgency than Holcroft had admitted to the First Engineer. He had not lied to Richards, but neither had he been entirely truthful. In the back of Holcroft's mind was a secret desire, irrespective of his ostensible duty to aid his comrades. Narrey – he wanted to get close to Narrey.

Yet where was the French murderer hiding among all this bloody chaos? Had he fled at the first reverse of the battle? Was he out there somewhere among the wounded and the dead? Holcroft had seen no Frenchmen in white uniforms lying among the corpses – nor a slight, ginger-haired figure in black curled among the crushed wheat stalks. Was Narrey even now with the retreating Irish Army, flooding towards the river crossing at Duleek, where they might be forced to turn and stand and fight again? Where Holcroft might have his chance? By God, he hoped so.

They saw several units of cavalry in the distance, galloping across their line of march, but Holcroft had no idea whether they were

friend or foe. They were moving slowly, at the pace of the Inniskillinger infantrymen who marched in two files of thirty men each on
either side of the little train. After an hour they were on the eastern
slopes of the Hill of Donore, and above him, to the right, Holcroft
could see the church burning beneath a thick column of smoke
and groups of redcoats sitting on the slopes, peacefully eating and
drinking, sleeping, or tending their wounds. Donore belonged to
King William now.

They came past a stately old mansion, with a large walled garden
where there had recently been a cavalry fight. There were several
dead horses on the grass, dead men, too, and patches of fresh blood,
scarlet on the mown green grass, puddling in the deep hoofprints.

A mounted Inniskillinger corporal – a neighbour of Sergeant
Hawkins, of all strange coincidences – told them that this was Platin
Hall, and the Jacobites had waited for their pursuers, attacked and
fought them to a standstill, killing a dozen of his comrades and
scattering his squadron. The enemy still had teeth, Holcroft noted.
The Ulster corporal directed them to a cart track, half a mile to the
east of the hall, which slanted down towards the town of Duleek.

Another half hour and even on this established path through
the fields the ground was becoming treacherous and boggy, as
they came into the flood plain of the River Nanny. Roaring Meg,
drawn by six horses at the head of the train, became stuck, and she
needed to be lifted bodily by a dozen strong matrosses to higher,
drier ground beside the track. Holcroft, up on the bank, waiting for
the gun to be hauled from the mire, could see the dark mass of the
enemy troops a mile ahead just by sitting up straight in his saddle.

Half a dozen muddy horsemen came clattering up the track
towards them from the direction of Duleek – all wore red coats but
which side did they favour? Holcroft put his hand on the butt of
the Lorenzoni pistol that was shoved in his officer's sash. He heard
Sergeant Hawkins bark the order for the company to form a triple
line across the track, swiftly obeyed. With a small part of his mind

that was not fixed on the oncoming cavalry force, Holcroft was gratified to see the Tiffin's men taking their places smoothly and without fuss. They had not forgotten their parade-ground drill while he had been away.

Lieutenant Francis Waters, his voice booming with new authority, gave the order for the company to present their muskets, and sixty-two barrels swung up into place as one. A single volley from their massed ranks would have wiped these horsemen – only forty paces away – clean off the face of the Earth.

'Stand down, the fourth,' said Holcroft. 'At ease, men.'

He recognised the leading rider. It was Brigadier William Wolseley, his old commander in Inniskilling.

'Good day, Brevet Major Blood,' said Wolseley, reining in a few yards for the first rank of muskets. 'You've brought me some cannon. Good man!'

'It's Captain Blood again, sir, since I rejoined His Majesty's Ordnance.'

'Looks to me as if you are now in command of the famous fourth company of Tiffin's Foot. Finest company in one of my finest regiments. That would make you still a brevet major, to my mind. But I'll call you captain, if you wish. Good to see you alive after that fearful wound you took at Cavan.'

'Likewise, sir,' said Holcroft, and he found it was true. The beaming men of the fourth were also pleased to see their old commander unharmed.

The pleasantries concluded, Brigadier Wolseley proceeded to outline the situation. Both Holcroft and he urged their horses on to the bank and while Holcroft took out his brass telescope to make his observations, Wolseley pointed out the deployments of the enemy with his drawn sword blade.

'The rearguard are French,' he said. 'Four battalions. About a couple of thousand men, I'd say, drawn from General Lauzun's Brigade.'

Holcroft examined the blocks of white-clad troops, drawn up in four groups under their French banners on the north bank of the River Nanny about half a mile away. Between each white-grey rectangle of musket men, Holcroft could see the shapes of wheels and the bronze barrels of guns, a pair of small cannon, three pounders by the look of them, between each battalion. Six pieces in all. There were groups of horsemen, too, on the flanks of the infantry. A sensible formation. The taller houses and a church spire of the town of Duleek could be made out a hundred yards or so behind, and to the right of the French position. Holcroft could make out the two low stone walls of the old bridge over the river, which was packed with jostling men and horses, struggling to get over the water and into the town and to make their way south to safety. Hundreds more, a vast multi-coloured crowd, were pushing forward urgently trying to get on to the bridge. This was the bottleneck.

'The ground makes it very difficult for us to attack,' said Wolseley. 'My troops are almost entirely cavalry and they can't gallop well over this soggy, treacherous ground. Worse than that, the horses won't charge home into well-formed infantry. Certainly not infantry of the quality of the French Brigade. On the approach we would be mauled by their volleys; when we got close the horses would shy away from their bayonets. Those damned cannon batteries between the battalions would also cause havoc in our attacking squadrons.'

'Where are our infantry?' asked Holcroft.

'Oh, they are coming up, fast as they can. King William is leading them himself, or so I'm told. But they are not here *now* and every minute we wait allows more of them to escape across the bridge. The Jacobite army will soon slip away, if we're not careful and then this whole bloody mess will have to be fought all over again. And there hasn't been a thing I can do about it – until now.'

Holcroft was only half listening to Wolseley. He was scanning the three batteries of light artillery between the French battalions, looking at the faces of the gunners and their officers.

'I said . . . until now, Captain Blood. You understand me?'

'You wish me to bombard the French infantry, sir?'

'I want you to soften them up so I can get my cavalry in amongst them. I would also like you to take out some of their gun batteries, if you can. I know you've only two small pieces but anything you do to weaken them will help.'

Holcroft nodded. 'Yes, sir,' he said. 'It would be my pleasure, sir.'

His glass was still scanning the faces of the men in the enemy batteries – and *there!* There was one he knew. In the central battery, the one nearest the Duleek bridge. It was Major Guillaume du Clos, late of his Most Christian Majesty's *Corps Royal d'Artillerie*. Narrey's henchman. And, in a time of battle, Du Clos was sure to be close to his master.

Holcroft took the glass from his eye. He saluted Wolseley, and said: 'We will set up on that patch of ground over there, sir, and begin as soon as we can.'

He pointed to a slightly higher, flattish area of grass a dozen yards from the road and about four hundred yards from the French left flank.

'I can give you an hour, Captain, to wreak as much damage as you can,' said Wolseley. 'Then I must send in my cavalry.'

The cannon ball screamed into the battery, clanging against the iron rim and exploding the big wooden spoked wheel in a thousand spinning shards, before skipping away behind the lines and splashing into the River Nanny. Major Guillaume du Clos took an involuntary leap backwards. He was no coward but three pounds of hot iron smashing into a bronze cannon beside your knee can have that effect on even the bravest souls.

Du Clos took command of himself. One of the matrosses was down, his face torn apart by wooden splinters, and he was blubbering through the gore, probably dying. The cannon barrel was leaning drunkenly off the side of the carriage, the barrel pointing at the turf.

The gun would not fire again – not unless a spare wheel was brought up and a competent carpenter found with the right tools to re-attach it. And that would not happen this day – the artillery equipment, all but a few dozen balls and a couple of barrels of powder and necessities, was far to the south by now on the road back to Dublin. They had what they had here and no more.

The second cannon in the central battery – a three-pounder stationed a dozen yards from where he stood, and unharmed by the disastrous strike on its sister piece – was about to fire. Du Clos listened to the master gunner give the time-honoured commands. The crew stepped back, the match was brought forward, smouldering on its long pole. He covered his ears; the match touched the vent and the gun belched fire, rocking backwards on its wheeled carriage.

He watched the flight of the ball – a faint streak of grey across the clear blue sky – and saw it bounce once on the spongy turf, twenty yards wide of the enemy battery – *his* God-damned battery, Blood's battery – spraying a rainbow of water, leaping away like a salmon and harming no one.

'Can none of you useless bastards shoot straight?' he growled.

The captain of the remaining gun, a veteran called Matthieu who was well into his sixth decade, wore a thick red woollen cap pulled low over his ears. He was, anyway, about three parts deaf after years of firing off his guns and gave no sign of having heard Du Clos' insult. Guillaume was certain that the man had noted his slur but had not deigned . . . *oh, so what? What did it matter?* Matthieu might be a veteran gunner but he was still a poor marksman, and indeed, an incompetent old fool. Guillaume considered taking over the gun himself. He was certain he could do better. But, no. His duty lay elsewhere.

The matrosse with the torn-up face was screaming like a soul in torment – which he would no doubt soon be – and his comrades were vainly trying to comfort him and keep him quiet, giving him cold water and soft words. The noise was deeply irritating. Why did they not cut his throat and be done with it?

Major du Clos walked away from the battery, heading for his horse which was tied up to an alder bush twenty yards behind the last line of French musketeers in the neighbouring battalion. He left the battery without a word – what was there to say? They knew their duty. It was a pity they could not seem to accomplish it. He would seek out the Comte. There was only one surefire way of killing this pestilential English gunner – and that was with pistol or sword. This time he would run him through the heart, make sure he was dead.

Major du Clos had been surprised to see, when he took out his glass half an hour ago, that the English officer commanding the two-gun enemy battery that had suddenly popped up on that grassy hillock a quarter of a mile away was in fact Captain Holcroft Blood. Alive. He felt sure that he had put a bullet through his head at Cavan – but he'd not checked to see he was dead. There had been enemies all around, savage Ulstermen in grey with a feral bloodlust in their eyes, and he had been forced to flee with the rest of the Duke of Berwick's men.

Perhaps the Englishman was protected by some dark witchcraft – he could easily believe it. He was a Protestant, after all, and therefore a damned heretic, which meant he was already halfway in league with the Devil. He would make sure of the man today. Blood had troubled his master for long enough.

As he reached for his horse's reins, he could hear the gun captain Matthieu going through the litany of reloading his piece, sponging out the barrel, recharging it with powder and ball – and then there was a far-off boom and gigantic clang, like a giant bell tolling the hour. He whipped round and saw that the enemy had struck again – so soon! – a direct hit on the half-loaded cannon, the second piece of the battery – smashing the long bronze barrel off its carriage. The gun crew were scattered away, bleeding, staggering, some lying dead or stunned. The screaming started . . .

As he climbed into the saddle, he reflected that the man Blood might be a heretic but by God he could shoot! That battery had been fired at only four times in the space of fifteen minutes and already it was destroyed. He kicked his horse into a canter. Enough.

Holcroft was pleased with his gun crews. In no more than twenty-five minutes of hot work by his watch, they had put the two nearest batteries out of action – one in which he was sure he had seen Major du Clos directing the fire.

'Concentrate your fire on the French battalions now, Enoch,' he said to the ancient captain of the equally ancient Roaring Meg. 'You take the one on the extreme right, I'll take the one inside that. Let's see if we can't knock some of the impudence out of them before Wolseley sends in his horse.'

'Very good, sir,' said Enoch Jackson. 'As the Good Book says: "We shall execute vengeance upon the heathen, and punishments upon the people".'

Holcroft's mind went blank. *Was that Genesis? No, it was . . . I have no idea. God, was this small memory loss the first sign of age?* He played for time: 'I'm not sure the French count as heathens,' he said. 'But punish 'em anyway.'

Jackson frowned at him. 'You've forgotten it, sir?'

And then it came back to him – and with it a huge flood of relief. 'Of course not, Enoch, how could I forget: Psalms chapter 149, verse seven!'

Jackson nodded and turned back to the crew. 'You heard the Captain, get the piece shifted. Jones, bring up that barrel, lively now . . .'

The two guns were nicely warmed by now and the crews served them with a brisk efficiency that came of months, indeed years, of practising together. With the closest enemy guns out of action, they no longer faced the hazard of enemy counter-battery fire. The furthest two guns were partly screened by the French infantry formations, which were standing, the men in white uniforms still as statues in their ranks and files under their flapping banners. This last battery was about eight hundred yards away, and while easily within range of Holcroft's guns, they were a more difficult target. The Ordnance officer's reasoning was that he would do Wolseley a greater service if he could smash the structure of the battalions in front of him, and in front of the bridge, and allow his cavalry to ride through their ranks, slaughtering at will.

Skill, enthusiasm and long familiarity allowed Holcroft's crews to fire their two light cannon every five minutes – an unusually swift rate of fire. The balls crashed into the standing lines of Frenchmen, ploughing through the ranks and doing the most appalling destruction. A single cannon ball bouncing through a formed battalion could kill three or four men and wound half a dozen others.

The Frenchmen stood and took their punishment. Bodies crushed, bones cracked, limbs ripped off by the flying balls. With every belch of the two English guns, blood sprayed in the French battalions and men were tumbled away. The lines began to waver; the sergeants shouting to restore order found their task ever more difficult. Another cannon shot would carve a bloody furrow through the mass of white-clad men, and another, and yet another. In short order, the crisp precision of the blocks of infantry turned into chaos.

The French were becoming a rabble.

'Advance the sponge,' said Holcroft for the seventh or eighth time in the past three quarters of an hour. He was blackened by smoke and was partially deafened by the roar of his Falcon, and the accompanying thunder of the Saker ten yards away. 'Sponge the piece now . . .'

'Sir, look yonder,' said Lieutenant Waters. He was tugging at Holcroft's sleeve and pointing to the right-hand side of the western-most battalion.

Holcroft looked up from the hot barrel of the Falcon and over in the direction the officer was pointing. He saw a small body of horse emerging from behind the shattered mass of the French battalion. They were an irregular formation – that was clear from the variety of uniform colours and styles – but no less a formidable one for it. They walked their mounts out from behind the block of infantry and began to order themselves in ranks and files with two men out in front of the others, seemingly the officers or leaders. One of them, a middle-aged man in a muddy green coat, seemed vaguely familiar; he was hatless with long iron-grey hair tied at the back and a drawn sword in his right hand. The other, Holcroft was certain, was Major Guillaume du Clos.

'Thank you, Francis,' he said. 'You know what to do, don't you?' The younger man nodded. Holcroft looked across at the other gun, which had just been noisily discharged. He yelled: 'Enoch Jackson – do you hear me, you deaf old rascal? Break out the cases of "partridge". Prepare to receive cavalry!'

The company of cavalry, some forty horsemen – Holcroft could now count them individually, when he looked up from his frantic work – advanced across the four hundred yards between the French flank battalion and the hillock with a deliberate slowness. They began at a walk, the squadron coming forward in three lines of a dozen or so men and then, at two hundred yards, they came up to a trot. Holcroft finished priming the vent, a delicate job with the powder horn, and looked up, straightening his back. He wiped the sweat from his face with the back of his hand. And then checked that the Lorenzoni pistol was still in the sash, and that his officers' small sword was by his side.

He glanced at Enoch Jackson, who was scowling along the barrel of Roaring Meg at the approaching enemy. They were a hundred yards away now and coming on at a stately trot. It was a rather magnificent sight, Holcroft thought: the perfect lines of horsemen bobbing slowly towards them. If they were not intent on slaughtering every one of the dozen English gunners toiling on that hillock, Holcroft might even have rather enjoyed the spectacle.

He searched his feelings for a moment. There was fear there, certainly. Death was no more than seventy yards away. But he was aware also of a calm acceptance of whatever fate God had in store for him. If he was to die, this day, so be it.

The cavalry came up into a canter. Holcroft could feel the ground shaking under the hooves of the horses, a tremor vibrating his own boot soles.

'Tend the match,' he said, casually over his shoulder.

The lines of horsemen were no more than fifty yards away – and they were spreading out, putting an extra yard between each rider and the next, coming on in open order, it was called. And finally, at no more than thirty yards distance, they came up to the full gallop. Holcroft could see the individual faces of the men, some scared, some ferocious, some merely concentrating hard on their riding. The grey haired man in the muddy green coat, stood in the saddle, waved his sword and shouted: 'Charge, my lads. Charge for Ireland and honour. *Charge!*'

Chapter Nineteen

The same day: 6 p.m.

One more attack, that's what the Frenchman had said. One more bit of reckless devilry – then he could take his remaining men to the crush around the bridge, push their way to the other side and gallop south for Dublin and safety.

Hogan could see why they wanted him to do it. The cannon on the grassy hillock were playing merry Hell with the infantry battalions of the rearguard. The two pieces were manned by magicians – or so it seemed to Hogan, who had little experience of field artillery – and they were killing the Frenchmen with a steady, methodical, machine-like horror. Hogan did not know how the men in the battered, bloody French formations could stand it. Perhaps a quarter of them in the nearest battalion must be dead or wounded, and yet they did not move – well, not all that much. There was a certain amount of swaying, and cringing away from the first line and the regular smash of those cannon balls. The sergeants were hauling away the dead and wounded and the others shuffled into their comrades' former positions; so yes, there was a little movement. But they had not run away. And that was a marvel to Michael 'Galloping' Hogan.

To stand tall and stare as enemy cannon pumped ball after lethal ball into their ranks: that took courage; it took discipline. It was partly respect for the infantry's steadiness that had made him agree to make this one last charge – that, and the identity of the man who commanded the English battery.

'He is right *there*!' the Comte d'Erloncourt had said loudly, pointing. 'The man I told you about in Longford, at the Bull. Captain

Holcroft Blood. The tall man on the right with the blue coat and red sash. Go, sir, and kill him. Major du Clos will ride along with you, to offer his strong right arm in aid. And the price has gone up, sir. I will pay you a hundred pounds in gold for his head. Do you hear me, Mister Hogan? One hundred pounds in *louis d'or*! How does that sound?'

Hogan had heard him. It sounded good. Worth the hazard, he thought, to himself and to his men. They would doubtless fire a dangerous cannon ball or two at him as he attacked. But he could see only a dozen enemy on the hillock, barely armed except with their big cannon, a sword or two, maybe a pistol between the lot of them. Beyond them was long grass and scrubby bush, a munitions wagon and all the draught horses tethered at their lines. The danger was minimal. And if Hogan's men went in fast, in open order, the risk would be acceptable. One or two of his men would not outlive the day – but this was war. And he would compensate the widows or sweethearts of the fallen well from the great hoard of golden French coins that would shortly be in his possession.

The enemy were thirty yards away now, and Hogan rose in his stirrups and shouted: 'Charge, my lads. Charge for Ireland and honour. *Charge!*'

The gun on the right, the smaller one, roared and a blast of 'partridge' – a thin metal canister packed with several hundred musket balls – exploded outwards in a vast cone of flame and fury. Hogan felt the hot wind of it on his cheek. He snatched a look round and was astounded to see that a massive hole had been punched into the centre of his galloping men. Three horses were down, kicking on the turf and four men too, bleeding, and sprawled like babies.

Ten yards to go and the second cannon fired. Another huge blast of noise and almost the whole remaining front line of Hogan's company were wiped from the Earth – five, six men snatched away in an instant. Like magic.

But the rest of Hogan's men were within spitting distance of the gunners and their now empty cannon. The tall officer in the blue coat stared coldly at Hogan, as if he was some guttersnipe who had gatecrashed a society ball. He pointed his peculiar pistol at the raparee captain, aimed and pulled the trigger.

At the last moment, Hogan hunched down behind his horse's head and the bullet slapped into the white blaze on the old mare's forehead, killing her instantly. Her legs faltered on the slope of the hillock, she collapsed in a heap and Hogan was hurled head over heels, up in the air, up, up, and came crashing down a yard or two on the far side of the Falcon. He lay there like an upturned beetle, all the living breath knocked out of him, unable to move.

The tall officer seemed to have forgotten him as he pistolled a charging raparee through the chest – Liam Fitzwilliam, a good man, if a little fond of the drink – and when the rider, mortally wounded but still in the saddle, slashed at him with his sabre, the officer shot the top of poor Liam's head clean off.

The company was all about the hillock now, shooting down gunners, swiping at those who tried to hide under the guns. Hogan saw Major du Clos skewer an old man, bald as an egg, with his sword. He leant down from the back of his horse and punched the blade through the old fella's ribs. The man Blood stood tall, indifferent to the horses and screaming men that flashed by on either side, felling Hogan's comrades with cool and carefully aimed shots of that strange pistol of his, which never seemed to need reloading.

And then, a wall of grey rose up on one side of him. God's blood – English soldiers, formed infantry. Where the Hell had they come from?

A fat little sergeant shouted a command, and a volley lanced out, thirty jets of smoke, and half a dozen saddles were emptied. And there were more on the other side, now. More of these damned grey-clad infantry, lined up, muskets levelled. Must have been hidden, crouching down in the long grass, or lying flat till the attack came in. Sneaky bastards. They were the same ones he had fought – fought? – been massacred by in that God-damned winter ambush. Inniskillingers. He was sure of it. Same officer, same first-class troops. Another crashing volley, and his poor men were decimated yet again. Hogan forced himself up on an elbow. His body throbbed. He levered himself to his feet.

He picked up his cutlass from the turf a yard away.

Another volley crashed out. More of his men were swept screaming from their saddles. A severed hand thumped to the ground near his boot. The fingers twitched once and were still. The tall officer pistolled a wounded raparee who was limping bloody-faced from the hillock. Shot him through the back.

Hogan screamed a war cry. He raised his sword, determined to make the Englishman pay for his foul murder. Blood turned. Faster than thought, he pointed the pistol, pulled the trigger – and nothing. Perhaps the damn machine was finally empty. Hogan struck at the man's head, a hard overhand blow that would have split his skull had it landed. Blood blocked it with an upward sweep of his empty pistol. The clang of steel on steel, as the octagonal barrel met Hogan's plunging cutlass blade, sent a shock all the way up his right arm.

Hogan swung again, slashing for the head once more. The man ducked under the blow, struggling to pull his own small-sword out of the scabbard.

'I'll have your fucking head, laddie,' Hogan snarled. 'The most expensive nob in all of God's green Ireland. I'll claim my prize yet, ye English bastard.'

He hacked with the cutlass, but the Englishman easily blocked with his blade. Blood lunged swiftly, and nearly spiked Hogan's forward leg. The Irishman retracted his front foot just in time. They exchanged two more passes, the steel clashed, sparks flew, Hogan felt the sweat start all over his body – the Englishman could fence, he had to give the bastard that. And with every grunt and swipe of the heavy blade, Hogan knew his time was running out. The grey-clad Inniskillinger infantry were reloading their flintlocks – in a few seconds one of them – Hell, maybe all of 'em – would shoot him down like a rabid dog.

His own men, mauled and shocked, were in full retreat, some still a-horse, most not, though, just running across the body-strewn meadow. He was almost the last man on that blood-smeared hillock who did not own Dutch Billy as rightful King of Ireland. The Englishman stabbed at his body, a lightning fast lunge that nearly skewered him. At the last moment he got his cutlass down and across, pushing the small-sword wide of his waist. Hogan saw a loose mount nearby, yards from the larger of the two cannon, a grey gelding with the reins trailing, and knew he must take his chance. Or he would never leave this field.

He screamed and hurled himself at Blood, his sword slicing and hacking the air near his face; the big man turned and slipped under the assault, and Hogan, driven on by his own momentum, allowed himself to plunge past the man and down the hillock at a full run, his left arm reaching for the reins of the horse just beyond. In two seconds he was in the saddle and spurring like a highwayman. A volley of musket shots behind him. He felt the urgent pluck of a bullet at his sleeve. But he was thirty yards away, forty, galloping for his life.

Holcroft leant forward with his hands on his knees, gasping for breath. That last bastard – the long-haired man with the heavy cutlass – had nearly had him. He lifted his eyes and saw that the man was already halfway back to the French lines on the grey and riding like a centaur. That had been close – Lieutenant Waters had been slow to bring up his company from the long grass. The cavalry had been all over them when the musket volleys began. Perhaps he had been waiting till the enemy were fully committed. Whatever the reason – he'd joined the fight too late. But there was no use in recriminations. Holcroft was alive – and unwounded. And the enemy had been driven off. He decided to say nothing to young Francis Waters but some vague words of congratulation.

A movement on the far left caught his eye. It was Wolseley and his cavalry force advancing diagonally across the field against the cannon-shattered battalions by the bridge. Holcroft watched in admiration as the perfect lines of red-coated horsemen came on, swords drawn and glittering in the sunlight.

They came up to the trot, their dressing immaculate. Two regiments of five hundred horsemen, each regiment advancing in three lines. At a hundred yards out they came up to the canter – and Holcroft could see the nearest French battalion already crumbling as if under some invisible pressure. The men in the front ranks were trying to squirm back into the mass of their fellows; the men at the back were dropping muskets, shedding packs and streaming away towards the Nanny. Forty yards out, the lead regiment moved up into the gallop – five hundred swords raised, pointed ahead of their mounts' heads like steel lances.

They struck. The first wave of horsemen crashed into the battalion and drove deep into its moving heart. The English cavalry were now riding in the centre of the mass of Frenchmen, slashing with their sabres, hacking down the footmen, droplets of blood flying from their long, curved blades. The second wave followed after them, and then the third came crashing in on their heels – a few muskets were fired off by the terrified foot men. A feeble token defence from a broken and doomed formation. Mostly they ran for their lives.

The battalion became a mob. A mass of panicked individuals streaming south towards the riverbanks. And the horsemen came after them, riding them down, overtaking and hacking backwards at their faces as they passed. Others shot down the running Frenchmen with their carbines or pistols. It was carnage, a horrible blood-soaked shambolic massacre of a helpless foe.

Holcroft tore his eyes way from the destruction of the French. He reached into his coat pocket and pulled out his telescope. Ignoring the one-sided cavalry action on the banks of the Nanny, he focused on the bridge, north of the town of Duleek. Strangely the crush seemed to have lessened – perhaps with the collapse of the French rearguard, many of the folk trying to cross had decided, in desperation, to chance swimming over the Nanny instead.

But *they* were there. A few yards from the north entrance to the stone bridge, hemmed in on all sides by a pack of men and horses. Henri, Comte d'Erloncourt and his henchman Major Guillaume du Clos. Just five hundred yards from where Holcroft was standing. Here was his chance – here it was.

'Enoch!' he shouted across to the Saker. He could see Jackson slumped in exhaustion over the barrel of Roaring Meg, almost seeming to cuddle the old bronze cannon. 'Wake up, man; it's no time for a nap. We're all bone tired.'

Enoch Jackson did not move. And Holcroft felt a cold hand close around his heart. 'He's dead, sir, I'm afraid,' said a voice from behind him.

Holcroft turned and saw Lieutenant Waters standing looking forlorn. 'All of Roaring Meg's gunners are dead, sir. They died trying to protect her.'

Holcroft stared at him. He could feel the grief slowly welling up inside his chest, sour and hot – but this was not the time for the luxury of tears.

'Help me, Francis. Help me now. My enemy – the Frenchman I told you about is on the bridge. He will cross very soon.'

Holcroft turned to two unhurt men standing dumbly beside the Falcon. 'Hodges, Jones, get this gun sponged and reloaded. Now, on the double. Francis, bring up two or three balls from the munitions wagon. Three-pound balls. Bonner, go with him. Quick now. Quick as you can.'

Holcroft turned and examined the bridge with his glass. *Five hundred yards, maybe a shade more. Enoch would know.* He gave a little gasp of grief. Pushed down hard on his heart. *Concentrate. So . . . five hundred and ten yards.*

The Falcon was slowly being reloaded. The men awkward and clumsy. The bloody battle for the hillock seemed to have made them unusually stupid.

He looked again – and saw that the two Frenchmen were pushing their way on to the bridge. He had no time, no time at all.

'Hurry, for God's sake, hurry.'

Francis Waters came lumbering up with a three-pound cannon ball. John Hodges was ramming a charge of powder into the Falcon's barrel.

Holcroft crouched behind the gun, he sighted along the barrel. 'A shade to the left, I think. Bonner, pass me the handspike.'

A little more elevation was needed, too. Holcroft seized a quoin from the rack, a wedge-shaped piece of wood; he examined it, tossed it angrily aside and selected another, smaller one. He tapped it into the gap between the gun carriage and the barrel of the Falcon with a wooden mallet, tapped it in a little further, raising the angle of the gun a fraction. *Yes, that should do it. God, why did you take Enoch from me? Why? I need him now more than ever.*

Finally it was ready. Holcroft looked one last time down the barrel.

He stepped back, put the telescope to his eye. 'Hodges – you've got the match? Good. You do it. Stand back, everyone. Have a care. Fire at will, man.'

Holcroft fixed his glass on the bridge. The Frenchmen were the only two mounted men on the stone structure, elevated above the mass of foot traffic. Guillaume du Clos was about two horse-lengths ahead of Henri d'Erloncourt, forcing a way through the crush of bodies, making a path for his master to follow. The major was only a yard or two from the south end of the bridge. In a moment, he and Narrey would be over the river and galloping free. And if that happened then . . .

Holcroft turned angrily; he snapped, 'God damn it, Hodges. Will you—'

With a roaring cough, the Falcon fired. A long plume of smoke jetted from the barrel. Holcroft whipped the glass to his eye and watched as the ball soared high and arced towards the bridge. It came in on a slanting trajectory, missed Henri d'Erloncourt by an arm's length, crashed into the stone wall of the bridge, bounced off and smashed straight into the broad back of Major du Clos. The artilleryman was snatched from the saddle of his horse by the cannon ball as if he had never been there at all. The horse went wild: bucking, kicking. The folk on foot scattered, some leaping over the side of the bridge and into the water below. Through the chaos, Henri d'Erloncourt's mount trotted over the other side and on to the main road. Once there, digging in his spurs, the Frenchman brought his horse briskly up to the canter and swiftly rode away.

Chapter Twenty

Friday, 4 July, 1690: 6 a.m.

There was definitely a symmetry to it, Henri d'Erloncourt thought to himself. Although he could not say it was a very pleasing pattern. King James had landed at this very spot, on this same damp, slimy and fish-stinking quay in the old port of Kinsale in March of the previous year. Henri remembered the occasion well. The King, splendid in purple embroidered with gold and silver threads, his head magnificently bewigged with flowing chestnut curls, his torso adorned with a green silk sash from shoulder to hip, a gold-handled sword at his waist, his fine silver-buckled shoes fashioned from softest lavender kidskin . . .

He had made a speech, saying that as monarch of three lands, the Irish nation were the closest to his heart, their courage and devotion was boundless, as was his love for them and their religion. He claimed this day would go down in history as the first in the glorious struggle for the recovery of his kingdoms.

He was cheered to the rooftops. The whole of Kinsale harbour had echoed with the sound of the local populace huzzah-ing, and calling down God's blessing on their handsome, glorious and rightful prince. They had turned out in hundreds to catch a glimpse of their champion. They had loved him loudly.

How different today was, fifteen months later. There were no more than a handful of curious onlookers – and no one was cheering. They knew James had lost his great battle with the Protestants at the River Boyne and was leaving their shores, most likely for ever. Most of them were scowling or even sneering at the man that Henri had heard being called *Séamus an Chaca* behind his back – which in the Irish language, he had been told, meant James the Shit.

The King was much thinner today, and drab-looking, too. No purple gold-embroidered coat, no green silk sash – just a plain grey riding cloak over his filthy once-white linen shirt. He had ridden exceedingly fast from the battlefield, embarrassingly fast, arriving that same night at the capital, then pausing only for a few hours at Dublin Castle to give orders that the city was to be surrendered without a fight. He had climbed back into the saddle before dawn and ridden south to Waterford with more unseemly haste, where he had taken a small ship along the coast on the short voyage to Kinsale.

The reasons he had come here were clearly visible out in the grey waters of the harbour, where the wide River Bandon debouched into the Irish Sea. The sleek black shapes of ten French frigates riding comfortably at anchor, nearly filling the harbour, which James had commandeered to take him and his depleted entourage back to France. He claimed the rapacious ships of the Royal Navy were lying in wait for him in St George's Channel and only a sizeable French force such as this squadron could return him in safety to the port of Brest.

James was now conferring with General Lauzun, a few last words before his departure; indeed with the crew of the rowing launch that would soon take him to the frigate *Hirondelle* standing by, James was surrounded by Frenchmen.

The man who would be King made no speeches today, not even a brief thank you to the nation that had sacrificed so many of its brave young men in his doomed cause. He simply nodded at the assembled French officers, and the handful of scornful Irish onlookers, and started to climb down the ladder to the launch. The men and women who had come to see the King depart did not tarry either. They began to disperse before James had reached the rowing boat.

Henri turned away, too, and began to walk back along the shore towards the centre of Kinsale. He thought briefly about Guillaume du Clos – what would he have made of today's muted royal departure. *Ah, Guillaume. My friend. My lover. My protector. My strong right hand. Cut down by that snake Holcroft Blood.* There would be a reckoning – Henri promised the soul of his dead friend – a bloody final reckoning with the Englishman. He vowed that he would not leave this damp and dismal country till he had at least achieved that aim. Holcroft Blood must die screaming in agony, paying the price for his crimes . . . He felt a heavy hand on his sleeve, jumped slightly, and turned to see General Lauzun's square, brutal face scowling at him.

'Breakfast with me, d'Erloncourt. I'm at the Market House.'

It was more an order than an invitation.

They ate smoked herring and coddled eggs with toasted bread and butter in a broad room above the courthouse, which looked over a busy market place – the Irish stallholders setting out their wares for the day's trade, seemingly indifferent to the ignominious departure of their rightful sovereign – and they drank a surprisingly good chilled white Burgundy wine with the meal.

'King James will not return to these shores,' said Lauzun, swallowing a mouthful of buttered eggs. 'He might say that he will, but his war is finished.'

'I think you're right,' said Henri. 'But does Louis le Grand know this?'

'He does. Although, of course, His Majesty will not – cannot – admit this to James. But we must now consider what course of action we are to follow in Ireland. If we are to remain here at all. I must confess, my dear d'Erloncourt, that a part of me wishes I too was on the *Hirondelle*, heading back to France.'

Henri said nothing. He finished his glass and poured another for himself and the general. He glanced around the room to see no one was within earshot.

'We shall depart soon enough, my dear Lauzun,' he said quietly. 'You and I and the French Brigade will take a ship and make it safely back to France in due course. But I have a little more work to do before we leave these shores.'

He took a sip of the Burgundy. It was truly excellent. 'My mission, general, has not altered with the departure of James Stuart,' he said. 'Indeed the departure of the would-be King, while unfortunate for his cause, may not be quite so disastrous for ours, I mean, for the cause of His Majesty King Louis.'

'How so?'

'My mission was *not* primarily to put James Stuart on the thrones of the Three Kingdoms. I sought – and still seek – only to advance the interests of La Belle France and of the Sun King himself – as I believe you do too, monsieur.'

'Indeed,' said Lauzun.

'Furthermore, I believe that the interests of France are best served by the war in Ireland continuing for as long as possible. I would even say that the catastrophic defeat at the Boyne may well be a blessing in disguise for us.'

Lauzun frowned at him.

'If James had triumphed in the battle, if let us imagine for a moment he had trounced William at the Boyne and sent him reeling back across the Irish Sea to England – what would he have done next? I suggest to you, sir, that if he managed to evict William and his army from this land, he might well be content to end the war there and then. Make peace; sign a treaty with William. There are many among his closest advisers – General Sarsfield for one, perhaps the Duke of Tyrconnell, too – who might urge him to settle for merely being King of Ireland. He knew in his heart, I think, that he could not rule in England, with most of her nobility, both Houses of Parliament, the Protestant clergy, the squires in the counties, even the common people themselves set against him.'

'You are claiming that defeat for James is somehow a victory for us?'

'A victory for James might have ended the war, my dear general. And then William would be able to concentrate his military power in his homeland, the Netherlands, and bring the troops to bear in the war in the Low Countries. He would bring his considerable might down on the armies of France, which, under the Duc de Luxembourg, are presently engaged against him there. A victory for James here might have been disastrous for us.'

Lauzun took a forkful of smoked fish. He chewed it slowly, then said: 'The Irish Army is largely intact. The Brigade took a pounding at the bridge of Duleek but enough of the men got away to fight again. We could concentrate all our forces, rebuild our battalions and make a lightning march on Dublin . . .'

'No, general, no – if you will forgive me. But that might lead to either a definitive victory or a resounding defeat. I wish for neither. Both would be disastrous for us. I hope for the war in Ireland to continue for years, for decades even, bubbling along like a vast stewpot of hatred and violence, with Catholic killing Protestant and vice versa, and never an end to the bloodshed in sight.'

Lauzun stared at him. 'Perpetual war? Is that even possible?'

'We must emulate the great Roman general Quintus Fabius Maximus.'

'Yes, I believe you may have mentioned him once or twice . . . So your new strategy would be hit-and-run, avoidance of battle at all costs, attacking the enemy lines of communication, swift bandit raids and so on. Is that it?'

'That has always been *my* strategy. King James had other ideas. We must keep the English troops here in Ireland – and the Dutch and the Danes and the Germans, too – for as long as possible. More troops here mean fewer troops available to fight against our forces in the Low Countries. Do you follow me?'

'The Duke of Tyrconnell and the bulk of the Irish Army has pulled back west behind the line of the River Shannon. My Brigade is with them. Tyrconnell holds the city of Limerick. He's determined to defend it to the last.'

'Let him – aid him, even, if you feel so inclined. But I say this: although the Irish Army may have retreated to the west, the war must continue throughout the whole of Ireland. I shall be mobilising all of my resources to gather information about the movements of William's troops all across the land. My spies will watch them constantly, they will pass along the information to our irregular forces – seemingly harmless men and women who hide among the civilian population – then we shall strike them hard when they least expect it.'

Lauzun took a sip of wine and raised an eyebrow at his companion.

'We must quit these shores – you and I and the Brigade – in a short while, *mon général*. But, with a little work, a little gold and a little persuasion before we go, we can ensure that the fighting here continues for years, for decades.'

Lauzun nodded and smiled grimly. 'I must admit it, d'Erloncourt, I am impressed with you. You have given me fresh purpose, sir.' He raised his glass. 'I give you a toast, monsieur, to war without end in Ireland. To perpetual war!'

Henri raised his own glass: 'Perpetual war!'

Part Three

Chapter Twenty-One

Saturday, July 19, 1690

Holcroft tapped the excess ink from his quill and wrote . . .

Whale and Crow Inn,
Dame Street, Dublin
Saturday, July 19th, 1690

Madam,
Of all the qualities that I admire in a woman, and particularly in
a wife, one of the foremost is discretion. However, it has come to my
attention that this most admirable quality appears to be distress-
ingly lacking in your character, since I have heard from numerous
reliable sources of your disgraceful . . .

Holcroft paused to recharge his pen and tried to think of the correct word to use. *Infidelity? Betrayal? Treachery?* None of them
seemed to hit the right note. He looked around the small, wood-
panelled upper room that he had taken at the Whale and Crow
for inspiration, at the small peat fire smouldering in the grate.
This fine new Dublin establishment, conveniently close to the
Castle, was warm and comfortable, the large four-poster bed
soft, and Holcroft – for an extra fee – had arranged to be the
only occupant, yet he could find no rest in its comfort since the
episode at the Ordnance mess two days previously when he had
seen the reflection of Claudius Barden in a mirror making the
sign of the horns behind his back and laughing with one of the
Gentlemen of the Ordnance.

He had rounded on Barden, meaning to call him out, to fight him, for the insult – the sign of the horns, the index finger and little finger of the right hand extended with the two middle ones curled into the palm – was an age-old sign that he was a cuckold. Barden, it seemed clear to Holcroft, was mocking him by suggesting that his wife Elizabeth had been unfaithful to him.

When confronted with his actions, Barden had pretended that he meant no insult – he had even apologised for any offence he might have caused. It was a silly misunderstanding; he said he was recounting to the other officer the events of the siege of Carrickfergus, when the Irish garrison had filled the breach in the town walls with a herd of slaughtered cattle, hence the hand sign to indicate the lead bullock, which had happily galloped away unscathed.

Holcroft had been forced to let it pass – Jacob Richards, the First Engineer and Comptroller of the Train, had been firm that he must accept Barden's explanation and his apology. He had already killed one Ordnance officer in a duel the year before – he would not be forgiven if he dispatched another.

However, Holcroft could not shake off the feeling that everyone in the mess was secretly laughing at him: a most unpleasant sensation. By protesting at Barden's humiliating hand-sign, he had revealed to those who did not already know it – and there were few of those, he suspected – that his Elizabeth had been conducting a very public affair with a handsome young Dutch officer named Markus van Dijk who was stationed in White Hall at Queen Mary's court.

Holcroft had previously turned a blind eye to numerous reports of the pair going out into society together. He had ignored the unpleasant anonymous letter. He was now forced to recognise that even his friend Jack Churchill, Lord Marlborough, had made a passing reference to it in one of his letters. He decided that he must act. And so he had begun this letter that sat before him on the paper-strewn table. One of the most difficult he'd ever had to write.

Dalliance. He decided 'dalliance' was the correct word to use.

I have heard from numerous reliable sources of your disgraceful dulliance with this Captain van Dijk, which news has caused me considerable distress, not to mention a large amount of personal embarrassment and humiliation . . .

He thought for a moment. Did he really want to do this? In a few strokes of his pen he could destroy a bond that had survived for nearly three years. How did he feel about Elizabeth consorting with this lustful young Dutchman? He did not like it, certainly. But he *had* been away a long time. On the other hand, this was not how a wife was supposed to act. She had broken the rules of marriage. And rules were important to Holcroft. There was no question of a divorce: an Act of Parliament would be required to formally end the marriage, and that would be expensive, and worse, would expose him to more public ridicule. No, no divorce. He would simply cast her off. An image leapt into his mind of Barden's gleeful drink-reddened face in the mirror, when he had made the sign of the horns behind his back . . . and Holcroft dipped the quill and wrote.

Accordingly I must ask you to remove your person and all of your possessions from the house we have shared in Mincing Lane. I do not care in the slightest where you go, although I suggest that you return to your father's house and confess to him the sins you have committed that have destroyed my honour.

He dipped the quill again, buoyed up, indeed surprisingly invigorated by a righteous, almost a joyous anger.

I shall not be renewing the lease on the house in Mincing Lane, which falls due at Michaelmas, a few weeks from now, and I shall be sending my agents in London to collect my belongings as soon as possible. I shall also instruct my goldsmith Richard Hoare, at the sign of the Golden Bottle in Cheapside, that you are to receive a sum of one hundred pounds on the first day of January every year — but not another penny. Furthermore, after this missive, I do not intend to communicate with you. Once this campaign is over, and it cannot be very long now, I am considering making Ireland, the land of my forefathers, my permanent home. If, for some unforeseen reason you should wish to contact me, a letter delivered into the hands of Richard Hoare, at the address above, will find me in due course. It is most unlikely, however, that I shall choose to reply.

Yours, etc,

Holcroft Blood.

A part of him knew that he was being unjust, perhaps even a little cruel. But a hundred pounds a year was a reasonable sum for her to live in some comfort. And perhaps this Dutch lothario van Dijk would support her as his official mistress. He shook fine-grained sand over the wet ink from the pewter shaker on the desk and rang the bell to summon the boy, who would take the letter, folded and sealed, to the General Post Office over the river in Fishamble Street.

It should reach Elizabeth at Mincing Lane in three days.

There was a knock at the door, but when Holcroft called 'Come in!' he was surprised to see, rather than the inn's tiny weasel-like errand boy, the lean, elegant, grey-uniformed figure of Francis Waters in the doorway.

'Good evening, Major Blood,' he said.

Major – Holcroft's heart quickened slightly at the sound of his new rank. King William, rejoicing at his victory at the Boyne, had been lavish with his promotions. Holcroft had been recommended for the step by Brigadier Wolseley, who had praised him for his action at the bridge at Duleek, telling the King that without Blood's gunnery, the French Brigade would have been able to escape unscathed. With the Duke of Schomberg dead – and no replacement yet as Master-General of the Ordnance – there had been no one to oppose the move and the ebullient King had been well pleased to raise Holcroft to his majority.

Holcroft was not the only combatant to be so honoured. Jacob Richards now gloried in the appellation Lieutenant-Colonel Richards and Francis Waters was raised to the dizzy heights of captain.

Captain Waters had also been given a new and covert role. He had been seconded from the fourth company of Tiffin's Regiment of Foot and set to work in a secret government department in Dublin Castle. This was also the work of Brigadier Wolseley, whom he had impressed with his hard work in the intelligence outfit that he and Holcroft had set up in Inniskilling. Wolseley had asked if Holcroft wished to join the new Dublin Castle set-up but he had demurred and insisted that he wished to remain with the Board of Ordnance, with his beloved guns. Nevertheless, Francis treated Holcroft as his mentor and was often less than perfectly discreet with him about his work.

'Are you ready, sir?' asked Captain Waters.

'Ready for what?' said Holcroft.

'You surely cannot have forgotten, sir – it is the ball tonight. I said I would come and collect you at six of the clock and that we should go along together.'

The ball. Holcroft had indeed forgotten it. Or perhaps he had deliberately blocked its hideousness from his mind.

The Grand Ball at Dublin Castle, given by the Governor of the City, was to celebrate the victory at the Boyne. King William would be the guest of honour. All those officers who had distinguished themselves at the battle were invited – particularly those who had received a promotion – and were expected to attend.

'It is six now?'

'Yes, indeed.'

'I suppose I had better put on my coat.'

'I think, Major Blood, that you might need a clean shirt and cravat. And perhaps some stockings that aren't spattered with mud. Where's your wig, sir?'

Captain Waters cosseted and bullied Holcroft into decent ball-going attire, placed the barely used wig on his cropped head, followed by his plumed hat, gave his court shoes a wipe with his silk kerchief and pronounced them smart enough to dance in. Then he led Holcroft from the tavern into Dame Street.

Before they left the Whale and Crow, Holcroft gave the errand boy his letter to Elizabeth, with a shilling and instructions to take it to the Post Office.

There! It is done, he thought. He was a free man. As they strolled along Dame Street, he gradually became aware that Francis was speaking about his secret business in the castle. He knew that he ought to tell the boy to be silent about such matters but curiosity got the better of him. He began to listen.

'. . . Anyway, a large quantity of letters were found in the baggage which was captured after the battle. Letters to and from James and his officers sent by all sorts of people – some the strangest characters, great men who pretend to love William and Mary but who are also in regular correspondence with James, just to be on the safe side, in case his royal fortunes should suddenly change.'

'Anyone I know?' asked Holcroft. A group of three obviously drunken junior guards officers came towards them in the street, arm in arm, singing a bawdy ditty, and the two officers stepped aside to give them a wide berth.

'Well, yes, actually,' said Francis. 'Which is why I bring the subject up. Your particular friend Lord Marlborough has been writing to James Stuart. He is discreet, of course, and never says what might be constituted as treason to King William, or even outright disloyalty. But he apologised several times for his betrayal in the Glorious

Revolution. Makes excuses, talks about the good of the country and so on. But the very fact that he is in communication with our enemy is . . . well, it doesn't make him look very trustworthy. And William has been informed of this. I thought that you might like to tell him that his letters have been read and, well, he should be careful not to anger the King.'

Holcroft digested this intelligence. *Damn Jack, why must he always be meddling in dangerous political waters?* He suddenly wondered why Francis had told him this. He felt a sudden shaft of suspicion. If Jack were suspected of treason, it would be the height of stupidity to tip him off. And Francis was not stupid. Was this some ploy? Where they expecting him to reveal something – or do something – that would incriminate Jack? No, he did not believe it. That was the problem with intelligence work. There was always the suspicion of some dark ulterior motive. He realised that Francis had told him merely as a kindness. To help him to keep his friend out of serious trouble.

'Thank you, Francis. I shall pass on what you say to Lord Marlborough.'

'You know he has been lobbying to come to Ireland?' Francis said. 'He wants to bring a combined-arms force here to attack the Irish-held harbours.'

'I know. He told me that he plans to come, if he can persuade the King.'

'Well, tell him that this commerce with the enemy will not help his cause.'

Holcroft said nothing. They were entering the gatehouse of Dublin Castle, passing by the saluting sentries without comment, and coming out into a vast rectangular courtyard with dozens of carriages arriving at the main building and depositing their passengers, who joined a queue to enter the castle itself.

'There is something else that I wanted to tell you, if I may,' said Waters. 'A number of the letters were written in code, and since you indicated you did not wish to be involved in these matters any longer, we sent a few of them to a retired mathematician in Cambridge, Professor Wallis, who has a reputation for this kind of work. And Professor Wallis was able to decipher the few we sent him remarkably swiftly, in a matter of hours – he is a very clever gentleman.'

Holcroft knew of John Wallis, an old man now who, in his youth, had broken codes for Oliver Cromwell during the civil wars, and later on for King Charles II. He *was* a very clever man – he was actually brilliant, to Holcroft's mind. He had been impressed by Wallis's musings on the subject of infinity.

'The encrypted letters, it seems, were written by an agent of the enemy. A spy within our ranks, to put it bluntly. And they were all signed with the code name Agricola. Have you heard this name, sir?'

Holcroft admitted that he had not.

'It is just that this spy was at Carrickfergus, it seems, during the siege. One of the letters makes a joke about Agricola revealing the location of the Duke of Schomberg's tent. I thought that might interest you. It is possible that he may be an English or a Dutch officer. Can you think of anyone who might fit the bill?'

Holcroft shook his head. The two men had joined the queue to enter the castle, they were standing on the stone steps that led to the entrance. There were a dozen people around them: the men mostly in military finery, the women in peacock-splendid silks and satins, with wide fans and plunging necklines.

'Have you any more information about this Agricola?' Holcroft asked, keeping his voice low. 'Who does he report to? Whom does he serve?'

'We've sent the rest of the letters to Cambridge for Wallis to decode – a great mass of them – and we expect to have more information about this spy in due course. But we have discovered this:

Agricola is the agent of your old enemy Henri d'Erloncourt, who is addressed in the letters simply as Narrey.'

Holcroft was drunk. He did not dance and he was bored with watching the elegantly dressed gentlemen and ladies circling each other in the minuet and making their graceful shapes on the dance floor. The ball was a rather subdued affair, in any case, and sparsely populated. The King had not attended, much to the Governor's chagrin, saying regretfully he must decline as he was deeply occupied with affairs of state. Everyone knew what that meant: news had been widely circulated about two catastrophic turns of events that put a dampener on the joy of the victory at the Boyne; indeed they made the whole bloody business seem no more than an unimportant skirmish in the context of the wider war.

A great sea battle had been fought off Beachy Head nine days earlier between the combined English and Dutch fleets and the French navy – and the men of Louis XIV had triumphed, sinking ten Anglo-Dutch ships for no loss of their own. With the Royal Navy thoroughly bested, there was much talk of a French invasion of England, which was expected imminently. As if that was not bad enough, news of the naval disaster came hard on the heels of a crushing defeat on land at the Battle of Fleurus, which took place in the Spanish Netherlands on the same day as the armies had been killing each other on the Boyne. The Duc de Luxembourg, commanding some forty thousand of King Louis' finest troops, had routed the slightly inferior force of the Dutch field marshal Prince Waldeck, forcing him back to Brussels and conquering swathes of new territory. King William, it was said, was considering leaving Ireland and returning to England to deal with the situation personally. The result of this news and the attendant rumours meant that there was an undercurrent of gloom at the ball, which many tried to dispel with forced jollity and reckless drinking. The room was also too warm, lit with hundreds of candles – even a fire at one end – and was filled with the body heat given off by Dublin's dancing gentlefolk.

When Holcroft's mind was deeply troubled, he often found in alcohol a soothing balm. He found the same tonight and had taken up a station beside the huge bowl of bright red gin punch, from which he helped himself freely as he watched the revellers. But he was not genuinely admiring the elegant gyrations of the dancers: he was thinking about the letter he had written to Elizabeth, and already regretting the haste with which he had composed and dispatched it. He was casting off his wife on the basis of gossip, a momentous decision that surely merited a little more sober reflection. But the letter had been dispatched and presumably was now in some post-rider's satchel on its way to London.

The other emotion troubling him was grief, a river of painful sadness running under the surface of his mind, over the death of Enoch Jackson. He had not been a good friend to Jackson, although the old man had been a staunch supporter and ally since he first joined the Ordnance six years ago. He had barely spoken to him this year, except to give him orders. And he had never thanked him for his steadfast loyalty and all the times he had followed Holcroft's wilder schemes, even when he knew it was against the rules. The business with the Humpty at Joymount House, for example. And now he was dead. He would never be able to tell the old man what his friendship had meant.

He dipped his crystal cup into the punch once more. He was not used to drinking gin and they had clearly not stinted on the newly fashionable Dutch spirit in the mix – but he was beginning to feel rather better. As he sipped his drink, he pondered the other matter that was exercising his mind. This spy Agricola – who could he possibly be? Holcroft looked at the reddened faces of the officers from William's various legions as they whirled past him, somewhat blurredly, on the floor. Was Agricola perhaps here this night?

There was Claudius Barden grinning like a monkey as usual and dancing showily with a pretty red-headed girl. Holcroft wondered if she knew what an ass he truly was. Could Barden be the spy – no, surely he was too stupid to attract Narrey's attention. And Holcroft could not imagine Barden keeping a secret of that magnitude for long. He would be sure to make a silly joke about it. There was the Quartermaster, Edmund Vallance – he was a venal brute, if ever there was one. If Narrey was offering his agent bright gold for their service, which was the Frenchman's usual practice, Holcroft could imagine Vallance passing on all manner of secrets without the faintest qualm.

And what about Brigadier-General Wolseley – on the far side of the room, talking to Captain Francis Waters. Could Wolseley be the traitor? Unlikely, but who could know the secrets of a man's heart? Perhaps he hated King William for some reason or was so horribly mired in debt that only French cash could keep him out of the sponging house. He had not been at Carrickfergus during the siege but he *had* been in Belfast – only twelve miles away. And somebody – most probably the spy Agricola – had told the defenders of Cavan that the Williamites were coming to attack them in February. They had plenty of notice of that attack – so much that they had time to be reinforced by the Duke of Berwick's horse and foot. Was it William Wolseley himself who tipped them off? There was no way to tell. How about Captain Jan van Zwyk there – the tall, handsome commander of the Blue Guards at Cavan – had he also been at Carrickfergus? Holcroft had no idea. But he found he now thoroughly disliked *all* tall, handsome Dutchmen. It would be most satisfying if it *was* van Zwyk.

This was the problem with intelligence. After a while you looked at everyone, no matter how blameless they truly were, as if they might be a traitor.

Lieutenant-Colonel Richards whirled past his eyes – it could not be his friend Jacob, at least. He had been in the Duke of

Schomberg's tent and had been grievously wounded when the French had fired on it from the roof of Joymount House. No spymaster in his right mind would fire cannon at his own secret agent. And Agricola had apparently joked about the attack on the tent afterwards – which was not something that Jacob would very likely do.

Holcroft's eye was drawn by Jacob Richards' partner, a slim, dark-haired woman, neat and graceful, obviously well trained in the dance, wearing a lovely sky-blue gown with a necklace of blue sapphires around her white neck.

It was Lady Caroline Chichester, of course.

Holcroft watched her for a while, entranced. What was she doing dancing with Richards? He was quite unsuitable – he was too dull for her and too poor. She was probably just being kind. Humouring him. Dancing out of duty. That was so like her. But she was encouraging him, which was unwise. He would take her a glass of gin punch when she next sat down and tell her so. She would surely appreciate his advice. He refilled his own crystal cup again, drank it off in one swallow and then filled two cups, ready to take some refreshment to the beautiful young lady when she finished her irksome chore.

But when the minuet came to its stately conclusion, Caroline did not sit down. She and Richards seemed to be laughing with each other, exchanging some pleasantries; then when the band struck up another tune, an allemande this time, Francis Waters approached her, bowed, seized her hand and they began to move in complement to each on the floor. Holcroft felt suddenly very foolish, standing alone with two cups of red punch in his hand. Of course, Caroline would be in demand at the ball. She was one of the most beautiful women there. And Holcroft did not care to dance. Why should she choose to sit and drink gin punch? Delightful as that would be for him.

As he watched her on the floor, he could not help but compare Caroline to Elizabeth. His wife was handsome, to be sure, but not elegant. Never elegant. She was a large-bodied woman, not fat but far from dainty. And she was loud. God, she was loud. Even when they were making love in Mincing Lane, trying for her longed-for baby, her voice had been like a trumpet blast in his ear. It had at times been difficult to concentrate on the task at hand. Caroline, he was sure, would not bellow at him like a sergeant-major, if they went to bed together . . .

Holcroft suddenly realised that he was standing at the edge of the floor and staring at Caroline as she danced. He took command of himself, drained both drinks, rid himself of the glassware and went to sit beside a large potted plant to wait out evolutions of this interminable allemande. The plant, some kind of extravagant fern, partly screened him from the rest of the room, and as he sat and leant his head back against the wall, he realised that he was extremely tired – the stress and exertions of the great battle, the deaths of so many of his friends, the heat of the ballroom, the gin punch warming his belly so very pleasantly. He closed his eyes, just for a moment or two . . .

Holcroft woke with a start. The ball was over and the room was half empty. Servants were clearing away the detritus of the party, broken glass, plates of half-eaten food, dropped gloves and fans. There were other revellers who had also succumbed to the gin punch, it seemed; one officer in splendid scarlet and gold was snoring on the floor half under a table, using his wig for a pillow.

Holcroft got up – mouth like bone, tongue leathery – reached for a half-full glass of crimson punch on the table, thought better of it and grasped a jug of lukewarm spring water, which he poured gratefully into himself . . .

As he stumbled home in the milky light just before dawn, now feeling decidedly queasy, he thought about what the day ahead held for him. Nothing urgent. Nothing that could not be done from the inn or put off until tomorrow if he felt too indisposed to work. He had some paperwork to read and sign on his desk in the room concerning a shipment of black powder expected to arrive in Carlingford from England any day now, as well as some other reports about the state of the Ordnance, and he was supposed to be inspecting the new eighteen-pounders after noon, and getting the Train ready for the resumption of the war.

The battle at the Boyne had not ended the conflict in Ireland. Not by any means. King James might have fled to France but there were still large numbers of Jacobite troops in the south and west of Ireland, many of whom had not yet faced the hard men of King William's armies, and were the braver for it. And they had no doubt been encouraged by the recent French successes on land and at sea. The Jacobites were strong in Connaught and were defending the line of the River Shannon in the west. And they held Cork and Kinsale and all of the wild lands on the south-western coast. The main force had retreated to Limerick, and he had heard they were fortifying the old medieval town and summoning their troops from across Ireland to defend it. It was thought that they had as many as twenty thousand men in arms in and around that city – the third largest in Ireland after Dublin and Waterford. Holcroft knew that there would be hard fighting before the war was over and the Jacobite cause put down for good.

As he approached the inn, he saw that Joseph Murphy, the man who owned the establishment, was already up and about. He was sluicing down the front steps of the Whale and Crow where some reveller had vomited during the night.

'Morning to you, Major Blood,' said the man cheerily. 'You enjoyed the governor's ball to the fullest, I see.'

Holcroft said nothing. He nodded at the man and made to move past him.

'Hold on just a wee moment, Major,' said Murphy. 'I must tell ye that you've a visitor this fine summer morning.'

'A visitor?' Holcroft stopped in surprise.

'Aye, sir, a young lady – unaccompanied, too! She didn't give a name.'

'Where is she?'

'She said she had to see you, sir, most urgent, and when I told her you were not yet returned from the castle, she insisted that she would wait for you. I put her in your room, to keep her from getting under my feet as I get the place ready. Hope that's satisfactory. I didn't know what else to do with her.'

Holcroft bounded up the stairs and threw open the door to his small room, and there, sitting demurely on the large four-poster bed in her sky-blue ball gown, chain of sapphires twinkling around her neck, was Caroline Chichester.

Chapter Twenty-Two

Sunday, August 10, 1690

Hogan stood up in his saddle and looked west where he could see the glint of water in the late afternoon sun – the River Shannon – and the smoke rising from the chimneys of the village of Ballina on the nearer, the eastern bank. To his left were the dark slopes of the Silvermine Mountains, an inhospitable rugged terrain he had known since boyhood.

Hogan had thought his part in the conflict was over after surviving the carnage at the Boyne. He now realised he had been fooling himself. The irresistible twin forces of Henri d'Erloncourt and Patrick Sarsfield had combined to keep Mick Hogan in arms, and there was not a damn thing he could do about it, save run for the mountains or the bogs and hide until the last echo of the last musket shot had died away – and that was not Hogan's way. No man would have cause to call him a coward after the war.

General Sarsfield had offered him a regiment of cavalry of his own to command and, when Hogan had demurred, had repeated his woo-ing words of patriotism, saying Hogan was needed by his country. He had also hinted that if he went back to his old ways – the thieving life of the wild raparee – he would immediately be declared an outlaw. If that was the cudgel that threatened him, Narrey had lured him with a sweetmeat instead. Gold, and plenty of it, ten pounds a week in *louis d'or* if Hogan would agree to lead raids on the supply lines and foraging parties of the English Army in the mid-lands between Dublin, which Dutch Billy now possessed, and Athlone, on the Shannon, which was still held by the Irish adherents of that cowardly runaway *Séamus an Chaca*.

It had been no contest for Mick Hogan. He disliked the pomp and formality of regimental life, and he was sure he would have made a poor lieutenant-colonel of cavalry. Much better to have his own band of loyal ruffians, sleeping under the stars, and causing mayhem whenever and wherever he could. He had enjoyed telling General Sarsfield that he had accepted the nominal rank of major in the royal army of His Majesty Louis XIV, that he was now detached on special operations in Ireland, and therefore must reluctantly decline his offer.

'I'd rather you fought with me, Mick. But I don't care who you fight with as long as you *do* fight,' said Sarsfield. 'And, laddie, I *shall* be watching you!'

The drawback to accepting all that filthy lucre to join the French service was that he was forced to spend a good deal more time in the company of Henri d'Erloncourt – a man for whom he had no respect, indeed an ever-growing dislike. The French colonel seemed to regard him as a ready replacement for his dead hench- man Guillaume du Clos, killed by a cannon ball outside Duleek, which meant that a good deal of errand-boy work was expected of him. But Hogan found that, if he concentrated on the little linen bags of gold the man was paying him each week, he could just about stomach his discomfiture.

Hogan was of a mind to buy himself a small farm when this bloody war was over and the English were expelled from his fine green home- land. He had decided that he would get married to some nice buxom lass and raise sheep and even a few children in a bare but bucolic heaven down by Lough Leane, near Killarney. That was the plan. In truth, he wasn't much of a farmer and suspected that he would die of boredom, but every man should have a dream, and this was Hogan's – and if he earned enough of the Frenchman's gold he might set up as a gentleman and leave all the dirt-grubbing to his tenants.

Hogan pulled himself back to the present with a start. This was no time for day-dreaming. He reined in his mount. A horseman in a dark blue cloak was riding towards him over the rough sheep pastures from the direction of Ballina, one of his scouts, probably, coming in to report. Hogan raised his hand in the signal for a halt and glanced over his shoulder at the double line of thirty mud-daubed, weapon-draped rascals slouched in their saddles behind him.

He did not know many of these men well – there were few enough of the old crew who had survived Cavan *and* the bloodbath of the Boyne – but these new comrades had shaped up well enough in the past few weeks of raiding and robbing around enemy-held Mullingar, fighting hard when called upon to do so, and retreating at speed – never fleeing in panic – when necessary, and grumbling only a reasonable amount at the privations of life on the road.

He had had no difficulty in recruiting riders. The two armies, both of Irishmen and William's brutal foreigners, had pillaged the mid-lands again and again as they crossed over them, killing livestock and burning what plunder they could not carry away. With many a Catholic smallholder facing starvation on his torched fields, finding good men to swear a solemn oath to ride with him had been absurdly easy and he had been able to pick and choose the likeliest.

The scout approached and made his report: the river was low enough to ford at Ballina, and there was no sign of any English soldiers. Hogan muttered some words of praise and sent him back to join the column with a jerk of his head. They would cross here and ride south-west for ten miles – in an hour or two, at around sunset, with the blessing, they would be safely in Limerick.

He had been summoned. His master – God how he hated that word, for all that it was the truth – had summoned him in from the wilds to a conference in Limerick with, of all people, Patrick Sarsfield. Something was afoot. William's legions, thousands of the godless Protestant bastards, he had heard, were now outside the decrepit, half-ruined walls of old Limerick. But they had not yet the man-power to surround the whole city – it was still wide open to the north and west across the Shannon on the County Clare side. Hogan's fear was that d'Erloncourt and Sarsfield between them would make him stay and defend the old town – in some God damned heroic last stand. If that were the case, he would not countenance it. Fuck them both. He had signed on the ride and raid, not to stand behind a crumbling stone wall with a musket and be blasted by English cannon fire from half a mile away. He would desert, yes he would, if that was what the two madmen asked him. He *would* hide in the bogs till it was over – and to the Devil with the Frenchman's gold *and* Sarsfield's threats of outlawry. And let any man afterwards dare to say he had not done his part.

Patrick Sarsfield seemed to have aged several years in the few weeks since Hogan had last seen him. There were fresh lines of worry carved into his strong, handsome face and his hands seemed to tremble slightly as he poured Hogan a large glass of brandy from the small wooden cask. Henri d'Erloncourt, on the other hand, seemed as fresh as a dewy meadow, and splendid this evening in a spotless lavender suit of clothes, with snowy lace at his collar and cuffs, and a shining blond periwig, the heavy curls hanging either side of his foxy little face.

The city of Limerick was made up of two parts: the ancient English Town to the north was beside the River Shannon, surrounded by water. The second part, the newer although still venerable Irish Town, lay to the south, across a bridge over the Abbey River, a tributary of the slow Shannon.

Irish Town, a jumble of workshops and warehouses and mean little houses, was the nearest to the enemy and was mostly surrounded by a wall of decaying stone hundreds of years old, held together by rotting mortar, mould, mud and the constant prayers of the defenders. From the decrepit, half-collapsing walls of Irish Town, the soggy trenches of the besieging English were only seven hundred yards away – and creeping closer as the sappers dug forward each day.

Hogan, Sarsfield and Henri were alone in a low, circular room at the top of one of the towers of King John's Castle – a stronghold built by Lackland in the twelfth century on the western side of English Town by the Thomond Bridge. It was about as far from the enemy as it was possible to be and still be in the city. Looking out of a medieval arrow-slit window, Hogan could see the campfires of the horse lines of the Irish cavalry brigades bivouacked on the far side of the river, although he could not locate the billet of his own handful of men, who were located somewhere near Sarsfield's Regiment of Horse.

'Good of you to come, Mick,' said Sarsfield passing him the brandy.

'Not at all. I always come a-running when I'm whistled for,' said Hogan taking a gulp of the spirit. It was the real stuff, as French as his master – and just as rarefied. 'A good and faithful hound-dog, Paddy, that's me.'

'I know you're not,' said Sarsfield. 'I know you can on occasion be a disobedient cur.' But he laughed a little and raised his own glass in salute.

'Could we get to our business?' said Henri, looking at the two Irishmen with contempt.

'To business then,' said Sarsfield, suddenly formal. 'As you will no doubt have gathered, Major Hogan, the Prince of Orange himself is at our gates with a substantial force – we think about twenty-five thousand foot and horse. We have slightly fewer men to oppose him; inside the walls of Limerick and including our cavalry across the river, we have a total of nineteen thousand. We have sufficient food and fodder, wine and brandy a-plenty, as well as powder, muskets and ball, courtesy of our munificent friends in France and their victorious navy. The magazines are full. And summer is nearly over. The rains of autumn are just around the corner. You follow me so far?'

It's not as bad as it might be, Hogan thought, his mood warming with the brandy. 'Panting hot on your heels, sir,' he said.

'The enemy is digging his saps, pushing the trenches closer and closer to our walls, and in due course they will make a massed assault on the walls of Irish Town. But they are proceeding slowly. Very slowly. At a snail's pace, you might say. Can you guess why that might be, Major Hogan?'

'They don't have sufficient guns,' said Hogan immediately. One noise had been conspicuous by its absence in the few short hours he had been in the city. The booming of the great wall-breaking cannon, the background music to every modern siege, was absent. There had been sporadic reports from lighter pieces – three-pounders, most likely – but not the big bruisers. It had struck him as odd then, and now, suddenly, he felt a glow of real excitement.

'Very good, Major. Yes, they don't have their big guns. They can't make much of a dent, even in our decrepit old stones. At least not yet. Your patron Colonel d'Erloncourt here has had news from his sources that they are hauling up their big Ordnance, the real smashers, as fast as they can from Dublin. But the English Artillery Train moves slowly – it seems that they do not find our narrow, muddy, winding Irish roads congenial for the swift movement of heavy guns.'

'Where is the English Train now?' said Hogan.

Sarsfield walked over to a map of southern Ireland that was pinned on a wooden board set up on an artist's easel against the curved wall of the tower. 'Here, we think. On the southern road somewhere near . . .' he squinted at the map, 'Doon. They could be before our walls in two or three days.'

Hogan thrust his head forward to see better; he traced the fine country road on the map with a blunt forefinger. 'So tomorrow morning they'll be about . . . here.' He stabbed the board with his less-than-clean digit. 'Ballyneety.'

'You know this region well, Major Hogan?' said Henri.

'Like the back of my hand, monsieur. I've been riding and hunting over the Silvermine Mountains and down to Tipperary since I was a lad. My father had a farm near Doon, good cattle country, till the landlord, a grasping bastard of an Englishman, threw him out on his ear over a trifle of arrears in the rent.'

'You do fully grasp the vital significance of the arrival of King William's Train here at Limerick?' said Henri looking doubtfully at Hogan.

'I'm not a fool, monsieur,' the Irishman replied, clearly nettled. 'If the big English guns get here soon, they can make a breach in the walls or, better for them, several breaches, in just a few days. Then they will ram their superior numbers into Limerick and we are lost. Maybe the whole war is lost, if they take Limerick, our last great stronghold. But, if we can capture or destroy their big guns, if we can delay the making of a practicable breach in any way, then maybe we can hold out till the rains come and the bastards must go away into their winter quarters. With the war suspended over the long cold months, well, anything could happen. We saw what sickness did to them at Dundalk – their army was decimated. Thousands dead or too ill to fight. They could all pack up and go home to England, with the blessing – or your master King Louis might send us a proper army, to push them back into the sea. Everything changes if we can hold out till the end of this campaigning season. And *that* will probably be at the end of this month, or the beginning of September. So, yes, monsieur, I do fully grasp the *vital significance* of delaying the arrival of the English Train.'

'Very good, Major Hogan,' said Henri with an arch smile. 'You are a quick student, I see. I was right to choose you. So, the sooner you depart on your mission the better, I would say. I wish you God-speed, and good luck!'

Hogan took a deep breath and tried to control his anger. He thought about the gold. Lots of French gold – and a sheep farm on the shores of Lough Leane.

'I don't have enough men,' he said, through clenched teeth. 'The English Train will be guarded – they would be fools not to have a substantial military escort. Fusiliers, cavalry, maybe a regiment of dragoons . . .'

'They *are* fools,' said Henri. 'My information is that the escort for the Train is light, a few cavalry, no more than a squadron or two.'

'I need more men – you said this was of *vital significance*. And it is.'

'I shall come with you,' said Patrick Sarsfield. 'My own regiment should be enough, even if your intelligence of their numbers is inaccurate, monsieur. We may leave Limerick in the tender care of General Lauzun for a day or two.'

Hogan winked at the Irish general. 'Anything for a bit of fame and glory, eh, Paddy?' But he was grateful nonetheless. With Sarsfield's men they would number a good six hundred cavalry, more than enough to cause some mischief. 'And would *you* like to ride along with us, monsieur, purely for the fun of it?'

Henri held up his pale hands in horror. 'Alas, Major, I have important business in Cork and it cannot wait. Sadly, I must ride this night for the coast.'

'Very well, Paddy. Just you and me. We ride for Ireland – and for glory!'

Chapter Twenty-Three

Monday, August 11, 1690

It felt odd to be on campaign again after so many weeks in the relative comforts of the Whale and Crow in Dublin and, for possibly the first time in his military career, Holcroft wished he were not with the guns. The heart of the Train was the great siege cannon: six twenty-four-pounders and two eighteen-pounders that should be powerful enough to blast through the ancient walls of Limerick with ease. As well as the big 'smashers', Holcroft had charge of five mortars, which would drop exploding shells into the streets of the old city, and he had sixty wagons of powder and shot, match cord and wadding, tools and equipment, all the necessities to keep the guns firing until victory was achieved.

The Train, which stretched nearly two miles along the narrow road, was hauled by hundreds of heavy draught horses and oxen, and was guarded by two troops of Sir Edward Villiers's Horse, eighty-two red-coated men armed with sword and carbine, under a languid dandy named Captain Thomas Pulteney. For once, Holcroft was thoroughly exasperated with the snail-like progress of the Train. In normal circumstances, he would have been content with its steady, almost sedate pace – none of the wagons had broken an axle so far on the week-and-a-half long rattling journey from Dublin over the execrable Irish roads – but this afternoon he felt tetchy, deeply irritated and impatient with the bucolic ambling of the oxen teams and their drowsing yokel drivers.

He wanted to get this business done; get the Train to Limerick, reduce the city walls and allow King William's infantry to storm the last great bastion of the Jacobite cause; then return to Dublin. He wanted to get back to Caroline.

When he had got over his shock at seeing Caroline sitting on his bed in the Whale and Crow, and had splashed his face with water and ordered up a pot of strong coffee from Joe Murphy, he asked her what she was doing in his room.

The tale she related to him made him feel uneasy, indeed it was profoundly disturbing. When she had complained about feeling hot from too much dancing, Lieutenant-Colonel Richards had gallantly taken her for a cooling stroll in the formal gardens at the back of the ballroom. He had led her to a discreet spot, taken her hand, kissed it, declared that he adored her, was passionately in love with her, and proposed marriage there and then.

Caroline had been totally surprised by this development. She was flattered, of course, by such a declaration but she did not think of Richards in a similar way. He was, she told him, a dear friend but she looked on him more as an elder brother, than a suitor. In any case she could not possibly consider a match without the consent of her older brother and guardian, the Earl of Donegall, who was still in Belfast. Richards had tried to argue with her; he even suggested a swift elopement, and swore that he would leave the Ordnance and run away with her to England or Scotland. She told him he was mad. Then he seized her and tried to kiss her and she slapped him once, very hard, and left him sobbing like a child in the garden while she went back towards the safety of the ballroom. All this had taken place while Holcroft had been passed out behind the shadow of the plant in the corner of the dancing hall.

On the way inside, at the doors of the ballroom, Caroline had been waylaid by Captain Waters, who had made an impertinent suggestion – one that she would not repeat – and having rebuffed him with a few choice phrases, she made her way, unescorted, out of the castle and down Dame Street to the Whale and Crow to wait for Holcroft's return.

'I will be no man's whore,' she told him, her face white with emotion, as they stood in the centre of the bedroom an arm's length apart. Her brilliant blue eyes glistened with tears. 'Neither will I be bullied into a grubby little marriage to some jumped-up powder monkey from the Ordnance – and a damned papist, to boot. I came to you, my dear Holcroft, to beg your protection. I know you are an honourable, decent man, a gentleman, and I place my person in your care.'

Holcroft was battered by a gale of emotions. On the one hand, he was pleased and flattered that she should choose him for her protector in this unfamiliar city thronging with lonely lustful soldiers. On the other, his feelings towards her were far from being either decent or honourable: indeed, as he stared into her lovely, tear-stained face, he longed more than anything to clasp her in his arms and kiss her. That would not do. She would be no man's whore.

'You cannot stay in here with me but I shall speak to old Joe Murphy and arrange for you to take the room next to mine – you have a maid, yes?'

Caroline admitted that she did and that she was lodged in an old house by the river with an ancient servant of her brother's, a feeble old man, past seventy and nearly blind. 'You shall all of you move into the Whale,' Holcroft decreed. 'Where I can keep an eye on you until I can arrange for you to travel safely back to Belfast. And I shall speak with both Francis Waters and Jacob Richards this day and make it plain that their advances are unwelcome and that you are not to be molested any further. Do not trouble yourself, my dear, I shall be firm and you will suffer no further affronts to your honour from either of these men.'

Holcroft was as good as his word when it came to Colonel Richards. He sought out his superior officer in the Ordnance's new headquarters in a set of cramped rooms in the west wing of Dublin Castle in the early afternoon. Jacobs was badly hungover and red-eyed from weeping, and before Holcroft had a chance to speak, Richards said: 'I suppose you heard about it. Every awful detail. How I humiliated myself with Caroline. I suppose you have come to say: "I told you so". Well, I can't blame you. I've been a damn fool. No doubt all Dublin today is sniggering behind their hands at this love-struck buffoon . . .'

Holcroft wisely said nothing.

Richards snuffled a little, cleared his throat and blew his nose loudly: 'You know the worst thing, Blood, the very worst thing about the whole horrible episode? She did not consider my proposal even for a moment. Not for a single instant did she think: shall I marry this gentleman? It was completely out of the question. It wasn't even a question. And the look on her face, when I asked for her hand. It was a look of horror, as if I had suggested she lie down with a hog.'

Richards, that controlled, taciturn man, went on in this sad vein for ten minutes or so, occasionally mopping his steaming eyes, before finally running dry of self-pity. He blew his nose one final time and straightened his spine.

Then they spoke of Ordnance matters, of the complicated preparations for the transportation of part of the Train to Limerick under Blood's command, and finally as he was about to take his leave, Holcroft said: 'I must tell you this – you will hear it anyway, so it had better come from me: Caroline and her people are moving into the Whale and Crow, into the rooms next to mine.'

Jacob Richards looked at him. His eyes narrowed briefly in puzzled anger and then his whole face fell apart. He looked defeated, utterly destroyed.

'She is not my mistress, Richards,' said Holcroft. 'I swear to you. She asked for my protection, that is all. I'll send her back to her family . . . intact.'

Richards half smiled. 'She is not your mistress,' he said, 'yet. But good luck to you, Blood. Seriously, I wish you joy. I shall never speak to her again.'

Holcroft was unable to locate Francis Waters. When he called at the offices of the new intelligence department, he was told that Captain Waters was not in the castle that day. And when he pushed for more information, he was shown the door by a pair of burly Inniskillingers and told to take himself away.

It took a surprisingly long time for Holcroft to arrange passage back to Belfast for Caroline, her maid Henny and Stevens the old manservant. Raparee activity across the whole of Ireland had greatly increased since the battle at the Boyne, the numbers of these irregular soldiers swelled by desperate men from the Jacobite Army who had ignored the call to regroup at Limerick and who instead had taken to the bandit life.

So, it was extremely risky to send Caroline home by land, unless Holcroft could drum up a sizeable armed escort, and the passage by sea between Dublin and Belfast – also not without risk from the French navy, which was resurgent in the Irish Sea after their great victory at Beachy Head – was booked for weeks in advance. The days passed, one after the other, after Caroline and her small entourage was ensconced in the Whale and Crow and every day, Holcroft's efforts to arrange transport of whatever kind for the lady slackened a little more.

In truth, he did not want her to leave. He was enjoying her company. She was subtle, graceful, soothing to be around. She did not intrude when he was working on his Ordnance papers, nor did she grow bored in her confinement and demand that he take her out to see plays or entertainments, to have dinner or to see the sights of Dublin. She was demure, humble, quiet – she was, in fact, Holcroft realised one fine morning, quite perfect.

When he wished to speak about his Ordnance affairs or of his love for the great guns, she listened with fascinated attention; when he was busy, she kept her distance. She took over the role of supervising his wardrobe, sending his linen out to be cleaned and pressed, arranging meals to be delivered to his room when he was engaged in work, keeping visitors at bay, occasionally bringing him wine or some small treat when he had been too busy to eat all day. They had long conversations about her likes and dislikes: she revealed a deep love of Ireland, of its bogs and mountains, of the lush green pastures and bluebell-crowned woods. She loved its people, she told him, their humour and courage, their quiet enduring strength. She said that she could never live anywhere else.

There were times when he was alone with her when he felt an almost overwhelming urge to embrace her, to kiss her and kiss her, and take her up and tumble her into his bed – but he found that the angry words she had spoken on the morning after the ball were somehow stuck in his head. *I will be no man's whore.* Also, humming in the background was the ugly description she had used for Jacob Richards: *some jumped-up powder monkey from the Ordnance.* Was Holcroft, too, merely a jumped-up powder monkey in her lovely blue eyes?

He made a few feeble efforts to secure her passage on a ship to Belfast, visiting the harbourmaster's office every other day to make enquiries, but his heart was not in it. He could not help but compare Caroline with Elizabeth. He had loved Elizabeth, or so he had thought, but she *had* been a daily irritation to him. He was less troubled now with his decision to cast her off. Perhaps she would take up with the Dutchman, her lover Marcus van Dijk, and all would be well. He had received no reply to his letter.

And so, with his own busy-ness preparing for the Train to march to Limerick, and Caroline's quiet congeniality as his neighbour in the Whale, by the time he finally set off for Limerick, she was still firmly in residence in Joe Murphy's establishment and likely to stay there till he returned from the siege. Surely that could not be too long. King William had sufficient men, he would shortly have the guns to breach the walls of Limerick, and with luck the whole business could be swiftly achieved and Holcroft could return to Caroline.

In any case, since it was now nearly mid-August, the campaigning season would be over in a few short weeks whether Limerick was captured or not, and the Williamite army would go into winter quarters. Holcroft allowed himself to contemplate the luxury of several months mewed up in the Whale with Caroline. There would be time enough then for plays, if she wished to see them, and fine dinners, and cosy evenings, just the two of them, by the fire . . .

Captain Thomas Pulteney cantered up to Holcroft's position midway along the length of the lumbering Train. He was resplendent in a long scarlet velvet coat with golden buttons, a grey periwig and a hat with matching grey ostrich plume.

'Major Blood, my scouts report that there is a ruined castle about a half a mile ahead, at a quiet, deserted place known locally as Ballyneety. I would suggest, sir, that we make camp there tonight. There is a spring and some shelter from the old tumbled-down castle walls, a few trees too for firewood. It is less than six miles from Limerick, or so they tell me, and if we bide there tonight we should be able to join the King and main force outside the city by noon tomorrow.'

Holcroft looked at the sun, and to confirm, he pulled out his brass pocket watch. It was a little before six of the clock and darkness was about two hours away. Not enough time to reach Limerick – and they would need daylight to make their camp. 'Very well, Pulteney, we shall make our camp at Ballyneety. You'll oblige me by scouting the area thoroughly for enemy troops.'

'Yes, sir. And the watchword, sir. What should it be tonight?'

Holcroft considered for a moment or two. They had been using the names of Jacobite generals each evening as a password so that scouts and foragers could identify themselves when they returned to the camp. Last night's had been Tyrconnell. The day before had been Berwick. It had been Lieutenant Claudius Barden's idea – he was the second-in-command of the Train – to use the names of their enemies – probably a joke of some sort, which Holcroft did not truly understand. But one name was as good as another as a code word.

'Let the word tonight be "Sarsfield",' he said. He remembered Caroline speaking of the dashing young Irish general in scathing terms on the night before he left her – *a glory-hunting little popinjay*, she had called him.

Holcroft lay in his blankets, half asleep, and looked at the bright scatter of stars overhead in the vast black sweep of sky. Nearly there, he thought, nearly at Limerick, and inside a week, or maybe ten days he would be riding back to Dublin, triumphant, the soldier returned from the war to his beautiful lady . . .

It had taken the best part of two hours to get the Train encamped in the partial shelter of the old castle, in what would have been the main courtyard. But now, in the brief darkness of the summer night, the horses and oxen were tethered in the fields beyond the ruins, the tents were set up for the wagon crews, the campfires were lit, and Holcroft could hear the snores, and a few snatches of laughter and song as the men of the Train, the Ordnance gunners and the off-duty cavalrymen took their ease and smoked their pipes. There was a small, flat-topped mound of rock in the centre of the soft green turf of the camp, what would once, he assumed, have been the tower or keep of the fortress and to the west and north the crumbled remains of a low curtain wall, a few yards of tottering man-high stone here and there, with wide gaps in between. It must have been several hundreds of years since Ballyneety Castle had been capable of withstanding any kind of enemy attack.

Holcroft had left the setting of sentries to Captain Pulteney, just this once, since they were so close to the main army at Limerick, and the cavalry officer had declared the area secure. And from time to time he saw a pacing musket-man at the fringes of the fire-lit camp. Lieutenant Barden had the first watch for the Ordnance and he had orders to wake Holcroft in three hours at midnight so he could take his turn on duty. Holcroft turned in his thick blankets to find a more comfortable spot on the spongy turf, closed his eyes, let out a long, long breath and went swiftly down into the deepest sleep.

He awoke with the strongest feeling that something was wrong. He sat up, looked around. The camp was quiet, the fires had burnt low into grey embers. The men were fast asleep. He looked at the black sky and saw that the constellations had rotated halfway around the heavens. He had slept far too long. It was well past midnight. That lazy dog Barden had not awakened him. Probably sleeping himself. He sat up and pulled on his boots, struggled into his blue coat, buttoned it and tied the officer's sash around his middle. He found the Lorenzoni and shoved it into his sash, slung his sword and muttered foul curses under his breath. This was too much – Barden must be disciplined for this egregious breach of military law. There was no excuse whatsoever...

He jerked around at the sound of a sentry's call. 'Who goes there?'

Holcroft saw a redcoat forty yards away, his broad back half turned to the camp, pointing his musket into the darkness. 'Who goes there?' he said again, an edge of panic in his voice. 'Give the watchword or I shall fire on you!'

Beyond the sentry, Holcroft could see shapes moving in the wall of grey. Horses, men on horseback, many men. He was immediately drenched in fear.

A voice rang out, loud, Irish and proud: 'Sarsfield's the word . . . and Sarsfield's the man.' And there were suddenly scores of horsemen pouring into the encampment, halloo-ing, bright swords unsheathed. A wall of cavalry falling on them like a collapsing sea-cliff.

Holcroft was shouting: 'To arms, to arms, the enemy is upon us!'

The Irish cavalry were in the rows of tents now, the horsemen slashing and stabbing at the befuddled wagoners and the half-dressed cavalry as they lurched awake. Many a sleep-drunk man stumbled to his feet only to be cut down an instant later. The horses trampled the tents, with men still inside them. The air was ripped with screams of terror and pain and the crack of horse pistols. There were hundreds of them, Holcroft saw, and more enemy horsemen coming in out of the darkness – the surprise was complete. He saw a rider coming for him, the man wielding a half-pike, tucked under his arm like a lance. Holcroft whipped out the Lorenzoni pistol, pulled back the cock, straightened his arm, aimed and shot the man through the centre of his chest. The horse thundered past, a foot from Holcroft's shoulder, the rider stone dead and flopping in the saddle.

Holcroft turned and ran for the stone mound in the centre of the courtyard, and scrambled to the summit. The horsemen could not easily follow him up there. He reloaded and cocked the Lorenzoni, and, holding the pistol in his left hand, drew his sword. He looked over the encampment and recognised that the battle was lost. The courtyard was filled with Irish cavalry, milling about, cutting down the men of the Train at will. His people were running, barelegged men in nightshirts, sprinting away from the horses, and into the darkness. Not all of them made it. Some were pistolled as they ran. Others were skewered on lunging sword-blades or trampled under the Irish chargers' hooves. He saw Barden, dressed but coatless, running across a suddenly open stretch of turf, leaping a campfire. A horseman, a rascally fellow in a rusty coat and woollen workman's cap, fired a pistol at Barden, and missed. The Ordnance officer ducked under a wagon, appeared on the other side and hared away into the night and disappeared. Holcroft breathed a sigh of relief.

But not for long. A horseman was trying to coax his horse into climbing the rocky slope of the mound, ten yards from Holcroft. He shot the Irishman through the throat, and reloaded the Lorenzoni awkwardly with his sword hand. A simple twist of the lever. The mound was surrounded, with a dozen men all about, some trying to loose their pistols at him. One dismounted fellow in a grey coat, leather cross belts and red turn-backs was nearly up the side of the mound, a long sword in his hand. Holcroft coolly shot him in the mouth – the bullet smashing through his skull and spraying brains, teeth and gore out the other side. But Holcroft was taking fire too. A pistol cracked and he felt a tug as the bullet ripped through the flapping skirt of his coat. He felt the wind of another and a zip as it went past his ear. *This is it,* he thought. *I'll never see Caroline in this life again.*

Then a miracle.

'You, sir, you on the mound. Surrender, sir. I call on you to yield now. Drop your weapons immediately, sir, or I'll shoot you down like a mad dog.'

Holcroft stared at the speaker. He seemed somehow familiar. A broad suntanned face under a black tricorn hat with a pheasant's feather, a green muddy coat, a horse pistol pointing at his head from a killing distance of fifteen feet.

A pistol banged from behind Holcroft and he felt the punch of a bullet as it ripped though his wide yellow coat-cuff, just grazing the meat of his right arm, but knocking it hard enough so that the Lorenzoni flew out of his hand and clattered to the mound's rocky floor.

'Cease fire, you bloodthirsty bastards. Hold your fire, I say. This one is mine,' the tanned fellow was yelling to the horsemen who encircled the mound. Then he said 'Drop your sword, sir; surrender – or you will die this instant.'

Holcroft looked at the encampment; he could see none of his Ordnance men, none of Captain Pulteney's cavalry either. All were either dead or had fled.

He opened his fingers and the small-sword clanged down on to the rock.

Chapter Twenty-Four

Tuesday, August 12, 1690

Michael Hogan could see the pain in the face of the tall officer he had captured. Not that he cared a fig for the fellow's discomfort. This Englishman – Major Holcroft Blood, he had confirmed as his identity – had killed at least three good men in the night-fight at Ballyneety, and had been responsible for dozens of the deaths of Hogan's comrades at the ambush in County Cavan in the winter and at the bloody fight at the bridge of Duleek six weeks ago. But what intrigued Hogan about the fellow was that he seemed to feel more anguish at witnessing the desecration of the siege guns of the Train than he did at either his own wounded arm or at the sight of the scores of dead Englishmen, his own countrymen, who littered the torn turf of Ballyneety in the sunny morning.

At dawn's first light, with Blood bound tightly to the back of a tethered horse and watching in angry silence, Sarsfield and Hogan had ordered their men to fill each of the big cannon's barrels with gunpowder – right to the brim and packed down tight, for they had captured more than a hundred and twenty casks of the explosive – and they then rammed the gun barrels into the soft earth, and piled all the rest of the powder, match, broken wooden gun carriages, empty wagons and equipment over the top, creating a huge flammable hillock as big as a house. The draught horses and oxen had mostly fled during the battle; and it would have taken too long anyway to hitch up the gun carriages and bring the guns over the Silvermine Mountains and across the Shannon into County Clare.

They laid a forty-yard powder trail and hastily mounted up. Patrick Sarsfield's men and the raparees galloped off, a great, dusty, thunderous cavalcade, leaving Hogan and his prisoner alone. As Hogan crouched by the small pile of black powder that marked the beginning of the trail, with a battered tinder box in his hands, he said: 'You best get ready to ride hard, Major. This will make a din that will be heard by every living soul from here to Limerick. And your boys will be on us like a wasp swarm on a broken pot of honey.'

Holcroft said nothing in response. He stared hard at Hogan. His hands were tied and lashed to the pommel of his saddle. His legs were roped together under the horse's belly. The horse, a dun mare, was tethered securely by its reins to a stout alder bush. If this Irishman expected him to ride hard, he was going to have to explain that to the horse.

A spark struck, flint on steel, and the pile of gunpowder burst into fizzing, smoking life. Hogan freed Holcroft's horse, kept hold of the dun's reins and swung up into his own saddle. 'Be a good lad and keep your seat – and don't give me any trouble, Major Blood, or I'll happily put a pair of bullets through your kneecaps, and you'll *still* have to ride. Now, let's get going!'

Seeing the glow of fire running merrily along the train of powder towards the mound of cannon, wagons and equipment, Holcroft was content to put as much distance between himself and the coming holocaust as possible. He gripped the horse with his thighs and, at Hogan's command, they set off at a fast canter.

They managed to put a good half mile between them and Ballyneety Castle before the explosion. But when it came the noise – a great, shattering whump – felt like the rending of the earth. Holcroft felt the force of the blast like a hard slap on his whole back, his ears rang like church bells, his vision swam sickeningly before him. The horses – his and Hogan's – panicked, kicking out and snorting with fear, and then began galloping across the open fields, with Holcroft having to use all the strength in his legs to remain in the saddle. After two miles, Hogan mastered his mount and got Holcroft's mare to finally cease her headlong flight. They paused by a thick hawthorn hedge; Hogan exultant: 'Did you ever hear such a thing?' he said. 'I'll warrant that there never was a louder bang in all recorded time. Never!'

Holcroft scowled at him: he could imagine the state of his eight big guns, their brass barrels splayed open like flowers by the force of the explosion, those beautiful machines rendered for ever useless. No more than scrap metal.

'Don't go all sad and sulky on me, Major. We've a long ride ahead of us and I can't abide a companion who doesn't provide some light diversion on the lonely road, a little amusing conversation to pass the time. A joke or two.'

Hogan was leading them to a gate in the field and, once through, they entered a muddy track through a dark and tangled wood. Holcroft was damned to Hell if he would provide amusing conversation – or, God forbid, jokes – but he did have a host of questions that he urgently wanted his captor to answer.

'Where are you taking me?' he said.

'Over the hills and far away,' said Hogan. 'Isn't that what you boys like to sing on the march – when you're off to slaughter some poor bloody Irishmen?'

Holcroft knew the tune; he had heard it sung by the redcoats on the march to the Boyne. 'You consider *that* an amusing topic of conversation?' he said.

Hogan looked at him. 'Granted, it's not the wittiest jest I've ever made. Can you do better, sir?'

Holcroft could not. He looked at the rising sun to his left and said: 'We are heading more or less due south. So . . . are we going to Mallow, or Fermoy, or somewhere else on the Blackwater River?'

'Further than that. But, tell me, Major, if you don't like my cracks about your butchering soldiers, would you like to hear a few choice jests about your sweet King Billy, the cheeky wee mouse who's gobbled up all of the cheese?'

Holcroft said: 'Mouse? Oh, yes, a cheese-eating Dutchman. I understand the joke. So witty. I collect then that you love King James, Major Hogan, is that so?'

'Hmpff,' said his captor.

'I've heard your countrymen now call him *Séamus an Chaca*, after his performance at the Boyne – how would you put that into English, I wonder?'

'That's enough conversation,' growled Hogan. 'Now shut up and ride.'

The two men rode all day, stopping only once at noon for watered ale and bread and cheese from Hogan's saddlebags. The ropes were badly chafing Holcroft's wrists but he was too proud to mention his pains to the Irishman. They saw patrols of English cavalry in the distance – the noise of the explosion must have been heard far and wide, as Hogan had said – and the cavalry were out in force in the hunt for Sarsfield and his men. In the afternoon, they had to hide in a barn off the road, while a squadron of English redcoats trotted past, with Hogan holding his pistol to the back of Holcroft's head and whispering dire threats of extinction if the Englishman made the smallest peep.

They swung west, almost as far as Killarney, to avoid the patrols, and dusk found them on the Blackwater River, making camp in a wood near the water's edge. It was only then that Hogan noticed the fresh blood on Holcroft's wrists.

'You're a damn fool. You should have said something,' he muttered. In the dying light, filtered through the trees, he made Holcroft swear that he would not attack him or try to escape that night. 'I want your true word of honour, Major Blood,' Hogan said sternly. 'Give it to me and I will tend your wounds.'

Holcroft was exhausted, weakened by blood loss, and hungry. He reluctantly gave his parole not to attempt violence against Hogan nor try to flee from his captor until dawn. Hogan dressed his wrists with a concoction of goose fat and herbs, bandaged them, and checked the bullet graze on his forearm, and bandaged that too. He gruffly said that Holcroft might remain untied till the morning. 'Break your word and God will smite you – that is, if I don't get ye first,' Hogan said, before sending Holcroft off to gather firewood.

There was a moment, when Holcroft was out of sight of the camp with an armful of broken branches, when temptation seized him. What if he ran now? Hared away into the trees and kept on running? Hogan would be unlikely to find him ... But Holcroft was essentially a man of rules, of laws, of order. He had given his word. He sighed, picked up a final branch and began to walk back to the camp. It was only then he saw Hogan, five yards away, half hidden by a thick trunk, watching him and holding a cocked pistol upright in his hand.

They ate a thin stew of boiled dried beef strips and spongy carrots and settled down on either side of the small fire. Hogan pulled out a bottle of some clear spirit from his pack, took a huge swig and offered it to Holcroft.

The Ordnance officer drank, coughed like a dying beggar, felt his eyes smart and stream with fiery tears and said, 'What the Hell is that? Gin?'

'Poteen,' said Hogan with a wink. 'Fine stuff. Put hairs on your arse.'

They sat in silence for a while, then Holcroft said, 'We are going to Cork, aren't we?'

'That we are.'

'But why? What's in Cork? Why was I not taken to Limerick? To your main army? Are you worried you'll lose me when the city falls?'

Hogan chuckled. 'Limerick won't fall,' he said. 'Not now. Not this year.'

'You think you can win this war?'

'It's not impossible. And I – and many good men like me – will fight until we rid Ireland of the last Englishman. Your people have no business here.'

'My father was an Irishman – he never claimed to be English.'

'Is that so?' said Hogan. 'Blood, Blood . . . I knew some Bloods over in County Clare. A man called Neptune Blood. Some of your brood, perhaps?'

'My father's family came from there.'

'They were double-damned Protestants, of course, godless heretics to a man, but not such bad people, down in the bone. Wild as devils when the drink was in them, and a little too proud, but not bad folk. I'll admit that to you now.'

They sat in silence for a while, passing the liquor, watching the fire.

'Cosy, isn't it,' said Hogan. 'A fire and bottle at the end of a long day's ride – what else does a man need, eh?'

Holcroft said nothing.

'There are folk who say every man needs a woman and I can't deny the pleasure of a good wench. But this is fine and dandy, too.' Hogan drank again.

He passed the bottle to Holcroft. 'So what do you say, Englishman?'

'About what?'

'You got yourself a woman? Or are you a fire-and-bottle man?'

Holcroft said nothing for a spell but it was clear that the man was attempting to be friendly and he could see no harm in being civil to his captor.

'There is a woman in Dublin that I . . .' He stopped. How could he tell this hairy bandit how he felt about Caroline? 'There is a woman in Dublin who is under my protection. At least, she was, until . . .' Holcroft trailed off.

'Under your protection, eh? Is that what you lusty English fellows are calling it now? She got a name, this beautiful lady who needs protecting?'

'Caroline Chichester.'

'*Jesus!* Not her. Lady Caroline. Belfast girl, brother's Lord Donegall?'

'You know her?'

'I don't *know* her. But she does have something of a reputation.'

Holcroft was suddenly angry. 'What the Devil d'you mean by that, sir?'

His unbound hands were clenched into large fists. And he saw that Hogan had his hand on his horse pistol.

'Easy, now, Major Blood. No need to fly off the handle. Have yourself another drink and we'll just let the subject drop. All right?'

Hogan passed the bottle left-handed, his right on the gun. Holcroft drank.

They sat quietly for a few moments then Holcroft said: 'So, why Cork?'

'There is a man there, a Frenchman, who says he wants to speak to you,' said Hogan. 'And he will pay handsomely for the privilege. That's why.'

Despite the warm night, the heat of the fire and the poteen in his belly, Holcroft felt an uncomfortable chill run down his spine.

'A Frenchman,' he said. 'Red hair, short stature, very fancy clothes, goes by the name of Narrey or the Comte d'Erloncourt? Yes?'

'That's the fella.'

'You know that he's likely to murder me, don't you?' said Holcroft.

'Maybe,' said Hogan. 'That's for him to decide. But I will promise you this: I'll not harm you unless you try to run from me. Remember your parole.'

Despite his exhaustion, Holcroft slept badly that night. He thought once again about breaking his word and running from the Irishman but his honour kept him where he was – that, and the paradoxical thought that he was, in fact, being brought face to face at last with the man who had been responsible for the deaths of Aphra Behn and less directly Enoch Jackson. Perhaps there might be some way he could strike a lethal blow at the murderous spymaster, perhaps . . .

After a cold breakfast they crossed the Blackwater and rode south-east. Hogan insisted – at pistol point – that Holcroft allow his wrists to be bound again. 'It never does to strain a man's word of honour too far, Major Blood,' he said jovially as he tied the rope. 'We are all of us only human!'

When they stopped for a drink and to rest the horses a few miles north of Cork, Holcroft made a last attempt to persuade the Irishman to set him free.

'Why are you doing this, man? You are taking me to my certain death.'

'For the best reason there is, Major, for gold. Narrey has promised me a hundred pounds for your head. That is an offer I'd be foolish to turn down. You possess the most valuable poll in Ireland, Major. A fortune on your shoulders.'

'If it's just about the money, I'll give you two hundred to set me free.'

'Got all that coin in your pocket, have you?'

Holcroft sighed. 'I'll write you a promissory note. For *three* hundred.'

'I'll take Monsieur Narrey's cash in hand, Major, if ye don't mind.'

'How can you serve this foreigner, this Frenchman, and do his bidding? You claim to be a patriot, you claim to want to rid the land of foreigners . . .'

'The enemy of my enemy, Major.' Hogan sounded irritated. 'And who are you to accuse me of serving a foreigner. How English is your King Billy, eh?'

They entered Cork by the North Gate and clattered their horses down the main street. The Irish redcoats on the walls and the ordinary townsfolk in the main thoroughfare gawped at Holcroft, a big man, hatless, scarred shaven head with his tied hands before him, his horse being led by the Irishman. Holcroft racked his brains for a way to break free.

They stopped about halfway down the street and turned left into a wide open courtyard with several large brick buildings – soldiers' barracks by the look of the flags on top and the redcoat sentries outside them – and a grim medieval-looking round stone tower in the north-east corner set into the city's wall. They dismounted, with Hogan helping Holcroft to climb down from the saddle, and then the Irishman bundled him towards the ancient tower by the scruff of his coat and pushed in through the open iron-bound door.

'I'm here to see the Frenchman,' said Hogan to a bald clerk who sat at a lectern just inside the door. 'Comte d'Erloncourt. They tell me this is his lair.'

'On the first floor,' said the clerk. 'But I should warn you, sir . . .'

'I'll find it,' said Hogan. He frogmarched Holcroft up a spiral stair that followed the tower's curving wall, past several noisome cells populated by a half dozen malnourished prisoners, who stared at the two of them mutely from the bars as they passed by. Then Hogan crossed the landing, knocked briskly at a plain wooden door and, without waiting to be invited, pushed his way inside.

Holcroft, who had been bracing himself for another sight of his enemy, was surprised to find himself face to face with a powerfully built man in his early twenties, with cropped hair, a lumpy, badly scarred face under a shapeless cap of the kind worn by French fishermen or sailors.

He looked round the room. To the right of the door was a broad shelf on which Holcroft could see a jumble of ironmongery: chains, manacles, spare keys to the cells, a broad surgical knife, a pair of heavy pincers, what looked very much like a rusty thumbscrew. He looked away hastily and fixed his eyes on the scarred, tough-looking young man, who was leaning casually against a beautiful escritoire, a carved desk, painted and inlaid with polished ivory and walnut. He had a bottle tipped up to his lips. He ignored them till he had drunk his fill then:

'What the fuck do you mean by bursting in here, you ill-mannered turds?' he said in a gutter dialect of Parisian French. 'The fuck you want here?'

'I'm Mick Hogan. Where is Monsieur d'Erloncourt? I must see him now.'

The man put down his bottle on the top of the escritoire. Holcroft could not help but think of the ugly ring the wet bottle would make on the inlaid wood.

'Ah, yes, of course,' the French sailor said in English, wiping his mouth on his ragged sleeve, 'you are Hogan, the one who gallops about. The monsieur has spoken often of you. It is a pleasure, sir, to make your acquaintance.'

'Where's your man?'

'Not here,' he replied. 'My name is Matisse, I have the honour to serve monsieur le comte. He's been summoned to Limerick by General Lauzun.'

'Is that so?' said Hogan, with a grim smile. 'Well, I'm not lugging this awkward bastard all the way back up there. So I will put him in your charge, Matisse. Take very good care of him or you will pay for it with your life. You hear me? Monsieur d'Erloncourt has promised me a hundred pounds in gold for his head. And I shall claim it in due course. You can tell monsieur le comte that I shall require cash for the Englishman's head. But that I'll throw in the neck and the rest of his body absolutely free. Gratis. It is my gift to him.'

Chapter Twenty-Five

Saturday, August 23, 1690

The constant noise of the big English guns had given Henri d'Erloncourt a monstrous headache – and this was only the first day that they had come into action against the decrepit walls of the besieged city of Limerick. He sat at his desk in the side of the room at the top of King John's Castle, and cradled his sore head in his hands. It did not help.

The Frenchman had been surprised by the speed with which the great guns that General Sarsfield boasted of utterly destroying had been replaced. The Duke of Tyrconnell said the replacement Ordnance had probably been brought across from the fortifications of the city of Waterford, which William's men had captured shortly after the battle of the Boyne. But Henri suspected that not all of the big guns at Ballyneety had been completely destroyed, the astounding success that Sarsfield claimed for his daring raid notwithstanding.

Whatever the truth, Henri was disappointed with the two senior Irish commanders in Limerick. They could not seem to do anything right. The defences of the old city were woefully disorganised. Morale among the Jacobite troops was lower than at any time. And, worst of all, ten days after the biggest man-made explosion that Henri had ever heard – it had shattered house windows and toppled solid oak dressers, even six miles away in Limerick – the English had simply replaced their cannon with others and the new guns were even now hammering steadily at the walls. In a matter of three or four days they would have a practicable breach and then all would be lost. Their troops would pour into the city and overwhelm it in a matter of hours.

The war would be over.

But it was not only the siege guns that were giving Henri an aching head that morning. His best secret agent, Agricola, had gone strangely silent – not a peep for more than two weeks. Usually the agent would send something via the courier networks that stretched across Ireland: well-paid tinkers, travelling priests and a few well-chosen and well-mounted raparees who delivered close-written notes in code every few days – even if it was just a background assessment of changes in King William's military capabilities or a few items of gossip from the officers' mess. But the last Henri had heard from his most valuable asset in the heart of the English establishment in Dublin had been the report in early August about the powerful Train of Artillery heading for Limerick. Deep in his belly, Henri knew that Agricola had been unmasked and was now dead, or facing execution. Well . . . *tant pis*, that was the fate of most secret agents in wartime, and Agricola had served France for a whole year – and been paid handsomely in gold for that service. There was little that Agricola could divulge to his enemies of Henri's covert activities, few vital secrets to betray under torture. So then, Agricola, *merci* and *adieu*!

But Henri had another source of disquiet, another problem to make his poor head throb: the Irishman Michael Hogan, the Galloper. The Major had, according to Sarsfield, captured an English officer at the fight at Ballyneety and had ridden south to Cork with him – for reasons unclear to Sarsfield – and he had not been seen since. The Irish general, flushed with his great success in destroying the enemy guns, had not tried to prevent Hogan's mission or dissuade him from his path. According to the general, the English cavalry had been buzzing about like flies on a dung-heap after the explosion and it had been every man for himself. Sarsfield had only just managed to get his own surviving men safely back across the Shannon by riding all day like demons. Two men, travelling alone, in a countryside crawling with vengeful English cavalry . . . their chances of evading the enemy were slim to none.

Was Hogan then dead or captured? This was to Henri potentially worse news than the loss of Agricola. He had been grooming Hogan to take the role that poor dear Guillaume du Clos had filled so admirably. Hogan had been destined to be Henri's strong right hand – the man was brave and ruthless enough, and while his bottomless lust for gold was still the prime motivating force, Henri was fairly sure that he could bind the Galloper to him with more subtle and enduring bonds. The man Hogan was a true Christian, a devout son of Holy Mother Church, and his deep commitment to the land of his birth, too, could be used to manipulate him. But if he was dead, incapacitated or rotting in an English gaol, then he could be of no further use to Henri – or to France. And all the time and money he had lavished on the man was wasted. That would be a blow. Yet one he could survive.

The new fellow they had sent him from Paris, Premier-Maitre Jean Matisse of the Sun King's navy, who was manning the bureau in Cork, was a reliable sort, loyal and strong, and apparently a gifted sailor, although he was a little uncouth and not perhaps as intelligent or well bred as he might be. It was odd that he had not heard from him either. Although the English patrols might easily have intercepted any messages from Cork.

Such was the incessant din from the English guns – audible even here in King John's Castle on the far side of the city from the barrage – that Henri did not at first hear the knocking on the door of his round office on the top floor.

'Enter!' he called, wondering if it were time for dinner in the hall on the ground floor – it was long past noon. He was hungry, tired and his head pounded like a kettledrum. Perhaps he would order hot wine to be sent up after the meal. Or a little brandy. Maybe he would take a long nap later.

He was surprised to see a young French officer pushing open the door and holding it for the squat, square form of General Lauzan, who strode inside.

'Shut the door and stand guard outside,' Lauzun growled at the junior officer. 'We do not wish to be disturbed.'

They exchanged the usual pleasantries and Lauzun, who seemed preoccupied, wandered over to the curved wall and peered out of an arrow slit at the bustling cavalry encampment on the County Clare side of the Shannon.

'It is nearly time, d'Erloncourt,' he said.

Henri said: 'Do you think that I don't know that?'

General Lauzun appeared not to hear him. 'It's just a matter of days now and I don't want us to be caught here when they break through,' he said.

'So we leave?' said Henri. 'What will our gallant allies say to that?'

'I've spoken to Tyrconnell,' said Lauzun, 'persuaded him. He agrees with me. This war is lost and it is time to recognise that uncomfortable fact. You will have heard that the Earl of Marlborough is preparing to bring thousands of fresh troops to Ireland by ship? You read the secret report from the *cabinet noir*?'

Henri nodded.

'So, it is time for us to go home, my friend. Ireland is doomed.'

So much for perpetual war, thought Henri. *Yet I do not wish to sacrifice my own life for this land of brutes and savages. Agricola is dead, or captured. Hogan most likely, too. There will be other wars. The King has need of me yet.*

He said aloud: 'So the Duke of Tyrconnell and all his men will come with us then? To Galway? We are simply to abandon Limerick to the English?'

'Yes, Tyrconnell and his regiments will take ship with us in Galway Bay – I have arranged for the navy transports to meet us there – and he and his men will serve Louis in the Low Countries.

The King made a generous invitation to all Irishmen who wish to serve him. But there's a problem . . .'

'I believe I can guess: General Sarsfield, yes?'

'He says he will not yield Limerick to the enemy. He says he will fight on for as long as he is able. He genuinely thinks he can win the battle here.'

'Then there is no problem. Let Sarsfield fight here – and die – if the fool wishes to, and with as many of his men as choose to throw away their lives.'

The sound of loud voices could be heard from beyond the door. Someone was arguing with General Lauzun's aide. There was the unmistakable meaty sound of a blow and the door flew open to reveal Michael Hogan standing over the prone body of the junior French officer. The Irishman was rubbing at the red knuckles of his right fist.

'Morning to you, Henri,' said Hogan. 'I'd like a brief moment of your time, if you don't mind. It is fairly urgent, I believe, but I am afraid I was not able to communicate that urgency with sufficient force to your wee man here.'

'It seems to me that you used far more than sufficient force,' growled Lauzun. 'If you have killed him, I shall make you pay for it, monsieur!'

'Major Michael Hogan, may I introduce to you General Antoine de Caumont, Duc de Lauzun, commander of the French Brigade here in Limerick.'

'Your servant, General. I wish you joy – and all the usual non-sense. But, if you don't mind excusing us, sir, I need to speak to old Henri here alone.'

The past ten days had been a strange, dream-like time for Michael Hogan. After leaving Holcroft Blood in the hands of the crude French sailor in Cork he had headed north towards Limerick, but slowly. He rode with a heavy heart.

In truth, he felt a deep sense of guilt about handing over the English officer to his doom. Sure, Blood was an enemy, even though he claimed an Irish father; sure, he had killed more than a few of Hogan's friends. But he liked the man. There was something about the fellow that sparked respect in him, the kinship of fellow warriors, perhaps, or the acknowledgement that they were both at bottom honourable men, a feeling which Hogan found hard to ignore. He would have fought the tall Englishman hand to hand – indeed, he had done so more than once – and he would have killed him if he could, just as he was sure that Blood would slaughter him in the heat of battle without a second thought. But delivering the man up to torture and death at the hands of that foppish piece-of-shit and his drunken minion – well, that stuck in his gullet. He thought about the gold – the hundred pounds in *louis d'or* that Narrey had promised him for his head, his usual moral panacea – but it didn't make him feel any better about what he had done. Indeed, when he looked deeply into his heart he felt dirty and dishonoured by his recent actions.

And honour meant a great deal to Hogan. So when he rode out of Cork, he was not clear in his mind where he wanted to go. Obviously, he wanted the money, and the gold was with Narrey in Limerick. But if he went back there, he would be putting himself under the control of the Frenchman, accepting servitude: the money notwithstanding, he wasn't sure he wished to do that.

In the event, the decision was made for him. Ten miles north of Cork, near the village of Grenagh, he ran into an English patrol, a small company of red-coated dragoons, who enthusiastically chased him west all the way into folds of the Boggeragh Mountains before he managed to lose them. He was dog tired, he realised, when he was able finally to stop running, and so was his poor sweat-lathered horse. He slept fitfully in a damp ditch that night with his pistol in his hand and the next morning he pushed on west, towards Killarney, but avoided the town and the people he knew, and eventually found himself in a small wood on the southern shores of Lough Leane. There he made his camp.

At first, alone, hidden by the trees beside a stretch of smooth water, he felt isolated and a little uncomfortable in his solitude – then after several days of tickling brown trout from the streams, hunting squirrels and rabbits for the pot with his carbine, swimming before breakfast every day, he began to feel calmer, at peace with himself. He was stealing time from his own life. And it was a joyous theft. He thought a great deal about Henri d'Erloncourt who would no doubt be chafing at his absence; he thought about Holcroft Blood – and the doom that awaited him. In his idle hours, he recalled all the women he had known and loved, the men he had fought, the adventures he had enjoyed, the wild midnight rides. He thought about the situation of the little untenanted sheep farm he hoped to buy with Narrey's gold, when the war was over, and spent a morning riding over to it and across its heathery slopes and small, neglected fields. It was a humble place in the lee of the Purple Mountain, wild, remote and beautiful. He believed he would have enough money to swing the deal, and if it cost more he would find it somehow. A decision was made. After more than a week of living like a savage, ten pounds lighter but clearer of mind, he saddled up his horse and set off at a brisk trot for Limerick.

'Where the Devil have you been?' said Henri, when General Lauzun had reluctantly yielded the room, and taken his stunned but living aide with him.

'Never you mind. I have been about my own business in the south.'

'Your business *is* my business – you serve at the pleasure of His Majesty King Louis, Major, as I'm sure I do not have to remind you. His Majesty is the man who pays your stipend. And I am His Majesty's deputy here in Ireland.'

'I hereby resign my commission. As of this moment. Draw up some papers, or whatever is necessary, but I can no longer serve either you or Louis.'

'You've lost your taste for my gold?' said Henri, putting his head on one side and considering the Irishman. 'You've come into an inheritance, perhaps.'

'I've lost my taste for service,' said Hogan. 'But there is a matter of business that remains between us. And I mean to hold you to your word on it.'

'Oh, yes?'

'You once offered me a hundred pounds for the head of Holcroft Blood. I now claim that prize. I'll take my money in gold, and my leave of you. Today.'

Henri looked pointedly at the Irishman's hands. 'I see no severed head,' he said. 'And no head means no prize money for you.'

'His head is still attached to his neck and is currently in the cells with the rest of his living body in the Old Tower at Cork, guarded by your man Matisse. I captured him at Ballyneety, took him to Cork, where I believed you were to be found. I delivered Holcroft Blood's head to your new man – and now I want my money.'

'Blood's head is fifty miles away. You have not delivered it to me.'

'Do not trifle with me, Monsieur d'Erloncourt,' said Hogan. 'You have had good service from me. I have fulfilled all my bargains with you. Know this: if you try to cheat me in this matter you will suffer for it.'

'Threats now? And you were so scornful of them when we first met.'

'Pay me or you will die, monsieur, I cannot say it clearer than that.'

'Well, that is certainly crystal clear, Major Hogan. But consider this: this old castle, built by Jean Sansterre – the Lackland, as you call him – is occupied by more than a hundred stout men of the French Brigade. I have but to call out . . .'

'You would die before they came through that door.' Hogan's right hand moved across his belly to rest lightly on the brass hilt of his cutlass.

'And you would die shortly afterwards. But there is a way that we can avoid all this unpleasant bloodshed, Major. A way that both of us can continue to breathe – and, furthermore, a way in which you can receive your money.'

'I'm listening.'

'The money – the gold – is not here. It is safe in my strong box in Cork. And the enemy, I am told, are thick on the roads between here and that port. Now, I have some business in Galway over the next week or so, ten days maximum. I have affairs that need to be put in order before my departure . . .'

'You are leaving Ireland?'

'With the French Brigade, and some of your men, too. Shortly, in a few weeks, Major Hogan, it seems that we must bid each other a fond farewell.'

'And my money?'

'I am getting to that, Major. Have a little patience. As I say, I must attend to some private matters in Galway, which will occupy me for about ten days, and then, if you would be so good, you may meet me there at the sign of the Blue Anchor in Harbour Street – shall we say on the third day of September? – and escort me safely across the territory controlled by the enemy to Cork, where I shall interrogate the prisoner Blood – and pay you what you're owed in full.'

'How do I know that you will not just sail merrily away from Galway, and back to France, never to return?'

'You must trust me . . .'

Hogan scoffed.

'You *must* trust me,' Henri repeated, 'because you have no other choice. I cannot pay you – the money is in Cork, not here. All you can do is kill me – and die yourself. If you follow my suggestion, you shall have your money in less than two weeks and our business will be done. You need never see me again. The French ships can pick me up from Cork and take me home from there.'

Hogan stared at him for a few moments. The urge was very strong to draw his blade and hack the little shit-weasel into chunks. He controlled it.

'Think on this, Major Hogan, before you decide. I was willing to pay a hundred pounds in gold to end the miserable life of Holcroft Blood. Do you think I would pass up that opportunity? Consider how much his life, his death, means to me. You might also consider, that my strong box – my whole treasury, if you will – is in Cork. You *will* find me in Galway, at the Blue Anchor, in ten days!'

Hogan gave an angry jerk of the head. 'I'd better find you there,' he said. 'Because I *will* come after you, follow you all the way to France, if you're not.'

Chapter Twenty-Six

Wednesday, August 27, 1690

The rain falling on Hogan's upturned face was warm and welcome. He did not care that his riding cloak was soaked, and the muddy green coat beneath it too, nor that the jaunty pheasant feather in his hat was a bedraggled reed. The rain meant the approach of winter. Rain meant winter quarters; an end to hostilities for months.

The rain, which had started an hour after dawn, had also briefly silenced the English guns. Open powder kegs could be spoiled by the wet; lit matches were often extinguished, unlit ones ruined. When the sky turned black, the gun batteries were hastily covered with tarpaulins, and the crews stood down till it passed. It would not last, Hogan knew that, the sky to the south-west, behind the gusting wind, was a pale innocent blue. It was a squall that had drenched him, nothing more, and by noon the sun would return and with it the anger of the siege guns.

For the past three days Hogan had stood his duty on the parapet of the old wall in Irish Town. He had thrown off his major's rank, which had always made him feel like an impostor, and dismissed what was left of his band of raparees to fend for themselves. Many had drifted away during his sojourn in Lough Leane – gone home to their farms, or signed up with one of the regular cavalry units – and as a mere volunteer, a private soldier, Michael Hogan found himself doing his part in the fight for Irish freedom as a musketeer. He wasn't sure why – only that men were needed on the walls to keep the enemy out. And he found that he could not shirk when the call went out for volunteers.

He spent the hours on duty idly taking pot shots at the Williamite sappers toiling in the trenches that wormed their way a little closer to the walls every day. The nearest sappers, a company of Danes, Hogan believed, were no more than sixty yards away now. He had missed his mark dozens of times – even his modern French-made flintlock carbine was not an accurate weapon. Like all muskets it was meant to be fired by a company of soldiers at another company – in other words, at a very large target – and at a maximum range of perhaps fifty or sixty yards. In these conditions about half of the company's fifty or so bullets would strike a man in the enemy formation. Hogan had always used the carbine as a close-range weapon, riding up to an enemy and firing at a distance of only twenty or thirty feet, which gave him a reasonable chance of a kill. But the defenders had plenty of ammunition, and he and his new comrades of the hastily formed First Limerick Volunteers all blazed away at the enemy from time to time during their watches, often just for something to do. In the past three days, Hogan had killed or badly wounded at least two of the sappers. But despite these small victories over the foe, when Hogan killed like this, firing from a distance at some dog-tired, mud-smeared workman, despite the loud cheers from his comrades on the parapet, it still felt like cold-blooded murder.

When he was not harassing the enemy at their digging, and when the siege guns were playing on his stretch of wall, he spent much of the time cowering on the shuddering walkway, hugging the wall – even doing a bit of praying from time to time – as the enemy's bombardment crashed again and again into the crumbling east wall. Three of his comrades had been wounded by flying shards of rock. One man had gone mad and, frothing at the mouth and stripping off all his clothing, had run back into the city never to be seen again.

More than half of the French troops – some three thousand men – had gone north to Galway to prepare for their departure, but two thousand of King Louis' troops under the Marquis de Boisseleau, a veteran of the wars against the Dutch and an expert in all manner of siegecraft, remained behind in Limerick. General Alexandre de Boisseleau was one of the few brave souls in the Jacobite army – along with the irrepressible Patrick Sarsfield – who believed that the old city could be successfully defended, and the energetic Frenchman's reward for arguing this point insistently with his superior officers was to be left behind and personally charged with Limerick's defence. He had also been granted the title of Governor by the Duke of Tyrconnell, King James's official representative in Ireland, just before that doddery old fool fled the city with General Lauzun and the slippery worm Henri, Comte d'Erloncourt.

Mercifully, the city of Limerick had *not* been stripped of all its fighting men by the departure of the three senior commanders. A total of fourteen thousand Irish and French infantry remained behind its battered walls, under the command of Boisseleau; and across the River Shannon in County Clare, General Sarsfield had command of some two thousand five hundred cavalry.

Limerick was not yet lost. And though they were badly outnumbered by their enemies – there were twenty-five thousand of King Billy's men in a semi-circular sweep of trenches, redoubts and fortification to the east and south – they were still not fully surrounded. Nor were they cut off from supplies from the rest of Ireland, which came in thorough County Clare. And, best of all, it seemed the rains were coming, heralding the end of the campaign season.

The squall passed, and Hogan could feel the warmth of the returning sun on his wet shoulders. Mortars from one of the enemy batteries on Singland Hill opened up again – a strange distant coughing sound – and bombs arced up in the clearing sky and sailed down to explode in the streets of Irish Town or crash through tile roofs and detonate inside the walls of houses and workshops. The brunt of the enemy fire over the past few days had been absorbed by this southern part of Limerick, an area filled with shops, warehouses, manufactories, slaughter yards, taverns, pawn shops and the houses of the poorer citizens, which were connected by networks of narrow, filthy lanes.

In a while, the big siege guns would resume their work on widening the breach. They had already cracked open the ancient wall about seventy yards to Hogan's right, a V-shaped hole had been blown in the mossy medieval stones, revealing a glimpse of the town inside to the enemy in their trenches, and tumbling down a rough staircase of rubble on the outside.

As Hogan watched, a pair of siege guns in Singland Hill gave a double bark, one gun firing an instant before the other, and the two sixteen-pound iron balls screamed through the air and cracked into Limerick's wall a few feet apart on the northern side of the breach. There was a rumbling shower of stones and detritus, a thin plume of dust rising like smoke, and then a large section of the wall slowly peeled away and crashed into the outer ditch. From where Hogan was watching, the dust-wreathed breach seemed infinitely wider, like an invitingly open door. *Welcome to Limerick, please do come in.* A few more like that last and there'd be a gap you could drive a carriage though.

The English knew this as well as Hogan did. Even now, the raparee could see files of men coming forward, tall, blue-coated Dutchmen, the elite guards, he thought, as well as big-framed redcoats from the English regiments. These would be their grenadiers, he supposed, selected from the besieging battalions to make a Forlorn Hope. When the breach was deemed practicable, the great guns would cease again, and these veterans would surge forward in attack.

Another pair of enemy guns fired from Singland Hill; another double impact crack against the walls and a crumbling tumble of ancient stones.

The enemy were filing forward into the attack trenches, great snakes of men winding on through the trenches in red or blue coats, muskets slung over their shoulders, hats pulled over their eyes. It would certainly be today; he knew it. Today was the day they would make their grand attack.

He wondered if he should seek out an officer, maybe Paddy Sarsfield or someone else he knew well, and share this insight. But he decided against it. Alexandre de Boisseleau was no novice when it came to siege warfare. He knew where the breach was and probably to the very minute when it would be practicable. He was doubtless already anticipating a massed assault on this day and had made appropriate preparations. Besides, Hogan was no longer an officer. His task was to stand on the parapet, do his sworn duty and shoot straight when the attack came. Nothing more.

Another cannon ball – just one this time – cracked into the eastern wall, on the far side of the breach, another dusty shower of rock and grit cascaded into the ditch below. *Not long,* thought Hogan. *Not long till the true contest begins.*

Hogan heard the bells of St Mary's Cathedral toll the hour. It was three o'clock, and he felt a great weight of relief float off his still-damp shoulders. This was the hour when his company – the second company of the Limerick Volunteers – was due to be relieved by a regular company of Irish Foot Guards on this section of the wall for the evening watch. He looked over his shoulder down at the narrow streets of Irish Town below him – there was no sign of the relieving company of redcoats, just the usual packs of scurrying civilians, haggard men, women and children who were trying to go about their daily business in the city amid the irregularly falling mortar bombs. One young woman was trying to sell mussels from a tray around her neck to a pair of slovenly, drunken dragoons, who were more interested in the charms of her person than her wares.

The Foot Guards would be along shortly, no doubt. But Hogan wished they would hurry. Looking out at the enemy trenches, he could see that the nearest ones were almost completely filled with men, Dutchmen in blue and Danes in yellow, English, too, in the red coats so similar to the Irish troops. He saw that the redcoats wore a sprig of green in their black hats to identify them to friend and foe alike. The cannon fire had grown in volume and regularity; and Hogan could feel every pounding strike against the wall through the soles of his boots.

There was a call from below, an Irish officer, and a company of His Majesty's King James's Foot Guards all around him. They were a smart lot, Hogan admitted, their redcoats brushed, their buttons shined, their blue breeches and stockings untarnished by mud and filth. Each man carried a long and heavy matchlock musket – there were no pikemen on wall duty – and a curved sword, and they looked as fierce a crew as any Hogan had seen.

As he and his colleagues filed meekly down the stone steps and into the street, Hogan nodded to the guards officer in a friendly way, but the man stared back coldly and turned away to urge his men briskly up on to the parapet.

The Volunteers' company officer, Captain Paul Johns, a scarlet-cheeked drunk who had been a successful grain merchant in another life, muttered for them to hurry along the narrow street. He no doubt wished to get back to his bottles – and Hogan himself was thinking in terms of a swig or two of brandy, and something hot to eat, when he arrived back at his mean lodgings by the cathedral on the King's Island. He suddenly realised that the English guns had stopped. The silence was oddly loud and eerie. He tried to think when he had last heard a cannon's report. On the wall, he was sure of it, but not since.

'Wait up, captain.' Hogan seized Johns' sleeve. 'Just halt for a wee minute.'

The officer looked at him angrily. Hogan released the officer and lifted a hand for silence. The men around him – apprentices, dockworkers, labourers, shopmen, civilians all – glared at him impatiently but they held their tongues.

'We need to be getting along,' said Johns.

'Wait,' said Hogan. *Was he being foolish? No, all the signs were there.*

He heard a gun, a small one, a Falcon or Saker, the kind used for giving signals. It fired once, then another fired a moment later, and then a third. Then all quiet. Then a sound of distant cheering, hundreds of men all shouting at once.

'They are coming,' Hogan said. 'We must get back to the walls.'

'The walls?' said the captain. 'No, our watch is over. We're due a rest.'

'Hear that?' said Hogan. There was the distant popping of muskets, and the shouts and calls of many men. 'The English are making their attack . . .'

'You men!' A man in blue and gold, with long black moustaches, was calling to them from the corner of the street ahead. 'You men come with me. We must man the barricades with every musket. Look alive. Quickly!'

Hogan recognised Lieutenant-Colonel de Beaupré of the French Brigade, one of Governor Boisseleau's arrogant young officers, a notorious fire-eater.

'We'd best do what the colonel orders,' said Hogan to Johns. The captain nodded sadly. He and the rest of the company began to jog after the Frenchman.

Governor Boisseleau had been most industrious over the past few days since the first serious cracks appeared in the crumbling east wall. He had ordered his men to clear the street behind that section, knocking down obstacles, pulling apart several sagging timber-and-turf hovels, demolishing a blacksmith's forge and carting away the debris. He removed anything that might provide cover to the enemy and then sealed off the side streets with barricades of upturned wagons and carts, reinforcing the spaces between them with sacks filled with earth and baulks of timbers. The main route into Limerick he blocked with bricks and paving slabs and broken masonry from the wall, stacked chest high, along with heavy items of furniture and huge wine barrels filled with water. He placed cannon on the various barricades and manned them with Irish sailors from the port of Limerick who were used to working the guns at sea. Then he filled the barricades between the cannon with hundreds of musket men.

He had created a *coupure* – a secondary wall inside the section of the ancient city wall that was steadily being blasted apart. And between the breach and the new barricades, he cleared a broad expanse of ground inside the tumbled rubble of the wall, fifty yards deep and thirty wide – a killing zone.

King William's Forlorn Hope – five hundred of his finest grenadiers from a dozen regiments and almost as many nations, roaring their challenges, shouting away their fears – came spilling out of their damp trenches, and began to run at the breach. They suffered a galling fire from the walls, where the musketeers of the Irish Foot Guards plied their lethal trade, shooting down from both sides into the charging grenadiers as fast as they could fire. Dozens of men dropped as bullets from above smashed into their blue and red and yellow bodies, falling and being trampled by their comrades' boots as they rushed for the breach. But the grenadiers were brave men, they soaked up their punishment and surged forward, scrambling up the tumbled rubble outside the breach, some with flintlocks slung, using their bare hands to tear their way upwards, jostling each other, panting, a swarming tide of men, desperate to make it to the summit and through the twelve-yard-wide gap at the top and into the city.

Hogan, his body jammed against the wooden bed of an upturned hay wagon, his cheek against the iron rim of one of its wheels, looked on with awe as the wave of grenadiers crested the breach fifty yards away, a jumble of men in different uniforms, some blood streaked or bleeding, all looking as fearsome as devils. They brushed away the thin line of Irish redcoats behind the breach, shooting down their foes, slashing at them with swords, or merely batting the men aside with their musket butts. They began to spill down the inside of the rubble staircase, forty, sixty, now a hundred big men inside the bounds of Limerick. They roared like beasts as they came on, scenting victory, knowing they had done the hard, bloody part and made it through the city walls. Now came the slaughter and sack; now the people of Limerick and all their goods were at their mercy.

The first cannon belched flame a dozen yards to Hogan's right. Loaded with 'partridge', the cannon sprayed the rubble slope with bullets in a wide cone like a giant fowling piece, cutting down swathes of grenadiers, smashing them back against the rocky stair-case, severing limbs, crushing skulls, flensing the flesh from bones. Blood sprayed, the shrieks echoed round the killing zone.

'Kill them! Kill them all!' Colonel de Beaupré was shouting. Hogan put his carbine to his shoulder, then resting the barrel on a wheel spoke, he pulled back the cock, aimed briefly at the mass of staggering, slipping, blood-painted men on the slope and fired. His bullet cracked into the head of a Dutch blue-coat, blowing the skull apart and splashing the man next to him with his matter.

A hundred other muskets fired from the barricade at the same time, pelting the grenadiers with a lethal rain of lead. The enemy bodies danced and jerked like puppets under the onslaught. It was a miracle, to Hogan's eyes, that any were left standing. But one man, a redcoat, stood tall at the bottom of the rubble slope, pulled a round black object from a bag at his side, touched it to a burning fuse and bowled it hard underarm towards the barri-cades. The grenade bounced once, bounced again, trailing smoke and exploded.

There was a flash of white and red and Hogan felt a hot wind knock him staggering back. A great section of the wagon bed was blown out, a jagged hole the size of a bucket remaining; two spokes from the wheel had disappeared, too. But Hogan was miraculously whole but for a tear in his coat at the shoulder. He stepped forward again and began unthinkingly to reload his carbine. He glanced up and saw the tall grenadier in the act of hurling another one of his grenades, when a pair of musket balls slammed into his chest and dropped him like a sack full of sand. The numbers of the enemy in the breach and on the slope seemed, bizarrely, to have swelled. And Hogan, as he snatched rapid glances between his carbine-loading actions, saw that many more men were surging up and over the breach, hundreds more enemies were appearing. It occurred to Hogan that the enemy could not see the carnage that was taking place inside the killing zone and was feeding more and more men into the meat-grinder inside the *coupure*.

Cannon and muskets were firing from both sides now as the barricades on the side streets joined in the slaughter. The noise was deafening. A cannon to Hogan's left detonated massively, and wiped a dozen red-coated men from the face of the Earth. But more were spilling down the slope, now strewn with bodies and slick with blood. Hogan put the carbine to his shoulder and pulled the trigger. He did not wait to see if he had killed – he immediately set about reloading, biting the cartridge, priming the pan, pouring the pow-der down the barrel, spitting in the musket ball, ramming down the paper of the cartridge, aiming and firing. And again, not bothering to peer through the eggy-smelling smoke of his own firing and the men next to him. Reloading, aiming, firing. Repeat once more. The man to his left – one of the Volunteers – gave out a huge cry and fell back, half of his face missing. Hogan fired and began to reload.

When he paused to catch his breath, a gust of wind swept clear the smoke bank before him. He saw to his horror that the enemy had advanced into the killing zone, and were only twenty yards away. And still more were coming over the top of the breach. The enemy was committing all his strength to this little patch of blood-splashed Hell. Hogan shot a man in the chest and knocked him down but when he tried to reload he found that his carbine was now fouled, his wooden rammer would not penetrate more than halfway down the barrel.

There were enemy redcoats at his barricade, green sprigs in their hats marking them out – not that that was necessary; their enmity was plain from the ferocity with which they slashed and hacked at the wooden barrier with their swords, or pounded it with musket butts or tore greedily with their bare hands, ripping out chairs, pulling away tables. Hogan felt the urge to run deep in his belly. These people were maniacs. Devils. He drew his cutlass and shoved the blade through the hole in the wagon and into a snarling redcoat's stomach.

'At them, push them back.' Somewhere to Hogan's right, Colonel de Beaupré was screaming: 'Come on, you Irish, show yourselves to be men. Kill the English! Kill the bastards. Come with me!'

The cannon roared again and cleared a space in front of the barricade. Hogan saw Colonel de Beaupré clamber on to the top of the makeshift wall, his blue and gold uniform now powder-grimed and splashed with blood. He stood upright with the sword in his hand. 'Come with me now, men of Limerick. Let us end this. Who is with me? For your faith. For your country! For Ireland!' And the Frenchman punched his small-sword into the air and leapt down on to the far side, as the surge of enemies swept forwards to meet him.

Hogan found himself climbing up the side of the wagon, cutlass in hand, and leaping down on the other side. He had made no decision. He made no choice. He seemed to have no say in this at all. And he was not alone. All the Irishmen, hundreds of them along the barricade, were spilling over the top and coming forward in a great human wave to get to grips with the enemy. Even the

Irish Foot Guards were jumping down from the walls to join in the mêlée.

The two sides met and mashed into each other, no time for musketry, blade to blade, muscle against muscle, hatred and fear driving men to claw and bite, hack and stab; the noise was that of a howling mob, shouts of outrage, screams of pain and terror. Hogan slashed a grenadier laterally across the face, crunching through teeth and lips and half severing the skull itself. He stabbed a yellow-coated Dane through the thigh, dropping the man, then stamped on his anguished face as he moved past him. He felt a whirlwind of rage and fear buoy him up, give strength to his limbs. Like a warrior of old, he slashed, he sliced, his cutlass swinging and thudding into meat. His enemies fell back before the sweeps of his blade, and Hogan advanced again. The French colonel was still calling the men to come forward and fight. A soldier with a green sprig in his hat rose up from nowhere and pointed a pistol at Hogan. He pulled the trigger but the gun misfired as Hogan began his down stroke. The cutlass chopped through the man's extended arm. He screamed and curled away.

Hogan paused, panting. Amazed at his closeness to his own death. Every breath in his aching lungs was a burning miracle. From the rooftops on either side of the killing zone, Hogan could see the figures of men and women, and children even. They were hurling bricks and slates down on the boiling mass of the enemy; bottles too smashed down, splitting scalps, slicing faces and necks.

The Irish were shouting for their own victory. 'For Ireland; for James!'

And the enemy was being pushed back, slowly, surely. They were retreating. Hogan found himself at the foot of the rubble slope, the stones slick with blood, the dead and wounded a carpet of flesh that writhed and moaned.

He cut down a musket man, no more than a frightened boy, with a chop to his skinny neck. And stepped on to the rubble stair, then he was running up, up, towards the summit of the breach. Pushing the enemy up and away. And there, he stood in the breach and looked down on the enemy lines, for the first time in hours.

The enemy were not done yet. There were formations: red-coats, some blocks of men in grey a hundred yards away and they were marching in good discipline – every man in step, towards the breach in the walls. Hundreds of fresh soldiers. The might of William's army. And coming for them.

Hogan's countrymen were around him now. He could feel their joy, their courage and pride in what they had done. His own blood was fizzing in his veins. And Colonel de Beaupré was there, his raised sword slathered in red.

'Come on, *mes enfants*, one more charge. For Ireland! For France!'

The man set off down the slope of the breach at a full run, stumbling on the uneven surface. *He's mad*, thought Hogan. *The Frenchman is moon-struck.*

Along with hundreds of his compatriots he found himself gal-loping down the rubble slope, waving his own gory sword and bellowing like a furious bull. The Irishmen charged towards the formed bodies of the advancing enemy, screaming their war cries, as moon-mad as Colonel de Beaupré. And the Williamite troops saw them coming.

They halted. Dressed their ranks. Brought muskets up to their shoulders.

The first volley smashed into the charging Irish ranks, blow-ing scores of good men into the next life. The charge faltered, men stopped or hesitated, some stumbling over bodies. A line of smoke covered the first line of redcoats. And out of that grey bank the second volley lanced out, a hundred fiery spurts, which scythed through the Irish. Hogan felt a tug at his flapping coat that pulled him off course. He tripped over a dead man's leg, and fell on his face, the air knocked out of his lungs, winded, his cutlass sent flying, only a dozen yards from the nearest enemy sappers' trench.

He heard another disciplined English musket volley scream over his head. And he knew then that all was lost. Squirming round on his side he could see many of his comrades running back towards the breach. Their lunatic attack was over and done, and now it was their enemies' turn to advance and kill. There were redcoats running at him. Thirty yards away, red-faced men in scarlet coats, green sprigs in their hatbands, muskets plugged with bayonets grasped before them in both hands. They were coming to kill him – and that was all right – he had done his duty well enough – but they were coming to kill his comrades, too. And that was not. He could see Colonel de Beaupré, a dozen yards away, his back to the enemy, screaming at the running Irishmen to stand and fight. And some heeded him, halting their flight, and turning to face the wall of charging redcoats. A pistol shot and Colonel de Beaupré fell to his knees, his broad back a mass of dark blood.

Boots thundered past Hogan's face. He closed his eyes, spent, the fight gone from his body, waiting for the prick of steel, the agony of a death-wound.

He heard the sound of trumpets, a familiar fanfare. And felt the rumble of many hooves vibrate through the soil beneath him. *Could it be? No, surely that was impossible.* He forced himself to sit up. Looked south, and there they were – horsemen. Horsemen in emerald green, many hundreds of them, at least a regiment, more likely two. And, by God, could that really be old Paddy Sarsfield out in front – gleaming sabre drawn, a wicked smile on his boyish face?

It was.

The Irish cavalry smashed into the attacking redcoats. The horsemen set about them with sabres and pistol or rode them down with the sheer weight of their galloping horses. The redcoats stood no chance. Out of formation they were easy prey to the chopping blades of Sarsfield's battle-mad horsemen. The cavalry rode here and there hacking down the cowering infantry – those that did not run back towards their own lines or dive into their trenches were dead men. They were chased and sliced down in a couple of blows and the riders spurred on, laughing, to seek fresh targets. The remaining men of the Irish foot charge cheered their horse-borne comrades, urging them on to the slaughter of the foe. And in a few short minutes it was all over for the English. The victorious horsemen rode about the field between the breach and the sappers' trenches unchallenged – their enemies dead or fled. Some of Sars-field's troopers were still seeking blood. Hogan saw three of them chase down a single fleeing redcoat – the man had played dead and tried to run at the wrong moment. He was hounded across the field before being sliced and chopped and skewered till he collapsed in a bleeding heap of reeking cloth-bound meat.

Hogan, back on his feet, was menaced by a rider with a bloody sabre. Only just in time he recognised the man: 'You keep your fucking distance, John Reilly,' he growled. 'I rode with you to Ballyneety a few weeks past. Shared my flask with you. Don't pretend you don't know me now.'

The horseman grinned at Hogan and opened his mouth to say something – when the mortars opened up again. A shell screamed down into the outer rubble slope in the breach and exploded, the bodies of dead men – Irish, English, Dutch and Dane, or parts of them – were tossed high in the air and came thudding down again. Hogan ran for the breach, and scrambling up the gore-slimed slope, behind him he could hear Sarsfield recalling his horsemen, sound-ing the retreat; and the deadly crack-crack-crack of muskets from the English trenches.

The rain returned in the night. Hogan could hear it drumming insistently on the roof of his lodgings as he bathed a deep sword cut on the back of his hand and a bullet score on the outer flesh of his thigh – he had no recollection of receiving either of these wounds. He washed the injuries with brandy – and made them sting worse than ever. Then drank the rest of the bottle and slept like the dead.

In the morning, his body aching from scalp to shin, he reported for duty with the Limerick Volunteers. What was left of them. Hogan saw how battle-depleted the company was. Of the fifty-three men on the wall the afternoon before, only seventeen unharmed men reported for duty at nine of the clock in the cathedral square. But grief in the deaths of so many of his comrades was tempered with a savage, soaring joy. *Victory!*

For when they filed up on the parapet once more and looked out over the field of battle, Hogan saw that the enemy were gone. In the night, amid the gently falling rain, the massed legions of King William – his guns and horse, all his wagons, carriages and carts – had packed up and quit the field.

Chapter Twenty-Seven

Friday, September 5, 1690: Noon

Holcroft heard the voices coming up the stairs. *Surely that was the Irishman Hogan's genial baritone.* He recognised the voice even above the sad murmur of conversation from the next, larger cell where half a dozen Protestant merchants of the city of Cork were caged. He recognised it over the moans of Robinson, the poor man who lay on the filthy floor of the back of their cell dying of gaol fever. *And the other voice – who was that?* His heart grew cold. That was Henri d'Erloncourt. He was sure of it.

He heard Narrey saying: '. . . I'm expected at the Governor's House at one o'clock for dinner. It will no doubt be another of Colonel McElliot's truly disgusting repasts – he really should hang his cook – but I fear I must attend.'

'I won't trouble you a moment longer than necessary, monsieur. Once I have all my money, I shall be on my merry way . . .'

A moment later, the two men came to the top of the winding staircase and into view. Holcroft stood at the bars of his cell and stared at them. The broad, bow-legged shape of Michael 'Galloping' Hogan and the slight, delicate figure of Narrey. He had been in that small, cramped cell for nearly three weeks awaiting the arrival of Henri d'Erloncourt, sleeping on the cold stone floor with only a few scraps of filthy straw to cushion its bite, eating the lukewarm 'soup' that Matisse gave him twice a day: greasy water with a few scraps of gristle floating in it, accompanied by rinds of cheese, and heels of barley bread, too hard and stale for Matisse to chew.

It had been a miserable period – twenty-three days by Holcroft's reckoning – and he had longed to feel fresh air on his skin and eat and drink like a human being once more. To stretch out on a proper bed again, with sheets and blankets. But this was far worse. As Narrey stopped before the cells and smiled unpleasantly at him from beyond the bars, Holcroft knew he was looking at his death. He felt the cold fear grip his bowels tight. Henri d'Erloncourt took off his black hat and made Holcroft an elaborate bow.

'Major Blood,' he said. 'My old playmate, my old fellow Cockpit page. Holcroft Blood – I cannot tell you how much joy it gives me to see you today.'

'I cannot say the same,' said Holcroft.

'Ah, no? I thought we might have a pleasant little conversation about this and that. About how you humiliated our good master the Duke of Buckingham, for instance. Or about my poor friend Major Guillaume du Clos, whom you put to death on the bridge at Duleek with your lucky cannon shot. Or perhaps about the names of the perfidious men and women who spied on the court of the Sun King at your masters' behest those many years ago. It should be an illuminating conversation, my dear Holcroft, do you not agree?'

'I have nothing to say to you.'

'No? I expect over the next few days we can find a way to loosen your tongue. I have so longed to have a nice intimate chat with you, à deux.'

Michael Hogan cleared his throat noisily.

'Yes, Mister Hogan – you want your money.' He turned away and strode to the door, calling: 'Matisse, let joy be unconfined, your master's home!'

Holcroft found himself looking into the rugged suntanned face of Hogan.

'You again,' he said. 'I thought you'd be off fighting the good fight in Limerick. Busy slaughtering Englishmen.'

'I did my share. But the battle was won a week ago. Did you not hear?'

Holcroft said nothing. In the past three weeks, the only person from the outside world he had seen – apart from the clerk who manned the desk at the door, who twice ventured upstairs to drink wine with the gaoler – was Matisse. And Matisse had never said anything but a few foul curses and the odd brusque order at pistol point to stand back while he brought in the so-called soup.

'Limerick was saved, Major Blood, and I played a not inconsiderable part in its salvation. And, furthermore, your own King Billy has quit Ireland and gone back home. Went to England, tail between his legs, right after Limerick.'

'Truly?' said Holcroft. His world seemed to be lurching sideways. 'Is the war over then?'

'Not by a long shot,' said Hogan. 'Your soldier-boys still hold Dublin, Waterford and all the north. And they say the Earl of Marlborough is on his way from England with reinforcements. But you got your arses properly kicked in the west – and it looks as if the fighting is done for this season.'

Holcroft looked down at his filthy bare feet. Matisse had stolen his boots and, worse, his coat – his beloved Ordnance coat, his identity, his very soul – the gaoler saying something about prisoners paying for their lodgings. He felt weak and naked without them – unmanned by their absence.

'So is the famous hospitality of the fine old city of Cork to your liking?'

Holcroft stared at Hogan, who had stepped a little closer to the bars.

'Because if you are not satisfied with your accommodation *here*, next time you are at liberty in the city, I'd recommend you try the sign of the Dolphin by the South Gate.' Hogan's voice was a murmur. 'A fine place to rest up, take your ease. They are discreet. Good food and drink, too.'

'Do you mock me, sir?' said Holcroft, very angry. He could hear Narrey speaking to Matisse in the office next door, telling him to fetch out the prisoner.

'I do not. Mention my name if you ever find yourself there, say the Galloper sent you, and you will find a warm welcome. Remember my words.'

Matisse was at the cell door. He had a cocked pistol in his right hand and the big iron key to the cell door. 'Back, *connard*; get back, you dog,' he said. Holcroft obediently moved to the rear of the cell while Matisse worked the key and swung open the door. Hogan stepped well out of the way and then followed Holcroft – with Matisse at the prisoner's back with the pistol – into the office.

Hogan lounged casually against the wall on the right of the door by the shelf of ironmongery and watched as Holcroft was lashed into a heavy wooden chair in the centre of the room by the sailor Matisse – with Henri keeping the pistol on him. When the Englishman was bound, Henri slapped him hard across the face. Holcroft rode the slap easily and fixed the Frenchman with a glare.

'I demand satisfaction for that blow – and for the treatment I have suffered as a prisoner of war in Cork,' he said. 'If you were a gentleman, you'd fight me.'

Hogan laughed out loud, and Henri too emitted a little giggle.

'I am a gentleman of France, a count of ancient lineage, a personal friend of His Majesty Louis XIV, I shall not sully my honour by treating you as an equal. But neither shall I even take the trouble to punish you myself for your gross impudence. Matisse!'

Matisse came forward and punched Holcroft four times hard in the face. Four measured pounding blows that knocked his head left and right, split his lip and loosened at least one tooth in his jaw. Holcroft was reeling; he could feel his mouth fill with blood and a thread trickle out and down his chin. His left eye was throbbing and he could feel the flesh around the socket beginning to swell.

'You punch like a little girl,' he said in French.

Matisse went wild. He smashed a barrage of punches at Holcroft's face and body, striking almost at random. Holcroft rocked back and forth, restrained only by his bonds. Eventually, panting like an exhausted dog, the sailor ceased.

'Now then, while that was delightfully invigorating,' said Henri, 'we must get down to business. It is time for a little chat. What *shall* we talk about? Ah, I have it. Shall we talk about your time as a spy in Paris? And the friends who helped you during that period. I nearly caught you once, did you know that?'

Holcroft, barely conscious, spat a mouthful of blood on the floor.

'Well, heart-warming as it is to witness your little reunion,' said Hogan, 'if you don't mind, monsieur, I shall have my money now and take my leave.'

Henri looked at the Irishman crossly. 'You really are a man with only one thing on his mind. Can't you wait until I have finished interrogating this one?'

'I have things I wish to do today – my money, monsieur, if you please.' Hogan put a hand on his cutlass hilt. 'And do *you* not have an engagement yourself with the Governor at one? It must be very nearly that hour just now.'

'Very well, very well . . . I have it here.' Henri went over to the escritoire, opened the lid, pushed aside a mass of papers, and pulled out a small iron box from a narrow drawer at the back. He lifted the lid and extracted several small, knobbly linen sacks. 'Business before pleasure, as always. I see we must postpone our little chat, old playmate, His Excellency the Governor awaits . . .'

'There is one more thing, monsieur. This fellow slaughtered several of my dear friends. Perhaps you will permit me one small measure of revenge. Yes?' Hogan lifted his right hand, bunched into a formidable gnarled fist.

'Indeed, sir, as you wish. But do not kill him – I have many important questions for him to answer when I return from the Governor's dinner.'

Holcroft strained at his ropes as Hogan approached. The raparee seized Holcroft's shirt collar with his left hand, lifted his right and punched him hard on the point of the jaw. Holcroft's head snapped back, and his vision exploded into red and black shapes and he sensed himself spinning out of the world. But before he lost consciousness he felt, unmistakably, the slide of something cold and hard down inside his shirt against his skin, an object that came to rest inside at his belly where the shirt was tucked into his breeches.

Holcroft only fully recovered his senses a half hour later. He was back in his cell lying on the stone floor and his face was swollen to twice its normal size. He could barely see out of his eyes. But he shrugged off the words of consolation from the worried men in the next cell and his hands fumbled at his waist. He could feel the object still there. Small, but iron hard. He knew what it was, and offered up a silent prayer to God to shower His blessings upon Michael Hogan. He went to the bars and peered to his left. The door of the office was half open and he could see part of the room, if he twisted his head at an uncomfortable angle. He could see the lower legs of Matisse, his baggy seaman's trousers, and – with a flash of anger – he saw that the man was wearing Holcroft's boots. There was no sound but a gentle snoring. Narrey was, no doubt, still at his dinner with the Governor.

There was no time to lose.

He reached inside his shirt and his fingers closed around the iron key. He tried it in the lock of the cell's door and, holding his breath, found that the lock turned easily. *Clever Hogan!* he thought. Urging his fellow prisoners to silence with a finger to his lips, Holcroft crept into the office. Matisse was fast asleep in the chair, a half-full bottle beside him. Holcroft wasted no time. He stepped over to the seaman, snatched up his bottle and cracked it hard over the man's head. Matisse did not wake. He gave a jerk as the bottle smashed over his scalp. The air filled with the smell of cheap brandy, and the man's scalp began to bleed profusely. But Matisse slumped down lower in the chair and was still.

Holcroft crossed the room and looked out of the window. The sun was away up to his right, so he was looking more or less due east. It was perhaps two o'clock, maybe a little later. He could see a channel of the River Lee running outside the ancient walls, and beyond it a suburb of small, gaily painted houses in neat rows on a low-lying island. To the south-east he could see a large bowling green and the tiny figures of men at play on the smooth turf.

How long would Narrey be at his dinner? An hour, two, at most, three? He would surely be returning soon – perhaps with soldiers, or with armed friends? He turned back to the room. First things first. He knelt down next to the unconscious form of Matisse and pulled off his boots. With them back on the rightful feet, Holcroft felt a good deal stronger. He took down a small-sword and scabbard from a hook on the walls, and slung them over his shoulder. Now booted and armed, he felt almost human again.

He went over to the escritoire and tried the lid. It was locked. But levering with the sword blade, he burst it open in a few moments. He seized a mass of papers, some written in a numerical code, some *en clair*, all that he could find, and shoved them inside his filthy shirt. He pulled out the iron box and found two small sacks of *louis d'or* inside – about forty pounds' worth of gold. That made him smile! He looked for anything else he could profitably carry away. There was a copy of a popular book, a small, leather-bound volume with a gilt-decorated spine. He took that too, shoving it inside his shirt with the papers.

It was time to go.

He seized a pair of keys from the shelf with all the iron implements of torture. He walked out into the corridor by the cells and went over to the larger cell. 'Paul Smithson,' he whispered. The Protestant merchant came to the bars. 'Give me your cloak and hat now and I will give you the keys to your cell.'

The prisoner nodded. The exchange was made.

With the hat pulled low over his battered, swollen face, and swathed in the raggedy, mildew-smelling cloak, Holcroft went quietly down the curved staircase. The clerk at his desk looked up once, looked again at the man approaching him. He opened his mouth to say something, or call for help, and Holcroft was on him like a tiger. He seized the man by the scruff of his scrawny neck and slammed his head down on to the desk in front of him. He did it twice, hard as he could, and a third time, until the man slid unconscious from his stool.

Holcroft peered out of the door. The courtyard was empty but for an old man humping a basket of firewood to one of the brick barrack houses, and a couple of red-coated sentries on either side of the door. But the soldiers would not move without orders. There was no sign of Narrey nor of anyone who might be a threat to him. He could hear the sound of the Protestant prisoners upstairs, calling to each other in delight at their newfound liberty, laughing. He walked out of the door, hat low over his eyes, pulling the cloak close around him.

He reached the exit of the courtyard, a pair of wide-open double gates, and still no one had challenged him. He could not believe it was this easy. Outside the flow of foot traffic was heavy, he glanced to his right, looking north, and saw no one he recognised. No one seemed to pay him the slightest attention. In the distance he could make out the North Gate to the city by the bridge over the north channel of the River Lee and a knot of red-coated soldiery stopping people on foot and asking for papers before allowing them to pass through the portal. He turned south instinctively, hunching his back, keeping his head low.

He remembered Hogan's words to him that morning. '... Next time you are at liberty in the city, I'd recommend that you try the sign of the Dolphin by the South Gate. A fine place to rest up, take your ease ... Mention my name if you ever find yourself there, say the Galloper sent you ...'

Could Hogan be setting a trap for him? Trying to lure him into some place where he could be found easily and recaptured?

That didn't make any sense. Hogan had slipped him the key to facilitate his escape. He had already been 'trapped' in the cell and facing torture and death at Narrey's hands. No, Hogan was a friend. Well, he was an enemy. But he had dealt straight with him, so far, and perhaps he was trying to make amends for leading him to his death. He'd have to trust Hogan. He didn't have a choice.

The Dolphin was a mean, narrow house, which seemed to be slumped between its two neighbours like a drunk being escorted home on wavering legs between two more sober and taller companions. It was made of dirty bricks, with small, infrequent windows and backed on to the southern channel of the River Lee.

Holcroft peered through a greasy window set in the low wide door and saw half a dozen drinkers inside, two at a counter and the rest gathered around a peat fire. Someone was playing a fiddle and he could hear the sounds of several voices singing. But when he pushed open the door and stepped inside all the conversations ceased, and the man on the fiddle stopped playing. It was a most uncomfortable sensation. There were seven people in the small, low, smoke-filled room, and all their eyes were fixed upon Holcroft. He noticed that several of them had a striking resemblance to each other: family members, no doubt.

In the brittle silence, Holcroft walked over to the counter and said: 'Brandy. A large tot of brandy.' There were two men, one at either end of the beam. The man on the right looked Holcroft up and down slowly along his long, broken nose, studying him minutely from his dirty boots to the mildewed cloak to his battered, grossly swollen, blood-streaked face to his old torn hat.

'Brandy,' said Holcroft, slightly louder.

The man behind the counter, a bald fellow with a straggly reddish beard, stared at him as if he had never heard of the spirit before.

Holcroft said: 'If you have no brandy, I will take a measure of gin, then.'

'We are closed, Englishman,' said the bearded man behind the counter.

Holcroft fumbled in his waistband and fetched out a coin from one of the linen sacks he had purloined from Narrey's strong box. He put the gold coin on the greasy counter with a click.

'I'll take that drink, sir, and buy one for every man in this place.'

'Are you deaf? The tavern's closed.' The broken-nosed man was speaking. 'This is a private gathering of friends. Go back to London, where you belong.'

Holcroft could hear the scraping of stools behind him and feel the heavy approach of the men who had been by the fire. Holcroft made himself ready.

'Go along, sir, there's a good fellow,' said the barman. 'Go along to the Red Bear on the other side of South Gate Bridge. They'll happily give you whatever it is you require there. No need for any unpleasantness in this house.'

Holcroft's character held a wide streak of stubbornness. It was not his finest trait, he knew, but he could sometimes not deny it. He often did things that he knew would result in trouble for him and for others. He did them anyway. Even weakened by weeks of prison, he believed he was a match, physically, for any man in this room. Maybe for several of them. And he was perfectly happy to prove it. Indeed, there was a part of him that welcomed the violence.

'I will have my drink here. Not at the Red Bear, not in London. Here. This place was recommended to me by a friend. I will not leave till I'm served.'

'And who might this friend be, then?' said Broken-nose.

Holcroft looked across at the man. He had taken the initiative by speaking while the other men were silent. Broken-nose was their leader. This man was the one he would knock down first. Holcroft

was a head taller than him. It should not be difficult. Holcroft shook
his shoulders a little to loosen the muscles in his arms.

'The man who recommended this fine establishment to me
was called Hogan. Michael Hogan. He told me to tell you that
the Galloper sent me. He said I'd receive a warm welcome at the
Dolphin. Good food and drink, he said.'

Broken-nose's face cracked into a smile. He chuckled. 'Good
food? Old Mick always did have a sense of humour. But you shall
have your drink. I can't help but admire a fella who has already
had seven shades kicked out of him but is still prepared to fight
another seven men for a nip of brandy.'

Someone laughed. The fiddler began to play once more.

Broken-nose was truly named Patrick McCarthy, and known uni-
versally as Mack. He was the owner of the Dolphin with his brother
Seamus, the red-bearded man who tended the counter, and they
were distant cousins of Michael Hogan's, as were three of the other
men in the tavern that afternoon. More importantly than their
kinship, Mack and Hogan were old friends who had done plenty
of lucrative private business together in Cork and along the coast
before the wars.

Mack's business was contraband. Brandy, wine, tobacco and tea
were the main commodities he dealt in – but he had also on occasion smuggled gunpowder, gold and even people to England or
France or even across the ocean to the American colonies. The
war had been both good and bad for business. With the French
and English navies in the Irish Sea, stopping and searching shipping at will, many a valuable illegal cargo had been lost to the
authorities. On the other hand, the war bred scarcity, and that
pushed up the prices of certain items that many people required
for their pleasures.

Mack and his friends had no stake in the war, they claimed. The
English had always taxed trade, and that was resented, but that

taxation on brandy and tea and so on gave birth to Mack's business. Then King James had landed less than twenty miles down the road in the port of Kinsale. Had the Catholic King abolished taxes on wine from France and tobacco from Virginia? He had not. Mack and the men of the Dolphin did not care who ruled in Dublin as long as they were left in peace to carry on their businesses. Their loyalties were to the people they trusted, family and friends. Not to causes or countries. Holcroft was a friend of Hogan's therefore Holcroft was to be treated as a friend. If he should betray them, he would be treated as a mortal enemy. No threats were made but it was clear that should Holcroft transgress in any way he would be killed.

Mack cheerfully shared this information with Holcroft when he showed him down a carefully hidden trap-door in the kitchen into a tunnel that led into a dim, damp cellar underneath the next-door house – which Mack also owned through intermediaries. The cellar was large, filled with barrels and boxes of merchandise and open to the River Lee through an iron-barred watergate. It was not especially warm, and Mack warned Holcroft that he could not have a light after sunset, as it would shine through the one small barred window high on the street-side wall. It was, in fact, disturbingly like a prison. However, Mack provided Holcroft with a dozen blankets and cushions; a basin of hot water, soap and a towel, and a clean shirt and drawers. And furnished him with a bottle of brandy and a small keg of ale. His wife, a well-fed matron, brought him a tray containing a tureen of hot turnip soup, a large chunk of ham, a small round cheese, two loaves of bread and a pat of fresh butter.

Holcroft, when he had washed himself, changed his linen, eaten and drunk to his heart's content, felt like the fairy earl of some underground realm.

Three days later, he no longer felt like an earl: he was bored and restless and, although he was well fed, clean and comfortable – apart from his face which still throbbed and ached like the devil – he wondered if by escaping from the Old Tower he had merely exchanged one prison for another.

Michael Hogan came to see him on the fifth day. He was suddenly just there in the cellar leaning on a huge box of tea, marked 'Property of the Honourable Company', holding out a bottle of brandy and grinning at Holcroft.

Holcroft had been sitting in a nest of blankets and cushions in the patch of light from the window, reading the book he had stolen from Narrey's escritoire – a tedious religious allegory that was not at all suited to his straightforward tastes – and he jumped to his feet when he saw Hogan.

'Look at the state of you,' said the Irishman. 'I've eaten beefsteaks that were more beautiful and less battered than your ugly map.'

Holcroft touched his still-swollen unshaven jaw, and the lumps around his eye sockets. He had not seen a mirror for longer than he could remember but he was sure that in the aftermath of Matisse's beating he looked gruesome.

'I've you to thank for some of it,' he said. 'And I do thank you, sincerely.'

'Think nothing of it. Can't stand the wee French shite. Once I'd had my money, there was nothing between us . . . So, here you are. In the pink, then?'

'I'm fine. Bored. I want to get out of Cork but Mack tells me the soldiers are still searching for me. He says I must lay low here for a week or more.'

'Aye, seems sensible. They're scouring the countryside – horse patrols on every road – saying there is a murderous English spy on the loose. There's a bounty of two hundred pounds in gold on your head. That would be the Frenchman's doing. I even saw a squad of redcoats knocking on doors in Tuckey's Lane as I passed on the way here. Asking for a tall man with a face like a ploughed field.'

Holcroft said nothing. He had hoped that his escape might somehow have been forgotten. But Henri d'Erloncourt was not a man to forget or forgive. He thought – two hundred pounds for his head! That would tempt a saint. He looked suspiciously at Hogan – he was no saint. The Irishman smiled at him. 'Have a drink,' he said, throwing over the brandy bottle.

Holcroft caught the half-full bottle in the air and pulled out the stopper. He took a long swallow. Fine stuff. He passed the bottle back to Hogan.

'I know what you're thinking,' Hogan said.

'What am I thinking?'

'You're surely thinking – can I really trust this handsome Irish fella not to betray me for the gold? Well, let me set your suspicious English heart at rest, my friend. I cannot go anywhere near Monsieur le Comte d'Erloncourt for the rest of my life. Or his. Those Protestant merchants you set free – most of them went straight home to their wives and families and were rounded up again by the city militia the very same day. They were only given the merest glimpse of those instruments in the fire before they were squealing to monsieur exactly what happened, how you had a key in your shirt, opened the door your own self – and who is the only man who could possibly have given you that key? The famous Michael "Galloping" Hogan, that's who. If I go near Henri d'Erloncourt again, I'm in the same leaky boat as you, my ugly English friend.'

Holcroft nodded. 'I am sorry for it. So you will hide down here with me?'

'No, I leave Cork in an hour or so. I've business to attend to in the west. A transaction to make. I'm putting the Frenchman's gold to good use, Major Blood. Buying myself a little piece of hillside near Killarney, a ram and fifty ewes. If you're ever down that way, when this nonsense is done, come and find me and we'll share a tankard or two and a bite of my own roast mutton.'

'I'll do that, Hogan. Once again, I thank you for your kindness. But before you go, I must ask something. It is a delicate matter. May I ask?'

Hogan looked puzzled. 'Ask away, then.'

'You told me, on the road, that Lady Caroline Chichester had something of a reputation. What did you mean by that?'

'Now, don't let us fall out, Major. I meant nothing much by the remark. I collect you are besotted with the girl. I meant no disrespect to your lady-love.'

'No, I won't take offence. My word on it. It is just that I have been sitting and thinking of her a good deal and I wondered why you said what you did.'

Hogan looked a little embarrassed. 'Well, she . . . well, Lady Caroline has something of an ill reputation. As a tease. And a troublemaker. She flirts with all the men, but won't take it any further, if you know what I mean. Promises Heaven but actually gives men Hell . . . by which I mean nothing but angry frustration. She often has several fellas on her line – she enjoys it most, they say, when they fight each other for her favours. Apologies, Blood, but that is what the gossips say about Lady Caroline. Her mother died giving birth to her, and she had no aunts or elder sisters to raise her the right way. She's always done as she pleased. Plays with men as if they were her dolls. Paddy Sarsfield had a go-around with her before the war; they stepped out a dozen times – and you should hear him rant about her. He fought a duel for her honour, too, and killed a man. Another poor deluded fool who thought he was in love with her.'

'I see,' said Holcroft. He could not meet Hogan's eye.

'Well, I'd best be off then,' said the Irishman. 'Mack's got a man who will take me over the walls tonight. So . . . I'll take my leave of you.'

'Goodbye, Hogan,' said Holcroft dully. 'Travel safely.'

'Don't you worry yourself too much down here, Blood. Mack will not betray you, and neither will any of his folk. And I have a snippet of news that will lift your heathen Protestant heart. The great Earl of Marlborough is on the way here.'

'Yes,' said Holcroft. 'You told me that before. In the cell.'

'No, you misunderstand. Your man, the Earl of Marlborough, is coming *here* with an English army. To Cork. Most of our lads are at Limerick recovering from the fight. A good many of them have gone back to their farms and families for the winter. The French have mostly gone now too. How long do you think Governor McElliot and a couple of thousand half-trained militia can hold out in Cork against a professional English army? A day? Two whole days? You sit tight in this nice cosy cellar and the city will be in English hands afore you know it.'

Chapter Twenty-Eight

Saturday, September 20, 1690

'What in God's name are we going to do?' Governor Roger McElliot's voice was a plaintive whine. He was a small man who tried to make himself look taller by donning a towering black periwig. He was standing in a vast reception hall in the Governor's House with the Comte d'Erloncourt, and a pair of very different Irish peers – the lined, tired, sixty-year-old Earl of Tyrone and the young Earl of Clancarty, who at twenty-two years was bursting with excitement at the prospect of his first battle. He was accompanied by Lieutenant-Colonel Philip Ricautt, who actually commanded Lord Clancarty's troops, and who had arrived that morning with reinforcements, two full regiments of infantry from Charles Fort, which overlooked the port of Kinsale, seventeen miles to the south.

The matter at hand was the sighting just after dawn of a veritable armada of English ships off the coast at the mouth of Cork Harbour. Civilian observers claimed to have seen sixty, seventy, even eighty ships in the first rays of dawn.

It is Marlborough himself, they whispered. The Earl and his new army of brutal Englishmen come to slaughter them all and burn Cork to the ground.

As if that were not bad enough, Henri d'Erloncourt had presented fresh intelligence that suggested that Ferdinand Wilhelm, Duke of Würtemberg-Neuenstadt, one of King William's more ferocious generals, was even now heading south towards Cork with another army of five thousand Danish, Dutch and Huguenot soldiers, men who'd been withdrawn from the siege of Limerick.

Cork was between the jaws of a pincer, menaced by land and sea.

'We are doomed, surely, is that not so, gentlemen?' said McElliot. 'What can we do but surrender?'

'We must fight them!' said the Earl of Clancarty, his young face flushing with battle ardour. 'We must show them we are not trembling cowards, that we will no longer submit to the tyranny of a foreign ruler. We will fight them from the walls, in the streets, in the houses, with every man, woman and child – we'll show them that a single honest Irishman is worth at least ten Englishmen.'

'Cork cannot be defended,' said the Earl of Tyrone flatly. 'Everyone with half a brain knows that. The city lies in a bowl, a marshland, with higher ground both north and south. The geography is against us. They will put their artillery up on the hills and rain death down upon us. We will be helpless. Pounded to rubble. But if we surrender at the first asking, perhaps Lord Marlborough will spare the city from pillage and sack. That, gentlemen, is the best we can hope for.'

'What say you, Colonel Ricautt – you have most experience in these matters?' The Governor looked up at the veteran soldier beseechingly. 'What, in your opinion, is the best course of action for us to follow?'

The colonel opened his mouth to speak but Clancarty answered for him.

'Colonel Ricautt commands my best troops – they are brave as lions, every man, and he will surely wish to lead them to a swift and glorious victory!'

Ricautt looked uncomfortable. It was plain to Henri that the soldier knew it was useless to resist the combined might of the two huge Williamite forces set against them but found it hard to contradict his patron Lord Clancarty, a man who, for all his youth and idiocy, was one of the richest and most influential landowners in the south-west of Ireland. He said nothing for several heartbeats.

'The marshland and the River Lee can be used to our advantage,' he said finally. 'They will find it difficult to assault the walls of Cork over this terrain. But, in all honesty, I do not think that we have very much chance of—'

'If I might interject,' said Henri. 'There is one piece of this puzzle that I have not mentioned. It is a very great secret, and I was told not to reveal it, but I think I should ignore that instruction in the light of the present circumstances.'

Every man in the room looked at him expectantly.

'I have been informed by my sources that the Duke of Berwick, King James's own son, has plans to come to our aid. He is raising a relief force in Connaught and will be at Cork with at least ten thousand men in a week, or perhaps ten days at the most. If we can but hold out till then behind our walls, Cork will be saved and the English will be handed another humiliating defeat.'

The Earl of Tyrone frowned at him. 'I have heard nothing of this,' he said. 'Not a word. I did not even realise that my lord Berwick still had so great a force under arms. Are you certain that this is true? If we are to base our future actions on this information, we must be absolutely certain.'

'My dear sir,' said Henri, smiling warmly at Tyrone, 'I am sure that you know that nothing in life is absolutely certain – except God's infinite love and the promise of Salvation in Christ. But I have this intelligence on the highest authority. The Duke of Berwick will come to our aid. You may count on it.'

'Very well then,' said Governor McElliot, 'it seems that we must fight. Now, as to our dispositions – I shall command the city and its walls and Lord Clancarty, will you take possession of Shandon Castle and the smaller forts north of the city? Will you, Lord Tyrone, take control of the Elizabeth Fort, St Finn Barre's Cathedral and the southern sector? Let us consult the maps . . .'

As Henri d'Erloncourt walked briskly back down the main street to the Old Tower, he felt not the tiniest twinge of guilt that he had lied to the Governor's war council. He knew for a fact the Duke of

Berwick considered the city of Cork to be indefensible and, as far as he knew, the King's eldest son was now ensconced comfortably in newly liberated Limerick and had no plans at all to ride to Cork's rescue. The Duke was, in fact, considering taking ship at Galway and following his father into exile.

But the commanders of Cork did not know that – communications between Cork and Limerick had recently been severed – and from Henri's point of view, it was vitally important that they continue in their ignorance. Cork must be defended for as long as possible against the English. And for reasons far more important than the saving of one small Irish city from the ravages of war.

Cork must hold out, so that the port of Kinsale should remain open to French shipping for at least another three and a half weeks. After Cork fell, and he was sure it would fall very soon, Kinsale would be next. And that must be delayed at all costs.

When Henri had made the arrangements for his own departure, the war in Ireland, although obviously lost even then, had had a completely different aspect to his eye. The south-westen ports of Cork and Kinsale had seemed secure, or at least he had thought they would be, until spring. Accordingly he had arranged the rendezvous with the French frigate *Hirondelle* for the middle of October, before sea travel became seriously disrupted by winter storms, in Kinsale.

Jean-Baptiste Trudeau, the captain of the *Hirondelle*, and a man who had been on the spymaster's payroll for some years, was engaged to collect Henri, along with his man Matisse and possibly some of his agents, at dusk on Wednesday, October 15, and take him back to France. He had sent and received messages to this effect when he was in Galway, and he had no method of changing the date of the rendezvous. He had no idea where the *Hirondelle* was at present, somewhere in the Atlantic, he thought, although he was certain that Captain Trudeau would make the rendezvous – Trudeau knew what would happen to him if he did not.

So Henri must remain in County Cork for the time being, and Cork city must resist the forces of King William for as long as possible.

There was another reason for Henri wishing to remain a little longer in Cork. The Englishman Blood had escaped his grip with the connivance of that treacherous rat Hogan and taken with him various materials, papers and so on, which he very much wished to retrieve. That it was *crucial* he should retrieve.

Holcroft Blood had not been seen, let alone captured, in the two weeks since he had escaped, despite a twenty-four-hour watch in the walls and all the gates of Cork. Neither had he been picked up by the regular Jacobite patrols on the roads leading to or from the city. Cork harbour, too, was watched all hours of the day and night, and every ship heading out to sea had been thoroughly searched. The manhunt had been vigorously prosecuted – and yet, nothing, not a hair of Blood's had been seen. The bounty in gold he had placed on the Englishman's head had been more than generous – yet no man had stepped forward with any information that might lead to his recapture.

However, he had finally begun receiving reports from Agricola once more – Narrey had no idea why his agent had been silent for so long, but the renewed contact was welcome – and the spy had mentioned that Major Holcroft Blood was still posted on the missing list in the Board of Ordnance. Missing believed dead or captured. The man had apparently simply disappeared.

In fact, in Henri's estimation, it was most likely that Blood had gone to ground inside Cork – was indeed still in the city. In some traitor's house. And Henri fully intended to sniff him out and take his revenge for the death of poor Guillaume du Clos before he had to quit Ireland for good.

Henri entered the door of the Old Tower, and greeted the clerk, Jacob, who was sitting at his usual place. The man had a pair of pistols on the desk in front of him, which he was using as paperweights, and he looked up quickly when he heard Henri's step, clutching at one of the weapons with his right hand. His face, still sadly cut and bruised from Blood's assault, was pinched with fear.

Once back in his office on the first floor, and having confirmed with Matisse that there was no new information about Blood, Henri sat down at the escritoire and pulled out the deciphered version of Agricola's latest report. Much of the information in it he was already familiar with – the Earl of Marlborough's imminent arrival, the ill-discipline of some of the veteran English troops in Dublin – but some of it was new. At Henri's months-old request, Agricola had included a lengthy report on Michael Hogan and his large family, which made interesting reading. Apparently the Galloper had a number of family members, distant cousins by blood but comrades in various illicit businesses, in Cork itself. These cousins might bear investigation.

However, reading through the document, once again Henri found himself distracted – in fact greatly irritated – by Agricola's often repeated demand for more money, saying it was urgently needed to pay sub-agents who supplied small items of military information to Agricola.

Henri had nothing against greed. He based the majority of his operations on the lure of gold. He trusted greed. It was a clear motive for treachery. He did not trust agents who said they loved France or King Louis enough to risk their necks, or those who said they hated the English so much that they would enlist in their ranks only to betray them. He felt that wild passions had no place in serious espionage. Greed, he liked. Greed, he preferred. He knew where he stood when an agent in the field asked for payment for their services.

But Agricola's greed was excessive. Almost every time they corresponded, the agent found another reason why Henri should part with more of his master's gold. And of greater irritation were the

lies: these sub-agents that Agricola claimed required extra pay-
ments. They were all fictitious, he believed, all fabricated by Agricola
as a method of extracting more money from Henri.

In other circumstances, Henri would have sent a threatening
note of admonishment to Agricola. But that would have been
pointless as he had no method of safely dispatching the note to
Dublin. Michael Hogan had deserted him and the Irishman had
been his link to a network of riders who carried his messages.
Fortunately, it did not matter. Agricola was coming to Cork with
the forces of the Duke of Wurttemberg-Neuenstadt. And there
would most likely be an opportunity for a meeting once the enemy
was encamped outside the walls of Cork. If nothing else, Agricola
was always resourceful in these matters.

Henri put the message down on his desk. He decided to wait
for the agent to contact him. The reliable lure of gold would ensure
that Agricola did.

'Matisse,' he said, 'take a message to the Governor's House for
me. Tell McElliot that I shall require a file of redcoats first thing
tomorrow – twenty men should do it. You may tell him I intend to
search the whole city for deserters.'

'Deserters, monsieur?'

'Yes, Matisse. Deserters. That is what I wish you to tell our
esteemed governor. Tell him that I deem it of the greatest importance that every available fighting man is found and compelled to
do his duty in defence of this fair city.'

Matisse knuckled his brow and disappeared out of the door.

Deserters, thought Henri. *Why not?* In the course of his searches,
he might even discover some. But of greater interest to him would
be a thorough search of a tavern known as the Dolphin by the
South Gate. A place that his own enquiries had revealed was
owned by members of Hogan's clan.

Chapter Twenty-Nine

Saturday, September 27, 1690

Holcroft had been increasingly irked by his voluntary incarceration. Particularly when he could hear the guns of the English cannon pounding the walls of Cork, and even feel them trembling the bricks of the cellar in which he languished. He had passed the time in thought and sleep, in eating and drinking the dull fare Mack and his friends brought down to him. And in trying to solve the puzzles contained in the secret papers he'd stolen from the escritoire in Narrey's lair.

By the time he could hear the rattle of musketry from outside the city, he had decoded every last one. But it had taken him two whole weeks before he realised how fortunate he had been in the items he had purloined from the office. The book he had stolen was, of course, the key. It was *The Pilgrim's Progress* by John Bunyan, published twelve years before but still selling in great numbers. A book that any good Christian might wish to have in his or her collection. Close examination of the groups of numbers in the encoded papers led him to believe that they corresponded to letters printed in Bunyan's tale. Both correspondents would need to have the same edition of the book, of course, but after that it was relatively simple to exchange messages. It turned out that the day of the date written *en clair* on the top of each letter dictated which page of the text was to be used for the code, and the numbers in the message corresponded to which line on that page and how many letters from the left of the beginning of the line. For example, on page nine of the book, lines twenty-two and twenty-three had the hero, a man named Christian, saying:

'I cannot go so fast as I would,
by reason of this burden that is upon . . .'

So if the writer wished to indicate the letter A, and was writing the message on the ninth day of the month, he would put in the numbers '22/3', to indicate the third letter of the twenty-second line on page nine. Similarly, in a missive of the same date, '23/1' would indicate the letter B.

Holcroft discovered this by guessing that the letters would be written originally in French, Narrey's own language, and a further line of defence against someone being able to decipher the message, and by knowing that the most commonly used letter in the French language was E, as it was, in fact, in English. Once he had worked this out he went through page after page of Bunyan's work until he had discovered the exact mechanism. At the end of his three weeks in the cellar beneath the Dolphin, Holcroft knew a great deal about Narrey's secret operations in Ireland, who among the Williamite Army had been compromised, who had taken bribes, who was just a credulous fool. But, most importantly, Holcroft knew the true identity of the spy known as Agricola. At first he could not believe it. He checked again, and again. There was no mistake. The revelation shocked him. He was also deeply saddened by the knowledge, mixed with the pain of personal betrayal. There was a good deal of raw anger, too.

However, he soon realised that, while his sentence in the cellar had been long and tedious, it had proved worthwhile. And tedious it certainly had been. The only break in the boredom during the seventeen days since Hogan's brief visit, had come on the eleventh day, when a breathless Mack had burst into his hiding place and told him that there were redcoats at the door. Holcroft had been bundled into an empty brandy cask and the lid quickly nailed shut, to the Englishman's distress. As he had breathed in the fumes of the brandy-soaked wood at close range, so strong that he felt almost drunk, he listened to Mack chatting amiably to a sergeant of

Clancarty's Regiment of Foot, who made only the most cursory of searches before repairing upstairs to the tap room for a restorative pint of ale and a nip or two of poteen.

Released from the barrel, with the redcoats long gone, Holcroft began to plan what he would do, and how, when the city of Cork had finally fallen to Lord Marlborough. There was a reckoning to be made. Two reckonings, in fact.

In the early afternoon of his twenty-second day in that dank, dull cellar, Mack opened the door and stepped into Holcroft's domain. He was carrying a blue military-style woollen coat with yellow turned-back sleeves and big brass buttons.

'A little gift for you, Major Blood,' said the smuggler, handing over the garment. 'It took some finding – your man Matisse sold it to a gentleman, who gave it to his godson – but we managed to sniff it out. May it bring you joy.'

Holcroft was overwhelmed with gratitude. He was speechless, in fact. He had not properly understood until that moment how much the old blue coat meant to him. A vital part of his being had been stripped away from him when he had been made a prisoner. And now it was returned – he was made whole.

'You must allow me to pay you for your trouble,' Holcroft said when he'd donned the wonderfully familiar coat and could finally work his tongue again.

'Now, Major Blood, it wouldn't be a gift then, would it?'

'I have so much kindness to repay you, Mack,' he said. 'I have been your guest for so long. If there is ever anything I can do, you must let me know.'

'Well, since you are kind enough to offer . . .'

'Yes?'

'The English soldiers are now in the city, Major Blood. They are looting, stealing whatever they can. They broke through this morning, with heavy casualties – they say the Duke of Grafton, the

son of old King Charles, was killed before the walls. There is a lot
of anger – well, I don't have to tell you about the passions of war.
There are Danes and Dutchmen running riot and—'

'You wish me to arrange protection for your people and your
goods?'

'That would be most kind, Major. And thereafter we would
consider any obligation you might feel towards us fully repaid.'

'Consider it done, sir,' said Holcroft. He slung his stolen sword
over his shoulders and began to button up the front of his blue
coat – a beautiful, warm, homecoming feeling, like a mother's
embrace. 'Can you tell me where the English have made their
headquarters, Mack? I'll go to them straightaway.'

'Why, sir, they are just where you would expect – in the Governor's House, the big white building on the main street, up towards
the North Gate.'

Cork was receiving its punishment for resisting the foe. As Holcroft
walked briskly up the main thoroughfare that led from the South
Gate to the North, he saw the full chaos of a city in the throes of a
sack.

Drunken redcoats stumbled about, their arms full of stolen merchandise; out of the corner of his eye Holcroft thought he saw a
couple rutting shamelessly in a graveyard, with other men standing
around and cheering them on. There were bodies lying here and
there, some dead, some just dead drunk.

One bald man had swathed himself in long bolts of purple and
white silk, like a Roman senator, and was capering on top of a carriage while one friend played a fife and a skinny, tear-stained drummer boy rapped out a dancing beat on his skin. Men fired off their
muskets into the air in celebration, sang wild tuneless snatches of
their marching songs. One house had been ransacked, doors and
windows hanging open, another next to it was filled with laughing
redcoats gleefully carrying out furniture and piling it in the street

to make a celebratory bonfire. Someone had rolled a barrel of ale out of a ruined tavern across the street and was hacking at it with an axe. A gang of men around the barrel – some still bleeding from minor wounds taken in the assault – were waiting eagerly to dip their mess tankards into the smashed open top.

A lurching Dutch sergeant, his blue coat open to the waist, approached Holcroft and asked his business, then asked if he were a God-damned Papist. Holcroft brushed him aside and when the man seized his elbow, Holcroft turned and knocked him down with a fine right to the side of the jaw.

When he reached the Governor's House, he saw a formed company of redcoats guarding the door, sober and under strict discipline. He gave his name and rank and was ushered into the building.

Once through the doors, he was waved by a redcoat towards a huge reception room, where a servant in immaculate forest green livery offered him a brimming glass of Champagne – which took him rather aback, although he accepted the fizzy wine gratefully. Such gentility after the chaos in the teeming streets of Cork. He recognised that a sort of informal party was in progress with more than a hundred officers from dozens of different units celebrating the victory in their own way. A string quartet was playing too loudly in the corner of the long room. Knots of men were talking and laughing together, the Champagne was flowing with dozens of servants circulating with full trays.

His eye was drawn to the blue coats and yellow turn-backs of the Ordnance, his comrades: there was Jacob Richards with roly-poly Claudius Barden, who seemed to be telling some sort of joke. Richards was laughing uproariously anyway. And there was Francis Waters, now wearing the sash of a captain, and engaged in a serious discussion with the Duke of Würtemberg-Neuenstadt and Mcinhard Schomberg, son of the dead Master-General of the Ordnance, and an older Danish commander whom Holcroft did not recognise.

He spied the Quartermaster Edmund Vallance, that damned thief, who seemed to have collared a bottle of Champagne to himself; he was taking animatedly to a guards lieutenant, wagging his finger like a conductor's baton.

Paul Smithson, the Protestant merchant who had been imprisoned in the cell beside him in the Old Tower, was collapsed in a large chair, unconscious.

There were so many other faces he recognised: Sir William Russell, Colonel Harry Fenton, Brigadier-General William Wolseley, who gave him a cheery wave from across the room. Yet Holcroft suddenly felt stricken with a paralysing shyness – these were his people but he felt he did not know them. He did not know who to speak to first; he felt excluded from their merry ranks because of his weeks' long absence from the war. How could he join in their celebrations when he had not fought at Cork, nor captured it?

'Good day, Hol,' said a voice behind him. He turned and there was Jack Churchill, the Earl of Marlborough himself, the victor of the hour, grinning at him from a yard away with a half-empty glass of Champagne in his hand.

'Oh, Jack,' said Holcroft. And at the sight of his old, dear friend all his silly qualms seemed to fade away. 'I am so very glad to see you.'

'And I you. I heard you were dead,' said Jack, frowning at his friend. 'I saw your name on the missing list after the affair at Ballyneety and my heart almost stopped. You look thin and pale. You've been a prisoner, I take it?'

'Yes, but more recently I've been in hiding in the cellar of a tavern called the Dolphin. Which reminds me: can you arrange for a squad – a half company, say – to guard it? The people there were very kind to me and I am beholden.'

'Certainly,' said Jack. He beckoned a red-coated junior officer, an aide of some kind, and gave him his instructions.

As he was talking to the aide, Holcroft saw a vision of beauty in clinging blue silk approaching him. Diamonds at her slim white neck and glinting in her night-dark hair, which was swept up and piled on top of her head. It was Caroline, his Caroline, and her grace quite took his breath away. The sudden urge to kiss her struck him like a blow – he'd never felt it more strongly. He felt dizzy from the mere sight of her lovely face.

'Darling Holcroft! I've been worried sick – I heard you were dead, and then captured, and imprisoned. I cannot tell you how happy I am to see you returned to us unscathed. I have missed you so much, my dearest friend!'

She put a cool hand on his, and squeezed. He felt the jolt go up his arm.

'You must tell me all about your adventures, I cannot wait to hear them. But first, my brave protector, I need you to do one tiny thing for me. You see the young man over there: Lieutenant Barden is his name, one of yours, isn't he?'

Holcroft nodded.

'Well, I regret to tell you that he is no gentleman. He seized me the other day, quite roughly by the shoulders, and tried to kiss me, while we were resting on a blanket after riding in the woods together up by White's Cross. Dear Holcroft, would you be kind enough to tell him that he must behave himself. Admonish him. I know he would listen to you. Talk to him sternly; tell him that he must curb his foolish notions.'

'You went riding in the woods with Lieutenant Barden? Is that correct? Alone? And during this jaunt, while you lay down together on a blanket, he tried – unsuccessfully – to kiss you?'

'Yes, he suggested that we go on a picnic, and it seemed such a jolly idea while the sun was shining, that I said yes. And then, well, as you said . . .'

'And it did not occur to you that young Claudius Barden might take your easy acceptance to mean something more was on offer than a jolly excursion?'

'Why no, I expected him to behave like a gentleman. What are you saying, Holcroft? If you're going to be difficult about this, I shall ask someone else.'

'I'm saying, Lady Caroline, that I am sick and tired of your manipulations. You are a beautiful woman – you know that. You must also recognise that you flirt and tease men shamelessly; you give them false encouragement. Naturally, they fall in love with you; they seek more than your friendship. I do not condone Lieutenant Barden's actions. But I understand them and believe that you, yourself are at least partly to blame. So, no, Lady Caroline, I will not admonish Lieutenant Barden for you. I will not tell him to curb his foolish notions. Furthermore, I must tell you, Caroline, and make you comprehend it fully, that from now on you may no longer consider your person under my protection.'

'Holcroft, how can you be so beastly? I thought we were friends.'

'Madam, you will bring disaster down upon yourself if you continue to behave towards men in this fashion. And you will bring death to any man who tries to be your champion. Either he will kill or he will die as a result of your games. Why on earth do you not pick out one man from among your admirers – and marry the poor fellow?'

'Where would be the fun in that?' said Caroline, her cold blue eyes like drawn daggers. And without another word, she turned and swept away.

Holcroft found that his heart was beating like a kettledrum, the blood pumping hot in his veins. He felt breathless, clammy – also strangely, joyously victorious. He was aware that Jack was standing silently at his shoulder.

'Dangerous woman, that,' Jack said. 'She only arrived in the camp a week ago and already half my junior officers are in love with her.'

'Tell them to steer well clear of her. She is poison,' said Holcroft.

'They won't listen.'

'No,' said Holcroft. 'I don't suppose they will. Tell me, Jack, who is that tall, blond, one-legged man over there by the orchestra? He seems to be staring at me, and only at me. But I do not think I have yet made his acquaintance.'

Jack looked at Holcroft. 'You do not know him?' he said.

'Never set eyes on him before.'

'He is a distinguished Dutch officer. He lost his leg at the siege of Phillipsburg in Germany in '88. A grenade exploded under his feet. He serves King William as a military adviser now and has been has moved to London with the court. But he asked to accompany me to Ireland. And I could not refuse.'

The one-legged man, seeing that Holcroft was looking back at him, advanced towards them, stumping along quite nimbly on his wooden leg.

Jack said quietly: 'The leg was not the only wound he took. The French grenade also blew away his manhood. All his private parts are gone.'

Holcroft looked at his friend. They both winced at the same time.

Jack said: 'Major Holcroft Blood, may I have the honour of naming Jongheer Markus van Dijk, lately of King William's famous Third Guards.'

Holcroft looked at the tall, thin man, saw the pain etched into his features.

'Your servant, sir,' he said.

'And I am yours,' said the Dutchman, in perfect English. 'I also have the honour to have the acquaintance of your lady wife, Elizabeth. She has shown the utmost kindness to me as a stranger newly come to London.'

Holcroft stared hard at the man. So this was the bastard who had been squiring Elizabeth around the city of London, taking her to racing meets, taking her to balls . . . Balls! Dear God, the poor fellow. Holcroft managed to smile at him.

'It seems, Major Blood, that an unfortunate misunderstanding has arisen. I have been greatly favoured by the company of your wife, this is true. However I wish to assure you that our association has been entirely blameless, *sans reproche*. She has lately been most distressed by the fear, which I'm sure is groundless, that she has alienated your affections by her association with me.

'I came to Ireland to reassure you that there is no cause for alarm. That Elizabeth and I are no more than friends. However, I know that as a gentleman, your good name must be dear to you, and so I am here to offer you satisfaction – a discreet meeting of blades – should you insist that your honour demands it.'

Holcroft straightened his spine. He looked the Dutchman full in the face and said: 'That will not be necessary, sir. I should like, instead, to offer you my gratitude for providing some pleasantly diverting company for my wife while she has been alone in London and I have been overseas. I thank you, sir, most sincerely and from the bottom of my heart.'

And the two men bowed to each other.

Holcroft ran nimbly up the stairs of the Old Tower. The clerk had disappeared from his lectern on the ground floor and been replaced by a trio of redcoats, armed and awake but the worse for drink. Holcroft's Ordnance coat, officer-like bearing and English accent were enough to gain him admittance.

It had grown dark since he had left the celebration – which he had done immediately after his *raprochement* with the wounded Dutch officer. He had enquired of Jack where the prisoners of war were being held and quit the party. He fought the urge to run through the dark streets towards the Old Tower, such was his eagerness to return to the place of his own imprisonment. But he was to be disappointed when he reached the top of the stairs and searched the faces of the unhappy-looking men who were now occupying the cells.

Henri d'Erloncourt's face was not among them.

There were about a dozen men, all apart from the Governor McElliot military men in uniforms of one kind or another. He looked at them and even insisted that one of the redcoat guards woke up a small thin man who was sleeping at the back of the cell. Narrey was not there.

'I seek a Frenchman,' he said, addressing Governor McElliot, and the trio of men standing at the bars around him. 'His name is Henri d'Erloncourt. A count. But he also uses the code name Narrey. Can you tell me where he is?'

'Do I look like an informer to you?' said McElliot, drawing himself up to his full, though still sadly unimpressive, height.

'He is an evil man. He is a spy and murderer and no friend to Ireland.'

'We will not say a single word to you – Englishman,' said the man next to the Governor, belying his own words. 'We would die before we delivered up our comrade, our good friend Henri, to your cruel English justice! Die, I say!'

Holcroft looked at the man who had spoken. He was young, red-faced, proud and clearly very stupid. 'But you *do* know where he is,' said Holcroft.

'My lord does not know where the Frenchman is,' said an older military type who stood by his side. 'None of us do. It is not worth putting him – nor any of us – to the question. Your hot irons and devices will avail you nothing.'

'Actually, I *do* have a pretty good idea where he is,' said the third man.

The other three men turned and stared at him. The young one said: 'Lord Tyrone – keep your silence, sir. Tell the enemy nothing. What of your honour?'

'What of it? D'Erloncourt did us no great service. He acted in all ways and at all times, so far as I could tell, only in the interests of his royal master Louis. He cared not a fig for Cork, nor for Ireland nor for Irish lives. Indeed, I believe he deliberately lied to us about the imminent approach of the Duke of Berwick, in order to force us to fight on here. Without his words in council, we would have surrendered a week ago and avoided many hundreds of deaths. We owe him nothing.'

Holcroft grasped the bars of the cell. 'So tell me, sir, where is he?'

'He is, I imagine, in Kinsale.'

'You are sure?'

'No, but I know he and his man slipped out of Cork the day before the city fell – probably over the wall in the dead of night and away by small boat on the river. I came looking for him yesterday morning and found him gone. The Protestant prisoners told me as much. They watched him clear his office, and two of them overheard talk of Kinsale, too, with his servant. I cannot be certain, of course, but my guess is that you'll find your man down there.'

The sack of Cork had ground, exhausted, to a halt. As Holcroft walked down the main street, heading south, he saw marching patrols of redcoats, disciplined squads of twenty men, arresting the most egregious looters, beating them into submission and leading them away. The worst fires had been put out, or had burnt out by now and order was returning to the streets. There was still the occasional musket shot or terrified scream from the darkness, but the Earl of Marlborough, having allowed his victorious men to run riot for a dozen hours, had by now re-established control over the bruised city.

Holcroft pushed open the door of the Dolphin and walked slowly up to the wooden counter. Once again the place fell silent. Holcroft nodded to the few local drinkers, and noticed a young lieutenant of the First Foot Guards and an older man, a sergeant, sipping from pewter pots by the fire, and through a small, greasy window he glimpsed a dozen more redcoats armed with flintlocks, at their ease in the candle-lit courtyard at the side of the old building.

He reached into his coat pocket, pulled out a small, lumpy linen sack, and slapped it with a chinking noise on the counter.

'I want supper and a room for the night, Seamus,' he said to the red-bearded man. 'The best you have. This should cover the expense and trouble.'

Seamus grinned at him. 'We do have a very comfortable cellar that I believe has just become available, if you don't mind the damp and a few rats.'

'No more cellars, Seamus. Something with a comfortable bed. I'd be obliged if you'd send up some bread and soup and a bottle of wine – no, make that two bottles.'

In a large, warm, oak-beamed room at the top of the Dolphin, Holcroft dipped his quill into the ink pot, gently shook off a drop of excess ink and, with his left hand he straightened the large sheet of paper in front of him so that its bottom edge was exactly in line with the edge of the table at which he sat. He composed his thoughts as best he could in his disordered state, then wrote:

The Dolphin Tavern, Cork, Ireland
Saturday, 27th September, 1690

My darling wife,
I have been a complete and utter fool, Elizabeth, and my behaviour towards you has been cruel and inexcusable. I can only hope that, in due course, you can find it in your heart to forgive my gross stupidity. I spoke tonight with Jack Churchill – who, as you may know by now, has captured the city of Cork – and I have arranged to take passage with him to England as soon as possible. I do have a small matter of business to attend to in the port of Kinsale over the next few days but once that is concluded I shall be sailing for home, where I hope we can effect a loving reconciliation . . .

Chapter Thirty

Wednesday, October 15, 1690: 9 a.m.

Not long. Not long now and he'd be free of this accursed country.
Henri peered through the gap in the battlements of the North
Bastion at the enemy siege lines on the hillside above. Charles
Fort was a low, thick, powerful construction on the eastern side
of the mouth of the Bandon River, two miles as the crow flies
south-east of Kinsale town. The Fort had five bastions: fat, stone,
spear-points that jutted out from the walls into the green surrounding countryside, all mounted with heavy cannon which
were set to cover every approach. It was a well-made fort, built
in the modern style, and yet the enemy encampment and their
massive siege guns easily overshadowed it on the landward side.
*Why do these Irish imbeciles insist on building their fortresses at
the bottom of hills?*

A gun fired from one of the English batteries on the left of the
enemy lines. A blossom of red. A faint line of black. A massive
shuddering impact in the thick wall beyond the gatehouse and
beyond the Flagstaff Bastion fifty yards to his right. A cloud of
smoke and grit flew up in the air and pattered around Henri, who
hunched his shoulders in reflex. The breach was a few feet wider.
This was the twelfth strike on the area of the breach in ten minutes.

A few more hours, he told himself. Tonight the *Hirondelle* would
surely be here and he and Matisse could shake the dust of this siege,
and this whole damned nation, from their heels. After tonight, he
did not care if the whole of Ireland surrendered to the forces of King
William – not just this badly sited, oversized gun redoubt. His royal
master could not complain – Henri had done his duty. For eighteen
long months he had fought his own private war in this damp island,

with scant thanks and little reward. He had, he believed, been a considerable thorn in the side of His Most Christian Majesty's enemies for all of that period. And now it was over. Time to go home. He had persuaded the citizens of Cork to hold out far longer than they might have, and he had done the same here in Charles Fort, the largest fortress of the port of Kinsale.

In truth, the Governor of Kinsale, Sir Edward Scott, a white-haired but still peppery seventy-year-old, had needed little persuasion. Henri had made his familiar false claims that the Duke of Berwick was on his way, and had repeated more recent rumours that Sarsfield was coming with a thousand fresh cavalry – but it had not been necessary. Sir Edward Scott knew his duty. He would resist the foe until he could realistically resist them no more.

The enemy had arrived two weeks ago, and Scott had abandoned the town of Kinsale, and given orders that it should be burnt to the ground to deny the enemy its comforts. He had pulled all his military personnel into Kinsale's two forts: James Fort and Charles Fort, which faced each other over the width of the Bandon River, the only access route by sea into Kinsale Harbour. But the fires set in the town had been swiftly extinguished by the arriving enemy cavalry, and these two fortresses – impressive though they undoubtedly appeared – were designed only to guard the mouth of the river, and keep out pirates and enemy shipping. They were no more than fortified coastal defence batteries, orientated toward the water. Perfect for trapping enemy vessels between two lethal fires. But when the enemy came at them by land, they were quite useless.

Würtemberg's Danes and Marlborough's English troops had overrun James Fort – the smaller of the two Kinsale fortresses – in half a day, coming round by sea in small boats, landing in the south and attacking it from there. Henri had watched from the safety of Charles Fort across the River Bandon in appalled, almost stunned silence as the lines of hundreds of red-jacketed men poured down the hill and swarmed over the stone walls. A massive explosion, a fountain of red and gold fire mantled in black – caused by a careless spark in the magazine, most likely – marked the end of the battle, and now the cross of St George fluttered from the ragged and powder-blackened battlements.

Marlborough and Würtemberg then turned their attention to Charles Fort.

It had been twelve days since Marlborough had sent in an officer under a flag of truce to demand the surrender of the garrison. Sir Edward Scott had replied with cool hauteur that, since the defenders had ample quantities of food and ammunition, and since they expected to be relieved very soon, it might be more suitable if Lord Marlborough were to apply again in one month's time.

Another English gun fired on the hillside. Another massive explosion in the breach, showering the defenders with grit and sand.

Henri had had enough. The breach in the north wall of Charles Fort, beyond the Flagstaff Bastion, was big enough, by his own calculations, to be deemed practicable. Today or tomorrow, Sir Edward Scott would hang out the white flag, and it would be over. And Henri had no intention of being part of the mass surrender. He knew that if he handed himself to the English, he would swiftly find himself at the wrong end of a rope. That bastard Holcroft Blood was out there somewhere, still alive, and no doubt slavering for his petty revenge. No, he would decline their kind invitation to render himself up to the foe. He and Matisse would make other arrangements.

He brushed some loose dirt off his shoulder and turned to descend the battlement, smiling at a young, rather pretty Irish captain, who was in charge of the North Bastion. He would go and find Matisse. It was time to start packing.

The same day: 2 p.m.

Another siege. Another breach in the walls that must be made wide enough by his cannon before the men of the Forlorn Hope were sent in to die in its jaws. Holcroft was struck with a sense of the familiarity of his position on this day – his beloved guns on a bare hillside above a castle by the wide grey sea; if he half closed his eyes he could almost be back at Carrickfergus – and, as he nodded the order to fire to Claudius Barden, who had command of this No. 3 Battery, he was also struck by the futility of this war. The Catholic Irish had not been brought to love King William, nor to tolerate their neighbours, his loyal Protestant Ulstermen. Quite the opposite. And how did the stout farming folk of Tyrone and Armagh feel about the papist raparees who had ridden, raped and robbed across their lands? James's cause might be finished, all hope gone, but the hatred on both sides showed no sign of abating. This conflict in Ireland, to Holcroft's mind, would smoulder on, enduring for generations.

He wondered what Hogan was doing now. Had he bought himself that sheep farm? Could he turn a deaf ear to the trumpet's call for ever?

So many good men killed or maimed. So many widows and orphans made.

And here he was outside the walls of Charles Fort, with three powerful English batteries under his hand – placed in his charge by Lieutenant-Colonel Jacob Richards, who had been called to Lord Marlborough's council tent – and he was still pounding away at another set of men, probably decent men, who fought him only because they differed over his choice of king. *Déjà vu.*

Were it not for his driving urge for justice, he might have resigned his Ordnance commission two weeks ago in Cork and caught the first available ship home to Elizabeth. But he had not, and he would not. Not until the issue with Narrey, with that bastard Henri d'Erloncourt, was settled. And not until he had unmasked and brought to justice the spy known as Agricola. Not until the two reckonings had been made. Narrey was evil. He must be stopped, and not only for the sake of revenge, although the Frenchman's casual and callous poisoning of his dear friend Aphra Behn was still a burning coal in his belly.

Henri d'Erloncourt must be stopped because, if not, he would continue to spread his poison, both literally and figuratively, unless he was put down. Agricola was a case in point. Narrey had recruited Agricola and used him as an agent of his evil: Agricola had betrayed the site of Schomberg's tent and caused the wounding of Jacob Richards; Agricola had most likely betrayed the attack on Cavan, and caused far greater casualties than necessary, including the deaths of many of his own friends and comrades in Tiffin's Inniskillingers; Agricola had betrayed the route and timing of the Artillery Train as it headed to Limerick, and caused the demise of many good men in that night attack at Ballyneety and, almost as heinous to Holcroft's mind, the destruction of many fine pieces of Ordnance. And those were only the betrayals that Holcroft knew about and could readily identify as perpetrated by the spy Agricola. There must be dozens more.

So Agricola must be stopped. Henri d'Erloncourt must be stopped.

And thus Holcroft's war continued.

The tall Ordnance officer walked across the gun platform to the nearest cannon, and seeing its familiar shape, he felt a further pang. It was Roaring Meg. But crewed by a group of men he did not know well. There was Enoch Jackson's death to be taken into account too. How he missed his friend!

He gave terse instructions to the crew to fire more to the west, a fraction. The last ball had sailed through the centre of the breach and bounded away inside the Fort. The cannon fire should chip away at the edges of the breach, or just outside them, if possible, widening the hole with every ball.

The gun captain was a young man who had unfortunately been named Peaceable Bonner by his earnest parents. Claudius Barden, who overheard Holcroft giving his orders to Meg's crew, called out cheerily: 'No time to be peaceable now, Peaceable. Major Blood wants to see blood today! Ha ha!'

Holcroft was suddenly consumed with an almost overwhelming wave of hatred for Barden. For a moment his vision was filmed with red. It took every atom of his will to prevent himself from walking over to the lieutenant and beating him senseless. Then Peaceable Bonner, cried: 'Sir, look, sir. A white flag.'

Holcroft whipped round, and there it was. From the Flagstaff Bastion, east of the gateway, a limp, dirty grey sheet was hanging from the pole.

'Cease fire.' Holcroft gave the order in a loud carrying voice. And along the No. 3 Battery, the men stopped what they were doing, frozen in their tasks – a couple of men carrying a sixteen-pound cannon ball on a hurdle, another with a big scoop full of gunpowder in his hands, a fellow with his rammer poised at the cannon's muzzle. For an instant, the only thing that moved was a knot of infantry in grey fifty yards away who were marching towards them, muskets on their shoulders, accompanied by two officers on horseback.

'At ease, everybody,' said Holcroft. 'Set your stations in order.'

'Do you mind, Major, if I give at least *some* of the orders on the No. 3,' said Barden. 'Makes me look bad in front of the men if you do all my work for me,' he continued. 'Makes it look, ha ha, as if you don't have confidence in me!'

Claudius might have been joking but he did indeed look more than a little hurt by Holcroft's usurpation of his powers. His senior officer, while in command of all the three English batteries on the hillside, had spent much of the day at the No. 3 Battery, barely visiting the other emplacements.

Holcroft ignored the younger man. He was watching the approach of the infantry and the two mounted officers. They were a company of Inniskillingers. The fourth company of Tiffin's Regiment. He could make out the brick-red features of Sergeant Hawkins in front. And the two horsemen walking their beasts on either side of the company were Captain Francis Waters and Lieutenant-Colonel Jacob Richards. His friends.

Holcroft smiled at the men as they arrived – so many familiar faces. And watched as they formed up in beautiful order, fifty men in two exactly straight lines slightly to the right of the battery. Waters and Richards came closer, they dismounted, and casually handed their reins to Sergeant Hawkins, who looped them over the wheel of a gun carriage.

Francis saluted; Jacob said, 'Blood,' to which Holcroft replied, 'Richards.'

Then Francis Waters glanced beyond Holcroft at the assembled men of the No. 3 Battery and said, 'Are you sure you want to do this now, Major Blood?'

'I'm sure. The white flag is out. The surrender will be this afternoon, most likely. Narrey will be in custody by nightfall and then we shall have our proof.'

'What are you talking about?' said Barden. 'Who is Narrey? What proof?'

Holcroft turned to the Ordnance lieutenant and said, 'Narrey is the code name for the French spymaster Henri d'Erloncourt – who is inside Charles Fort. Once he is in our hands, he will identify his agent, the spy known as Agricola, to us. He will trade that information for his life. He will tell us tonight who Agricola is. He will also provide written proof – several secret documents that may be used in a court of law. To save his own greasy neck, Henri, Comte d'Erloncourt will name you, Claudius Barden, as the notorious spy Agricola.'

Barden went as white as milk. He looked wildly between Holcroft, Waters and Richards. He shook his head, 'No, no, Henri would never do that . . .'

Francis Waters said formally: 'Lieutenant Claudius Barden, I am arresting you for the grave crimes of treason and espionage . . .'

But Barden was already moving. He lunged past the trio of officers, knocking Jacob Richards flying with his shoulder. At the same time his hand went to the large pocket in his blue Ordnance coat. He took three running steps, pulled out a small steel pistol, cocked it and shot Hawkins between the eyes as the fat man stood there beside the horses. Even as the sergeant was slumping to the ground, Holcroft was diving for the fugitive. He got a hand on the spy's boot just as he hit into the saddle. But Barden swept a hand across his body and smashed the steel pistol on to the top of Holcroft's head. And Holcroft splashed down in the mud, breathless, his black hat knocked free by the blow.

Barden spurred savagely, sawing the reins on his borrowed horse at the same time. The animal was spooked by the strange rider and set off at a mad canter, downhill towards the Fort. Holcroft lurched to his feet, blood running freely down the side of his pale face. 'Men of the fourth company,' he gasped. 'Tiffin's Regiment! Front Rank! Make ready!'

The front line of the Inniskillingers, twenty-five tough men, brought their flintlocks smoothly up to their right shoulders.

'He's killed Sergeant Hawkins. He betrayed us at the fight at Cavan. Remember that . . . and take aim!' Holcroft's voice was stronger.

Twenty-five cocked and loaded muskets were pointing down the slope.

'Give fire!'

The line of muskets barked, and Holcroft saw two bullets strike Barden, now thirty yards away, in the back and shoulder. But the spy miraculously kept his seat. The horse was tearing down the hill, galloping.

'Second rank, step forward one pace. Make ready . . . take aim.'

Barden was fifty yards away. He was within hailing distance of the Fort.

'Give fire!'

Twenty-five muskets spoke. Twenty-five lethal tongues of fire lashed out. A lone bullet smashed into the back of Barden's skull, blowing away his wig and hat and severing the top of his head like the opening of a soft boiled egg. The Ordnance man flopped in the saddle, body swaying. The horse kept charging onwards towards the Fort. But the body slipped, hanging sideways out of the saddle, blood and matter spilling freely, then it thumped to the turf.

The same day: 5 p.m.

'What do you mean he's not there?' snapped Holcroft. 'He must be there. We know he *was* in there. Is he in disguise? Is he hiding?'

'I don't know what to say,' said Francis Waters. He was shocked at the passion, the rage, that he saw in the eyes of his mentor. 'We've examined all of the prisoners, we've looked every man in the face and d'Erloncourt is not among them. Your description was most detailed and exact. He's not there.'

'He must still be in the Fort, hiding somewhere. Have the place searched.'

At a little before four o'clock, the garrison of Charles Fort – their honourable surrender magnanimously granted by Lord Marlborough – had marched out of the front gate with Governor Sir Edward Scott at their head followed by his senior officers. Fifes had played and trumpets, too, and the drums had beaten spritely marches. The officers had carried their swords.

They were gathered in a huge group, more than a thousand men, on an area of flattish ground at the head of the road back to Cork. They were to be escorted under flag of truce to Limerick by a single company of Danish cavalry.

Yet Narrey was not among them.

Think, Holcroft told himself. *Where does Narrey wish to go? Home. Yes, but by what method?*

'Is there a boathouse?' he asked Waters. They were standing on the battered battlements of the Flagstaff Bastion, which overlooked the Charles Fort. The place was bustling with redcoats, parties of men and officers, exploring the Fort, auditing the stores. The sun had sunk behind the headland to a red glow in the west.

It would be full dark in half an hour or perhaps less.

'Over on the other side,' said Waters. 'There is a boathouse set into the sea wall, with a watergate.'

'Come on, Francis – and you two men as well!' Holcroft beckoned to two of the larger Inniskillingers in fourth company, John Ellis and Joe Cully.

He crossed from the bastion to the curtain wall and began jogging clockwise around the top of the curtain wall, along a cart-wide road designed to allow the easy transference of troops, the three soldiers following behind.

He passed the Cockpit Bastion without stopping and arrived minutes later at the first of two huge rectangular block-like seaward bastions, this south-easterly one called Charles's, and named like the Fort itself after the English King Charles II, who had commissioned its construction.

Francis, panting, said: 'The boathouse is under there!' He pointed to a dark opening below the walls. But Holcroft seemed not to hear him, he was instead now bounding up the stairs that led up to the roof of Charles's Bastion.

Once at the top, Holcroft looked almost due west, squinting into the last red gleams of the sun. Across the mouth of the River Bandon, half a mile away, he could make out James Fort on the headland.

And in the water, midway between the two forts but heading south out to sea, was a small rowing boat, with two figures on board. One a burly type in a shapeless seaman's hat efficiently manning the oars; the other slight and wrapped in a huge black cloak, with a black hat pulled low over his face.

They were about a hundred yards away, far beyond an accurate pistol or musket shot. Holcroft screamed, 'Narrey!' as loud as he could and the black-clad figure in the stern of the boat turned and looked back at the tall figure outlined by the setting sun on the seaward bastion. He raised a lazy hand in salute, twirling it elegantly at the wrist, and then turned back to the seaman and said a few words, evidently urging him to row faster.

'This is not the end,' said Holcroft. 'This cannot be the end of this.'

He looked at the three men, the two big Inniskillingers, the doubled-over and wheezing form of Francis Waters – it was clear the officer was finished for a while at least. 'Francis,' he said to the gasping man, 'give me your glass. Quick now. And you two men come along with me.'

He accepted the small collapsed telescope from Francis's trembling hand, cast one final furious look at the rowing boat now in the middle of the Bandon channel and pulling steadily southwards, measuring distances with his eye. The two men in the boat cast monstrous black shadows in the last of the sun's light.

'Come on! Run with me, men, run!' And Holcroft dashed down the steps.

The three of them pelted along the curtain wall, past the Cockpit Bastion, past the Flagstaff Bastion. They skidded to a halt by the main gate and fought their way through the crush of soldiery coming in and going out of the Fort across the bridge over the wide ditch. Once outside, the three men ran north, up the sloping road that led to the heights. Across fields scarred by the sappers' assault trenches, past campfires and idling redcoats. Until at last they reached the No. 3 Battery. The twenty-four-pounders had already been hooked up to their carriages, ready to be hauled away in the morning. But God was good to Holcroft, for Roaring Meg was still emplaced, and Peaceable Bonner was polishing its bronze barrel with a rag, and looking up shocked, even fearful, as Holcroft and two huge infantrymen came charging up the hill towards him.

'Is she . . . primed and . . . charged?' Holcroft demanded, between gasps of agonising breath. His sides ached; his lungs were ablaze.

'What?' said Peaceable.

'Is Roaring Meg loaded?' asked Holcroft.

'Of course not,' said Peaceable, indignantly.

'Load her now. Round shot. Fast as you can. Help him, Cully, and you, Ellis, go and find some gunners, matrosses, any man of the Ordnance – *now!*'

'But why are we—' said Bonner.

'Don't ask questions. Just do it. Time is vital.'

Fighting to regain his breath, Holcroft pulled out Francis's telescope and trained it on the Bandon channel. *There, there it was.* He could see the boat was nearly at the open sea, at a distance of – perhaps – three thousand five hundred yards. It was impossible to say with true accuracy. The sea had no markers for reference. Holcroft lifted the glass a fraction, beyond the rowing boat, he could see the sleek, dark shape of a ship skulking behind the southernmost tip of the isthmus on which James Fort stood. A frigate, a damned French frigate, no doubt. It was clear where Narrey and his man were heading. If the ship did not move, the rowing boat would reach its side in about ten minutes.

There was just time. The Saker's maximum range, Holcroft knew well, was four thousand yards. The rowing boat was just about within range. But the chances of hitting it were very slight indeed.

Holcroft whirled round. He saw Bonner at the muzzle, shoving a bag of powder inside its mouth. It was nearly full dark.

'Give it an extra half pound,' he said. 'It's a long shot.'

'You'll burst her breach, sir,' said Bonner. 'She's a very old lady.'

'Do it, Peaceable. And quickly.'

Holcroft attended to the sighting of the piece himself. There were a swarm of Ordnance men around Roaring Meg by now, summoned by John Ellis and also by the excitement in the air. Holcroft banged in the last wedge-shaped quoin, giving old Meg almost her maximum possible elevation.

'Pierce the charge,' bawled Holcroft. And Bonner plunged a thin spike through the vent hole to make a hole in the bag of powder in the barrel.

'Prime the piece!' Bonner slid a straw of fine powder into the vent hole.

'Tend the match.' A gunner brought up the burning cord on a linstock.

'Have a care, everyone,' said Holcroft. 'Stay back in case she bursts.'

He took the linstock from the nervous-looking gunner and waved him away. 'Give fire,' he muttered to himself to complete the beloved ritual, and he touched the burning match to the vent hole.

Meg roared. And in the dying light Holcroft saw the flight of the ball as a darker line against the grey of dusk. The missile soared, arced, and sank down towards the slowly moving rowing boat.

It flew high overhead and splashed into the water fifty yards beyond it.

Holcroft said: 'One more time, lads.' He began the sacred and familiar litany of firing once again: 'Advance the worm.'

'Search the piece.'

'Advance the sponge . . .'

Holcroft kept the glass to his eye as he spoke the soothing words. The boat was four hundred yards from the frigate, which had not moved.

The gun was loaded, charged and primed.

'Give fire,' said Holcroft.

The shot was long again and a few feet wide of the mark; it seemed the boat had changed its course slightly.

'One last shot – take over charging,' said Holcroft to Peaceable Bonner.

He knelt beside the barrel as the ritual began again. He put his right hand on the warm bronze of Roaring Meg's body and closed his eyes.

No words were spoken out loud, but in his mind he said: '*Enoch, can you hear me? Enoch Jackson, wherever you are now – in Heaven or in the other place, aid me now. Send your spirit to guide me. You know Meg as well as any man, you and she have fought together more times than I can count. For our long friendship, lend me your aid now.*' He opened his eyes and looked along the barrel. A little more elevation. Just a touch, and perhaps a fraction to the left. Was that Enoch's advice or his own?

'Joe Cully, come here,' he said, 'and bring that handspike.'

Between them, he and the big Inniskillinger shifted Meg no more than half an inch to the left. He slid an eighth-of-an-inch quoin under the barrel, tapped it home.

It was ready. It was nigh on full dark. Even with the glass trained on the rowing boat, now a short two hundred yards from the enemy frigate, he could barely make out more than a dark, moving lump on the water.

'Give fire,' he said quietly, and behind him he heard the old battle cannon roar one last time.

In the circle of the glass, for the longest time, the little boat ploughed on, the oars splashing gently in the black, black sea. Then the ball struck.

The iron sphere smashed down in the centre of the boat, crashing through the flimsy wooden floor, snapping the wooden craft in two. One moment, two men in a skiff were pulling slowly, placidly towards Salvation, the next chaos – broken wreckage, men struggling madly in the white-whipped water.

Then quiet again; all Holcroft could see was a few pieces of floating wood.

Historical note

Holcroft Blood was a real soldier, in fact, a minor historical hero. He is listed among the two dozen or so officers of the English Artillery Train destined for Ireland in June 1689 as the Second Engineer; along with Jacob Richards, First Engineer; Claudius Barden, Third Engineer; and Obadiah Field, Gentleman of the Ordnance – all under the command of His Grace the Duke of Schomberg.

Yet I admit I have taken some artistic liberties with Holcroft's character and career. For example, I have no good reason to suggest that he was, as I have described him, somewhere on the autism spectrum – not that his idiosyncrasies would have been described as such in the 17th century. My Holcroft is, I would say, semi-fictional.

I have tried, however, whenever possible, to recount the true course of Holcroft's life from the little we know of him. He was the third son of the notorious crown-stealer 'Colonel' Thomas Blood and his wife Mary. He enlisted in the Royal Navy in 1672 and served during the Third Anglo-Dutch War. He later joined the French service as a cadet and studied engineering and gunnery. During this period, I have my fictional Holcroft spying for Charles II, although I have no evidence except that the real man was mysteriously granted a sinecure in Ireland by the King, a job that would pay him a salary for which he never, as far as I can tell, did a stroke of work. He could well have been a spy for King Charles II – his father almost certainly was at various times.

In 1686, now back in London, Holcroft married Elizabeth, daughter of the barrister Richard King, and, before the Glorious Revolution in 1688, he served as a captain of pioneers in James II's Royal Train of Artillery. Despite his loyal service with the old regime, when William and Mary came to the thrones of England,

Scotland and Ireland, he remained with the Ordnance. And, in May 1689, he was appointed Second Engineer on the Artillery Train bound for Ireland to fight the rebels under James II – who after his ignominious departure from England had landed in the port of Kinsale in March 1689, with a small but efficient French army of six thousand men provided by his patron Louis XIV.

Unfortunately, I don't know very much about Holcroft's service in Ireland. One source says he fought at the siege of Carrickfergus in August 1689. The *Oxford Dictionary of National Biography* says only: 'He served in all the major sieges and battles in the campaign in Ireland, and was wounded at Cavan in February 1690.' It's not a lot to go on – but it also gives a storyteller a lot of latitude. I hope the reader will not feel I have abused the privilege of ignorance.

Michael 'Galloping' Hogan was a real man, too. And I know even less about him. Even his name might be wrong. The respected historian John Childs, author of *The Williamite Wars in Ireland 1688–1691* – a brilliant book that I used as my main source – gives his first name as Daniel. But everywhere else he is referred to as Michael Hogan. It may be there was more than one dashing fellow called Hogan who was a famously hard-riding raparee.

'Galloping' Hogan, a local man, guided Patrick Sarsfield's cavalry to the ruins of Ballyneety Castle where they surprised the English Artillery Train camping there on August 11, 1690, on its approach to the siege of Limerick. The Irish killed or drove off the accompanying troops and, by stuffing the barrels of the cannon with captured gunpowder, they succeeded in destroying some, if not all of them, along with great quantities of other vital supplies. One English officer was captured at Ballyneety, and I decided, for my own narrative purposes, that this man should be Holcroft Blood.

The destruction of large amounts of war *matériel* at Ballyneety delayed the assault on Limerick, although not for very long. More guns were swiftly brought up, properly guarded this time, and on

August 27, 1690, after a suitable breach had been made in the city's medieval walls, the grenadiers of William's Forlorn Hope made their assault. They were bloodily repulsed, thanks to the military expertise of Limerick's French Governor Alexandre, Marquis de Boisseleau, who prepared the *coupure* described in the novel behind the breach and slaughtered hundreds of the attacking troops. Even the local civilians joined in the desperate fight, hurling missiles from the rooftops. The next day, with the autumn rains almost upon them, the superior English forces abandoned the siege of Limerick and, shortly afterwards, King William returned to England.

John Churchill, Earl of Marlborough (the future Duke) is also – obviously – a historical figure. Later in his glittering career, at the Battle of Blenheim in August 1704, the commander of all his field artillery was one Colonel Holcroft Blood, whose intelligent and courageous actions that victorious day brought the celebrated gunner a promotion to Brigadier-General.

I wanted John Churchill and Holcroft to be lifelong friends and have described them as such in all the novels, even going so far as to have Holcroft give him the affectionate nickname 'Jack'. However, while they certainly would have known each other well, both moving in the highest English military circles, their long friendship is sadly a fiction.

However, the Earl of Marlborough did lead reinforcements from England in September 1690 and he did capture both Cork and Kinsale in short order.

Henri d'Erloncourt, my evil French spymaster, is entirely fictional, as is his entrapment at Kinsale, and escape after Charles Fort surrendered. So is his agent Agricola. I am sure the real Claudius Barden, Third Engineer of the Train, was a good and loyal officer, not the lazy joker I have made him out to be. He was said to be a fine mathematician, but he had the misfortune to be shot dead at the siege of Charles Fort and so, since I wanted the bad guy to get his deserts at the end of the tale, I recruited him posthumously for Narrey's Irish network. My deepest apologies to any living members of his family for the slur on his name.

The war in Ireland did not end with the capture of the southern ports of Cork and Kinsale. The bulk of the French troops departed but the war rumbled on for another year. There was a terrible bloody battle at Aughrim, at which the Irish were crushed, and a second siege of Limerick, which ended when the city surrendered in September 1691. A peace treaty was signed in October that year and, as part of the agreement, the surviving men of the Jacobite Army, some fourteen thousand of them, and ten thousand women, were provided with ships and allowed to go into exile in France to continue serving James, an exodus known to history as the Flight of the Wild Geese. They were led by Patrick Sarsfield, and among their number was the hard-riding raparee nicknamed 'Galloping' Hogan.

Acknowledgements

Many people make a book and I'd like to thank just some of them here for their hard work on *Blood's Campaign* and the other novels in the Blood series. Firstly, Katherine Armstrong, Martin Fletcher and the rest of the excellent team at Zaffre, for their eagle-eyed editing of the text, their insightful suggestions for improvement, and their tireless support of the series. Secondly, my hard-working agent Ian Drury, who gave me the inspired idea that I should make Holcroft just a little bit autistic. I'm proud of my creation but Ian's superb notion helped to lift him out of the ordinary run of muscular military heroes.

On a trip to Drogheda in July 2017, my friend Ruadh Butler, author of *Swordland* and several other excellent novels about Irish medieval history, accompanied me on a tour of the Boyne battlefield on a blisteringly hot day, happily discussing where the English Artillery Train might have arrayed their cannon, showing me where the Dutch Blue Guards made their magnificent river crossing, and kindly driving me along some of the routes the foot-sore soldiers of the two warring kings would have tramped in victory and defeat.

My guru for all things related to 17th-century cannon is the immensely knowledgeable Roger Emmerson of, among other re-enactment organisations, the group Colonel Holcroft Blood's Ordnance, who demonstrated the firing of his field guns on several noisy occasions and patiently answered all my technical gunnery enquiries.

Finally there are the historians whom I have not had the pleasure of meeting but whose work I have read and greatly admired. John Childs, author of *The Williamite Wars*, I have mentioned above, but I would also like to thank Gerard Fitzgibbon, whose book

Kingdom Overthrown: Ireland and the Battle for Europe 1688–1691 was a joy to read, brilliantly researched and beautifully written. Michael McNally was extremely helpful on many details of the prominent people involved in this theatre and his Osprey book *Battle of the Boyne 1690: The Irish campaign for the English crown* is an excellent guide to this battle and the overall campaign. They have given me the building blocks with which to construct my own story and all I can offer in return are my sincere and heartfelt thanks. Any factual errors are, of course, entirely my own.

Angus Donald
Tonbridge, April 18, 2019

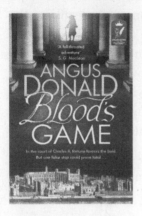